What People Are Saying about
Loree Lough and *Maverick Heart*...

Few can match Loree's ability to pen a page-turner. She is a master at making characters jump off the page, and I was right there next to Levee, Dan, Mack, and all the others in this captivating tale.

—*C. Maggie Woychik* ✦ Author, *I Run to the Hills*

Loree Lough is a gifted storyteller! Her characters come to life in a compelling fashion.

—*Ronie Kendig* ✦ Author, *Dead Reckoning* and *Nightshade*

When you pick up a Loree Lough novel, you can expect three things: fast-paced action, emotions that grab you by the heart, and a make-you-melt love story. *Maverick Heart* delivers all these and more.

—*Jennifer AlLee* ✦ Author, *The Pastor's Wife*

This gripping story wasted no time in whisking me to Texas in the 1880s, and Loree Lough's deft, fast-moving prose brought the characters to life. I loved the pluck and true grit of Levee and was touched by her compassion and faith.

—*Linda S. Clare* ✦ Author, *The Fence My Father Built*

Loree has a magical way of drawing in her readers, and this story has all the ingredients of a best seller—action, drama, and heart-tugging romance. Don't miss out on this one, dear readers!

—*Sharlene MacLaren* ✦ Award-winning author,
The Daughters of Jacob Kane series

Loree Lough artfully weaves together unforgettable characters and Old West culture in her latest action-packed adventure, another "keeper" for your bookshelf.

—*Heidi Main* ✦ Author, *Satisfy*

4/18/13

It doesn't get any better than *Maverick Heart*. You will be mesmerized from paragraph one, and when the last page has been turned, you'll be left begging for more. I give this book two thumbs up.

—*Laurean Brooks* ◆ Award-winning author, *Journey to Forgiveness*

Maverick Heart guarantees readers another wonderful love story that's filled with entertaining characters and an action-packed storyline. I was hooked from page one, and you will be, too.

—*Rita Gerlach* ◆ Award-winning author, *Surrender the Wind*

Once again, Loree Lough has created a world of vivid landscapes, delightful characters, and a storyline that grabs you by the heart and doesn't let go.

—*Lori Twichell* ◆ Reviewer, fictionaddict.com

Loree Lough writes with poignancy and a keen understanding of human nature. With her skillful style, readers will be immediately hooked and compelled through the final pages.

—*Annette M. Irby* ◆ Author, *Love Letters*

Maverick Heart

11/29/15

Loree Lough

WHITAKER
HOUSE

All Scripture quotations are taken from the King James Version of the Holy Bible.

MAVERICK HEART
Book Two in the Lone Star Legends Series

Loree Lough
www.loreelough.com

ISBN: 978-1-60374-226-9
Printed in the United States of America
© 2011 by Loree Lough

Whitaker House
1030 Hunt Valley Circle
New Kensington, PA 15068
www.whitakerhouse.com

Library of Congress Cataloging-in-Publication Data

Lough, Loree.
Maverick heart / by Loree Lough.
    p. cm. — (Lone star legends ; bk. 2)
    Summary: "When young widow Levee O'Reilly and rancher Dan Neville, a confirmed bachelor, are awakened to a long-ignored desire for love, they need to accept God's forgiveness—and forgive themselves—in order to pursue it"—Provided by publisher.
    ISBN 978-1-60374-226-9 (trade pbk.)
    1. Ranchers—Texas—Fiction. I. Title.
    PS3562.O8147M38 2011
    813'.54—dc22
                            2010040976

1 2 3 4 5 6 7 8 9 10 11 12 **W** 18 17 16 15 14 13 12 11

Dedication and Acknowledgments

Maverick Heart, like the seventy-four novels that preceded it, is dedicated to my reader-friends, whose warm letters inspire me to keep writing, and the grace-filled people at Whitaker House, whose faith in my talents made the Lone Star Legends series possible. To my exceptional editors, Courtney, Sharon, and Lois, whose eagle eyes put the final "shine" on this tale, and the talented folks in the graphics department for another dynamic cover. To Diana Flegal, my dedicated agent who introduced me to the Whitaker family, and Lee Raine of CowboyShowcase.com, whose knowledge of ranching is boundless! To Winter Peck, Annette Dashovy, and all my Facebook, ShoutLife, and Twitter friends who also shared "cow and horse" tidbits.

To my devoted husband, daughters, and grandkids, whose unwavering support and understanding helped keep my fingers on the keyboard, and Cash, faithful canine companion, for patiently waiting until his key-clacking mistress found Frisbee time. To my beloved grandfather, who went to paradise while I was just a teen, and who no doubt grinned when he learned this story is set in 1888, the year of his birth!

Most important of all, this novel—and my entire life—is dedicated to my Lord and Savior Jesus Christ, who called me to write faith-based fiction that touches hearts and changes lives—according to His design.

A Letter from Loree

Dear Readers,

What comes to mind when you hear the word *maverick*? Images of a beautiful stallion, running wild and free across the prairie? Unbranded cattle roaming the open range? An orphaned calf, searching for its mother?

And what about *heart*? Does it make you think of the hardworking organ that supplies us with life-sustaining blood from the moment we're conceived until we draw our final breath? The tenderness and compassion so often referred to as "heart"? Maybe it reminds you of the way sports announcers so often use *heart* in place of *courage*, *energy*, and *spirit*. You might have a change of heart, set your heart on something, or deliver a heartfelt message. In school, you learned your ABC's and the multiplication table "by heart," and at funerals, you comfort grieving friends by telling them to "take heart." Who hasn't experienced heartache and heartbreak, or discussed topics that get right to the "heart of the matter"? People can be heartless, evil deeds make us heartsick, sad stories are heartrending.

Put them together, and you have *Maverick Heart*, the title of this second book in the Lone Star Legends series. Join me for a rousing, Wild-West adventure that will take you back to Eagle Pass in 1888, where Levee O'Reilly and Dan Neville will face a killer tornado, gun-toting rustlers, and a long cattle drive. Share their joy at friends' weddings, laugh alongside them at children's Christmas pageants, and cry with them as they grieve the loss of beloved friends and family members. Then, drop me a note to let me know which scene from *Maverick Heart* was your favorite.

It's always a joy hearing from you, and, as some of you already know, I make a point of answering every letter personally. Happy reading, dear friends! I look forward to hearing from you soon.

Blessings to you and yours,
Loree

PS: Watch for *Unbridled Love*, book three in the Lone Star Legends series, coming in summer 2011!

May 1888 • Somewhere along the San Antonio Road

"You behave as though you're the first woman to have a miscarriage!" Liam scolded Levee. "Pull yourself together. Can't you see you're making everyone miserable?"

That had been three days ago, but the memory of the rebuff still stung like the gritty, windblown Texas dust. Levee huddled in a corner of the stagecoach and prayed that her husband wouldn't notice her tears. She'd never been the type to wallow in self-pity, but was it too much to ask her husband to show some warmth and compassion? As a doctor, he should have been able to acknowledge that her reaction to losing the baby was perfectly normal.

Frowning, she tucked her lace-trimmed handkerchief back into her purse—a mistake, for Liam saw and correctly guessed that she'd been crying. Again.

"You'll never get over it if you don't at least try to put it out of your mind," he grumbled.

The impatience and disappointment in his voice hurt almost as much as his earlier reprimand, and Levee heaved a sigh. Oh, if only she could put it out of her mind!

Maybe he had a point. Maybe thirty-four days of grieving her lost baby had been enough. As one of the first women in the country to earn a nursing degree, Levee understood the mental and physical aftereffects of a miscarriage. But could melancholia explain why she felt her husband was too preoccupied about opening his new clinic in Mexico to mourn the loss of yet another baby?

Like it or not, they would arrive in Mexico in a matter of days. Chihuahua, of all places, where she didn't know a soul, and the people spoke a language she didn't understand. Where, according to Boston newspapers, outlaw gangs roamed the—

"Hold on to your hats, folks!" the driver bellowed. "Bandits, ridin' in hard and fast!"

Amid the thunder of horses' hooves and the report of gunfire, their fellow passenger, who'd introduced himself only as Mack, calmly unholstered two six-shooters. "You got a gun, doc?" he asked Liam as he lifted the leather window covering and peeked outside.

Liam clutched his black medical bag tight to his chest. "Yes, but—"

"Then you'd best get 'er loaded and cocked. There're three of them and five of us. We might just have us a fightin' chance"—he fixed his brown eyes on Levee—"if you can shoot."

Just as she opened her mouth to confess that she'd never so much as held a gun, one of the stagecoach drivers cut loose a bloodcurdling scream. Quick as a blink, his body hurtled past the window and hit the ground with a sickening thump.

With a trembling hand, Levee clutched her throat, and Mack groaned. "Make that four of us." He spun the chamber of the second revolver and, after pulling back the hammer with a click, wrapped the fingers of Levee's other trembling hand around the grip. "Just aim and pull the trigger, and keep on doing that till you're out of bullets."

"B-but how will I know when I'm out of—"

"Are you two God-fearin' Christians?"

She heard Liam's dry swallow. "I don't know what that has to do with anything," he muttered.

Mack glared at him. "If you want to get out of this mess alive, you'd best start prayin'. Pray like you've never prayed—"

His warning was cut short by male voices shouting and terrified horses trumpeting. Gears and brakes screeched as the coach came to a jolting halt.

Then, a deadly hush rode in on a cloud of dust.

The door nearest Levee flew open with a bang. "Throw them guns into the dirt," growled a masked man with a rifle.

When Liam slid his revolver back into his doctor's bag, Mack gave a slight nod, then tossed his own pistol out the door. Taking his other gun back from Levee, he uncocked it and flung it to the ground, too.

The bandit raised his rifle barrel higher. "Git on outta there, one at a time, and don't try no funny business, neither."

Levee climbed down first, followed by Liam. *So much for Mack coming up with a last-minute scheme to save us,* she thought as he joined them in the shade of the coach.

A few yards away, two more bandits sat in their saddles. The smooth baritone and well-enunciated syllables of the tallest didn't fit the rudeness of his words: "Gather anything of value you find on their persons or in their valises," he told the rifleman. And then, using his chin as a pointer, he said to the man to his left, "You. Fetch the money."

Their immediate obedience made it clear that this man was one to be reckoned with. Levee's heart beat harder as his cohorts carried out his orders, but it wasn't until the strongbox hit the ground with a loud clang that she noticed the other stagecoach driver, hanging like a half-empty flour sack over the armrest of his seat. She could almost hear Mack thinking, *And now we're down to three.* Their only hope was the tiny pistol hidden in Liam's bag. But even if by some miracle the cowboy managed to retrieve it, would it be enough to disarm all three thieves?

The second bandit fired one round from his pistol, demolishing the heavy iron lock on the strongbox. If he noticed Levee's tiny squeal of fright or Liam's gasp of shock, it didn't show. "Must be fifty thousand dollars in here!" he said, pawing through the contents. He gave a rousing "Yee-haw!" and saluted his leader. "All's I can say is, you sure know how to pick 'em, Frank!"

"Shut up, fool!" bellowed the rifle-toting robber. "Now we'll hafta kill 'em, so's they won't be able to tell the rangers they was robbed by the Frank Michaels Gang!"

The Frank Michaels Gang? Why did that sound so familiar? Levee's question was quickly extinguished by a sickening admission: in her twenty-two years of life, she'd never given a thought to how she might leave this earth. Until now.

"No need to get your dander up," Mack drawled. "Y'all just keep right on helpin' yourselves to everything we've got. Think of us as the three wise monkeys. We didn't see a thing or hear a thing, and we won't speak a thing, either."

"That's right," Liam quickly agreed, "even if the Texas Rangers ask questions—an unlikely event, since we don't plan to seek them out."

Levee looked up at her husband, unable to decide which surprised her more: the fact that he'd opened his mouth or that he'd opened his medical bag. But in one beat of her hammering heart, his hand disappeared inside it. In the next, his puny revolver dangled from his fingertips. "I think you boys should—"

One shot rang out, and even before its echo fell silent, Liam slumped to the ground. "No-o-o!" Levee wailed, dropping to her knees. She cradled his head in her lap and, for the first time since graduating from the New England Hospital for Women, regretted her nursing degree. Because one look at the bloody wound in the middle of his chest told her that although he wasn't dead yet, he soon would be.

Liam gasped for breath. "I—I wanted to—give them—the gun," he sputtered, "to p-prove we—c-could be trusted—"

"Hush, now," she whispered, finger-combing dark curls from his forehead. "Shh."

Mack threw his Stetson to the ground and kicked it. "Of all the...." Arms whirling like a windmill, he kicked it again. "Did you hear what the man said? He's from *Boston*, for the luvva Pete. He meant you no harm. Why, I doubt he could've hit the broad side of a barn with that pea shooter of his, even if he'd tried!"

"Looked to *me* like he was aimin' to shoot," one of the bandits insisted, "an' nobody takes aim at Frank Michaels whilst I'm around."

The rifleman cursed under his breath. "Thought I tol' you to shut up, Tom."

"*All* of you shut up," Frank snarled.

But Levee paid him no mind. "Fight, Liam," she urged him. "Stay with me! You promised that as soon as we were settled, we'd—"

His eyelids fluttered open, and an enormous, silvery tear leaked from the corner of one eye. "S-sorry, Levee," he rasped, grabbing her hand. "S-sorry...."

"There's nothing to be sorry for, Liam. You're going to be fine." *Oh, please, God, let it be true!* "Just fine! Do you hear me?" No sooner had the words passed her lips than his body shuddered once, and the fingers that had been squeezing hers went limp. A dribble of blood trickled from the corner of his mouth to his chin. Then, one grating, ragged breath later, he was gone.

Levee couldn't help feeling guilty about her role in his death. These horrible men had murdered her husband, but if she hadn't put her dream of a nursing degree ahead of their wedding plans, they would have had a house to call their own. If she hadn't spent so many hours on her feet at the hospital, they would have had a child or two, instead of two unfruitful pregnancies to mourn. Perhaps, with a family to occupy his time and fill his heart, Liam wouldn't have reacted with such enthusiasm to the article in the *Boston Globe* that spoke of the need for doctors in Mexico. Why had she let him talk her into this move? And why had she bowed to the dictates of society and the Good Book regarding wifely submission? If only she'd been stronger and less self-centered!

She watched the thugs help themselves to Liam's hard-earned savings. Watched them poke through her small suitcase as Frank Michaels tucked Grandpa O'Reilly's gold pocket watch into his vest. He looked up, caught her staring, and touched a finger to his hat brim. "My apologies, ma'am," he said, aiming a steely smile her way. "And to prove my sincerity, we aren't going to kill you. You have my word on that." A grating chuckle passed through the red and black fabric of his bandanna. "At least, not today."

His implied threat hung on the parched air as Levee looked into her husband's ashy face. Almost from the moment they'd left Boston, Levee had been afraid. Afraid of ghastly-looking bugs and wild animals, afraid of the unrelenting wind and the dry, desolate land that seemed to stretch on forever. Afraid of the outlaws and bandits she'd read about. Distraught and anguished, she was beyond fear now. A swirl of self-blame, guilt, and shame roiled inside her like a cyclone, putting put her on her feet.

Fists balled at her sides, Levee marched up to the leader's horse. "You killed my husband for no reason, and you think a phony apology will make things right? You're—you're a lunatic, Frank Michaels, and so are these so-called men who ride with you." Levee wiped angrily at her traitorous tears. "Look at you, hiding behind your masks. Why, you're nothing but cowards, the lot of you. Heartless thieves and—and cold-blooded killers. You'd better shoot me good and dead, right here where I stand, because the very first chance I get, I *will* report you to the Texas Rangers, and nothing will please me more than to watch you hang for your crimes!"

Her hysterical tirade silenced even the chorusing insects and chirruping birds. Silenced the amused chortles of Frank and his cohorts, too. The men exchanged puzzled glances, and then the one named Tom said, "You want I should plug her, Frank, or d'you wanna do it?"

Frank rested one leather-gloved hand atop the other on his saddle horn, seeming to consider the idea. "I gave her my word, and I intend to keep it."

Tom snorted. "She'll probably die of thirst before she reaches the next town, anyway." Winking, he added, "If the coyotes don't get her first. Levee had been an unwilling eyewitness to what the mangy canines could do to a deer carcass, and in very little time, too. She pressed her fingertips to her closed eyes to block the grisly image, and when she did, the picture of Liam's lifeless body took its place. A dozen thoughts flitted through her head. Could she have used her medical training to do something to save him? Why hadn't she seen the gunman take aim before he fired at Liam? If she had, what might she have done to prevent the shooting?

"Coyotes," she heard the rifleman say. "You got that right, Tom. No chance she'll live long enough to tell anybody what happened here."

Mack's voice broke through. "That was uncalled for," he grumbled. "The poor woman just lost her husband."

As if she needed a reminder! *Please, Lord, please, let this be a terrible nightmare. Let me wake up and realize that—*

A deafening explosion ended her prayer. She wasn't dreaming, as evidenced by the whiff of smoke spiraling from Frank's gun barrel—and the ghastly sound of Mack's body hitting the ground. "No-o-o," she wailed for the second time today. "Not him, too! B-but you promised not to—"

"I only promised not to kill *you*," Frank said, then coolly holstered his revolver and faced Tom. "Tom? Unharness the team."

Frank and his men had ended four lives in barely more than four minutes, and with four words, he'd dismissed the matter. The howling wind whirled around them, gathering the dust into tiny twisters that hopped across the prairie like jackrabbits. Levee buried her face in her hands, unwilling to let the bandits witness one more moment of her misery. She had the rest of her life for that.

Life. She almost laughed at the notion. Sitting in the middle of the Texas prairie, waiting for only the good Lord knew what to kill her, wasn't her idea of *life.*

An idea dawned: perhaps, if she got them good and angry, they'd shoot her, too, and she could join Liam in paradise.

So, Levee began hurling insults and slurs, shrieking like a crazed fishwife, and waving her arms. But she might as well have been a cactus or tumbleweed for all the attention they paid her. Infuriated, she picked up rocks and pebbles and hurled those, too, yet the outlaws continued to ignore her. It seemed they really did intend to leave her out here in the middle of nowhere to wait for starvation and thirst—or hungry coyotes—to kill her. *Oh, Father, please let it be coyotes,* she prayed. As painful and terrifying as that would be, she'd die faster that way than by nature's cruel hand. Either way, she'd have ample time to repent of her sins of selfishness.

"You're no better than the coyotes!" But her words disappeared into their cloud of get-away dust and gleeful bellows. Hugging herself, Levee sunk to the dirt between Liam and Mack and sat on her boot heels, rocking and groaning, groaning and rocking, as she waited for the tears to start.

But not a single drop fell. Not for her husband or the babies they'd lost, not for the brave young cowboy who'd died defending her, not even for herself, alone and afraid, somewhere in West Texas.

She didn't know how many hours had passed when the sun began to sink below the horizon like a gold coin disappearing into a slot. A dark chill blanketed the plains, waking snaky shadows that slithered from bush to scrubby shrub. That's when strange, forlorn moans spilled forth from Levee's lips, ascended into the blackness, and merged with the midnight cacophony of night birds and bugs and coyote calls.

By the time exhaustion rendered her silent, the moon was high in the sky, and she found herself cuddled up to Liam. And, though his lanky body offered no warmth or comfort, that's where she stayed, praying that before morning, the Almighty in His loving mercy, would call her home, too.

*L*evee saw Becky cup a hand between her mouth and Samantha's ear and heard her whisper, "See, I *told* you he's teacher's pet."

Her seatmate rolled her eyes and sighed. "Shh, before your talking gets us into trouble."

Levee tapped her pointer on the blackboard. "Rebecca? Samantha? I'd hate to make you stay after school again."

"Sorry, Mrs. O'Reilly," the girls chorused.

Levee had done her best to look and sound stern, but her heart just wasn't in it. During the seven months she'd spent in Eagle Pass, she'd developed a deep affection for every one of her sixteen students, from four-year-old Willie Rogers to thirteen-year-old Tim Boone. "Now, let's pay attention, shall we? Go ahead, Eli."

The boy picked up where he'd left off in his *Parker's First Reader*. "You have seen a picture of a cat and a house."

It was Samantha's turn. "Did you see a sound?"

"No," Tim continued. "I can hear a sound, but I cannot see a sound."

As the children took turns reading the lesson, Levee's mind wandered. Was it possible that just last April, she'd been in Boston, a married woman with a baby on the way? Or that now, halfway through December, she was a widow, forced to accept the only position available to make ends meet until she could afford passage back to Boston? If she hadn't spent so much of her pay on classroom supplies, that's where she'd be right now.

You know better, Levee O'Reilly, she corrected herself. *Eagle Pass feels more like home than Boston ever did.*

Perched on the corner of her desk, she determined to concentrate on the children's reading lesson. Instead, her attention was drawn away again, this time to images of that terrible day on the prairie. The stagecoach robbery, those awful men, the gruesome sight of her young husband lying still, so very still, in the grainy Texas dust....

Levee crossed her arms, cupped her elbows with the palms of her hands, and focused on the fact that Frank Michaels was dead. *Thank God for Kate Neville,* she thought, *for firing the shot that killed him!* It was a horrible thought, one that would have sent any other Christian woman to her knees in a prayer of repentance, and she wished she could do the same. But she was not like other Christian women, and, right now, it seemed she would never be able to forgive again, thanks to the vile outlaws who had ended her husband's life.

"Somethin' wrong, Mrs. O'Reilly?"

Levee felt her cheeks go hot. "Of course not, Tim. What makes you ask such a thing?"

"It's just, well, you looked powerful mad just now," the boy said. He closed his reader. "I, uh, we're finished with the lesson."

So much for Reverend Peterson's assurances that you'd forgive that terrible man eventually. "I'm not mad," she assured him. *At least, not with you, dear boy!* "I didn't sleep very well last night, that's all." Forcing a smile, she glanced at the ornate clock in the corner, which had been donated, along with a huge crate of books, by Matilda Montgomery, a wealthy benefactress who lived in a beautiful home near the school. Levee had enjoyed getting to know her and was glad to have a friend.

With only thirty minutes left in the school day, she saw no point in moving on to the next lesson. "You all did such a wonderful job. Simply wonderful!"

Just as she opened her mouth to dismiss the class, Mack walked through the rear doors. "Howdy, young'uns," he said, holding up a brown sack. "Look what I've brought you!"

The girls giggled, and the boys shouted, and before Levee could say hello, Mack was surrounded by children. He looked so hale and hearty, doling out rock candy, one chunk per palm, that it was hard to believe what sorry shape he'd been in when they arrived in Eagle Pass.

At sunrise on the day after the stagecoach robbery, quiet whimpering had roused Levee. For a brief moment, hope had glimmered in her heart as she'd examined Liam, but a kiss to his cold, dry cheek was all it had taken to confirm the ugly truth. She'd then turned her attention to Mack, who'd been weak but somehow alive. Using ointments and tools and tape from Liam's medical bag, she'd patched him up as best she could. All day long, he'd slid in and out of consciousness as Levee had dug a shallow grave for Liam. By sundown, she'd fashioned a crude cross of boards pried from the drivers' seat, and Mack—God bless him—had carved her husband's name into the wood and said a quiet blessing over the discreet mound in the dirt. It had hardly been the burial Liam deserved, but it had been far better than leaving him for the buzzards and coyotes.

The next morning, Mack had been strong enough to walk, and they'd headed southwest by way of the San Antonio Road. With every step, Levee's bitterness toward Frank Michaels had grown. In the afternoon, a dust-covered stagecoach had appeared, and the driver had offered to take them as far as Eagle Pass, where the two friends, bonded by heartbreak on the prairie, had been ever since.

"Penny for your thoughts…."

He'd caught her daydreaming. She'd been doing a lot of that lately. *Make sure to pray about that later,* she told herself.

"I brought something for you, too." He patted his shirt pocket. "Early Christmas present."

She should have admitted straight-out that she had no intention of celebrating the holiday. Should have told him that theirs wasn't a "gift-exchanging" type of relationship. But in the months she'd known Mack, she'd learned the futility of arguing with the bighearted cowboy. "Just let me give the children their homework assignment," she whispered to him, "and I'll be right with you."

Nodding, Mack plopped into the seat nearest her desk while Levee instructed her pupils to practice their multiplication tables before returning to class the next day. To the youngest three, who hadn't progressed that far in arithmetic, she said, "Recite your ABC's ten times." Then, she ushered the students to the door and stood on the schoolhouse porch to watch them disperse. "Lift your skirts if you're going to run, girls!" she called after them. "Boys! Put down those sticks before someone loses an eye!"

Smiling and shaking her head, she walked back into the classroom. Oh, how she loved them! *Because they're likely the closest you'll ever get to having children?* The somber thought erased her smile, but a glimmer of it returned when she read what Mack had written on the blackboard: "Levee O'Reilly, the prettiest gal in Eagle Pass."

"As flattering as that might be," she teased, "you're not leaving here until you've washed that slate clean, Mack Burdette."

"All in good time, teacher, all in good time. But first," he said, holding out a brown paper-wrapped package, "you need to open your present."

She gawked at the small, flat rectangle. "But it's nearly two weeks until Christmas."

Mack shrugged. "I'll probably be out at the farthest acres of the ranch by then, rounding up strays."

On the very afternoon Doc Lane had given him a clean bill of health, Mack had hired on as a ranch hand for the Nevilles, who owned the Lazy N Ranch. He hadn't talked about where he'd been prior to boarding that stagecoach or how he'd earned his pay, and Levee had never asked. But Mack seemed born to the work, and during the months he'd been employed at the Lazy N, he'd grown lean and tan, and his brown eyes now glowed with contentment. Though it made her feel conceited and vain, Levee suspected that his happiness was due in part to the fact that he'd taken a shine to her. His boyish grin, his impromptu visits, and his thoughtful little gifts for her students and her made his feelings clear, and he probably hoped she'd return his feelings someday.

Yet Levee didn't expect that day would ever come. For one thing, she'd barely wrapped her mind around the fact that at twenty-two, she was a childless widow. For another, she knew how unfair it would be to saddle Mack—or any man, for that matter—with the feelings of guilt and shame that hung over her like a black cloud. She'd never atone for the sins of selfishness and weakness that had led to Liam's death. She loved Mack like a brother and, because of that, could never allow her fondness for him to grow into something more.

Gently, he pried open her fingers and set the parcel in her palm.

"You shouldn't have, really."

A grin lit his dark eyes. "Yes, I should." He stood a little taller. "Now, go on, open it."

When she peeled back the brown paper, a bar of chocolate appeared.

"It's imported," he explained, tapping the wrapper. "All the way from Switzerland."

Levee had seen the chocolates at J. W. Riddle's grocery store and knew they cost far more than he could afford to spend regularly. She also knew that gifts—mostly things she realized she'd never really needed or wanted—had been one of the many ways Liam had held sway over her. She had made the right decision where Mack was concerned, kindhearted though he was. "It's—it's too much." She started to refold the brown paper around the candy bar. "I'm sure Mr. Riddle will give you a refund, or exchange it for someth—"

Mack snatched it back, peeled back the wrapper, and bit off a corner. "Can't take it back now," he said, grinning around the mouthful as he handed it back to her, "so you might as well enjoy it."

Levee accepted it from him and took a tiny bite, telling herself as the sweet chocolate melted in her mouth that it was best to humor him. "I'll save the rest," she said, smiling, "and when you return from the 'farthest acres,' we'll share it." She carefully rewrapped the candy and tucked it into a pocket in her big canvas bag. "Thank you, Mack. But, really, you shouldn't have. You're too thoughtful and too generous for your own good sometimes."

"No such thing as 'too thoughtful and too generous' where you're concerned, Levee."

And he meant it. She could see the proof all over his handsome, mustached face, could hear it in his gravelly voice. The warmth of a blush crept across her cheeks, because now she felt awful for having mentally compared him to Liam, and to hide her discomfort, Levee led the way to the door. "Will you be here for the children's Christmas pageant? They've been practicing for weeks, and I'm sure they'd love to see you in the audience."

A strange expression skittered across his face—a look of hope and longing that told her nothing would please him more than to hear her say *she* would love seeing him in the audience. But it wouldn't be fair to mislead him. He deserved a woman who'd give him all the affection and attention he deserved, not one who'd second-guess every kindness, every gesture, simply because she'd made the mistake of marrying a cold, unloving man.

"Wouldn't miss it," he said from the porch. "Not for all the world. I'm going to miss—"

"Say, Burdette," interrupted a cheerful baritone, "you gonna stand there jabbering with the schoolmarm all the live-long day?"

Mack returned the man's smile. "Hey, Dan," he said, waving. "Finished at the granary already, are you?"

"Yep."

How was it possible that she had been in town all this time and never seen the fellow before? Not at Sunday services or church socials, not in the shops in town or on the roads leading to and from Eagle Pass. As Mack gathered up his gear and tossed it into the back of the wagon, the man's gaze locked with hers.

If she'd ever seen bluer eyes, Levee didn't know when. Gleaming golden curls peeked out from under his hat brim, and then he smiled, reminding her how it feels to glimpse the sun after days of dreary rain. The warmth made her tingle from the roots of her hair to the soles of her stockings.

Mack looked from Levee to the man and back again. "I take it you two haven't met?"

One corner of his mouth lifted in a bashful grin. "Can't say as I've had the pleasure."

Mack chuckled. "Well, that's easily remedied. Levee O'Reilly, Dan Neville." He cupped a hand over his mouth to add, "Be nice to this fella. He's my boss."

So, he was a member of the Neville clan, known throughout the area as the biggest, wealthiest family for miles and miles.

"Now, now," Dan said, leaning forward to see past Mack and look at Levee. "I'm sure the lady is always nice." When their gazes met, she found herself hoping she wouldn't exclaim, "I've never seen more beautiful eyes," or "What a delightful smile," or "If only my own hair was half as radiant as yours!" Because all of those comments—and more—were bouncing around in her head.

"It's *quite* lovely making your acquaintance," she heard herself say. And then she curtsied. *Curtsied!*

When Dan's eyebrows arched slightly as the corner of his mouth lifted again, the heat of another blush warmed her cheeks, and she blinked stupidly, wringing her hands in front of her. If only she could stuff the words back into her mouth and hide her silly, curtsying self on the other side of the thick schoolhouse doors!

"Well," Dan drawled, "guess we'd best be on our way."

Mack nodded in agreement. "You have a good evening, Levee."

"Pleasure meeting you, ma'am."

More of a pleasure meeting you! she almost said.

As he snapped the reins and urged the team forward, shame coursed through her. She'd never reacted that way to Liam— not on the day they'd met, not on the rainy afternoon when he'd listed the many logical reasons why they should marry, and not even on their wedding night, when she'd counted the hours until he put down his ledger book and came to bed.

You're a horrible, horrible person, Levee O'Reilly. Just horrible! she berated herself. *Poor Liam gone not even a year yet, and already you're flirting with strange men!*

Not that Daniel was strange. Far from it, actually. Much to his credit, he'd behaved like a perfect gentleman, even as she'd gushed and blushed and...and *curtsied*.

Levee hid behind her hands and groaned. Yes, it was a very good thing that she'd promised to spend the rest of her days alone. What man in his right mind wanted to spend his life with an empty-headed twit like herself? In time, perhaps she'd grow to enjoy being referred to as the Widow O'Reilly and the Eagle Pass schoolmarm. Perhaps there'd come a time when she would put her nursing degree to use doing something other than bandaging her students' skinned knees and bruised elbows. Funny how the job that was supposed to have lasted only until she'd earned enough to pay for passage back to Boston had become the focus of her life. Funnier still how each student had become a surrogate child.

She never would have guessed that a city-bred girl like herself, accustomed to crowds and noise and modern conveniences, could adapt so quickly to a place where the wind caused more ruckus than the people. But there was nothing for her back East. It was no surprise, then, that this little town on the banks of the Rio Grande felt like home, and the bighearted people who had donated furniture, curtains, and china to warm the atmosphere of her little cottage behind the schoolhouse felt like family.

When she came out of hiding, Dan Neville's wagon was little more than a dot on the horizon. If she closed her eyes, Levee could still picture him, and as she headed back into the schoolhouse, she wondered about the smile that never reached his beautiful eyes.

Was it, like hers, a mask donned to hide secret sorrows?

3

Dan gritted his teeth. His interest in Mack's relationship with Levee O'Reilly didn't make a lick of sense, considering the promise he'd made to himself ten years earlier. If his ranch hand and the local schoolteacher were sparking, well, it shouldn't make a whit of difference to him. Still, there was no denying that he was interested. She'd captured his attention with nothing more than a shy smile.

But he couldn't very well just come right out and ask Mack about her, especially considering how much he'd come to appreciate Mack and how afraid he was to put any bone of contention between them.

The day Mack had come looking for a job, Dan's attitude had been admittedly surly. "Man comes to town all shot up and tight-lipped about where he's been?" he'd told his family that night over dinner. "Why, he could be a gunman, for all we know."

"Seemed to me he knows plenty about horses and cows," his cousin Josh had said.

Usually, Josh was a pretty good judge of character. But that hadn't stopped Dan from saying, "Maybe, but what if he's just passin' through? We need to know we can count on him out there."

"You gave *me* a chance," Josh's wife, Kate, had pointed out.

Leave it to Kate to shine a different light on things. Dan had taken a liking to her the moment Josh had returned from a business trip in San Antone with her in tow, bruised and battered and even more guarded about her past than Mack. She made Josh happy, and every Neville had fallen in love with her, from his grizzled old pa to his sister's little boy, Willie. And that was good enough for Dan.

As it turned out, Mack more than earned his pay, doing the work of two men every day he'd been with them. If he said he'd be in the north fields, that's exactly where they'd find him, and he didn't consider himself above shoveling stalls or raking dung from the paddocks. If the man wanted to keep a secret or two, well, didn't he have that right? *Lord knows you're holding on to your share*, Dan reminded himself. He shook his head, hoping to shake free the ugly memories. Maybe asking Mack about Levee would clear the cobwebs from his mind, once and for all. To avoid upsetting their relationship of mutual respect, however, he would have to tread carefully. "Didn't realize you were so friendly with the schoolmarm," he said casually.

The steady clip-clop of the team's hooves counted out the seconds until Mack finally spoke. "So, what's your plan for those south pastures?" And then he yawned.

If the cowpoke's relationship with the teacher had teeth, why not admit it straight-out? That's what Dan would do if a woman like Levee ever deigned to include him in her life. He frowned at the improbability of that ever happening. Eventually, she'd get an eyeful of him hobbling around like an old man, or some old biddy in town would tell her about the terrible thing he'd done as a teen. No, Dan was smart to have pledged celibacy. It would save him the pain of inevitable rejection, deserved though it would be.

"Weather can be unpredictable this time of year," Mack added. "You've got a good idea there, rounding up those strays before the winter rains set in. Maybe we can even gather up any mavericks we find."

With the image of Levee O'Reilly still so clear in his mind, Dan found it difficult to focus. Mack was right. The weather was mighty unpredictable this time of year. And so were the uncharacteristic thoughts jumping around in his head. *Winter.* Dan grunted. It had never been his favorite season, but after that brisk November day when Daisy had died—

"She sure as shootin' is a purty one, I'll give her that," Mack finally admitted.

The comment caught him off guard. "Who?" As if he didn't know.

"Why, Levee, of course." Mack leaned forward in the wagon seat and cast Dan a quizzical look. "Don't tell me you didn't notice."

Before Dan could agree or protest, Mack whistled softly. "Bet she would be sweet to hold, too."

He pictured himself doing just that, and instantly, his heartbeat doubled. He cleared his throat as an ember of relief flickered in his heart, because Mack's musing made it clear he hadn't gotten that close to her. "I hear-tell you were there when her husband was gunned down," he said.

From the corner of his eye, Dan saw Mack lower his head. "Doubt she'll ever forgive me for that."

"What's to forgive? Way I heard it, the Frank Michaels Gang killed him."

Mack leaned back in the seat. "Don't mind saying, it seems a mite peculiar that I've worked for you going on a year, and we've never talked about that day before now."

"We haven't talked about much of anything, save for ranching." Most of the ranch hands joined the Neville family for dinner every chance they got, but Mack preferred taking his meals in the kitchen. If anybody had heard him talk about that day, it would be Lucinda, the cook, and her husband, George, who looked after the house and grounds.

"Not much time to talk about anything but, I reckon."

"I reckon."

Mack chuckled. "Read a poem once about some dude worrying that he might drown in his woman's eyes." Another chuckle. "Had no earthly idea what he was talking about until I met Levee." He heaved a long, shuddering sigh. "Can't shed the thought that I ought to have been able to save her man."

"My family had a run-in with that bunch," Dan put in, remembering the night when they surrounded Frank Michaels and his gang at their campfire. "I'd bet the ranch that there wasn't a thing you could have done to save the doc."

"Maybe." Mack looked pensive for a moment. "Wasn't it your cousin's wife who shot Michaels?"

In a flash, Dan was back on the prairie, watching helplessly as Josh lay bleeding, hearing horses' whinnies and men's shouts and gunshots like red-hot pokers slice through the darkness. He ground his molars together, thinking of the moment when Kate had picked up a revolver just as Frank had aimed to fire a second round at Josh. If she hadn't pulled the trigger precisely when she had....

Dan cleared his throat. "Yeah," he said quietly, reverently. "That li'l gal's got more backbone than all those outlaws put together."

If he'd known that the simple remark would release a flood of information from Mack, he might have kept it to himself.

Then again, that would have meant missing out on hearing how Levee had stood up to Frank Michaels, flinging insults and accusations and stones at him and his cohorts. Now, he was more interested in her than ever—and more determined to back off. Mack's voice and posture made it plain that he cared plenty for the pretty little schoolteacher.

Dan had been in love once and expected he'd remember Gwendolyn's parting words until his dying day. *"I suppose I could learn to live with your limp and that hideous scar on your face,"* she'd said, *"but you don't really expect me to spend the rest of my life with a man who killed his own sister, do you?"* Despite the reassurances of family and friends, all of whom insisted that what had happened to Daisy had been a tragic accident that he couldn't have prevented, Dan believed otherwise. And the slightest possibility of Levee reacting the same way once she found out was more than enough to help him keep his vow never to fall in love again.

Experience had taught him that once the painful memories rose to the surface, it took patience and hard work to push them down again. Maybe spending some time in the open country would accomplish that. "I'll head into town for supplies," he said, returning to the subject of ranching. "We can head out at first light Saturday."

Mack swiveled in the wagon seat. "We?"

Dan stared straight ahead, deliberately ignoring his surprise. "Yep," he said. "We."

The men rode the rest of the way to the Lazy N in companionable silence, Mack playing a gloomy tune on his harmonica, Dan trying to figure out why, after one brief meeting and a few words, he felt a keen kinship with the sad-eyed schoolteacher with the peculiar name.

4

Oh, don't make such a fuss, Susan," Aunt Eva scolded her daughter at the noontime meal the next day. "Willie is as hale and hearty as any man on this ranch."

Dan's cousin sighed and rolled her eyes—actions that would have earned her young son a wallop to his bottom. "Mother, you didn't see him when he left for school this morning, all sleepy and quiet and—"

"Should've kept the boy home, then," her father, Dan's uncle Matthew, brusquely interrupted her. "Pass the chicken."

As the platter traveled from cousin to cousin down the long, mahogany table, Dan helped himself to a piece. Anything to ignore the noise. Some days, he thought it sounded more like a henhouse in here than a dining room, which had produced two positive results: he'd become a master at staying out of family squabbles, and his gut didn't fold over his belt like his uncles', because no matter how tasty the meal, he rarely reached for second helpings. Too hard to digest food with so much bickering going on. He managed to live peacefully in a house smaller than this one with his own folks, two unmarried sisters, and another sister and her husband. Why couldn't Uncle Matthew, Aunt Eva, Susan, her husband, Sam, her sister, Sarah, and little Willie do the same?

"Makes no sense," Uncle Matthew was saying, "sending him to school if he's ailing. Waste of time for him and the schoolmarm." He held up one hand to fend off the defensive comment his daughter no doubt was fixing to deliver. "I didn't see the boy when he lit out for school, but I'd wager he just didn't get a good night's sleep."

"Your pa makes a good point," Aunt Eva agreed. "I declare, Susan, you worry enough for ten people!"

Dan's uncle chuckled. Meanwhile, tears filled Susan's eyes. She stood up and tossed her napkin onto her chair. "I do wish you'd both stop trying to make me feel like an overprotective hen. It's perfectly natural to be a little concerned, considering...." Her lower lip trembled, and it appeared she was trying to decide what to add to her sentence. "Considering he looked so small and pale. And with that long walk home and all—"

"Now, now, just settle down, darlin'," her husband said, giving her hand a squeeze. "After dinner, I'll hitch the team. Then we'll ride to town and—"

Susan snatched her hand away and pressed it to her slightly rounded belly. "You know perfectly well that the doctor said I'm not to sit a horse or ride in a wagon on these rutted roads. Not unless I want to have another miscarriage!"

There were few things Dan wanted more than a wife, some young'uns, and a home of his own, except at times like these. Right now, poor Sam looked as if he could commiserate with a beetle stuck on its back, and Dan hardly envied him.

"If you sit down and finish your dinner," Sam began again, "I'll ride into town and get him, myself. All right?"

"It most certainly is not all right." The exasperated baritone had come from the north end of the table, and all heads turned toward Uncle Matthew. "How do you expect Sam to get any work done if he's lollygagging in the wagon all the blessed afternoon?"

It appeared to Dan that Susan couldn't make up her mind whether to dart for the door, to stomp her foot, or both. Having been born sixth in a line of seven siblings, the other six of whom were girls, Dan had seen all manner of female drama. Daisy had been the only one never to give in to histrionics. According to his mother, his half-blind twin's sunny disposition was explained with two little words: "She's slow." But Dan had spent more time with her than anybody else and knew she deserved more credit than that. Not even perfect eyesight and a brilliant mind would have altered her calm, gentle personality.

As always happened when his sister came to mind, Dan pictured her before the tragedy—and after. He cleared his throat and pushed away from the table. The last thing he needed right now was to dwell on that. "I'm happy to fetch Willie at the schoolhouse," he volunteered. "I'll be in Eagle Pass later, fetching supplies for the—"

"Oh, would you, Dan?" Susan scuttled around to his side of the table. "You're the best cousin a girl ever had," she said, hugging him from behind. "You're always there for me, for everyone in this family, and I love you to pieces!"

"Careful, honey," Sam teased. "If you layer it on too thick, he'll get a swollen head."

"Can't have that," Dan agreed, "'specially not after I forked over five hard-earned dollars for my new Stetson!"

Susan mussed his hair. "You shouldn't be hiding all those curls under a silly old hat, anyway." Then she turned and headed for the parlor but stopped in the doorway to announce, "I do believe I'll just put my feet up and tackle that basket of darning. So, if anyone has a missing button or a holey sock, now's the time to fetch it."

Amazing, Dan thought, how quickly her sour mood had sweetened. Women were a puzzle, that much was certain.

"You're sure to turn heads in town today, cousin," Susan added. "That shirt of yours brings out the blue of your eyes, and the black bandanna makes your hair look like spun gold." She blew a kiss over her shoulder and added, "Thanks again, Dan!" before disappearing down the hall.

The family listened as her footsteps kept perfect time with each tick of the grandfather clock's heavy brass pendulum. "Eva," Uncle Matthew told his wife, "I don't mind admitting that I'll never understand women. Not if I live to be a hundred."

"Which is as the good Lord planned it to be, I'm sure." She chuckled and patted his hand. "Seriously, though, you know as well as I do that Susan isn't usually like this. After two miscarriages in such close succession, it's no wonder her emotions are in a knot."

"Biggest knot I've ever had the displeasure of seeing."

Every male at the table groaned in agreement with Uncle Matthew. Just then, Lucinda entered and began collecting the dinner dishes. "Men," she spat, clicking her tongue, "are just as big a riddle to women!"

Not wanting to hear her side of things, Dan thanked her for the meal, said good-bye to his aunt and uncle, and headed for the door. He couldn't escape fast enough. Outside, he took a deep breath of brisk, December air. If his pa had built a bigger barn, Dan could have tended his horses there instead of at his uncle's. "If only you'd built one, yourself!" he grumped.

Like every Neville heir, Dan was entitled to a generous slice of the enormous Lazy N Ranch once he came of age. At one time, he'd given serious thought to claiming that parcel just beyond the road. He fancied building a sprawling, L-shaped home that would face north on the knoll, giving him a clear view of his outbuildings, paddocks, and pastures from the wide porch. But then, Gwendolyn had gotten wind of his role in Daisy's death, turned tail, and run. After that, his heart just hadn't been in it, and he'd traded in his homestead plans for horse breeding.

Still, if he had a place of his own…. He pulled his Stetson low on his forehead and grunted. Life was depressing enough without dwelling on something that could never be.

He saddled his horse, thankful he'd been spared another round of his cousins' kidding for unsaddling it in the first place. If he had a nickel for every time he'd heard "Why go to all that bother for the few minutes it takes to wolf down a meal?" he'd have a pocketful of coins. And if they'd teased him today, Dan would have repeated the same old line: "Biscuit is a hardworking, dependable mount, and he deserves a little coddling from time to time."

His cousins' ribbing was a small price to pay for the privilege of sharing their company and good food. Each night, after putting in a long, hard day, he returned to his parents' house a few miles up the road, but it made no sense to ride all the way back there for meals when he spent most of his time in the barn on Uncle Matthew's land.

Older than his three brothers, his uncle had inherited the big, two-story home built by the family patriarch, Ezra Neville. There, Ezra and his wife, Esther, had raised the "Bible Boys": Matthew, Mark, Luke, and John, each of whom had fathered a son of his own, along with several daughters. With the house came the largest barn on Lazy N property, a perfect place for

Dan to conduct what his cousins called "horse-periments."
The trials had begun while Josh had been away at Yale, earning his law degree. In his cousin's absence, Dan had made it his
business to study animal husbandry and, under the watchful
eye of Joe Kingsley, local horse breeder-turned-veterinarian,
learned to breed dependable saddle horses. In short order, he'd
taken Joe's training to the next level, producing a herd of quality quarter horses whose progeny sold for top dollar at auction.

Wincing as he climbed into the saddle, Dan rubbed his
bum leg and wished, not for the first time, that he'd died in the
stampede of '85. As usual, he sent a silent *Sorry, Lord* heaven-
ward. But that never stopped horrific images, sounds, and sen-
sations from shuffling through his mind like a deck of cards:
pounding hooves and dust so thick he couldn't see his hand
in front of his face, the frenzied shouts of his cousins and the
ranch hands, then indescribable, searing, never-ending pain.

Rubbing his eyes, he headed to the barn, where he'd hitch
the team and drive the wagon to town to pick up Willie from
school and also fetch enough supplies to last him and Mack a
week. He hadn't written a list and figured he'd compile one in
his head to help pass the time as he drove to Eagle Pass.

Just that quick, the Widow O'Reilly came to mind.
Lucinda and George had the same nearly-black hair, but for
every straight and gleaming strand on their heads, Levee probably had three, and the mass of thick, dark curls framed her
pretty face like a tangled wreath.

He'd delivered cows to every major city in Texas and a
few in New Mexico and Oklahoma, had even gone as far as
Kansas and Nebraska a time or two. He'd likely seen hun-
dreds of women along the way, but not one with eyes the color
of lilacs, and none with long, inky lashes that made him think

of a delicate paintbrush. What was it Mack had said? That she would be sweet to hold? Oh, to have lived a different life, so he could at least hope to have that pleasure one day!

At the barn, Biscuit stopped on cue, and Dan leaned forward to pat the horse's neck appreciatively. Minutes later, unsaddled again and contentedly munching oats in his stall, Biscuit nodded, as if he approved of the thorough grooming his master was administering.

With every stroke of the brush, the high-strung stallion seemed to calm. "Think I'll see that purty li'l gal in town?" Dan asked as he stowed the cleaning box.

A brief snort was his answer.

"You're right. 'Course I'll see her—when I fetch Willie." Thankfully, he'd tucked a black bandanna into the band collar of his shirt. Would Levee notice how his shirt brought out the blue of his eyes, as Susan had? And could he keep his tan canvas trousers clean while harnessing the horses so that he wouldn't show up at the schoolhouse looking like he'd just plowed the north forty?

Dan took his time hitching the trusty mares to the wagon. Back they stepped, and once he'd secured the hames and untangled the reins, he climbed onto the seat. Just as he'd failed to write down a list of supplies to purchase, he'd forgotten money. That would mean making a stop at the bank, directly across the road from the schoolhouse.

If he knew why Levee O'Reilly kept popping into his head, he might have had a prayer of keeping his eyes on the road and his mind out of the clouds. Sighing, he raised a forearm to block the early-afternoon sun. Funny how nature could fool mere mortals. Today it was breezy and warm, but as early as next week, cold winds could blow across the prairie, drenching them with bone-chilling rains and maybe even a dusting of snow. He didn't have much choice but to trust that the good Lord would get him and the boys home again, strays in tow, before that happened.

But the threat of inclement weather did very little to distract his thoughts from Levee O'Reilly. In just over an hour, he'd stand at the back of the classroom, doing his best not to be noticed. For if Willie behaved the way he usually did at the sight of his uncle, Dan certainly wouldn't win any points with the teacher.

In an eyeblink, he pictured Willie, grinning from ear to ear, tiny boots pounding the floorboards as he ran toward him for a big hug. In the next moment, he pictured Levee, far too young and pretty to be a widow. As the familiar buildings came into view, the memory of Levee O'Reilly waving good-bye to him and Mack from the schoolhouse steps flashed in his mind.

Oh, to have a woman like that, waving hello....

Instantly, regret burned in his gut, because a woman like that deserved far better than a reformed sot like himself.

*L*evee's students were hunched over their desks, some practicing their multiplication tables, others working on long division, the youngest three trying their hands at simple addition. Willie Rogers put down his pencil and scrambled to the window. "Look, Mrs. O'Reilly," he said, tapping on the glass. "It's my uncle Dan!"

Coming to stand behind the four-year-old, Levee nodded. "Yes, I see." She'd nearly developed calluses on her knees from praying that the good Lord would erase the man's image from her mind. Now that the real thing sat not twenty feet away, her heartbeat doubled. But she couldn't let the children see her behaving like a boy-crazy schoolgirl. She cleared her throat and gave Willie's shoulder a gentle squeeze. "Get back to your seat now, please, and finish practicing your sums."

The boy frowned up at her. "Can't I go out and say hello?"

Half an hour ago, she'd seen Dan roll into town with an empty wagon. Now it was piled high with sacks and tins of what looked like pantry staples. She'd been in cattle country long enough to know it was the wrong time of year for a cattle drive. What did he need with so many supplies?

No matter. He looked so handsome in the bright, Texas sunshine, his arm muscles flexing under his pale blue shirt as he pulled back on the reins....

"Please?" Willie implored her. "I promise to come right back."

Quit gawking like an empty-headed nincompoop! Levee berated herself. Bending at the waist, she lifted the boy's chin on a bent forefinger. "You'll see him soon enough, dear Willie." Pointing at the big clock, she added, "School's out in another thirty minutes." As if to confirm her statement, the timepiece chimed, signaling the half hour.

"I hardly git to see him at home," he grumbled, "on account a' he'll be out in the barn with his dumb ol' horses, like always." The boy slogged back to his desk and crossed both arms over his chest. "Body can't even say hello to his kinfolk around here."

"Better watch out," Samantha whispered to him, "or you'll end up writing 'I shall not pout' on the board."

"Yeah," Becky agreed, "a hunnert times, like Mrs. Neville used to make us do 'fore she busted her leg."

"*Broke* her leg," Levee corrected her. Writing the same line over and over was a time-honored discipline tactic of teachers, one even Levee had been forced to do once or twice as a young student back in Boston. She'd never used it in her own classroom and had no intention to. In all her months of teaching, she had never needed to use anything more than a mild reprimand to bring the students back under control, even after a rousing game of baseball during recess. As for sweeping the porch, scrubbing desks, shoveling ashes out of the stove, and hauling firewood? Hard times and circumstances had most of the students laboring at home, so the only work Levee demanded of them was schoolwork.

Perhaps the children had exaggerated. Or perhaps Mrs. Neville really had been a harsh taskmaster. Levee would know if she had taken the time to visit the woman. But she had spent those first several months in Eagle Pass cleaning the cottage behind the schoolhouse. By midsummer, she'd coaxed a few vegetables to grow in her little garden. In September, her free time had been taken up with sewing new curtains for the schoolhouse, and in October, her evenings and weekends had gone to baking pies for the fall festival at church. Before she knew it, November had arrived, and she'd filled the weeks with planning lessons. Just last week, she'd led the children on a daylong nature hike, and this week, the Christmas pageant had kept her too busy for a trip to the Lazy N Ranch.

She stayed current on her predecessor's condition, thanks to prayer requests voiced during church services on Sundays, and lifted the woman in prayer. Now, as her students sat and ciphered quietly, guilt stung Levee's heart. It was unforgiveable that she hadn't made time in all these months to deliver a batch of cookies, at least, or a tureen of soup. But what if stopping by the Lazy N was just enough to inspire Mrs. Neville to reclaim her job?

Shame inspired a quiet gasp, and Levee hung her head. *Father, forgive my selfishness and mean-spiritedness!* No sooner had she formed the contrite prayer than an idea materialized in her mind, an idea that brought an excited smile to her mouth. "Children," she said, clapping her hands, "put away your arithmetic. I have the perfect project to round out our week!"

She'd been saving the thick, cream-colored notepaper for a special occasion. What could be more special than this? She walked up and down the tidy rows, placing one sheet on each desk.

"What's this?" Billy wanted to know as Levee slid the remaining sheets onto a shelf in the cupboard.

She picked up a piece of chalk and began writing on the board. "It's notepaper," she said over her shoulder.

"What are we s'posed to do with it?"

"You're each going to write Mrs. Neville a get-well note, that's what."

"Mrs. Neville?" Tim held his paper up to the light. "Now, why would you want to go and waste this fancy paper on the likes of her?"

Surly whispers drifted from desk to desk.

"I'll just pretend I didn't hear those rude remarks," Levee said, turning to the class and raising an eyebrow. "I'm sure Mrs. Neville had her reasons for every punishment she meted out." Yet, as she looked into the faces of her students, wide-eyed with innocence, she couldn't imagine what those reasons might be. "Each of you will write a letter telling her that you hope her leg heals very soon, and that you miss her very much." Hopefully this would make up for her self-centered fears of Mrs. Neville coming back to teach.

"But we don't miss her!" Becky blurted out. "She was grumpy an' mean, an' she didn't make learnin' fun th' way you do, Mrs. O'Reilly. Why, if we so much as looked sideways, she'd put us in a corner."

"Or make us clean somethin'," Steven added.

More murmurs of discontent rose up as the class recalled what was beginning to sound like the Judith Neville Method of Unfair Discipline. "Children! That's about all the disrespect I can tolerate for one day!" As expressions of penitence settled on their young faces, Levee set the chalk on the tray beneath the blackboard and dusted her hands together. Then, she pointed to what she'd written on the board. "This is an example to help you decide what to write in your notes." Moving to the aisle, she said, "Samantha, will you please read it for the class?"

The girl stood up at her desk, folded her hands primly in front of her, and began to read aloud. "Dear Mrs. Neville. We hope your leg is healing well and that you'll be back on your feet soon. We will pray that the good Lord mends your broken bones quickly. Yours truly...." The girl hesitated and wrinkled her nose. "What's that line for, Mrs. O'Reilly?"

Levee chuckled. "It's just there to show you where you're to sign your names." She clapped her hands twice. "Now then, let's get busy, shall we?" The children's sour expressions told her they would enjoy any assignment—even mathematics—more than this one! But Levee knew how to sweeten the mood. "I'll tell you what. If you do a nice, neat job on your notes, there will be no homework this weekend."

An eruption of whistles and whoops followed her announcement. Willie, however, was quiet. "I ain't never wrote this much in one place all at one time, not never in my whole entire life!"

As the youngest child in class, he couldn't copy the message as well or as quickly as her older students. "Just do your best, Willie," Levee coaxed him. "Mrs. Neville will appreciate knowing how hard you tried, and we'll keep it our little secret that I helped you." She made a point not to refer to the woman as Willie's great-aunt, because the good Lord knew he'd been the unhappy recipient of enough taunting and teasing for being related to the children's former teacher!

He bent over his desk with a sigh and said under his breath, "If I mess up, she's likely to make me do it over. A hunnert times, even. Or—or—or, she'll save up her 'mad,' and when she gets back here and takes her old job back, *then* she'll stand me in a corner, just 'cause she can."

Levee had known when she'd accepted the job that it wouldn't be permanent, and Willie's comment reminded her just how temporary it was. With her heart pounding, she rearranged some papers on her desk in an attempt to hide her uneasiness. For all she knew, the woman could be packing a bag with teaching supplies right now. What would Levee do to support herself then? Her nursing degree would do her no good in Eagle Pass, as the local physician had said he couldn't afford to employ an assistant.

No sense worrying about it now, she told herself. Tomorrow was Saturday. First thing in the morning, she'd bake something tasty and deliver it to the Lazy N, along with the children's notes. She'd rent a buggy and a horse from Bert to save her the long walk. If only he could tell her what sort of sweet treats Mrs. Neville liked!

The sound of pencil nibs scratching across the thick paper roused her from her daydream, and she scanned the classroom. Furrows of concentration lined the children's brows as pointy, pink tongues peeked out from between their lips. They looked so serious, focused on every stroke of their pencils. Oh, how she loved them all! *Please, Lord, no matter what happens to me when Mrs. Neville returns, let me keep in touch with these precious children!*

Levee was about to announce that they could be dismissed once they turned in their notes when movement at the back of the room stopped her. Straightaway, she recognized Daniel Neville, smiling and shuffling from one foot to the other. He removed his wide-brimmed hat and gave a two-fingered salute.

And all it took to get her heart fluttering was the slow smile on his face.

She tried to blame her response on the fact that she hadn't heard him come in—odd in itself, considering the shrill squeal the door usually made. But Levee knew better. She still wondered how so many months had passed without their meeting. It was just as well, because it simply wasn't proper or fitting for a widow to entertain thoughts about a man, even one as ruggedly good-looking as Daniel Neville. Besides, for all she knew, he had a wife and children waiting for him at home. The Neville clan was so large and complex that she still didn't know how many there were or how they were related.

So, what was he doing here?

She might have conjured a reasonable answer if he hadn't taken a halting step forward, planting his booted feet on the fringes of a sunbeam that spilled in from the window and spread across the floor like a golden carpet. His gaze again locked with hers. At the sight of the flirty grin that slanted his mustached mouth, she forced herself to look away. "Willie," she said, hoping to hide her discomfort, "look who's here."

The boy turned, squealed, and, in two ticks of the big clock, rushed over and threw himself into his uncle's arms. "I saw you from the window," he said excitedly. "Mrs. O'Reilly wouldn't let me go out to say howdy, so I'm glad you come inside."

"*Came* inside," Levee corrected him gently. "Is your note finished?"

He returned to his desk. "Almost." An audible sigh escaped his lips. "I can go with Uncle Dan when it's done, right?"

"Yes, you may." By now, the dialog had encouraged a rustle of whispers among her other students. "You may all leave once you've placed your notes to Mrs. Neville on my desk."

"Which Mrs. Neville?"

Dan's question startled Levee. How had he managed to cross twenty feet of wood-planked floor without making a sound?

Before she could answer, Willie blurted out, "Why, your maw, o'course." He waved his note in the air. "Mrs. O'Reilly maked us all write her a note to say we hope she's better soon."

"*Made* you, you mean," Dan said as his nephew slapped the paper onto Levee's desk.

Willie plopped his short-billed cap atop his head and looked up expectantly at his teacher. "So, I don't need to take home my slate, right?"

Levee winked. "That's right. No homework this weekend."

The rustle of papers mixed with the shuffle of boots on the floor as the children scrambled to turn in their assignments and race for the door. "Have a safe and happy weekend," she called after them.

"I'll wait for you in the wagon, Uncle Dan," Willie said, then hesitated, his little-boy face alight with mischief. "There's somethin' out there for me, ain't there?"

His uncle laughed. "Under the seat." The boy was already out the door as he added, "But save some of that licorice for the ride home." He chuckled and looked at Levee. "Think he heard me?"

"Not likely, but we can hope," Levee managed—a wonder, with all of the questions swirling in her head. What would that slightly raspy, wholly masculine voice sound like in song? And how blond would his hair be without the big hat to protect the curls from the bleaching effects of the sun? As light as his long, thick lashes?

"Didn't mean to disrupt your lesson."

She'd been staring, and he'd caught her at it. She turned to the blackboard to hide the blush that sprang to her cheeks. "Oh, I didn't mind," she said, picking up one of the two erasers from the chalk ledge. "We were nearly finished for the day, anyway."

Dan grabbed the other eraser and began helping her wipe away the sample note. "This was mighty thoughtful of you. My mother will sure enjoy reading their letters. She isn't used to having so little to do. All this sitting around is driving her to distraction."

Levee returned her eraser to the tray and brushed the dust off her hands. "How did she break her leg, if you don't mind my asking?"

He glanced out the window, and Levee followed his gaze and saw Willie waiting in the wagon, his cheeks so full of candy that he looked almost as much like a chipmunk as a boy. "His teeth will be as black as that candy by the time I get him home," he said, chuckling and shaking his head.

When he handed her his eraser, their fingers touched for an instant, and their eyes met, too. Dan abruptly ended the mesmerizing moment. "She was out riding one evening and a jackrabbit spooked her horse. Wouldn't have been an easy landing for a woman half her age, especially…."

Levee didn't know what he might have said if that shadow hadn't darkened his eyes. Once, as she'd stood at the mirror pinning her hair into a bun, images of that wretched day on the San Antonio Road had come alive in her mind and had glowed hot and fearsome in her eyes. She hadn't met her own gaze in the glass since. Dan's expression was a lot like that, and Levee couldn't help but wonder what dreadful event in his own history had put it there. Surely not his mother's broken leg. "I'm so sorry to hear it," she said, meaning it.

Both brows dipped slightly in the center of his forehead, and he stared at some unknown spot over her right shoulder. "Found her horse two days later, still saddled and grazing on field flowers." His frown deepened. "She fell just hours before a storm. No telling how long she'd have been out there once the rains had washed away the horse's tracks."

Dan shook his head, as much to clear the memory, she supposed, as to bring himself back to the here and now. "Well, then," she said, forcing a smile. "Thank the good Lord for leading you to her in time."

It was such a simple comment, really, so the sudden flash of anger in his eyes made no sense to her.

"God," he sneered disdainfully, "had *nothing* to do with it." He softened his tone only slightly to add, "Would've made more sense if He'd prevented the fall in the first place."

Now, Levee saw yet another trait that reminded her of herself. Not long ago, she'd blamed the Almighty, too, for the loss of her parents and brother, for the miscarriages, and for Liam's death. If He'd answered her prayers instead of Liam's, they wouldn't have been on the road that day, and her husband wouldn't have died at the hands of three murderous outlaws. If not for Reverend Peterson's patience and prayers, she might still be in the emotional state Dan seemed to be stuck in now. Still, his fury seemed disproportionate with this single event. Something else, Levee reasoned, must have caused the rift between him and his Creator. "How long ago did she fall?"

"May."

May had been an ugly, heartbreaking month for Levee, too, for that's when she'd landed in a town of strangers with nothing but the clothes on her back and a heart full of painful memories. But she knew from her medical training that seven months was a long time to nurse a broken bone. "Compound fractures?" she asked.

Dan nodded. "Doc Lane had to do two separate operations, one to reset the bones, one to cut out the gangrene."

Levee wondered what else had gone wrong to allow infection to set in. "Sorry to hear it," she said again.

"Well," he drawled, "better get the boy home."

He smiled, but Levee noticed once again that the smile never quite reached his eyes.

"I'm in enough trouble, spoiling his supper with candy. If I make him late, too?" He whistled. "My cousin Susan will tan my hide."

"Thanks for helping me," Levee said, nodding toward the blackboard.

Dan nodded, too, at the stack of letters on the corner of her desk. "Want me to deliver those?"

"Well, I was planning to deliver them myself tomorrow afternoon, along with some sort of baked good." She shrugged. "It's the least I can do, after waiting so long to visit her. I'm sure she has a thousand questions to ask me about the children and their lessons."

This time, the smile not only crinkled the corners of his eyes, but it glimmered in the blue orbs, too. "That's right nice of you, Mrs. O'Reilly. I'm sure she'll enjoy that."

"Tell me," she said, walking with him toward the door, "what shall I bake? Does your mother favor cake? Pie? Cookies?"

"Ma will tell you herself that her biggest weakness is cherry pie," Dan said. Winking, he added, "One of many things she passed down to me."

"Well, then, maybe I should bake two pies." Instantly, she regretted the comment. Would he misconstrue it as flirtation? *What's to misconstrue, you twit?*

On the porch, he donned his Stetson as Willie hollered, "I thought you were gonna be in there forever!"

"Did you save any licorice for me?"

The boy smiled, exposing two rows of teeth stained black. He held up one chunk of candy. "Yessir, I did!"

"Here's hoping you won't be visiting two invalids tomorrow," Dan said with a chuckle as he made his way carefully down the steps.

"Two?"

"When my cousin sees her boy's mouth?" He whistled again. "Any idea what time you might stop by tomorrow?"

"Early afternoon, I'd guess. I need to round up the ingredients for the pies, then see about borrowing a buggy and a horse."

"Borrowing? But why?"

"Because I don't own a horse or buggy," she said, giggling, "and I wouldn't have a place to store them if I did. And if I walk to the Lazy N, I'll be on the road for hours, that's why!"

"No need to go to all that bother. I'll stop by around noon and pick you up."

Levee started to protest when he held up a hand to silence her. "It's a big spread. You'd be half a day just trying to figure out which house is ours."

Before she could object, he'd covered the remaining distance to the wagon, and as she waved good-bye to her youngest student, Levee wondered what calamity had caused his pronounced limp, and if it was responsible for the haunted shadows in his eyes.

*D*an tossed and turned half the night, unable to get Levee out of his mind. When two hollow notes from the parlor clock announced the hour, he surrendered to wakefulness.

He flung the covers aside and sat on the edge of his bed, holding his breath as he attempted to massage the ache from his leg. It wasn't all that long ago that pain like this had driven him to a saloon in town, where he'd downed shot after shot of rye whiskey, hoping the fiery liquid would ease his misery.

Donning the shirt and trousers he'd worn the day before, Dan limped down the stairs, wool socks in one hand, boots in the other. Thankfully, no one else was up and about. He'd wandered the dark house so often that he knew every creaking board and squeaking door. Knew how to avoid them, too.

Hanging the socks over one shoulder, he used his free hand to grip the front door's bulbous brass doorknob and turned it clockwise, from the twelve o'clock to five o'clock position. When he heard the familiar click, he eased the door open and tiptoed outside. His ma was a light sleeper and, since the accident, had taken to bedding down on the parlor chaise. Waking her would guarantee an agonizing inquisition that could easily last for hours as she hammered him with one question after another, each intended to test the level of his sobriety. If he

passed, she'd try to figure out what had made him too agitated
to sleep.

He sat in his pa's old porch rocker to pull on his socks and
boots. As he tied the laces, he reminded himself that his mother's watchfulness was rooted in love. He then decided that life
would be a good sight easier if she didn't love him quite so
much.

You've got no one but yourself to blame for her suspicions, he
thought, settling back in the chair. How many times had he
sworn he'd given up the bottle, only to slide right back into it
again? Five? Ten? Dan sighed and shook his head. That last
bout had nearly killed him. It had nearly broken her heart, as
well, and the look of disappointment and sorrow on her face
had made him give it up, once and for all.

It hadn't been any sacrifice, really. While whiskey had the
power to blunt the throbbing in his leg, it did nothing to erase
the hard memories of what had happened to Daisy. What he'd
allowed to happen to her. Some nights, he reckoned, he just
wasn't supposed to sleep. Insomnia and the never-ending pain
seemed a small price to pay, for at least he was alive to feel
them. He could never explain any of this to his ma, of course,
because hearing it would only remind her that her youngest
daughter was dead and gone.

On nights like this, he liked to sit on the porch, watching his frosty breath hang on the night air and counting every
blessing he'd been granted and never could have earned. He
needed these quiet hours alone with his conscience to keep
him on the straight and narrow. Needed them as much as he
needed food and water. He didn't want to imagine what sort of
man he'd become without them.

"Dawn comes mighty early, boss."

"Mack!" Dan exclaimed. "What are you doing up at this hour?"

The cowboy climbed onto the porch. "Couldn't sleep." He pulled the makings of a cigarette from his shirt pocket and began rolling tobacco into the rectangle of paper. "Kept thinkin' 'bout the roundup." He scraped a match head on the heel of his boot, squinting when he brought the bright flame near his face. "How many head you reckon wandered off?"

"Several dozen cows, I expect. Maybe half that many horses." Dan grinned. "Better take care, or you're liable to light up that hair on your upper lip instead of your smoke."

Mack held out the tobacco and papers. "Care to roll yourself one?"

"Nah. Tried it once when I was a young'un. I've found other ways to keel over that aren't nearly as hard on my lungs."

Nodding, the cowboy returned the materials to his shirt pocket and leaned against the porch rail. "What time we gonna light out in the mornin'?"

Dan thought of his promise to Levee, whose lovely, lavender eyes had widened when he'd offered to drive her to and from the ranch. He hadn't given a thought to the fact that the errand would take him most of the day. Hadn't given a thought to canceling, either. "We'll head out at sunup, day after tomorrow."

Mack inclined his head, and Dan waited for him to ask why, but he didn't. Instead, he shrugged, then exhaled a stream of gray smoke. "You're the boss." Then, "Mind if I set a spell?"

Dan shook his head. Soon, the seats were rocking opposite each other, Dan's tilting back when Mack's went forward. The steady creak of chair joints created an eerie blend of notes high and low, and before long, Dan closed his eyes, content to listen to the tune whose tempo matched the beats of his heart. In his almost-drowsy state, he thought of what Mack had told him about Levee—how she'd stood up to the outlaws that day on the San Antonio Road, then tended his gunshot wound with quiet efficiency. What puzzled Dan most was the last thing Mack had said on the subject: "Levee never shed a tear, least none I saw."

Not one tear, though she'd lost her husband in such a horrific way? Did it mean she hadn't loved the man? Or was she the type who, like Dan, didn't want others to witness her despair? Then he pictured those big, innocent eyes and that warm, sincere smile, and decided that the latter was true. Either that, or she'd missed her calling and should have joined up with some Shakespearean acting troupe instead of becoming a teacher.

"I recollect you saying that Mrs. O'Reilly was a nurse back in Boston?"

"That's right."

"Wonder why she didn't hire on with Doc Lane. Bet his missus would have been happy for the help."

"She tried." Mack inspected the glowing tip of his cigarette. "He said he couldn't afford to pay her enough to keep a roof over her head. And when the town council got wind of the fact that a healthy young female had come to town, desperate and despondent, the mayor didn't let any grass grow under his feet. "Had her movin' in to the teacher's cottage behind the schoolhouse before she had a chance to spend her signing bonus."

Each time he'd made a trip to town, Dan had noticed an improvement to the cottage. First, lacy curtains had gone up, followed by fresh paint trimming the windows and doors. A tidy walk had been installed to lead visitors from the white picket fence to the covered porch, and two straight-backed chairs now flanked the bright-red door. He hadn't given a thought to who might sit in the second chair until now. "Did the council hire somebody to make all the improvements on the place?" he asked.

"Nope. I offered to help, but she turned me down flat. Said she liked the hard work, 'cause it took her mind off...things."

Like the murder of her husband? "Has she ever mentioned family back East?"

"Nope." Mack took a drag from his cigarette. "As far's I know, her husband was her only kin."

Dan's heart ached for Levee. But with no parents or siblings waiting for her back in Boston, perhaps she'd remain in Eagle Pass after her contract expired. Something told him a raise in pay wouldn't be necessary to encourage her to extend the agreement. He'd seen the way she looked at her students and knew she loved each one of them. Knew, too, that she would be a wonderful mother. What a shame that she didn't have a houseful of young'uns to love instead of having to spend her affections on other people's children.

But she'd need a husband for that, and hers was dead. Levee was young and beautiful, smart and spirited. Surely someday, when the pain of losing him ebbed, she'd want to remarry. Would Mack be the one she'd choose? Dan's heart fell. In a contest between him and Mack, the cowboy would win hands down. The man had little to call his own, except for a horse and a saddle, some boots, and a Stetson, but he hadn't caused a death and hadn't been addicted to alcohol. At least, not as far as Dan was aware. But what business was it of his, anyway? He sure as shootin' didn't qualify as "husband material." Not by a long shot! Still, if he thought for a minute she'd consider it, why, he'd— *You're losin' it, man.* He sat up straight and rested his right boot on his left knee. What sort of dolt entertained such thoughts about a li'l gal he barely knew? *If you don't get a grip, and get it soon—*

"Guess I'd best turn in," Mack said, getting to his feet. He stretched and yawned as he gazed out over the pastures. "Be daylight soon. You got anything in particular needs doing, seeing as how we ain't leavin' tomorrow?"

Dan rolled the question around in his mind for a moment. He would hate to give up one leg of the trip with Levee, but he would hate to start the rumor mill grinding even more. "When I picked Willie up at the schoolhouse yesterday, the kids were writing get-well letters to my ma. I guess Mrs. O'Reilly feels a mite guilty that she hasn't stopped by before now, so she's baking Ma's favorite pie, too, and wants to bring it by with the letters." He shrugged. "When she mentioned having to rent a horse and buggy to do it, I offered to see that she got to and from the Lazy N."

"Good," Mack said. "She spends half her pay on those young'uns."

"Few things pain me more than a damsel in distress."

Mack nodded.

"If you'll take the 'pick-up' leg of the trip off my hands, I'll run her home."

"I don't mind doing both."

I'll just bet you don't. "You've more than earned an afternoon off." *And I've earned some time alone with her.* "I'll run her home when she's done visiting with Ma."

"What time?"

Hopefully, his mother would invite Levee to supper so that he could drive her home under the stars. He was about to tell Mack that he could set out early for Eagle Pass when the cowboy said, "Not too early, I reckon, since she has a pie to bake." He pinched off the fiery end of his cigarette and ground it onto the flagstone walk, then pocketed the stub. "What flavor?"

"Cherry. I told her I'd stop by around noon."

"Be there by quarter of," Mack said, chuckling. "If I'm lucky, I'll get there before she has a chance to wash up all the mixin' bowls."

Dan bristled. He'd berated himself half a dozen times for being attracted to Levee, telling himself she deserved better than the likes of him. He had no right to be jealous of Mack. But jealous he was.

"Sounds good," Dan said at last. "You have the time?"

Mack fished his pocket watch from his trousers pocket and bent to catch a moonbeam. "Ten minutes till three," he said, closing its case with a quiet snap. "See you at sunup," he added, then ambled toward the bunkhouse.

Dan slid out of his boots and then tiptoed back inside the house, taking care again to avoid every creaking floorboard. For once, he hoped he wouldn't fall asleep the minute his head hit the pillow. Like it or not, right or wrong, smart or foolish, he wanted Levee for himself, and he needed time to think up some solid excuses for ditching his list of "Reasons You're Not Worthy of Levee."

Thoughts of spending time alone with Dan Neville on the ride to and from the Lazy N Ranch kept Levee awake. After hours of browbeating herself for entertaining such thoughts about another man so soon after losing Liam, she rose at two o'clock in hopes of finding wisdom for her situation in the Good Book. When she closed her Bible one hour later, she felt a sense of peace, even though it seemed the Lord was telling her to wait patiently—and, had patience been a subject of study in school, she would have flunked it!

Her mama used to say, "Idle hands are the devil's workshop." So, Levee put the Bible back on the bookshelf and went to the kitchen to work on the treat she'd promised to bake for Mrs. Neville. By six o'clock, two perfect pies sat cooling on the table. The children's notes, stacked in a neat pile beside them, were bound together by a wide satin ribbon that matched the blue checks in the towel she would use to cover the pies.

It was barely seven when she finished scrubbing the pots and pans and tidying her tiny kitchen, and morning devotions and Bible study passed an additional hour. A leisurely bath and shampoo ticked away thirty minutes more. After wrapping her wet hair in a towel, she picked up her carriage clock and shook it gently. "Are your gears rusty?" she asked. But the tiny silver clock on her bedside table told the same time. "Well,

I suppose that, just as a watched pot never boils, the hands of an observed clock never move." She covered her mouth to stifle a giggle, then flung her hand away and laughed out loud. Why hide her mirth when she was the only one around to witness it? The moment of levity was quickly silenced by a troubling question: How would she spend the remaining hours until Dan arrived?

She could take the rugs out back and beat them, but she'd already bathed. She could replace the buttons on the white shirt Matilda Montgomery had given her, but she hadn't thought to purchase any buttons. She might have tried catching a few winks of sleep if she hadn't already styled her hair into a fashionable twist like the one she'd seen in *Godey's Magazine*. "You could nap sitting upright in the rocking chair," Levee thought aloud. And then she giggled. What would the members of the town council say if they heard her? "Why, they'd think you're too daft to teach their children, and they'd tear up your contract!"

That thought sobered her quickly. Losing contact with her students would be painful enough, but without the job, she'd lose her home and means of support, too. If only Eagle Pass had a hospital, she wouldn't feel so dependent on the teaching position. "What would the council say," she wondered aloud, "to the idea of a clinic, like the one Liam planned to open in Mexico?"

Smiling at her genius, Levee raced to the small rolltop desk in the corner of her parlor and lit the lamp on the wall above it. She couldn't very well present her idea to the council without a plan. She'd need proof that it was a feasible goal. They'd need a building. Beds and bedding. Surgical tools and medications. Some of the start-up costs might be donated by the town's businessmen and solvent ranchers. If she could sell the idea to the Ladies' Auxiliary first, perhaps they'd help organize bake-offs and boxed lunch auctions to fund the set-up and plan similar events annually to assure the clinic's continued success.

She filled page after page with notes and could hardly believe it when she glanced at the clock. "Eleven fifteen!" That left her only thirty minutes to change out of her nightclothes and into the outfit she'd wear to the Lazy N! Levee pushed her paperwork into the desk and rolled the top down, then headed for her cozy room, where her freshly pressed skirt and shirt lay on the neatly made bed. She'd polished her boots, too, and dusted the shoulders of her seldom-worn walking jacket. Under the sunny sky, she wouldn't need it for the ride to the Neville ranch, but she'd heard plenty about how quickly the Texas weather could change this time of year. With that in mind, she decided to take along a bonnet and an umbrella, too. "Never hurts to be prepared," she said, fastening a wide belt around her waist.

The day Mack had introduced her to him, Dan had worn a navy blue shirt, and when he'd come to pick up Willie the previous day, the hue of his shirt had matched the sky. Levee hoped she was correct in assuming Daniel was partial to blue, for she'd chosen to wear her favorite outfit, a blue calico skirt and coordinating blouse, which she had ordered from *Godey's Magazine* and paid for with her hard-earned wages. Her other clothes, all of them hand-me-down dresses donated by the reverend's wife, were lovely, and Levee had altered them to fit her slimmer waist and smaller bust. Still, none seemed to flatter her like the blue ensemble.

Would Dan notice that she'd rubbed a dab of rouge onto her cheeks, or that she'd donned her only pair of earrings?

What would he think of the lavender perfume—a gift from Matilda—she'd sprayed from the crystal atomizer that sat on a mirrored tray on her bureau? What if, like Liam, he disapproved of such vanity and considered it excessive and frivolous? Or, what if he preferred his women with even more embellishment?

His women.... The very thought struck fear in her heart. Why, she'd never bothered to find out if Dan was married or engaged. What would folks think when he showed up to escort her to the Lazy N if he had a sweetheart somewhere? "If talking to yourself doesn't get you fired, that surely will!" she said to her reflection in the mirror.

She was startled by vigorous knocking on the front door. *That must be Dan*, she thought with a glance at the clock. Fifteen minutes early. Did it mean he was as eager to see her as she was to see him? "Good thing your boots are laced up good and tight," she whispered, heading for the front door, "or you'd have leaped clean out of them!"

"Mornin'," Mack said, tipping his hat when she opened the door. "Don't you look purty today?"

"Why, thank you!" She was happy to see him, albeit more than a little disappointed he wasn't Dan. "And you look rather dapper, yourself." He'd trimmed his dark mustache and shined his pointy-toed boots. "Well, come in! I'll make some tea, and you can keep me company while I wait for Dan to—"

"He sent me to fetch you."

"Oh." It was her own silly fault that the news stung. If that didn't teach her not to get all moony over a man she barely knew, what would? Levee stepped aside as Mack entered the parlor.

"Sorry to disappoint you."

Oh, that's grand! Now you've gone and hurt the poor man's feelings, you insensitive oaf. "Disappointed?" She laughed and waved the notion away. "I barely know the man. When I told him I planned to rent a horse and buggy so I could pay his mother a visit, he insisted on driving me." Why, she wondered, did she feel an incredible need to explain herself? "I'm pleased, actually, that he sent you in his stead." If her words rang hollow and insincere in her own ears, how false must they have sounded to poor Mack? "This will be a real treat," she added to soften the message, "having some time to chat with you."

Mack glanced around the room. "Place looks good."

Except for that terrible day when they'd been attacked by the Frank Michaels Gang, Levee had never seen Mack appear less at ease. "It's coming along." She felt awful for having caused his discomfort. "Can you keep a secret?"

"I reckon so."

"I baked two pies. One to bring to the Lazy N"—could she say it convincingly enough to fool him?—"and one for you." She stepped over to the table so he couldn't read her expression and whipped the tea towel away, revealing the pastries.

Mack grinned, but then his face fell. "Ain't like there's a cupboard in the bunkhouse. I walk in carrying that, it'll be a miracle if I'm not mowed down by the others."

"Oh," she said again. "I hadn't thought of that. How silly of me."

"Maybe you can keep it here for me, and I can stop by every few days to—" He slapped his Stetson against his thigh. "Aw, that won't work. We're headin' out at first light to round up the stray cattle."

"We?"

"Dan and George and me. We'll probably be gone till Christmas Eve."

She couldn't have planned it better if she'd tried! "Then why not take it along? I'm sure the others wouldn't mind sharing it with you."

"Okay, then," Mack said. "Well, we'd better head out. I told Dan I'd have you in his ma's parlor by one o'clock."

"I'm ready to go," Levee said. She covered the pies again with the towel, picked up the tray, and off they went.

Their amiable conversation during the first mile of the ride reminded her of that day on the San Antonio Road, when Mack and Liam had exchanged opinions about recent inventions. "Typewriters, light bulbs, telephones, and elevators might well be commonplace in Boston," Mack had pointed out, "but you'll be hard-pressed to find any of those in Chihuahua."

Liam's too-typical chortle had preceded his reply. "You talk as though the Mexicans are backward."

"Folks are poor where you're going," Mack had countered, "but they ain't dumb. I'm just wondering if you took into account how different things might be. Especially at first." He'd nodded toward Levee. "You ever lived in an adobe hut before?"

She hadn't, and said so.

"Slept on a pallet stuffed with straw?"

Nor that.

He'd listed other nuisances and inconveniences, like fleas and coyotes, *banditos*, and the language barrier. "Either of you speak Spanish?"

"As a doctor," Liam had huffed, "I'm fluent in Latin. It cannot be all that different, being a Romance language."

Mack's knee-slapping laughter had inspired one of the drivers to say, "Keep it down back there, 'fore you spook the horses!"

Levee didn't know which had amazed her more, her spouse's pomposity or the cowboy's familiarity with newfangled gadgets. He was full of information and gladly shared it, but not when it came to personal details. *How odd that I've known Mack all these months yet know next to nothing about him,* she thought. She decided it was time to change that.

"So, Mack," she said, "do you have a family somewhere?"

He hesitated, as if considering whether or not to share any information. "Last I heard, there was a cousin in Chicago."

Last he'd heard? "How sad that you've lost touch with him."

"Her. And there's nothin' sad about it. That scheming female took me for five hundred dollars last time I saw her."

"Goodness gracious! Why, that's a small fortune! What would make a woman swindle her own kin?" But the better question, Levee thought, was where Mack had come by such a sum of money. "Is Chicago where you lived? Before heading west, I mean?"

"Spent some time there."

But it wasn't home, Levee deduced. So, where had he been born? And what had happened to his parents? What sort of work had he done before signing on as a ranch hand at the Lazy N?

It dawned on her that Mack didn't know any of those details about her, either. Why, if he hadn't been traveling on the same stagecoach on that fateful day, he wouldn't know how she'd become a widow. "I was born and raised in Boston," she offered. "My mother's parents died of natural causes in Ireland, and I lived with my paternal grandparents after I lost my folks. Then, my brother died of the fever. That, along with my grandfather's dying of cancer, is what made me go into nursing, and nursing is how I met Liam. He never really wanted children, you know, so I suppose it was a blessing when I miscarried all those times."

It was astonishing to realize that she'd never told those things to anyone. Even more astonishing was that she'd summed up her entire life in just a few sentences. Poor Mack, the reluctant recipient of a flurry of personal information! "Sorry," she said, holding her hand over her mouth and blushing. "Sometimes when I get started, I don't know when to stop."

Mack simply pointed. "Just another mile or so and we'll be there."

Evidently he had no intention of playing the "story swap" game. At least, not today. It was just as well. If he confessed to having committed some egregious crime, she'd never be able to look at him quite the same way. What good would that be for their friendship? And then, there was the matter of the long ride back to town.

"So, how long will you be gone?" she asked, changing the subject. "On your roundup, I mean."

Mack shrugged. "Anywhere from a few days to a couple of weeks." Another shrug. "Depends on how many wanderers we come across."

"Have you gone on a roundup before?"

"Yep, but it's been a while." He exhaled a long breath, then chuckled softly. "Don't go volunteering that information to Dan, though, y'hear?"

"What are friends for if they can't be trusted with a secret or two?"

"Well, there's the house."

Levee barely noticed that he'd neatly evaded her hint. She was far too busy trying to figure out what she'd say to Mrs. Neville when they met, and how she'd hide her hurt feelings if and when she saw Dan.

*O*nce the wagon passed under the wrought-iron arch that spelled out "Lazy N Ranch," Levee saw the tidy split-rail fences bracketing the length of the lane. Longhorn and Angus cattle grazed leisurely in pastures to her right, while horses frolicked to the left.

The steel-rimmed wagon wheels ground on for what felt like miles before the house came into view. She'd expected a one-story structure built of stripped logs, like so many of the cabins she'd passed during the trip from Boston to Texas, or something fashioned from adobe, like the courthouse in Eagle Pass. Instead, she saw a stately three-story home of white clapboard, flanked by two towering trees that looked like giant sentries.

She tried counting the many-paned windows, each decorated with festooned draperies, and barely reached fourteen when Mack stopped the wagon in the circular drive. He wrapped the reins around the brake stick and leaped to the ground as Levee prepared to disembark. But she never got the chance, for the instant she was on her feet, he clamped both leather-gloved hands around her waist and gently deposited her on the flagstone walk.

"Can you manage the pies by yourself?" he asked.

"Of course, I can," she insisted, taking the pie tray out of the back of the wagon. "And I could've climbed down from there by myself, too, I'll have you know."

Grinning, he hoisted himself back up into the wagon. "Never doubted it for a minute. I just figured you'd want to make a good impression on Dan's ma. Kind of hard to do if you trip on your skirt or catch your sleeve on the brake."

"Thank you, Mack. Will you be joining us, I hope?"

"Not likely," he said, flapping the reins. The horses plodded forward, and he raised an arm to wave.

"Well, I'll see you when you come back to take me home, then."

"'Fraid not. Dan's gonna do that."

"He—he *is?*" Her heart raced. *Ninny!* she scolded herself. "Don't forget your pie in the back of the wagon," she called after Mack. Was it her imagination, or had he urged the horses to move faster? "You be careful out there on the open range, you hear?" And in a slightly louder voice, "And don't forget, you promised to attend the children's Christmas pa—"

"You look beautiful in blue."

She didn't have to turn around to know it was Dan, standing behind her on the path. She spun around and was about to tell him he looked nice, too, when he relieved her of the pie tray and nodded toward the wide, covered porch.

"Ma's in the parlor with my sister Dixie and her boy, Seth. I'll introduce you, then be on my way."

He'd already handed her off once today. Did he really think he could get away with it again? "Oh, won't you join us? I'm sure your mother would prefer that."

Dan held the door open for her. "Actually, it was Ma who hinted that I should make myself scarce."

"But—but why would she do such a th—"

"Danny? Is that you out there?"

"None other." He entered the parlor first and put the pie tray on a side table. "I think she made your favorite, Ma," he said, whipping off the blue-checked cloth.

Levee noticed how his eyes widened and his brow arched. No doubt he'd expected to see two pies, one for his mother and one for himself. He'd find out soon enough that the second pastry had ended up in Mack's hands. Maybe, just maybe, Levee would be inclined to explain herself as he drove her home. Unless, of course, he planned to hand her off again.

"Ma, this is Levee O'Reilly," Dan said. "Levee, meet my mother, Judith Neville."

The woman held out a hand, and Levee shook it heartily. "I'm so happy to meet you, Mrs. Neville."

"My sister, Dixie," Daniel said. "And that little tyke on her lap is Seth."

"I'm three," Seth said as Levee and his mother shook hands.

"Pleased to meet you, Seth," she said, shaking his hand, too.

"I want some pie," he added, wiggling his eyebrows. "Is it cherry? That's my fav'rite. Gramma's fav'rite, too." He looked at Mrs. Neville. "Right, Gramma?"

"That's right, dear. It's my favorite, too." Mrs. Neville met Levee's eyes. "It looks delicious, but you didn't have to make it."

"Oh, but I did," Levee protested. "The pie is a symbol of sorts, proof just how sorry I am, Mrs. Neville, that I haven't made time to visit you sooner." She accepted the woman's invitation and sat down at the foot of her chaise, then handed her the stack of letters. "These are for you from your students."

With hands trembling slightly, Mrs. Neville took the notes. "Thank you, Levee. And, please, call me Judith. Mrs. Neville was my mother-in-law." She held the stack to her bosom. "I think I'll read these later. Otherwise, my blubbering is bound to make conversation all but impossible." Laughing, she placed the papers on the table beside her, then turned back to Levee. "So, tell me, how do you like teaching?"

"Oh, I love it. And the children—I could just hug the stuffing out of every one of them."

"As much as I adore children, I'm afraid I never had much talent for the job. Never could coax much cooperation from them." She leaned forward. "Tell me, how do you do it?"

Levee didn't know how to answer, and so she said, "I pray a lot."

Judith laughed. "I can't tell you what a pleasure it is, knowing I'll never have to go back to that classroom—at least, not as the schoolmarm!"

Nothing could have pleased Levee more. And if that expression on Dan's face was any indication, it pleased him, too. "So, how is your leg?" she asked his mother. "Are you any closer to getting around as before?"

"If only I knew," Judith said with a sigh. "I've done everything the doctor ordered." Another sigh. "I hate the thought of a wheelchair, but it might be inevitable."

"It's better than sitting here alone all day, Mother dear," Dixie said, getting to her feet. "Now, how about if I take that pie into the kitchen and cut each of us a nice big slice?" She picked up the tray and headed for the door. "Would anyone care for a glass of milk to wash it down?"

"I'll stick with tea, dear," Judith said. "Levee, what can my daughter bring you?"

"Tea sounds lovely, but only if I can help prepare it."

She rose, intending to follow Dixie, but Judith said, "You'll do no such thing, young lady. It took you all these months to get here, and there's no telling when I might see you again." Pointing at the chair beside her chaise, she added, "Please, sit with me. Danny will help Dixie." She looked at her son. "Won't you, darling?"

"Nothing would please me more." He limped toward the hall, Seth close on his heels.

"So," Judith said once they were gone, "tell me all about yourself, starting with where you got your rather peculiar name."

"Well, as the story goes," Levee began, adopting a thick Irish brogue, "'twas a bitter feud 'tween Ma's folks an' Da's. For generations it went on, both sides bickerin' o'er who had rights to the river separatin' their farms, and which family ought to be in charge of the levee that kept it from floodin' the pastures. Then one bright, sunny day, my dear ma set eyes on the man who would become me da, and the two eloped into the night." Levee giggled and winked. "Seems all it took to bring peace to their slice o' County Kerry was for both sides to meet their first grandchild. And so they named me Levee, since 'twas me birth that kept hate from flowin' into another generation."

Judith chuckled, evidently satisfied with the story. Levee went on to repeat the life summary she'd recited for Mack, carefully omitting the events that had unfolded on the San Antonio Road. "I love it here," she admitted. "Almost from my first day in Eagle Pass, this place has felt more like home than Boston ever did." She laughed a little. "Isn't that odd?"

"No, no, of course not. I was an only child, born and raised in Baltimore. I met Danny's father when my pa brought me to Texas to choose stud bulls for our dairy farm." Judith's face showed a faraway smile. "We were married in Maryland, and I saw my parents only one more time after that. Much as I missed them, I never regretted my decision. We kept in touch by mail, and it was enough, until...."

Until they passed on, Levee finished mentally. She found herself wanting to reach out and squeeze the hand of this lovely woman to prove how closely she identified with her story. *How blessed you are,* she wanted to say, *that all your children and grandchildren live right here at the Lazy N.* Instead, she merely nodded.

Dixie, Seth, and Dan returned, and while Judith's daughter and grandson delivered her treat, her son handed Levee a plate with a slice of pie and a fork. This time, when their fingers touched, he didn't recoil. Rather, he allowed them to linger for a tick in time, his eyes locked with hers in a warm gaze.

Judith's good-natured titter severed the connection. "The poor dear can't eat until you turn her loose, son."

His lips slanted in a shy grin. "Sorry if I was staring," he said, "but I was trying to come up with a name for the color of her eyes." He sat down across from Levee. "What do you call it?" he asked her.

Looking down at her plate, she did her best to sound as nonchalant as possible. "Some say lilac."

"I'd say lavender," Dixie said.

"Sarah!" Seth shouted.

All heads turned to see a lovely blonde woman enter the room.

"Welcome home, my dear!" Judith greeted her. "Your mother didn't tell us you would be home so soon. How was your time in Amarillo?"

"It was lovely, thanks, but it's good to be home," Sarah said, bending at the waist to accept Seth's hug. "It's good to see you, too!" she said, laughing.

"Sarah, I'd like you to meet Levee O'Reilly," Judith said, gesturing to Levee. "She took my place as the schoolteacher in Eagle Pass." Then, gesturing to Sarah, who smiled warmly at Levee, she said, "Levee, meet my niece Sarah. She just returned from a five-month stay with her great-aunt in Amarillo."

"Pleased to meet you," Levee said, returning Sarah's smile.

"Likewise," Sarah said. "I hope that those little rascals aren't giving you too much trouble!" Then she looked around the room. "So, how are the rest of you?"

"Oh, as well as can be expected," Dixie offered, "considering...."

Considering what? Levee wondered. But since no one volunteered more information, she kept the question to herself. A quick glance at the downturned mouths and furrowed brows around her told her that the news wouldn't be good, and that Judith was the probable cause of everyone's concern. "Oh, Dixie," the woman said, "you worry far too much."

Her daughter's mouth formed a thin line. The family must have covered this ground many times.

"So, what else is new?" Judith asked Sarah.

With a furtive smile, Sarah disappeared out the door and returned with a garment draped over her arm. She unfurled it to reveal a beautiful gown. "While I was away, I had a chance to finish Dana's wedding dress." She held it up in front of her. "I think she'll make a lovely bride, don't you?"

Dan grunted. "I don't see why not. She was lovely at her other weddings."

Judith clicked her tongue and aimed a maternal glare at her son.

"Sorry," he said, shoulders raised. "Did I let the cat out of the bag or something?"

Sarah hung the dress over the back of a vacant chair. "It's no secret," she said to Levee, "that my beautiful cousin has had abysmal luck when it comes to choosing a husband."

This inspired another grunt from Dan. "She won't turn thirty until spring, but she's planted three of 'em so far."

Seth filled his mouth with pie, then said, "Is that why they call Aunt Dana the Black Widow? Cuz she bites her hubsbands an' kills 'em with her poison?"

"Land sakes, Seth, what a question!" Dixie exclaimed.

Seth blinked innocently. "Well, is it?"

Levee hoped never again to experience tension that felt thick enough to fry on a griddle.

"Eat your pie, sweetheart," Judith suggested.

"But, Gramma—"

"We'll talk about that later."

The boy stuck out his lower lip. "That's what you always say." He speared a cherry with his fork. "But we never do."

"I must say, I'm impressed that a child so young knows anything about black widow spiders," Levee said, hoping to lighten the mood with a compliment. "Wherever did he learn about them? I mean, he isn't even in school yet!" But Dixie gasped, Sarah's eyes widened, Dan shook his head, and Judith sighed. *Levee, Levee, Levee! Will you ever learn to keep your lips buttoned?*

"The pie is delicious," Dan said, waving his empty fork.

"Yes, yes," his mother agreed. "I do hope you'll agree to share your recipe, Levee."

"I'll write it out as soon as I get home." *Which will be soon,* she hoped. She glanced at Dan to see if he'd picked up on her subtle suggestion that they hit the road.

But Mack strode into the room, instead. "What?" he said when six dour expressions greeted him. "Did someone die?"

"Not yet," Dan said under his breath.

This comment earned him a giggle from Sarah and a glare from his mother.

"So, who's under the weather, then?" Mack pressed. "Anybody I know?"

By now, Dixie had joined the misbehaving ones and hid a grin behind one hand.

"What's so funny?" Seth demanded.

"Seth, li'l buddy," Mack said with a shrug, "if I had a clue, I'd tell you. And if you figure it out, I sure hope you'll do the same." Just then, he looked at Sarah, and a slow smile spread across his face. He stood, staring as if he'd spied an angel.

"I guess you haven't met my cousin Sarah," Dan said. "She's been in Amarillo for the past five months, and when she's home, she's usually working in her sewing room."

"Believe me, if we'd met, I would've remembered," Mack said, wiping his palm on the seat of his trousers. "Name's Mack," he said, offering her his hand.

When Sarah held it, a blush crept up from his collar and turned his whole face bright pink.

"Pleased to meet you," she said, looking just as intrigued as Mack had when he'd first noticed her.

Wouldn't it be lovely, Levee thought, *if Sarah and Mack struck up a romance!* She hoped it was a sign that she'd misjudged his feelings for her, that she could pay more attention to Dan without worrying about hurting Mack's feelings. A quick glance at Dan made her wonder if he'd had the same thought, for an affectionate smile brightened his face.

"Why don't you take Mack into the kitchen and get him a slice of pie?" Dixie suggested. "I'll just go upstairs and see if Dana is ready for her final fitting."

"Final fitting?" Now Dan looked confused.

His mother expelled an exasperated sigh. "Please don't tell me you've forgotten that your sister's wedding is in two weeks."

"Christmas Eve, remember?" Dixie said.

"I don't know...Mack, what do you think? Can we make it back in time?"

But Mack was already following Sarah out of the room toward the kitchen. "What would you prefer with your pie?" Sarah asked, linking her arm with his. "Tea or milk?"

Those seated in the parlor never heard his answer because the pair disappeared around the corner.

Judith sent Dan a warning glare. "You had better be back in time for your sister's wedding."

Nodding, he drained his milk. "When's supper, Ma?"

"Five o'clock, same as always."

He glanced at the clock. And so did Levee. "You're not in any rush to get home, are you?"

Levee's heart leaped when he fixed her with that alluring blue gaze. Smiling, she shook her head, knowing that even if she had been in a hurry, she never would have admitted it.

9

"You have a lovely family, Dan," Levee told him as they pulled out of the Lazy N drive and onto the road to Eagle Pass.

He chuckled. "Oh, I reckon they'll do."

"No, seriously. They're just so warm and welcoming, every last one of them. Why, they made me feel as though I've known them for years, instead of just hours, even after that horrid faux pas about Seth."

"What faux pas?"

From the corner of his eye, he saw her cringe a bit before saying, "That ridiculous remark about how intelligent he is for a boy so young. It opened the door to—" She bit her lower lip. "How *did* he learn about black widow spiders?"

"Guess when a young'un hears something mentioned enough times, it gets his curiosity up."

She gasped. "You don't mean to say people really call your sister—?"

Dan smiled grimly and nodded.

Another gasp. "How awful for her."

"Dana has a knack for picking sickly types. The first one had the cancer, and she knew it when she married him. Consumption took the second one. The jury's still out on what killed number three."

A long moment passed before she repeated, "How awful for her." Then, "Did she love them, do you think?"

Surely she was joking with a question like that. He sent her a quick glance and saw that she was dead serious. "Why would she have married 'em if she didn't? Ain't like we're living in the Dark Ages, when families put men and women together to merge kingdoms or married a girl off to save havin' to feed and clothe her."

It suddenly dawned on him that Levee wouldn't have said such a thing unless she hadn't married for love. "What about you?" he asked. "Was your marriage arranged?"

She took a deep breath. "Not in the traditional sense. My folks and Liam's didn't put us together, if that's what you mean. I met Liam while I was in nursing school, and our final exam involved assisting him at the hospital. He hadn't gotten on well with the other nurses. Too arrogant and bossy, they said of him. But I wasn't one to complain, and he liked that about me. Said that since we made such a good medical team, there was no reason to believe the same wouldn't be true of a marital partnership."

"You don't mean to say that's what he called it—a partnership?"

"It made sense at the time, so rational and logical, the way he explained it. And I thought—I prayed—that in time, perhaps we'd fall in love, the way people do in fairy tales."

He wanted to wrap her in a warm hug for believing in love and happy endings.

"And then he got it into his head that since Boston was crawling with doctors, we could do more good where there were no hospitals. Mexico was the last place I wanted to go, especially after...after having miscarried twice. I'd never been

outside the city limits of Boston, and the thought of traveling cross-country terrified me. But, before I knew it, there we
were, on a southbound train, then on a stagecoach, heading to
Mexico to set up a church-sponsored clinic, when...."

When we were robbed and my husband was murdered, Dan
finished mentally. Picturing Levee, hands in the air as the outlaws set upon the stagecoach, made him shudder. "Well," he
said to disguise it, "there's no reason to believe you wouldn't
have had your fairy-tale love eventually."

"You're very sweet to say that," Levee said with a smile.
"But I've since realized the impossibility of that having happened, even if Liam had lived to a ripe old age."

She sounded so certain and sad that he wanted to grab her
hand and press reassuring kisses into the palm. "Why not?"

"Because Liam loved his work and nothing else." After a
spurt of nervous giggles, she said, "Would you believe he actually told me on our wedding night that because doctoring was
his gift from God, it would have to come first, always? 'To do
less,'" she mimicked him, lowering her voice to sound manlier,
"'would be like spitting on that gift.'"

And yet she'd let him take her from the only home she'd
ever known and had stood up to murderous outlaws on his
behalf. Rare bravery for anyone, man or woman.

"I remember thinking what a twit I'd been, because, of
course, I believed him. All the signs were there, so why hadn't I
admitted it to myself before?" She took a deep breath. "I cried
myself to sleep that night and vowed never to shed another
tear over that man until I could convince myself that he loved
me."

So that's why she hadn't shed a tear when he was killed.
"How long were you married?"

"Nearly two years. We would have celebrated our second anniversary on the day of our arrival in Chihuahua. Liam saw that as proof that the Lord had blessed his decision."

What a fool the man had been! He'd married the most beautiful, spirited woman in the world and hadn't known what a prize he'd had.

"It's such a beautiful night!" Levee exclaimed in her habitually cheerful tone. She was looking up at the stars and smiling, and Dan could see three-quarters of her lovely face. The moon cast a milky glow on her skin, making her hair and eyelashes seem even darker than before. What would those amazing eyes look like in the lunar light? Maybe he'd find out when he got her home. Unfortunately, they would arrive at her cottage in no time.

"So, tell me, what do you think about Sarah and Mack? Is love in their future?"

He chuckled. "Never put much stock in that 'love at first sight' nonsense." He bristled a bit, hearing the half-lie in his words. "But the way those two looked at each other?"

"I know, I know! Wasn't it just the sweetest thing?"

No, he thought, *you are the sweetest thing.*

"Oh, look," she said, pointing at the sky. "The North Star."

While she looked up, Dan looked at her, instead. "They say when a man and woman kiss beneath the North Star, their love will last a lifetime."

She faced him, grinning mischievously. "Who's 'they'?"

For the first time in years, Dan felt bold. Felt hopeful and happy, too. What did he have to lose by testing the waters? "Me, myself, and I, that's who."

"Well, the three of you are just as silly as silly can be," she said, giggling merrily. When they heard the startled hoot and flapping wings of an owl, Levee cuddled closer to Dan, clutching his arm with both hands. "Goodness! I believe we just shaved two years off that owl's life!"

Dan hoped her fear wouldn't subside too quickly, because he liked having her so near. "I imagine he's thinking the same thing."

Levee rested her head on his shoulder. "And how can you be so certain it's a he?"

He was certain of only one thing at the moment: he cared for this woman as he'd never cared for Gwendolyn. Considering how their parting of ways had nearly destroyed him, he worried more than ever how he would feel if Levee reacted the same way when she found out about Daisy.

He'd tell her everything. Not tonight, because he wanted to enjoy the uncomplicated comfort of knowing she liked him, but soon, so it wouldn't hurt so much if she turned tail and ran when she learned the ugly truth about his past.

Levee had seen him walk and hadn't appeared the least bit fazed by his limp. Maybe that was a sign, a simple proof, that she could love him for the man he was, not the man he'd been.

He felt her tremble. "Cold?"

"A little. Guess I should have worn a warmer jacket."

Gripping the reins with his left hand, he draped his right arm around her shoulders, happy to share his warmth and only wishing she'd shivered earlier. The lights of downtown Eagle Pass glowed up ahead, meaning he had ten minutes at best to enjoy having her snuggled so close beside him.

Despite his plans to rise before daybreak the next day and hit the trail, Dan was busy searching his brain for suitable excuses to linger once he escorted Levee to her door. Dare he pray for ideas? He took a peek up at the heavens and saw a shooting star slice through the blackness above, winking once before it faded from view. And he read it as a sign from God.

*T*he sky blazed with the deep purple of early dawn when Dan, Mack, and George left the Lazy N, bellies full of Lucinda's fried eggs and griddle cakes, brains buzzing with thoughts of the long day ahead. For miles they rode, single file and silent, taking care to guide their mounts through clumps of prickly pear and white brush, and the only sound Dan heard was the low howling of the wind and the occasional flutter of birds, startled from their nests by the rumble of passing hooves.

He guessed they'd been riding for two hours by the time a thin strand of shimmering sunlight finally hugged the horizon, and he would have been hard-pressed to say which pleased him more, the sun coming up or going down, because, in his opinion, the world was never more stunning than when the daystar was kissing the world good morning or bidding it good night. In another hour or so, it would burn the frost off their hats and warm the air around them. At least he hoped it would, because if he tucked his face any deeper into his canvas coat, he wouldn't be able to see at all.

From experience, he knew they were likely to find the strays in any one of a handful of places where water and grass were plentiful, so he followed the Rio Grande until it branched off some fifteen miles from the road. If the ornery critters weren't gathered at Coyote Creek, he and the boys would split up and try the old watering hole near Rustlers' Ridge.

His best guess was they had two dozen head of cattle to find and round up—cows, mostly. It was a good thing, since the bulls behaved even more surly and stubborn this time of year. With any luck, they would have the lot of them bunched up by dusk and lumbering toward home by morning, because Mother Nature could be an unpredictable shrew, especially in December. Sleeping under the stars had its good points, he'd grant her that, but Dan didn't relish the idea of shivering under a soaked blanket while the skies poured rain on the campfire, their only source of heat and light.

He scanned the landscape and spied half a dozen black specks in the distance. Raising one hand to signal George and Mack to hold up, he narrowed his eyes. If the spots moved, chances were good he'd found the escapees. If they didn't budge, he thought with a frown, he couldn't very well use his branding iron on shrubs, now, could he?

Mack pulled up beside Dan. "Found 'em?"

"*Sí*," George said, coming up along his other side. "And more to the east."

"All I can say is, if those are Neville cows, this'll be a first," Dan said.

Mack tipped back his hat, exposing a white band of skin just below his hairline. "A first for what?"

George's saddle squeaked when he leaned forward to peer around Dan. "It is rare to find them all in one place, so soon," he told Mack, then sat back with a grin and nodded at Dan. "You were right, Meester Dan. This one, he really is a leppy."

"What's a—?"

"An orphaned calf," Dan explained. And when Mack's brow creased with confusion, he added, "Lost, young, and dumb."

Mack laughed good-naturedly. "I get it. Don't much like it, but I get it."

"We'd best be gettin'," Dan put in, "or we'll be out here till Christmas."

That inspired a chuckle from Mack. "Can't have that, now, can we? Wouldn't want to miss the Christmas pageant at the schoolhouse."

Dan pictured Levee as he'd last seen her, wearing a blue calico dress covered in lavender flowers that exactly matched her eyes. His heart thumped faster, and he gulped, willing it to slow. "My nephew would never let me forget it if I didn't show up," he said. But it was Levee he didn't want to disappoint.

He tugged his Stetson lower, just in case his thoughts were visible on his face. "We'll ride in slow and easy," he told Mack. "You'll go left, George will go right, and I'll circle around from the north. Once we get 'em bunched up, we'll lasso 'em, one at a time. Did you bring your tie-down ropes, like I told you?"

Mack patted the coils hanging from his saddle horn.

"George?"

"Never leave the ranch without them, Meester Dan."

"All right, then, let's show this beginner how it's done."

By now, they were so close to the herd that Dan could almost hear the cows' teeth grinding tufts of grass into pulp. In the months Mack had worked the Lazy N, he'd proven himself to be a fast learner. If he passed this test, he'd be a welcome addition on the trail drive come spring. "Ready?"

Mack nodded, and in minutes, the three succeeded in coaxing five cows, two heifers, and a steer into a tight cluster. Only the burly bull seemed flustered by the horses and their riders. He edged away from his harem and stood off to the side, head down, glaring at the cowboys.

"He's probably the one that led them out here in the first place. We'll have to get him first," Dan explained to Mack. "You mosey back and forth, keep him distracted, while I get a rope around his fat neck."

Mack gave a low whistle. "What do you figure he weighs?"

"Twelve or thirteen hundred pounds."

"Shoo-eee! He won't gore my horse, will he?"

"This horse of yours," George said, "she is smarter than you, *amigo!*"

Dan grinned. "Wasn't all that long ago you were raw, too, George."

"*Sí,*" he agreed, laughing, "but never *this* raw!"

The cowboys' quiet banter, together with the back-and-forth motion of their horses, kept the bull occupied while Dan whirled a lariat above his head, then let it fly, the near-silent hiss of rope skidding across his gloved palm alerting the formidable animal. But the bull looked up a tick too late, for Dan's rope had already landed around his thick neck. While it kicked and snorted, Dan unfurled a second rope and snagged both hind legs. One good jerk tightened the second rope. Dan wound the lasso around his saddle horn and, grabbing a tie-down rope, slid from the saddle. Before the bull could react, Dan wrestled it to its side, lashing one foreleg to the other, binding both rear legs to the front.

"There," Dan said, breathing hard. "The grumpy ol' cuss ain't goin' nowhere till we say he can." He wasted no time getting back into the saddle, wincing as he flung his bum leg over the horse's back. "Now let's get these girls roped so we can start on that other gang of runaways."

Less than an hour later, all seven beeves had been successfully roped and tied.

Once the job was done, Mack frowned. "We're not just gonna leave 'em here like that, are we?"

"*Sí*," was George's patient reply.

"But—but I thought they couldn't breathe on their sides!"

"Ain't pretty, I know," Dan said, "but it's the only way to keep 'em from wandering off again while we round up their cousins." He quirked an eyebrow. "You feel up to taking one down and getting her roped all by yourself?"

In place of an answer, Mack got into his saddle and urged his horse toward the other cows. "Well, what're you waitin' for, *amigos?* We're burnin' daylight!"

"This should be *muy interesante*," George said, grinning.

And interesting it was! Though Mack's first attempt was more comical than accomplished, he was soon roping like a seasoned cowpoke—a fact that pleased Dan, for it meant he wouldn't need to hire another hand for the spring drive.

By sundown, twenty-seven head—a mix of heifers and cows, one a young stud, and the tough old bull—had settled under a scrubby pine while the men hunkered down for a meal of stale bread and cold jerky. Their horses, covered in grit and sweat, drowsed behind them. Finally, all was quiet on the prairie.

After the meal, George sat whittling a gnarled branch while Mack leaned on his saddle, playing mournful tunes on his harmonica. After a while, George looked up from the shavings and said, "You not know any songs that are not *doloroso?*"

Mack wiggled his eyebrows and pointed at the herd with his harmonica. "If you think I'm gonna rile those cows after all we went through to get 'em, you've got another thing comin'."

He crossed one booted ankle over the other and launched into a century-old hymn. Dan recognized it from his boyhood days, when he'd attended Sunday services with his ma and pa. The melody reminded him of the lyrics, long asleep in his mind, and he closed his eyes. "Come, Thou Fount of every blessing, tune my heart to sing Thy grace...." If he concentrated, Dan could almost hear the strains of the pipe organ and the quavering off-key soprano of old Mrs. Willis.

He shook his head, hoping to clear the cobwebs from his brain, for he'd learned the hard way what happens when bitterness takes root where good memories once grew.

Oh, what he'd give for a mug of coffee and some biscuits with maple syrup. But the added weight of coffee beans, a brew pot, tin mugs, and flour for the biscuits would only have slowed them down. They had a fire and scratchy blankets to keep them warm, and an umbrella of stars in the inky sky that promised a dry night. He'd just have to be content with that.

"I'll take first watch," he said, draping his blanket around his shoulders. By the time it was his turn to bed down, he'd be too dog-tired to dwell on his past. At least, that's what Dan hoped.

George put his away his whittling and spread out his bedroll, and Mack did the same. "I don't rouse easy," Mack said, dropping the harmonica into his shirt pocket, "so don't be afraid to give me a good swift kick to the boots in an hour or so." Then, he rolled onto his side and, within seconds, began to snore.

"Ay yi yi," George grumbled, clapping a hand over his eyes. "We will be lucky if that noise no scare *las vacas*."

"Never heard-tell of a man's snoring being noise enough to spook 'em."

"My grandfather used to say there is first time for everything. I hope he was wrong." Then George flopped onto his back on the other side of the fire. Before long, his snorts were harmonizing with Mack's.

The breeze picked up, and Dan pulled his blanket tighter around him. Experience had taught him that the cows hated the howling wind almost as much as he did. He started a slow, wide circle around the herd, watching for signs of agitation or restlessness. Finding none, he let himself relax a mite and thought of Levee. For the Christmas pageant, would she bundle her thick, dark curls into a bun or let her hair drape around her delicate shoulders like an ebony waterfall? Would glittery earrings dangle from her earlobes, as they had when she'd visited his ma at the ranch?

He remembered how she'd cuddled up beside him, seeking warmth, as he'd driven her back to her cottage. It hadn't been easy letting her wriggle free from his grasp, but she'd made it bearable by inviting him inside for some tea while she'd copied the cherry pie recipe for his ma. He'd downed two more cups of the watery, sugary stuff after she'd finished writing, glad for any excuse to dally a while longer. It hadn't been easy saying good-bye, either, because with every fiber of his being he'd wanted to wrap his arms around her and find out if those pretty, pink lips tasted as good as they looked.

"Better take hold of yourself, man," he whispered, "or she's liable to take hold of your heart."

But it was too late to fret about that. She had accomplished it with the first smile aimed his way from the schoolhouse steps.

Yep, he'd better get hold of himself, all right, and quick, because if she didn't feel the way he did, he was in for a world of hurt.

11

*L*evee's students lined up beside the makeshift stage at the front of the church, trembling with anticipation. "There's nothing to worry about," Levee assured them. "You've all worked very hard, so just relax and have fun. I'll be off to the side of the stage in case you forget a line, all right?"

"Is Mr. Mack here?" Willie asked, brandishing his shepherd's staff.

"He wasn't the last time I checked, which was a whole minute ago," she said, grinning.

"He promised he'd be here," Samantha said solemnly, "and grown-ups never break their promises." She looked at her teacher. "Do they, Mrs. O'Reilly?"

Levee thought of the many times adults had let her down, both when she had been a child and since she herself had joined the world of adults, and tried to come up with some words of reassurance. "I believe in most cases, grown-ups never mean to break their promises."

"In other words," Becky said, "they'll have a good excuse every time they do."

Steven, who was dressed as one of the three Magi, adjusted his crown. "Maybe," he said, "but that ain't true 'bout Mr. Mack."

"Stevie's right," Willie piped up. "He said he'd be here, so he'll be here. He's with my uncle Dan, and he wouldn't let Mr. Mack show up late."

No one had heard a word from the men since they'd left on their winter roundup. Levee had been praying for their safe return since the night Dan had taken her home from the Lazy N, and those moments spent alone in her cozy kitchen as he'd waited for her to write out the recipe for his mother were emblazoned on her heart. How funny he'd looked, trying to fit his thick, calloused fingers through the tiny handle of his fragile china teacup! The memory of it encouraged a fond smile and inspired a silent prayer: *Father, stay with Dan and Mack. Keep them safe and bring them home to us soon, so the children will not be disappointed!*

"Need any help?"

Levee would have recognized that beautiful baritone in a crowd. "Dan!" she exclaimed, whirling around to face him. "You certainly like to arrive at the eleventh hour, don't you?"

A tender smile shone in his eyes. "Took longer to scrape off the trail dust than we figured."

One of the "angels" ran up to Dan. "Is Mr. Mack with you, Mr. Neville?"

"Yes, he sure is."

Willie peeked through the opening in the curtain Levee had fashioned from blankets draped over a clothesline. "Yep, he's there, all right," the boy said, jumping up and down, "and he's got a sack on his lap."

"Rock candy!" Steven said.

"Children, children!" Levee admonished them. "Mrs. Peterson will take her place at the piano any second now, and if you don't quiet down, you'll never hear her signal!"

"Guess that's my cue to get out front and take a seat—if my cousin Josh and his pretty wife, Kate, have saved me one, that is," Dan said. "See you after the show?"

"We've planned a cast party," she told him. "You know, like the ones Shakespearean actors have after a performance."

"Never had the privilege of attending one."

Before she had a chance to invite him, Dan ducked around to the other side of the curtain as the reverend's wife struck an inharmonious chord on the piano. "All right, now," Levee said in a loud whisper, clapping to get the children's attention. "Are we ready?"

Once her students had scrambled into place, Levee stepped in front of the curtain. "Ladies and gentlemen, boys and girls," she announced, "I now present the Eagle Pass Schoolhouse Players in 'O Holy Night: The Story of the Nativity.'" Those gathered in the church applauded while Levee opened the curtain. She then signaled Mrs. Peterson, who began the first song.

As promised, Levee stood off to the side, hands clenched beneath her chin as she mouthed every line and lyric of the children's recitations and songs. She'd spent hours sewing their costumes by the flickering light of an oil lantern, and now, as she watched them perform what they'd practiced countless times, her heart swelled with pride and affection. It had been well worth each needle prick, every eye-straining hour! The final burst of applause painted smiles of delight and satisfaction on every young performer's face, and on the faces of their friends and family members, too.

"The best Eagle Pass Christmas pageant ever!" bellowed a man from the back of the church.

"The first Eagle Pass Christmas pageant ever!" someone else yelled.

"Three cheers for Mrs. O'Reilly!" called a third voice.

"Thank the good Lord I was too poor to pay you!" said Doc Lane as laughter rippled through the pews like a wave.

Levee cheerfully accepted hugs from each of her students and shook the hands of their parents as they filed into the church basement for mulled cider and cookies. An hour later, she waved good-bye and listened to the children's giggles echo down the road as they retreated, aflutter with post-performance excitement and the effects of the sugary rock candy.

"Only a few more days until Christmas," Matilda Montgomery said as she helped Levee straighten up the sanctuary. "Where are you having dinner?"

She'd hoped to spend part of the day in quiet prayer, then scrub every desk and chair in the classroom and stack firewood alongside the schoolhouse. Then there were lessons to plan, and the cottage could use a good sweeping. She also had a dress to launder and a skirt to iron....

The older woman studied Levee's face. "Don't tell me you're spending the day alone."

"I've never been overly fond of the holiday," she said. And it was true, after all, especially thanks to Liam's stern lecture about the sinful and frivolous nature of festive dinners and decorations. "I just thought I'd catch up on a few chores while everyone else is busy celebrating."

"Nonsense! After services, you'll ride with me to the Lazy N. I have a standing invitation from Eva Neville, and I have it on good authority that a joyous announcement will be made after dinner. I wouldn't miss it for the world." She wagged a finger under Levee's nose. "And neither will you."

"Matilda," Levee began, "I appreciate the offer, really I do, but I'd much rather—"

"Nonsense," Matilda repeated, linking her arm with Levee's. "I have some things I'd like to donate to the school, but how can I know which you can use if we don't make time to discuss them?"

She'd already been so generous in her donations—the blackboard, the teacher's desk, and the grandfather clock, to name just a few items—that Levee couldn't imagine what more the dear lady could contribute! Matilda was also the reason the children didn't have to bring lunch pails to school. When she'd discovered that three of the sixteen students couldn't afford even a crust of bread in their buckets, she'd arranged for a local restaurant to deliver a lunch of fried chicken, boiled eggs, cheese, and biscuits for each student every day at noon.

"All right," Levee said, "if it's for the children." *I wonder if Dan will be at his aunt and uncle's house, or if he will spend the day with his parents.*

"You'll be happy to hear the entire Neville clan gathers at Matthew and Eva's house for the holiday."

"Goodness, Matilda! A person could get the idea you're a mind reader," Levee said, grinning.

"My eyesight is as good now as it was when I was sixteen. Don't need mind-reading skills to see how you and Dan Neville feel about each other."

Levee looked left and then right to see who might have heard her friend's remark.

"Don't worry, I've sent them all on their way. It's just the two of us, and I promised the reverend that we'd tidy this humble house of the Lord before leaving here tonight. And then?" Her boisterous laughter bounced off every wall of the church. "And then you're going to walk me home." She picked up her skirts and began walking through the pews, tidying hymnals and picking up the programs Levee had had printed for the pageant attendees. "I'll handle things out here while you turn the stage back into an altar."

Half an hour later, Levee found herself in Matilda's parlor, listening as the woman described her former life as a Shakespearean actress. She stopped only to spoon sugar into her gilt-rimmed teacup. "So," she said, balancing her cup and saucer near her ample bosom, "I understand you were one of the first women in the country to earn a nursing degree." She raised her cup as if giving a toast. "Well done. That's quite an accomplishment."

Levee would have thanked her if Matilda hadn't gone right on to say, "So, tell me, do you miss it?"

"Nursing, you mean?" Levee shook her head. "Not at all. Not even in my first days of teaching."

"That's because you're a natural-born mother. More's the pity you don't have any children of your own." Matilda sighed. "But your students have an advantage in that they receive your undivided attention. They couldn't be in better hands." She paused. "And neither could Dan."

Dan? What did he have to do with anything?

Matilda answered her unasked question. "You'd think a boy like that, born with the proverbial silver spoon in his mouth, would have enjoyed a happy, easy life, wouldn't you?"

"I—I suppose I never gave it much thought." And she hadn't, either, because she'd been captivated by his soft-spoken ways and gentle smile. And those haunted blue eyes....

"He had a twin, you know."

"No, I didn't know."

"Her name was Daisy. Poor little thing barely survived being born. She came into the world part deaf and nearly blind. Why, she was almost four when she took her first step, and I don't believe she ever really learned to run like a normal child." Matilda leaned forward to add, "If you ask me, it wasn't fair the way Mark and Judith put Dan in charge of the girl. I'm sure it wasn't easy, accepting the fact that she was less than perfect, like all their others, but still, the boy endured a lot of teasing from his pals and those rowdy cousins of his. 'Daisy Minder,' they called him, and 'Nanny,' among other things." Matilda shook her head. "Far be it from me to pass judgment, especially since I never had young'uns of my own, but...." Matilda frowned and grew pensive before adding, "The twins were thirteen when Daisy died."

"Such a shame," Levee said, shaking her head also.

"Yes, so much life ahead of her."

And such an enormous loss for Dan! "What took her, illness or accident?" was Levee's careful question.

"I guess to be perfectly accurate, it was both." Matilda took a sip of tea. "See, with Daisy's poor eyesight and hearing, she had to get right up on things to investigate them. One day, when Dan's folks went to town, they left him to look after the girl. He didn't tell them that he aimed to go fishing with his cousins Josh, Micah, and Paul that day." Her chest rose and fell with a deep breath. "I suppose he thought since she'd tagged along with them so many times before, there'd be no harm in taking her to the river that day."

Levee knew by the anguished expression on her friend's face that the story was about to take a tragic turn, and since it involved Dan, she wasn't at all sure she wanted to hear more.

"Seems the girl saw an injured dog off in the distance," Matilda said, closing her eyes. "That child had a heart as big as her head, I tell you." She clicked her tongue. "While the boys were busy roughhousing and bickering about who'd caught the biggest fish, Daisy went over to see how badly the dog was hurt, and it bit her. Her crying roused the boys, and they went running. Turned out it wasn't a dog at all but a coyote."

Levee gasped into the palm of her hand.

"Thank the Lord Dan had the good sense to bring his rifle. Shot the critter dead, and…."

Awestruck by the dreadful tale, Levee became aware that she'd leaned forward to pay even closer attention. It took all the willpower she could muster to sit back and keep herself from saying, "And *what?*"

"And it had frothy spittle around its lips."

"Rabies," Levee whispered, remembering everything she'd learned about the disease in nursing school. If the boys hadn't known to clean the wound, and to do it immediately, Daisy would have become infected with the virus, and—

"The child suffered for months before she died. It was the twins' thirteenth birthday. I was in her room when she spoke her last words."

Levee was afraid to ask what those last words were, but something told her she knew to whom she'd spoken them.

"Somehow, she found the strength to grab hold of Dan's hand. 'Wasn't your fault, Danny,' she said. 'My guardian angel told me just now that you'd need to hear that.'"

Levee now understood the forlorn look that seemed to have made a home in his eyes—dreadful proof that, even after all this time, he still blamed himself for his sister's death.

"And that isn't the whole of it," Matilda said, refilling her teacup. "That limp of his?"

Levee could see it without closing her eyes. She'd wondered how he'd come by it.

"Losing Daisy changed Dan. He hadn't been reckless before. Oh, he was a normal, boisterous boy, but never reckless. After Daisy died, he turned into a daredevil. Nothing scared him—or so it seemed by the bold things he did and the foolish risks he took. If you ask me, he was trying to join Daisy." She added another spoonful of sugar to her tea and stirred briskly.

Eyes closed, Matilda lowered her head, as if praying for the strength to finish the story. "Several years back, Dan and the boys were driving some cattle to Kansas when an afternoon storm blew in, and lightning spooked the cows. He saw that his cousin Josh was in trouble, and he rode straight into the teeth of a stampede to divert the herd. It worked, but not before he fell from his horse, and…."

Matilda patted her graying temples. "It's a miracle he survived at all." Her voice dropped to a near whisper. "He lay there in his bed," she said, hands folded as if in prayer, "still and quiet as a corpse. Stayed that way for months. Josh himself said that he would have been dead for sure if Dan hadn't ridden into the melee."

The mantel clock ticked as the wind rustled the trees on the terrace beyond the French doors. "When he came to, I prayed he'd lapse back into unconsciousness, because the pain was bad, so very bad. The only thing that dulled it was whiskey, and lots of it. By the time he was well enough to walk again, he couldn't last an hour without the stuff." Matilda reached for her teacup. "Oh, those were terrible, *terrible* years," she continued. "Seemed like every week, the sheriff was sending a deputy to ask one of the Nevilles to fetch Dan at the jail, where he'd had to put him for getting into fistfights and shouting matches down at the saloon."

Fistfights and shouting matches? Mild-mannered, soft-spoken Daniel Neville? Levee almost didn't believe it.

Almost. She'd seen the embers of heartbreak glowing in his eyes.

Matilda shook her head. "He carried on like a blamed fool for a few years. Once, as he stumbled past my place on his way home from the saloon, he stopped to get his balance. Sat on my porch and told me it was his own selfishness that had gotten Daisy killed. Said God was deaf and coldhearted for not taking him up on his offer to trade his life for his twin's. I tried to tell him that no one held him accountable for what happened. His ma and pa told him the same thing, and so did just about everybody in town."

As the woman fell silent, Levee closed her eyes, correctly anticipating the gist of what Matilda would say next.

"But it didn't matter what they said, not when he believed otherwise."

Levee had heard folks use the term "tortured soul," but she'd never met anyone who epitomized it more than Dan.

"Oh, don't look so down in the mouth, dearie," Matilda said. "It isn't all that bad. Dan is made of sturdy stuff. He pulled himself out of it, for the most part."

"*For the most part?*" It had taken Levee an incalculable number of hours reading the Good Book until her eyes burned to realize she'd been powerless to change what had happened on the San Antonio Road. If she had spent months of her life grappling with the shame and remorse of wondering what she might have done to save her husband, how much more excruciating had it been for poor Dan, a mere twelve-year-old boy when tragedy had touched his life?

"One day, he caught his mama crying," Matilda went on, "and it wasn't the first time. He realized who was the cause of her misery and gave up his whiskey, just like that."

And Levee got the message, loud and clear: the torment in his eyes wasn't just emotional; it was very much physical, too, without whiskey to numb the pain. Her eyes filled with tears and her heart ached for him. Oh, if only there was something she could do to help ease his agony!

"Aha," Matilda said. "So I was right!"

"Right? About…?"

"About young Dan." She winked. "And about you."

"Forgive my thickheadedness, but I'm not following."

"Dan Neville couldn't be in better or more loving hands."

An eddy of emotions swirled in her head and surged through her heart. "I'm flattered that you think so, but really, Matilda, you're giving me far more credit than I deserve. I barely know Daniel. We only just met a few—"

"How does that saying go?" Matilda tapped a forefinger to her chin. "Something like, 'You can fool some of the people all of the time, and all of the people some of the time, but you can't fool all of the people all of the time.'"

Yes, Levee had heard that line, but she failed to see what it had to do with the situation.

Matilda winked. "You can pretend not to care for him when other folks are around, but you can't fool me. You're bonnet-over-boots in love with that man. Why, it's written all over your pretty face."

Levee felt the heat of a blush rise from her throat to her cheeks. Had the rest of Eagle Pass seen what Matilda had? What would they think if they knew that the woman who spent hours with their impressionable children every day had fallen in love with a near stranger mere months after burying her husband?

No sooner had the question formed in her mind than another followed behind it: *Did* she love him?

"And he looks at you the same way," Matilda added with a conspiratorial smile.

Could it possibly be true? And if it was....

Rubbing her temples, Levee got to her feet. She needed time alone to think things through and pray about everything Matilda had just told her. "Goodness gracious! Will you look at the time?" she said, loading the silver serving tray with cups and saucers. "I'll just carry these into the kitchen for you," she said, hurrying toward the door, "and then I really must be on my way!"

When Levee returned to the parlor, she found her friend in the doorway, a glowing lantern in one hand, a lace-trimmed handkerchief in the other. It didn't take a genius to figure out that the lamp was to help light her way to the cottage, tucked neatly into the woods adjacent to Matilda's expansive back-yard. As for the handkerchief, she would just have to wait for the explanation that was sure to follow.

"It's been a pleasure getting to know you better," Matilda said. "I hope we'll visit this way again real soon."

"I do, too. Thank you kindly for the refreshments." Levee needed to change the subject, and do it fast, in case the woman had a mind to share more about Dan Neville's past. "That's a lovely tea service. I don't believe I've ever seen one quite like it."

"It's Staffordshire," Matilda said, glancing at it, "one of the two prized possessions my dear mama carried across the Atlantic."

Patience, Levee, and you'll find out soon enough what the other thing was.

Sure enough, Matilda extended her right hand so that Levee could see the gleaming ring on her pinkie.

"Mother gave it to me the week before she passed. It was the cancer that took her." She stared off into space and spun the ring around on her finger a time or two. "Guess she thought that by saving some poor fool the price of a wedding band, I might be spared an 'old maid's fate.'" Matilda laughed softly and looked at the ceiling. "Sorry, Mama." Laughing again, she met Levee's gaze. "I suppose by now she understands that her only daughter just wasn't meant to be a wife."

"Oh, I don't know about that. With a heart as big as yours? Maybe the Almighty is still looking for the man who's worthy of you."

Matilda pursed her lips, then giggled. "Levee O'Reilly, I never would have pegged you as a bluffer!" She handed off the lantern. "Tell me, why did your mama choose such a peculiar first name for her girl?"

Levee recounted the story she had told to Dan's mother just two weeks prior, Irish brogue and all.

When she was finished, Matilda used the hanky to blot her damp eyes. "My, my, my," she said, "that's one of the most romantic stories I've ever heard." She pulled Levee into a warm hug, then held her at arm's length. "And here I thought you'd inherited your 'Irish' by taking your husband's name."

Levee resisted the urge to scoff as she recalled that her Celtic heritage was another one of the reasons Liam had cited to prove to her what a smart union their marriage would be.

"Sorry, I'd hoped to give this to you, dear," Matilda said as she pressed the fabric to her eyes.

Levee smiled. "How kind and thoughtful you are. But, really, I have half a dozen at home, all donated by the good women of the church."

"But this was brand-new, a gift for you. I'm relieved to know you have others," Matilda said, wiping her nose. "Well, I've given you a lot to ponder tonight, and, unless I'm very wrong about you, a handkerchief will come in handy when you start ruminating about everything your Dan suffered and survived." She gave Levee one last hug and, with a wave of the lacy cloth, bid her good night.

Levee took her time walking from Matilda's to her little cottage. Tomorrow, she'd bake two loaves of bread and deliver one of them to Matilda when she returned her lantern. How like the woman to know that with so little moonlight, she'd need help navigating the path. Why, with all the tree roots and tilting flagstones, she could very well trip and end up like dear Mrs. Neville, with her leg in a splint, and—

"Pretty night, isn't it?"

Levee muffled a tiny yelp with her free hand. "Dan," she said, holding the lantern higher to see his face. "You scared me half to death!"

"Sorry. Guess that was thoughtless of me, wasn't it?"

Stepping out of nowhere on a dark, windy night and blurting out a greeting to a woman walking alone at the edge of the woods? Levee might have laughed at the imprudence of it if she hadn't been so delighted to see him. "I thought you left an hour ago, after the cast party."

"Should have, but couldn't."

"Goodness. I hope nothing happened to your horse."

Chuckling, Dan took a step closer. "No. Biscuit is fine."

He relieved her of the lantern as she said, "That's an interesting name for a horse. How'd you choose it?"

"Because she's sort of gold and sort of white, like—"

"—a biscuit," they said together, laughing.

"Well," she said, resuming her walk, "I'll give you an A for originality."

"Last time I checked, the word started with an *o*."

Levee glanced up at him, intent on countering his sarcastic remark with one of her own. She caught the toe of her boot on a tree root, instead.

"Careful there," Dan said, grabbing her elbow.

Oh, how easy it would have been to stare into his blue eyes, to let her gaze linger on that enticing, mustached mouth….

Levee suddenly realized that's exactly what she'd been doing. She realized, too, that he'd slid his arm around her waist to help steady her. Why, he was close enough to kiss, if she had a mind to kiss him. She cleared her throat. "Y-you— you never said why you couldn't go home after the pageant," she sputtered, taking a careful step away from him. And when the playful grin reappeared, her heart beat a little faster.

"I was hoping to get a few minutes alone with you," he said. "Before Matilda Montgomery stole you away, that is."

Levee heard herself giggle—a little too long and a little too loudly for the hour. "Alone with me? But—but whatever for?" *Idiot!* she thought, holding her breath. *What a silly thing to say!*

"To tell you what a good job you did pulling that show together, for starters."

So, there were other reasons—reasons her addled brain couldn't begin to conjecture with him looking at her that way! Thankfully, the darkness hid her blush. At least, Levee hoped it did. "Oh, all the credit goes to the children." Wasn't it bad enough he'd seen her trip over her own feet? Now he could add "moony-eyed" to the traits he no doubt associated with her. "They were just magnificent, weren't they?"

"Only because of their magnificent teacher."

He'd taken a step closer, lowered his voice almost to a whisper. An expectant, affectionate gleam radiated from his eyes, and he licked his lips. Was he about to kiss her, right there in front of her house?

Dan handed her the lantern. "Well, now that I've seen you safely home, I guess I'd better head home, myself."

Oh, to have the courage to flout the unspoken rules of etiquette that spelled out whom a lady could invite into her home without planting seeds of gossip! Especially at night, and particularly if the invitee happened to be a handsome, eligible bachelor. Levee cleared her throat again. "Take care on that road, you hear?" she said as he made his way back down the shadowy path. "There are ruts and holes, and   "

"Don't worry, Biscuit knows the way to the Lazy N even better than I do."

From taking you home all those nights you tarried in the saloon? Immediately, she regretted the thought.

Dan lifted the hat from his head for a second, then quickly donned it again. "Good night, Levee," he said, bowing slightly.

"Good night," she echoed. When he disappeared from view, she added, "Sleep soundly, dear Daniel, and may God's angels shield you from pain of any sort."

The wind kicked up, wrapping her skirts around her shins, and she hurried inside to stoke the fire. The gentle beam of the lantern flickered on her bureau as Levee changed into one of her two hand-me-down nightgowns, also donated by the church ladies. *How ironic*, she thought, grinning as she pictured the immense wardrobe that had dominated half a wall in her bedroom back in Boston. Dozens of silk dresses, brocade jackets, damask skirts, and satin blouses had hung neatly behind its bevel-mirrored doors, and the drawers had all but overflowed with the finest nightclothes, stockings, petticoats, and gloves. Fancy hats had lined the shelves, while boots and slippers of the finest quality had stood in orderly rows on its floor. Much to her dismay, Liam had limited her to one suitcase, and so she'd given everything that wouldn't fit to his sister, Bonnie. "How will it look if you show up in Chihuahua dressed like a princess when the local ladies are wearing simple cotton and muslin?" he'd asked her when she'd reminded him how much each frock had cost.

"I suppose the one bag will be easier to manage as we travel," she'd agreed. "But once we're settled, I'll need to have some new clothes made. We can't have the local doctor's wife looking like a ragamuffin, now, can we?"

The memory inspired a soft chuckle. "Oh, Liam," she whispered, "if you could only see me now!" She looked down at her patched robe and her stockings, which had been darned more times than she could count.

Sighing, Levee doused the lantern's flame, plunging the room into darkness. She snuggled deep beneath the covers, closed her eyes, and pictured Dan's fine-looking face. What a paradox it was that Liam, though blessed by a life of ease, had become a stuffy, imperious snob, while Daniel, who'd earned his comforts by dint of his own hard work and endured all manner of suffering, was gentle and generous.

You're a nasty, callous shrew for so much as thinking ill of the dead! she thought, giving her pillow a remorseful punch. Liam hadn't held a gun to her head, after all, and hadn't forced her to become his wife, either. He'd presented a good case, and her prudent grandfather had concurred with every sensible point on Liam's list. If she hadn't been raised by her well-mannered grandmother, a woman who would rather have eaten dirt than speak a cross word, might she have demanded a modicum of respect from her husband?

Not likely, she admitted. The only time she'd ever stood up for herself had been when she had pursued a nursing degree, but since the only "nursing" she did these days involved bandaging skinned knees and plucking splinters from chubby fingers, it seemed a feebly-fought battle. She wouldn't dream of trading any part of her teaching position for one that required her to wear a cap and apron. Still, that single triumph didn't exactly endow Levee with ample faith in herself. "Unless you focus on the possibility that all you need is the right thing to fight *for.*"

Dan instantly came to mind, forcing Levee to ask herself if she would fight for him. She turned onto her right side. What circumstances would require such a thing of her? Flopping to her left side, she couldn't help wondering if he'd even want her to fight for him.

On her back again, Levee tucked her hands under her head, remembering that Matilda had called him "her" Dan. Grinning, she clutched the bedsheet and pressed it to her lips. It wasn't likely, but it wasn't impossible, either, because hadn't he waited all alone in the cold just to tell her good night? What about how guilty he'd looked when his sudden appearance had frightened her? And she'd seen the pain in his beautiful eyes when he'd shifted to his bad leg to keep her from stumbling. Levee didn't know which touched her more, the way he'd quickly tried to hide it from her or the look of tenderness that had replaced it.

On her right side again, Levee faced the windows and bunched the pillow around her ears to drown out the woeful wail of the wind, but it did little to smother the sound of witch-fingered branches tapping the glass. Despite his huge family and the dozens who called him "friend," Dan had convinced himself that no one understood why he'd punished himself these many years. Levee didn't know this but rather sensed it, just as she didn't need to see his injured leg to believe it caused him great physical pain, pain that paled in comparison to the emotional injury of his guilt.

Too soon to have such powerful feelings for him? Perhaps. But certainly not too soon to want to ease his suffering, to hope that their friendship would provide him proof that someone did understand his grief, someone who cared about him—and for him—very much.

Dabbing her teary eyes with a corner of her pillowcase, Levee floated off to sleep, praying that sometime during the night, God would reveal His will for her life. Because, whether or not it was too soon to feel this way, she very much wanted Daniel to be part of it. A big part of it.

12

S lipped with the razor, did you?" Mack said, sitting down
across from Dan at the breakfast table the next morning.

Dan put down his fork and self-consciously traced
the still-raw nick on his cheek. Earlier, as he'd drawn the blade
across his soap-lathered jaw, an image of Levee had flashed in
his mind. It had been cloudy the night before, but for an instant,
the moon had peeked out from behind a cloud, swathing her in
silvery light. He'd been afraid to blink for fear he'd miss the halo
and wings that would complete the angelic illusion. The memory
had provoked a smile and cost him a few drops of blood. "Some
days," he admitted, "it just doesn't pay to get out of bed."

Mack speared a biscuit with his fork. "How'd you come by
that other scar, if you don't mind my asking?"

At least a dozen times, Dan had been tempted to shat-
ter a mirror to avoid looking at the ugly reminder of his tar-
nished past. Yes, he minded Mack's asking, but how could he
explain why without admitting what a scoundrel he'd been?
He drained his mug of coffee. If he was lucky, Mack would
recognize it as a stall tactic and take the hint to back off.

No such luck.

"Got it in the stampede, same as the bum leg?"

Groaning inwardly, Dan shoved away from the table and
limped over to the sideboard. He'd eaten his fill but heaped

another pile of fried potatoes on his plate, anyway. Better to pretend his appetite distracted him than have Mack think it was a touchy subject.

"Looks to me like an old wound," Mack murmured behind him.

Slowly, Dan lifted the china coffeepot, one of his ma's prized possessions, and held the lid in place with the pad of his thumb as he refilled his mug.

"Does it hurt?"

Only when folks ask me about it. "No."

"So, it *does* have something to do with that stampede, huh?"

"Which stampede?"

A second passed, maybe two, before Mack said, "What, you mean you've been in more than one?"

Dan carried his mug back to the table and stood behind his chair, studying Mack's face. Dan had never been the curious type, and he didn't understand folks who were. On more than one occasion, he'd seen what can happen when folks poked their noses into other people's business. "I was in a saloon once—Kansas City, to the best of my recollection—where a writer started prying into Frank Michaels's life."

Mack stopped chewing, and his eyebrows arched high on his forehead. "Frank Michaels the outlaw?"

Dan nodded.

Brows knitted in a frown now, Mack went back to eating. "What sort of fool meddles in a killer's private affairs?"

"The kind who ends up flat on his back with a hole in his belly."

Dan watched Mack's Adam's apple rise, then fall. "You mean to say Michaels really shot the man just for asking questions?"

"I reckon some fellas don't have the patience for busybodies." Would his brusque reply put an end to Mack's inquisition? *A man can hope.*

"Well, do tell," Mack said, getting to his feet. He carried his plate and silverware to the sideboard, then started for the door, stopping just inside the archway. Mustache slanted in a wry grin, he said, "You never did say how you came by that scar."

"Do tell," Dan echoed. "Are *you* writin' a book?"

Mack's eyes darkened—was it with fury? hostility?—and, in a blink, returned to normal. Dan didn't know what to make of the quick recovery. Was it a good sign or a warning?

"If I were writin' a book, you wouldn't shoot a hole in my belly," Mack said, blinking. "Right?"

His stance, tone, and flinty expression reminded Dan of the bravado displayed in too many barroom brawls and a showdown or two. He stood a little taller to say, "I declare, you ask more questions than an old woman."

Shoulders up, Mack sighed. "My mama always said it's the only way to learn anything." He donned his hat and gave a two-fingered wave. "But never let it be said that Mack Burdette can't take a hint. How you came by that scar is your business, and if you want to keep it a secret, well, that's your business, too, I guess."

The last two words hung on the air like the scent of boiled cabbage from last night's supper. Dan had been suspicious when Mack had first come to town, but in the months that had passed since then, he'd let his guard down, partly because the man worked harder than any he'd ever seen and partly because he was a right likeable fellow.

Until this morning.

Next time he was in town, Dan would talk to Matilda about getting a message to that Pinkerton nephew of hers, because what if Mack had ridden with an outlaw gang? Not that he'd jump to conclusions if that turned out to be true. He himself was walking, talking proof that a man could sink real low and bring himself back up if he had a mind to. Still, it made sense to find out if the unsettled feeling roiling in his gut had teeth, or if it could be chalked up to an overactive imagination.

"Who tied your socks in a knot?"

His pulse pounding in response to the sudden intrusion, Dan whirled around. "Land sakes, Pa! You just took five years off my life!"

His father chuckled. "Then, you owe me a thank-you, boy."

"For what?"

"Way I hear-tell, those last five years are the hardest."

Dan grinned, but his heart wasn't in it. The last fifteen or so years had soured him, and until Levee had breezed into his life, he'd half expected to meet his Maker long before his chronological age caught up with the grizzled old man who had taken up residence in his head and his heart.

His father poured himself a cup of coffee, then topped off Dan's mug. "Willie was over here earlier, looking for you."

Dan had planned to follow Mack outside to the barn, where a week's worth of work awaited him, but moments alone with his pa had always been few and far between, and he'd learned to take advantage of them whenever he could. "He came by himself?" Dan asked.

"Said he ran the whole way from his house." Chuckling, his pa added, "That young'un reminds me of you at that age—always in a hurry, always with a list of 'wants' longer than his arm."

Hard to believe I was once a boy, Dan thought, taking a swig of coffee. It seemed to him that he'd gone from thirteen to thirty-five in the time it had taken his sweet sister to say good-bye.

"Had a dog with him."

That snapped Dan back to attention. "What kind of dog?"

His pa started describing the animal, but Dan barely heard a word. He'd been about Willie's age when he'd found a raggedy pup in town, brought him home, cleaned him up, and named him Mischief for all the trouble he'd gotten into around the Lazy N. Dan had enjoyed six good years with his furry sidekick before Mischief got into a fracas with a wild dog who'd started the fight. For more than a month, Dan had hunted for the mangy instigator, hoping he'd been wrong about what he'd seen. Yet, all too soon, Mischief's behavior had gone from energetic and affectionate to cantankerous and sluggish. Dan hadn't bothered telling his family, and he hadn't waited for the telltale white spittle to appear, either. Instead, one rainy morning, he had lured the poor, sick critter far from the house and put him out of his misery.

His pa set down his coffee mug with a clank, rousing Dan from his reverie. "...he's fixin' to give it to the teacher as a Christmas present," he was saying as he shook his head. "I told him he'd best check with her first, see if she wants the work and responsibilities." He shook his head again. "That pup's full of spirit. Smart, too. With feet as large as dinner plates. Why, he'll be big enough to saddle before long. Dunno if he'll fit in that li'l place Mrs. O'Reilly calls home!"

"How'd Willie come by this dog?"

"Didn't ask him. Was you he come lookin' for."

"Where is he now?"

"At his grandpa's, I reckon. The boy knows as well as anybody you're likelier to be in Matthew's barn than just about anyplace else."

That was true, or it had been until a certain little lady had stepped out onto the schoolhouse porch. Dan cleared his throat, wondering what in tarnation was happening to him. How was it possible for a wisp of a gal to consume his thoughts, especially when he could practically count on his fingers the number of minutes he'd spent with her? Shoving his hat onto his head, he said, "Guess I'd best get on down there, then, and see what the boy's got up his sleeve. Wouldn't want him marching into town by his lonesome with that rascal in tow."

"Just be fair, son. Not every dog has rabies." His pa shrugged. "Maybe you'll get lucky and she won't want the pup."

"Lucky?"

"He could be a right fine herder, with a little work."

"See you at supper," Dan said, shoving through the screen door as he tried to fight the urge to find Willie and set him straight. He wanted desperately to get rid of that dog before it had a chance to infect anyone—Levee, in particular—with whatever diseases it might be carrying, and before anyone had a chance to get attached to it. Anything to protect her from danger and death.

13

*T*he carriage clock had just announced the nine o'clock hour when a steady rapping captured her attention. It had to be Matilda, stopping by as she did on most Sunday mornings to see if Levee wanted to walk to church with her. Levee stepped into her shoes and hurried toward the door. "You're in luck," Levee said as she opened it. "The kettle's still simmering, and we have time for a cup of tea before—"

But instead of Matilda, Willie Rogers stood on her porch, one hand holding his cap, the other gripping a frayed rope. And at the end of the rope was a furry, friendly-looking mutt.

"'Mornin', Mrs. O'Reilly," Willie said, beaming.

"And a very good morning to you, too, Willie." Levee stepped onto the porch and glanced up and down the street. Evidently, she'd misunderstood the conversation between Judith and Sarah during her visit to the Lazy N, and Susan hadn't been restricted from riding into town for the duration of her pregnancy after all. "Where are your parents?" Perhaps the Rogerses parked their wagon behind the church, where the horses could munch grass while the family sang hymns, prayed, and listened to Reverend Peterson's sermon.

"Back at home," Willie said.

"Then, how did you get here?"

"Why, by the power of my own two feet, of course," he said, his smile widening. "Papa says when there's work to be done, a man has to do what a man has to do."

What a precious, precocious youngster! Levee thought. How blessed Susan was to have him for a son. How blessed she was that, soon, Willie would have a brother or a sister. Would the baby be as bright and sociable as its older sibling?

"How is your mother?"

"She's fine, just fine. Doc Lane says long as she doesn't do anything foolish, the baby will be born hale and hearty."

"Well, that's good to hear." Rumor had it Willie's mother, like Levee, had endured two miscarriages. "I've been praying for her."

"That's right nice of you, ma'am. I'll be sure to tell her that."

She hadn't prayed to be nice, but because she understood exactly how complicated the aftereffects of a miscarriage could be, physical and emotional alike. If Susan managed to bring a third pregnancy to term, perhaps there was hope for her, too. *Stop thinking about yourself!* "So, tell me, Willie, what work has brought you to Eagle Pass, all alone?"

"Oh, I ain't alone, ma'am. I come to town with him." And as if on cue, the animal sat at attention and looked up at Levee.

"I know you've been coveting a dog," Willie said, "so I brung this one, to see if maybe he'd be the right one for you."

Coveting? What a big word for such a small boy! Did he even know what it meant?

"Coveting," he repeated, standing straighter. "It means 'wanting.' I been listenin' real close when grown-ups talk, tryin' to learn big-people words, so's they'll quit saying things like 'Oh, he's only four,' and 'He don't know nothin'; he's only a baby.'" He shuddered. "I just hate that!"

Levee resisted the urge to correct his grammar. "And how, exactly, did you come to the conclusion that I might want a dog?"

He got down on one knee and slung an arm around the pup's furry neck. "Well, it's like this," he said, squinting when the dog licked his cheek, "I saw you accost Mr. Riddle in the middle of the road couple weeks back. And when the pair of you got to swappin' sweet talk, I heard him ask how you're enjoying that cozy little teacher's cottage behind the school-house, and you said it was fine, 'cept for how quiet it gets after the sun goes down, and *he* said, 'What you need is a canine companion,' and *you* said, 'If I knew where to find one, I might just do that.' Asked my mama, 'Just what *is* a canine companion, anyway?' and she said it's a dog that becomes a stand-in friend for lonely folks." He ruffled the dog's fur. "Since you ain't got a husband or young'uns to amuse you when school's out, and you don't like how quiet your house is after dark, well, I took that to mean you're one of them lonely folks Mama was talkin' about. So, I decided to keep an eye open for *your* canine companion. And, well, here he is!"

Yes, there he was, indeed, big-eyed, woolly, and weighing probably twenty pounds.

But "accosted"? And "sweet talk"? Levee stifled a gasp and looked left and right, breathing a sigh of relief when it became apparent that no one could have heard the child. She was able to interpret his words, even though their usage was a mite creative, but what would the town gossips and busybodies do if they heard him say such things?

"So, anyways," Willie continued, "I found this feller in town, out behind the hotel. I was back there lookin' for sparkle-rocks, see, while Papa was in the bank, but instead of sparkle-rocks,

I found him, settin' in the shade of a wagon, gnawin' on a ham bone. Took some doin', let me tell you, talkin' Papa into sayin' I could take him home, but once he heard what I had in mind for this feller, he changed his tune like that." Willie snapped his fingers. "So, I cleaned him up and taught him some tricks, thinkin' he'd make a right fine Christmas present for you." He met Levee's gaze. "Unless you don't like dogs. Or already have one in mind. Or if dogs make you sneeze and wheeze. Uncle Mark said dogs make some folks do that. He said I should ask you about all of that first, before I tell you he's yours. And he is. Yours, I mean. If you want him, that is."

Levee got down on her knees and scratched the dog behind the ears. "He's quite the handsome lad, isn't he?" she said. "I had a dog when I was a little girl—a much smaller dog, but he had this same look about him. Grandmother said it was a sign of intelligence." The memory of Emmitt, named for the beloved grandfather who'd passed away several months before she and Liam had left Boston, brought on a blissful surge of nostalgia. The pet had been responsible for her only act of disobedience, for despite the "dogs belong outdoors" rule, Levee had snuck Emmitt into her room every night for the entire five years she lived with her grandmother. It wasn't until the dog died that she learned her grandmother had known and had looked the other way.

"Oh, this boy's smart, all right!" Willie said. "Only took me a little while to teach him some tricks." Jumping to his feet, the boy dug into his coat pocket and pulled out a small rubber ball. "Watch this, Mrs. O'Reilly. Fetch!" he said, tossing the ball down the flagstone path.

But the dog only sat, blinking and licking its lips.

"Well, what's wrong with you, boy? You did it before, back at the ranch!"

Eyes narrowed, Willie wagged a finger near the dog's shiny, black snout. "I think I know what's going on here," he said, nodding at Levee. "Guess he's bashful around purty girls, just like my Uncle Dan."

At the mention of Dan, Levee's heart beat faster, and her cheeks warmed with a blush, which she hoped this bright, intuitive child wouldn't notice. "Bashful?" she exclaimed, mostly to distract him. "Why, I like it! If you haven't named him already, that is." When, exactly, had she made the decision to accept the gift? Sometime between the warm memories of her childhood and Willie's admission that Dan had something to do with it, no doubt.

"So, you like him, then? And you want to keep him?"

"Who wouldn't like him? And, yes, I'd love to keep him." It was such a thoughtful, caring present that Levee gave in to the urge to wrap her arms around the boy, and then she pressed a gentle kiss to his cheek, which he promptly erased with the back of his hand. "Heavens to Betsy, Mrs. O'Reilly," he said, crinkling his nose.

"Sorry, Willie. I didn't mean to embarrass you."

Hands in his pockets now, he stared at the toes of his shoes. "Aw, it's all right. I know girls tend to get carried away by passionate gesticulations."

It was all she could do to keep from laughing out loud, for something told her he'd meant to say "caring gesture."

"Willie Rogers, you are a thoughtful and remarkable boy."

When he smiled, she noticed a missing lower incisor, and a lesson from her nursing classes came to mind. He was a tad young to have lost a baby tooth. Another lecture came to mind, and she could almost hear her professor saying, "Nothing about medicine is absolute." Perhaps Willie's little body had decided it had better work harder if it hoped to catch up with his incredible brain!

"So, you want I should help get things ready for him?"

"Get things ready?"

"Uncle Mark says he'll need a dog house, unless you're fixin' to keep him inside. I could help you build one. Not today, of course, but I'll be happy to come back with my tools someday soon."

"You have your own tools?"

A tiny furrow formed between his blond brows. "Well, o' course. Doesn't every man?"

It took all her willpower to keep herself from tousling his blond locks and saying, "Do you have any idea how adorable you are?" Instead, she said, "I'd prefer to have him indoors, where I know he'll be safe from the weather and critters and such."

Willie gave her comment a moment of consideration, then approved it with a serious nod. "Well, all right, then, but that means he'll need some special trainin', so's he won't do his...you know, so's he won't do his business in the house." Squinting, he counted on his fingers as he said, "And he's gonna need a food bowl, and a water bowl, and something to sleep on, like an old blanket or a quilt, unless—" He frowned again. "You ain't fixin' to have him up on your bed every night, are you?"

A pang of guilt, left over from sneaking Emmitt upstairs at bedtime, compelled her to swallow. "I—I'm not sure." How ironic that the situation had turned, putting him in the teacher's role and her in the student's!

"Still and all," he continued, "you'll need a good, strong rope, in case you need to leave him outside alone, like when you fetch groceries and such, so he won't get to wanderin' through the streets, pesterin' folks." He inhaled a loud breath.

"We have a lot to do, so we'd better get crackin'. I promised Mama I'd be home before dark."

"But what about the Sunday service?"

"What about it?"

She pointed, drawing his attention to the Eagle Pass residents who'd gathered on the church steps to shake Reverend Peterson's hand before filing inside. "I can hear the organ music starting up. Would you like to come with me?"

Willie exhaled a sigh of exasperation. "Now, Mrs. O'Reilly, I don't think the good Lord is gonna mind if you miss services just this once. Betcha if He was here, He'd say making a good home for Bashful is sorta like prayin', seein' how He made Bashful and all." He hung his cap on the end of the railing and dusted his hands together.

Levee considered his argument for a moment, but Willie must have taken her silence as consent, for he said, "Well, should we get started?"

The pair spent the next hour searching her cottage for things Willie believed were critical to the care and feeding of a dog. Before leaving, he started counting on his fingers again. "When he laps from his water bowl, wait an hour and take him out back, or he'll make a puddle on the floor. And after he eats? Same thing, sort of, only you can wait a little longer for that. He might cry when you turn in for the night, but only if you don't let him sleep in your room. Don't need to be *in* the bed, mind you, but if you're all right with that, I'm sure Bashful won't mind none."

"Goodness!" Levee said, laughing. "It's so much to remember! Where did you learn so much about dogs?"

"Papa taught me. And you'll do fine, just fine." He tapped his temple. "Mostly, it's horse sense. You'll have it all figured out in no time."

Bashful sat looking up at Levee, a doggy smile on his lips, as if he agreed. "He's the best Christmas present anyone ever gave me," she said, blinking back tears of gratitude. "I promise to take very good care of him. I won't let you down."

Willie patted her forearm. "Oh, I know that. I have reassurance in you!"

"Let me get my hat," Levee said, "and Bashful and I will walk you home."

"Aw, that's okay," Willie said, opening the door. "I'll ride home with Grampa. He's at the service, I think." The screen door banged closed behind him, and he pressed his nose to the wire mesh to add, "I'm real glad you like your gift, Mrs. O'Reilly."

Then he grabbed his cap, jammed it onto his head, and ran off, leaving Levee and Bashful alone in the tiny parlor. She sat cross-legged on the floor. "My, my, my," she said, combing her fingers through his thick, gray fur, "don't you smell delightful! I'll just have to ask Willie what kind of soap he used to bathe you, because I wouldn't mind smelling like this!"

When the carriage clock chimed twelve times, Levee realized she'd been playing with the dog for nearly an hour and remembered what Willie had said about putting it on a schedule. "Well, mister," she said to Bashful, "I suppose we'd better see about finding something for you to eat!"

"I'm told he's fond of boiled chicken liver and beef bones."

Bashful's barking drowned out Levee's startled yelp. The dog ran toward the screen door and skidded to a stop just shy of the threshold. "It's all right," Levee said, getting up and joining Bashful at the door. "It's only Dan Neville, the man who seems to take great pleasure in hearing me squeal with fright."

"Sorry," Dan said, removing his Stetson. "I'll try to make more noise next time I call on you."

Next time? Levee's heart thumped harder. My, but he looked handsome in his collarless white shirt and black trousers! "Please, come in," she said, holding open the door. "Are you on your way home from church?"

"Church? Me?" Dan scoffed and shook his head as he stepped inside and stroked Bashful's neck. "Nah. Haven't been in years."

She pretended not to have noticed the crease between his eyebrows and the flash of anger that darkened his eyes. Maybe in time, he'd tell her what had separated him from the congregation. "I missed the service, myself. Willie convinced me that making Bashful feel welcome could be viewed as an adequate substitute." When he smiled, her heart beat harder still. "But I told myself it would be just this once."

"Can't decide if that boy will be a salesman or a politician when he's grown," Dan said, spinning his hat around and around. "Why, I'd bet he could convince a bull that he could give milk. If I were a betting man, that is."

Levee laughed. "I know exactly what you mean!" She smoothed her skirts, hoping that playing on the floor with Bashful hadn't mussed her hair, too. "Would you like a cup of coffee?" she asked, tucking a curl behind her ear.

"Sure, thanks," he said, wiping his boots on the rug just inside the door. He nodded at Bashful. "So, you really want the dog?"

"Oh, yes. He's just wonderful." Levee put her back to him long enough to stoke the coals in the stove, then headed for the sink. "He's everything Willie said he was, and more." Raising and lowering the pump handle, she filled the coffeepot with water. "You're right. That nephew of yours is quite the little convincer."

"I reckon you know he isn't really my nephew. He's my cousin Susan's boy, which makes him a first cousin, once removed. One day, he asked me why he didn't have any uncles. It was easier for me to tell him to call me 'Uncle Dan' than to explain the family tree to a four-year-old."

Levee hadn't given the matter a thought, but Dan's relationship with Willie gave her yet another insight into his character. If she'd liked him before—and she most assuredly had!—she liked him even more now. "I baked an apple cobbler day before yesterday, and there's plenty left." She reached for the serving platter. "Would you like some to go with your coffee?"

Something flickered in those oh-so-blue eyes. Had she presumed too much, inviting him to stay?

"That'd be nice," he said, and she breathed a sigh of relief. "Right nice. But only if you'll have some, too."

"I really shouldn't."

"Why not?"

"Penance," she said. "For skipping church."

Dan laughed quietly. "I thought for a minute there you were going to say you're watching your figure, or something equally ridiculous...."

Ridiculous?

"...because your figure is...." He drove a hand through his hair. "...because I think you're...." He swallowed, then cleared his throat and exhaled an enormous sigh.

She couldn't stand to see him so uncomfortable, especially since his apparent intention to compliment her was at the root of it. "I skipped breakfast this morning, too, thinking I'd treat myself to some cobbler and milk after church." After placing two cups and saucers on the table, Levee said, "Willie was right, I think, that it *was* more important to get things ready for Bashful than—"

"You don't have to keep that name, you know. I'm sure Willie wouldn't mind if you chose something less…silly. He's your dog now, after all."

She set two folded napkins on the table. "I'll have you know that I chose that 'silly' name, not Willie."

His mustache tilted in a grin. "See, now you've learned something about me that I'd just as soon you didn't know."

"Oh?"

He nodded, and when he did, a golden curl fell across one eyebrow. He shoved it back into place and said, "I'm familiar with the taste of shoe leather."

She couldn't very well tease him by saying, "You mean, from putting your foot in your mouth so often?" Particularly not after he'd embarrassed himself in his clumsy attempt to compliment her figure. "Please, have a seat," she said instead as she took two plates out of the cupboard. "The coffee's nearly finished, and—"

"You've got a good heart, Levee O'Reilly."

And it's beating like a parade drum thanks to you, she thought. But she couldn't very well say that, either. "How old do you think Bashful is?"

"You're better off asking Joe Kingsley about a thing like that."

"Joe Kingsley, the horse breeder? But what would he know about—"

"He was a veterinarian before he started raising horses."

From Dan's tone, she got the feeling he wasn't admitting a shortage of knowledge about dogs so much as a lack of affection toward them. Was it because dogs were cousins to coyotes?

"Don't mean to sound hard-hearted," he began in a gentler voice. "Had a pup when I was a young'un, but he got into a scuffle with a wild dog. Wound up with rabies, and I had to put him down."

Levee took the lid off the sugar bowl and poked a spoon into it. "Oh, Dan, that's positively horrible! How old were you?"

"Ten."

"Only ten? Such a painful thing for a boy that young to have to do!" She pursed her lips and propped a fist on her hip. "That's the sort of thing a loving father should do for his son." She could hardly believe the level of ire in her voice, so she bit her tongue, waiting to hear the sorry excuse his father had given for making his son do a man's job. How she longed to wrap him in a comforting embrace!

"My pa would have done it, but he didn't know what I was planning."

Levee perched on the edge of her chair and folded her hands, waiting expectantly for the explanation that would follow.

"I spent every spare minute of six years with that hound, and when it was clear he had the sickness…." Dan's voice trailed off, and he stared at one callused palm, then folded his fingers into a fist. "When I got home all puffy-eyed and sniffling," he said, meeting Levee's eyes, "Pa said he would have done the job. But, like I told him, Mischief was my dog, and Pa trusted me to do what was best for him."

Levee reached out and laid a hand atop Dan's. "I can't imagine how hard that must have been."

His mustache tilted in another smile as a warm light glowed in his eyes. "Yep, you've got a good heart, all right."

Bashful trotted up and nudged his mistress's free hand, and when she gave him nothing more than a distracted pat, he rested a paw on Dan's thigh, only to get the same reaction. Looking from Daniel to Levee and back again, the dog flopped onto the floor, as if to say, "So much for being the center of attention around here!"

The coffeepot sizzled and hissed, commanding Levee's attention. "Goodness!" she said, jumping up. She picked up a towel and transferred the pot to a trivet on the table, then filled their cups with the steaming, black liquid. Would Daniel have tried to kiss her if not for the interruption? And, if he had, would she have let him?

"That could have been a mess," he muttered as she spooned cobbler onto his plate.

"Yes, it surely could have." She reached into the icebox and took out a pitcher of milk. "Would you like some on your cobbler?"

"No, but thanks."

Levee put the pitcher back in the icebox, happy to have an excuse to turn her back to him. For one glance at her telltale expression surely would have told him that she not only would have allowed a kiss—she also would have welcomed it!

*D*an was midway through reading a newspaper article when Willie strode into the barn, thumbs hooked in his pockets, just the way his pa so often did. The boy was one of a handful who could successfully distract him from his study of the Kickapoo, the Indians who'd settled the area in the mid-1700s. Back then, life had not been harmonious between the natives and the Texicans, and it had taken a sneak attack by the cavalry to quiet things down. Yes, the skirmish had produced the desired calm, but Dan believed it had been unfair and downright un-American to force the Kickapoo onto reservations shared with Sacs and Fox tribes, where life was nowhere near what it had been on the open prairie.

Someday, he'd tell Willie this story. For now, Dan contented himself with watching the boy stroll about, poking his nose into every nook and cranny within his reach. He'd inherited Susan's pale hair and bright eyes, but in every other way, he was the spitting image of his pa, Sam. What might it be like, Dan wondered, to walk in Sam's shoes, with a son at his heels, mimicking his every move and echoing his every word?

It'd be right nice, that's what, he decided, propping both boots on his battered old desk. Leaning back in the chair, he peered over the newspaper as Willie wandered from stall to stall, stepping up on overturned buckets and bales of hay to get a glimpse of the horses inside.

The big black stallion in the middle stall watched, too, and when Willie stopped at its gate, it snorted, blowing a puff of air through the knothole and startling the boy so much that he lost his balance and landed on his backside on the straw-covered floor. "Mama read me a story about a fire-breathing dragon once," he said, dusting hay bits from his britches, "but I'd wager that horse would give him a contest!"

Chuckling, Dan laid the newspaper on his desk.

"Is he fit to ride?"

"Yeah, but he's strong as an ox. Takes all the strength I can muster to keep him reined in. It'll be a while before you're able to handle him."

"How long is 'a while'?"

Dan stroked his mustache, giving the question serious consideration. "That's hard to say. Boys get into growth spurts, or so I'm told, so I reckon it'll depend on how long it takes you to get big enough."

Willie looked over his shoulder at the big black horse, bobbing its head over the stall wall. "He got a name?"

"Thunder."

He leaned both forearms on his uncle's desk. "So, how big would a boy have to be? To ride Thunder, I mean."

Dan plucked a number from the air. "Not how old, but how big. I'd say five foot five." Just to be safe, he added, "And weigh more than a hundred pounds."

Willie nodded. "How tall you reckon I am?"

"Easy enough to find out." Dan got to his feet and grabbed the yardstick from its hook on the wall. "Stand back against this post, and we'll see." Using his thumbnail, he etched

Willie's height into the wood, and when the boy stepped away, he measured the distance from the floor. "Three foot eleven."

Willie's eyes narrowed as he counted on his fingers. "You mean, I have to grow a whole eighteen inches before I can ride Thunder?"

"'Fraid so, son."

He frowned, then brightened. "I love Gran's biscuits and gravy, and Pop says sausage will put meat on my bones. What if I was a few inches shy of five foot five, but I weighed a hunnert pounds? Then could I ride him?"

Dan was beginning to get the picture. Crossing his arms over his chest, he said, "When was the last time you rode a horse?"

Willie aped his uncle's stance. "Ain't rode one, ever. Mama says it's a long way from the saddle to the ground for a boy my size, and Papa says he ain't brave enough to go against her."

Chuckling, Dan nudged the boy's shoulder. "I was about your age first time I sat a horse. Want me to have a word with her, see if I can talk her into letting you try your hand at riding?" *If his eyes get any bigger,* Dan thought, *they'll pop clean out of his head.*

"Oh, would you, Uncle Dan? Would you really?"

"I'll do it tonight, right after supper."

He was reviewing the list of chores he needed to do before then when Willie said, "Wonder how Mrs. O'Reilly and Bashful are getting along."

Yesterday, before Levee had realized Dan was at her door, she'd been on the floor, crawling around with that dog and giggling like a schoolgirl. The mental image made Dan grin. "Something tells me they're gonna get along just fine."

"You think she liked my Christmas present, then?"

"Yep, I do." Knowing Levee, though, she'd keep the mutt even if she didn't, just to spare Willie's feelings.

"So, what are *you* giving Mrs. O'Reilly for Christmas, Uncle Dan?"

The question caught him completely off guard. Until that moment, he hadn't given it a thought. They weren't courting, though he certainly wouldn't have minded that, and he wondered which rules of etiquette he might break by giving her a present. He knew this much: if it wasn't acceptable, the old biddies of Eagle Pass would let him know right quick! Ruffling the boy's hair, he said, "You know her better than I do. Any suggestions?"

Willie whistled through his teeth. "After coming up with ideas for Mama and Papa, and Gran and Pop—and you, of course—my head is about empty."

"The boy who ciphered that feet-and-inches problem in two seconds flat?" Dan chuckled. "I don't believe a head like that could ever get empty!"

A proud grin lit up Willie's face, but it faded as he wondered aloud what time it was. Dan snapped open his pocket watch. "It's nearly two."

"Better head on up to the house, then. I promised Mama I'd let her read me a story." He groaned. "I'll sure be glad when that baby of hers gets here. Maybe when she's got somebody else to worry over 'sides me, I'll get a little peace and quiet and privacy in my life!" On the heels of a noisy sigh, he added, "You have no idea what a lot of work it is, keeping a mother happy."

Dan had known Susan for most of his life and understood only too well what a worrier she could be. His heart went out to the boy, but more with envy than pity. His own ma hadn't been the hovering type, and the way that she'd foisted Daisy's care upon him as a boy had a lot to do with his inability to forgive himself for her death.

Willie sprinted toward the door, slowing just enough to shout over one shoulder, "Don't forget to talk to you-know-who about you-know-what!" And with that, he raced away.

Two days before Christmas, and Dan hadn't yet given a thought to presents. He picked up a pencil and began scribbling names on the back of an envelope. Ma, Pa, all six sisters, and Willie meant he'd need nine presents. Ten, if he counted Levee, and he very much wanted to count her, no matter what the biddies might think.

He checked his watch again. Five minutes past two. If he didn't lollygag, he could make it into town before Mr. Riddle closed his store. With any luck, the man would have some helpful suggestions of what to buy.

Dan made it to town in record time, thanks to Thunder. He felt a little guilty riding the big black instead of Biscuit, but he had a lot of ground to cover and only a little time to do it. The choice had been a wise one, he decided, as he headed home with a hefty parcel sandwiched between his stomach and the pommel of his saddle. By five, the horse had been groomed and was back in the stable, and Dan's biggest problem was figuring out where to stow the things he'd bought, as well as the single present he'd pulled from his wardrobe. Would Levee think him a miser for giving her something that had been his as a boy? Or would she understand the significance of his choice? "Only one way to find out," he said as he headed up to Susan's room. As soon as he convinced her to let him teach Willie to ride a horse, he'd wrap his gifts in the brown paper he'd bought from Riddle's and bunk down for the night.

He'd decided that when it came time to deliver Levee's present, he'd wear his whitest shirt, the one with those fancy buttons. His cousin Sarah, the seamstress, called them "opalescent" because of the way they reflected light in muted rainbow patterns. It was her favorite shirt because of the buttons, and if she liked it, maybe Levee would, too.

He'd trim his mustache and scrape every whisker from his chin, and after his bath, he'd use some of that fancy scented powder his pa was always raving about. With a spit-shine on his boots and a dusting of his hat, she might not mind the limp and the scar. Though, to give Levee her due, if she even noticed either, she'd never indicated as much.

Is that why he felt duty-bound to please her? And why her opinion mattered so much?

Partly, he admitted. But only partly. Her attitude had given him hope that maybe he could expect a normal life, regardless of his sins, despite his part in Daisy's death, and that it was possible for a woman like her to fall for a man like him.

A woman like her, whose smile would melt snow, whose curly-haired head barely reached as high as his shoulders, and whose big, long-lashed eyes flashed with intelligence and kindness....

Dan didn't dare list the reasons he believed she was too good for him, lest he lose his nerve and not deliver the present at all. He tossed and turned all through the night, unable to stop his brain from rehearsing what he'd say when he handed her the package:

"For you, Levee"? Too easy.

"I know it isn't much"? Too apologetic.

"I hope you like it"? A pathetic plea for approval.

"Merry Christmas, Mrs. O'Reilly"? Uncomplicated. Straightforward. Honest. Just like Levee.

Dan linked his fingers behind his head and stared at the ceiling, where shadows painted gray streaks across the plaster. The big clock in the front hall gonged twice. Had he really been thinking about Levee for all this time? He had no business feeling this way about a woman, especially not one he'd met just a few weeks ago. Had all those falls from the saddle addled his brain? Had punches to the chin and cheeks, received during fights in taverns and saloons from Eagle Pass to Kansas City, destroyed his common sense and torn down walls built to protect his heart from another beating like the one his former fiancée had given it?

Dan groaned softly and closed his eyes, then did something he hadn't done in a long, long time.

He prayed.

15

"I can hardly believe you've never had a Christmas tree," Matilda said. "Why, decorating for the holidays is something I look forward to all year!"

Despite Levee's attempts to pay attention to her friend, her mind locked on things she usually avoided dwelling on. Her parents, and her devout grandparents, too, had viewed Christmas trees—and almost every other holiday tradition—as a sinful pagan ritual. It was a moot point, really, since her mother and father, as missionaries, had spent most of their time on one remote Pacific island or another. Twice, they'd taken her along, but Levee had spent much of her childhood with her paternal grandparents. Then, one late-December day, a bedraggled-looking parson had knocked on the door. "Rest easy," he'd said to Levee, squeezing her hands, "knowing your mama and papa made the ultimate sacrifice for Christ Jesus. Celebrate, child," he'd all but shouted, "as they're celebrating with Him now in paradise!"

With those few words, he'd spoiled her twelfth birthday, turned her worst fears into reality, and made the Boston brownstone that she'd prayed would be a temporary residence into her permanent home. Had he really expected her to celebrate after hearing that her parents had been slaughtered by cannibals? And did the Almighty, Himself, expect that she'd praise Him for making her an orphan?

Matilda's voice penetrated her fog of self-pity. "Far be it from me to pass judgment, but it seems to me that a parent's first duty is to his children, not a bunch of coconut-worshipping heathens."

Levee might have chuckled at the comment if it hadn't expressed in a nutshell how she had felt for many years.

"I mean, really," the woman continued, "it's one thing for unmarried folks or those without children to traipse around the globe, spreading God's Word. But parents?" She clicked her tongue. "How can they teach their own children about Him if they're halfway around the world?"

Oh, how well Levee identified with that argument!

Immaturity, both age-related and spiritual, had separated her from God when she was a young girl. Levee had her grandfather to thank for her spiritual transformation. "Promise me that you'll go back to church," he'd wheezed on his deathbed, "because I can't leave this world without knowing I'll see you in heaven someday." *Whatever it takes to ease your suffering, Grandfather,* she'd thought at the time. She'd owed him that, considering all he had done for her. Two weeks after his passing, during a Sunday service, tears had filled her eyes when the preacher had quoted Jeremiah 3:12: "'*Return, thou backsliding Israel, saith the* LORD; *and I will not cause mine anger to fall upon you: for I am merciful, saith the* LORD, *and I will not keep anger for ever.*'" It had been one of her grandfather's favorite Scriptures, Levee had remembered, and she'd looked around to see if the words had struck home with any of the other parishioners. Bored yawns and sleepy expressions had told her that the phrase had been a personal invitation, and she'd accepted it then and there.

"Do you share their beliefs about Christmas?" Matilda was asking.

No, she most certainly did not. In fact, Levee could think of just one reason to explain why she didn't celebrate the holy festivities and customs of the day: the lack of someone special to share them with.

"I'll take your silence as a no," Matilda said, throwing open Levee's front door and disappearing for a moment. When she reentered the house, she carried a scrubby pine shrub that she'd carefully trimmed into a pyramid shape. After plopping it onto the parlor table, she ducked onto the porch again, this time returning with a small wooden box. "Ornaments and such to decorate it," she announced, placing the crate beside the tree. "I'll be back later to see your very first Christmas tree all adorned and embellished."

Levee barely noticed as Matilda waved and closed the door behind her.

Peeking into the box, she found tiny, hand-blown glass ornaments in iridescent shades of red, blue, and green, many of them in shapes that resembled stars and doves, and the sparkling silver links of a long, delicate chain.

Excitement buzzed in her veins as she glanced around the room, searching for the best spot for the tree. "The table in front of the window will do nicely," she told Bashful, and the dog trotted alongside her as she relocated the table's occupants—a doily, a white-globed whale oil lamp, and a carriage clock—to the mantel. "There," she said, standing the tree in its place. "Now, won't that look lovely, adorned with all of Matilda's decorations?"

She looked at Bashful, who cocked his head in apparent confusion. "I know, I know," she said, ruffling his fur. "We human beings really are a silly lot, aren't we, bringing shrubs inside, then trimming them with doodads?"

An hour later, Levee stood back to admire her handiwork. "What do you think, Bashful?" she asked, adjusting the silvery garland and repositioning two doves. "Is it perfectly balanced, or what?"

A quiet, breathy bark was his answer, and Levee hugged him. "After I tidy up all this tissue paper and stow Matilda's box into the cupboard under the stairs, I'll see if I have all the makings for sugar cookies." The dog's ears perked up, and she added, "Yes, of course, I'll make a few just for you."

Soon, sugar, flour, lard, and salt were placed on the table, and not long afterward, tea towels lined with dozens of crisp, golden-edged treats covered every inch of available space in the tiny kitchen. The heat of the stove had warmed the entire cottage, almost making her wish she hadn't built a fire that morning.

Almost, because the flickering flames, together with the sweet scents that filled the air, reminded her of her grandparents' Boston brownstone. How good it was to think of those days without the old feelings of bitterness and sadness to spoil her contented mood.

She opened the interior door and inhaled the crisp December breeze that slipped in through the screen. "If that doesn't cool you off, Bashful, I don't know what will!"

The dog followed her every step as she put away the cookie ingredients. "You know what you are?" she asked, bending to pat his forehead. "Adorable, that's what!"

"The perfect word to describe what I'm seeing."

Bashful barked, and Levee yelped, in reaction to the masculine voice. "Daniel Neville! If I didn't know better, I'd say your main goal in life is to scare me out of my wits!"

"Sorry," he said, grinning as he ducked inside the door, "I knocked, but I guess you were too busy talking to yourself to hear it."

"For your information, I wasn't talking to myself. I was talking to Bashful."

"Smells delicious in here," he said, the package he carried crinkling slightly as he walked into the parlor. And then he saw the cookies that blanketed the table. "I must have missed the bulletin that said an army would be passing through town."

Giggling, Levee brushed the bangs from her forehead. "I'm going to package them up and give them to my students tomorrow morning after the Christmas service." She pulled out a chair. "Please, have a seat. Coffee's hot, if you'd like a cup."

"Don't mind if I do."

"These should be cool enough to stack now," she said, gathering up several rows of cookies to clear a space for him at the table. "Just let me clean up those crumbs. I'll toss these outside later, a little Christmas treat for the birds." Why she felt the need to explain why she collected them in a mug, she couldn't say. Oh, how she loved the way his mustache slanted when he smiled!

"I'll wrap a few cookies for you to take home to your mother. And the rest of the family, of course."

He'd barely uttered a word. *Well, how could he, with the way you're chattering like a chipmunk?* Levee filled a mug with hot coffee, wondering about that package on his lap. A gift for Matilda, perhaps? Hopefully, it wasn't something for her, because Levee had nothing to give him in return. Well, that sweater she'd been knitting might do in a pinch, though the yarn would likely cling to Dan's broad chest and shoulders like a second skin. Why she'd made it Liam's size was anybody's guess.

"Brought you a little something," he said as she set the coffee mug on the table in front of him. "For Christmas."

"Oh, Dan, how very sweet of you, but—"

"Go on," he interrupted her. "Open it."

Levee sat down across from him and untied the twine that held the brown wrapper in place, then held up a fringed suede jacket.

"Something to keep you warm during cold December buggy rides."

"Oh, Dan," she repeated, "it's much too extravagant. I couldn't possibly accept a gift that cost this—"

"Didn't cost me anything, save for the time it took to wrap it." He nodded at the jacket. "That was mine, when I was a boy. Thought maybe…."

Was he *blushing*?

"…maybe, when you wear it, you'll remember our ride, and…." He swallowed. "And think of me."

As Levee put it all together—the memory of their ride from the Lazy N into town, how he'd put his arm around her when the chilly wind had made her shiver, the quiet conversation they'd shared under a canopy of stars—she felt the heat of a blush in her own cheeks. No one had ever given her such a thoughtful gift!

Tears filled her eyes and she bit her lower lip to still its trembling. Hugging the jacket tight, she stroked the velvetlike leather. Dare she hope this meant that Dan had feelings for her, too?

A pained expression crossed his face as he leaned forward. "Aw, Levee," he said, "I'm sorry. I half expected this might be a mistake."

When Dan reached out to take the jacket back, she clutched it tighter.

With his brow furrowed in confusion, he said, "You—you like it?"

She wiped away a tear. "It's by far one of the sweetest, nicest presents I've ever received!" And to prove it, she put it on.

His frown deepened slightly. "Then, why are you crying?"

Levee laughed past her tears, then sighed. "I'd think a man who grew up with so many sisters would know that when a woman weeps, it doesn't always mean she's sad or disappointed."

Ah, there it was, that charming tilt to his mustache she'd come to adore. She got to her feet and extended her arms so that the fringe of the sleeves waved gently as she did a slow twirl. "It fits perfectly, don't you think?"

Tenderness softened his smile. "Yeah. Perfectly."

The glint in his eyes told her that she, and not the jacket, was his idea of perfection. She'd entertained a suitor or two before Liam had come into her life, but not one had made her feel more cared for. If this wasn't what it appeared to be, she could be in for a heartache of gargantuan proportions! Her head told her to slow down, to take things easy, but her heart was singing too loudly to hear it. "Thank you, Dan," she said, bending to place a soft kiss on his cheek. "I'll treasure it always."

Just as she stood up and took a step back, he grabbed her wrist and got to his feet. Moving his free hand to the small of her back, he scanned her face, and when his eyes locked with hers, she thought her heart might leap clean out of her chest. If she didn't do something, and quick, he'd kiss her for sure. With the curtains drawn so that her little tree would be visible in the window, anyone passing by might see. It was bad enough she'd invited him inside, unchaperoned. If the townsfolk saw them kissing, why, they'd both have a lot of explaining to do!

Levee forced herself to look away from his mesmerizing eyes. "I have a little something for you, too," she said, taking a careful step back. "I'll just be a minute." And with that, she scampered off to her room.

When she emerged a minute later, Levee saw that Dan had helped himself to a cookie. "Delicious," he said, grinning around a mouthful.

He looked so comfortable munching sweets at her table, and it was a picture Levee wouldn't mind seeing every day for the rest of her life. "I—I'm sorry it isn't wrapped," she said, unfolding the sweater.

"You made this for me?" he asked, accepting it from her.

She felt so simpleminded, nodding and grinning and blinking as he held it up against his chest. "If it's too small, I can—"

"I'm sure it'll fit just fine." And, as she'd done earlier, he proved it by putting it on.

Just as she'd supposed, the yarn stretched and strained across his broad chest and arm muscles, and the hem barely covered his belt buckle. Levee couldn't help herself. The sight of him— hair mussed from poking his head through the too-small neck hole as he tugged at the cuffs and waistband—inspired a giggle that, in a matter of seconds, developed into full-blown, breathless laughter. "Please," she said, wiping tears of mirth from her eyes, "*please* take it off before it stops the flow of blood to your extremities. Leave it with me, and I'll undo the seams and add a row of cable to the sides. And the sleeves. And the hem."

"But then it won't be the sweater you made me for Christmas." A lop-sided grin brightened his face. "I can't believe you went to all this trouble, just for me."

Guilt smothered her laughter as surely as water douses hot coals. If Levee admitted that, out of habit, she'd made it with her deceased husband in mind, Dan would naturally presume she missed Liam and still loved him. And nothing could have been further from the truth. "I'm a terrible judge of distance. And of size, too, obviously. I feel awful, just *awful*, for misjudging—" If she had finished with "how big and strong you are," why, it would sound as if she had a schoolgirl crush on him, instead of…. Levee buried her face in her hands, shocked by her own admission: *instead of a boundless love beating within her heart.*

"All right," he said, struggling to remove the sweater. "I'll let you make it bigger. But only because you seem so distressed about the way it fits."

"I feel like such a ninny, letting you leave without your Christmas present," she said when he handed it back to her.

His eyebrows disappeared under his bangs. "So, you've changed your mind, then?"

"Changed my mind?" Levee had no idea what he was talking about.

"You said something about sending me home with cookies…."

A nervous giggle popped from her lips. "Oh, that. Yes. Of course." She slid a plate from the shelf above the stove, piled it high with cookies, and topped it with a blue-striped kitchen towel. "There you go," she said, handing it to him. "Now, promise you won't eat them all on the way home, okay?"

"Promise." He stepped onto the porch. "Your little tree is as cute as you are, by the way."

And then he was gone, leaving Levee to wallow in joy and wonder—and regret that she hadn't let him kiss her.

16

*I*t had been weeks since Levee had written in her journal, and longer still since she'd read the entries she'd made during her first days in Eagle Pass. She turned up the flame on her lantern and found the entry that described Christmas and the festive dinner the parishioners had shared in the church basement. Everyone had been there, laughing and joking and wishing one another a prosperous New Year.

Everyone but the Nevilles, that is.

Matilda had announced that with Susan so close to her due date and Judith still not quite able to walk, the family would spend the holiday at the Lazy N. Plus, there had been Dana's wedding on Christmas Eve, a small, family-only celebration at the ranch. Reverend Peterson had led the congregation in a prayer for the Nevilles, a prayer Levee had barely heard because she'd been too engrossed in one of her own, asking God to watch over Dan, whose caring Christmas gift had inspired many poems describing her infatuated state. She flicked past them so quickly that the pages created a breeze that gave her goose pimples. The book fell open to an entry that made her cheeks burn. "What would folks say," she'd written, "if they knew I've been sleeping with the lovely jacket Dan gave me?" And if they knew she still hugged it every night, all night? *They'd think you belong in an asylum!* she admitted, grinning.

Levee flipped back to the passage she'd scrawled in June, mere weeks after accepting the teaching position, and came across the sheet of crisp paper she'd tucked into the pages. "All of Chihuahua mourns the loss of your husband, dear lady. I pray that when your heartache has healed, you will change your mind about coming to work in our humble clinic," the mission priest had written. "Medical professionals such as yourself are still in short supply here, and we will welcome you with open arms." She would continue praying for the Mexican town and its residents every day of her life, but that was as much of herself as Levee could give the good people of Chihuahua. Too many reminders of sorrow and discontent....

She turned the page on that depressing part of her life and came across the letter of condolence from Liam's only sibling. "I do wish you'd take Mother up on her offer to send you money for passage home," Bonnie had written in her fanciful script. "We miss you so very much, and I think you know we couldn't love you more if you'd been born into our family."

Levee loved them, too, but Boston wasn't home. At least, not anymore. Yet she couldn't admit that to them without hurting them. She hadn't been able to go into detail when describing Liam's death for the same reason. Her mother-in-law's health had deteriorated in the months leading up to their departure. Levee should have been stunned that Liam wasn't apprehensive about traveling thousands of miles with his mother in such a frail state. Should have been shocked that after she'd offered to stay behind and nurse the poor woman back to health, he'd pitched a fit. Should have been offended when he'd thundered, "You're my wife, and your place is at my side!" But, by that time, very little about the young doctor had been able to surprise her. How ironic that the kindest, most caring words he'd spoken during their marriage had come as he'd lain dying on the parched prairie.

One line from her journal entry following Liam's death stood out from the rest: "Describing the events of that grisly day would only subject them to the same nightmarish images that will haunt me for the rest of my life." Even now, as she read the words penned by her own hand, Levee suffered no guilt about being vague in the telegram that informed them of his death. Her conscience was pinged, however, that so many of Bonnie's letters had gone unanswered.

"Soon," Levee said, patting Bashful's head. "I'll write her a long, chatty letter in a week or so." By then, school would be back in session, and she'd have some fun, uplifting stories about the children to share with Liam's family.

Levee turned to a blank page and stared down at it, chewing the tip of her pen and wondering what to write. A soft knock on the door broke into her thoughts, and Bashful sounded a quiet woof. "Shh, sweet boy," she whispered. "It might be Dan!"

Levee stood up and checked her reflection in the mirror above the sideboard, fluffing her curls and giving each cheek a pinch. "Oh!" she said when she flung open the door. "Matilda."

"Goodness, just look at that face! I'm so sorry to disappoint you," her friend said with a grin. "Expecting a certain gentleman caller, were you?"

Levee returned the woman's enthusiastic hug with one of her own. "No, not exactly. Well, maybe. Sort of."

The women laughed, and Matilda helped herself to a cup of coffee. "Remember when you told me the reason I didn't have a husband was because the good Lord was looking for the right man for the job?"

"I wouldn't put it quite that way," Levee said, filling a cup for herself, "but, yes, I remember."

"Well, my dear, I believe I've found him."

Levee had never seen her friend more enthused. She plopped on the sofa and patted the cushion beside her, inviting Matilda to sit. "Is he new in town? Do I know him? Is he handsome and strong? What sort of work does he do? Well, what are you waiting for? Tell me all about him!"

"I would," Matilda said, laughing, "if I could get a word in edgewise!" She took a sip of coffee, sat down, and set her mug on the side table. "His name is Ethan. Ethan Rourke." She fanned herself with one hand. "A gorgeous hunk of Irish, off the boat only three years. You should hear him talk, Levee. Why, everything out of his mouth sounds like poetry! Don't know how in the world I went so long without running into him, especially since he's been right up the road at the Lazy N all this time."

"He works for the Nevilles?" *Maybe someday, Matilda and I will share a double wedding!* Levee blushed at the thought, because, so far, she hadn't allowed herself to entertain such thoughts. Something to pray about, now that she had.

"He's a ranch hand when they're not on the trail, and when they are, he's the cook. Forty-seven years old," Matilda continued, "the perfect age for me, don't you think? And at five foot nine and a hundred seventy-five pounds, the perfect size, too!" She fanned herself again. "Though, I'll admit, the height and weight are just guesses."

"Where'd you meet him?"

"At J. W. Riddle's, day before yesterday, if you can believe it!"

"And it took you this long to tell me about him? I'm crushed!"

The women shared another spurt of laughter before Matilda sat back and sighed. "I've been far too busy thinking up excuses to visit Judith. And Eva. And every other woman at the Lazy N." She leaned in to say, "Did you know that Susan's baby is due in just a few days? What a relief that she's carried this one to term. The poor girl lost two babies to miscarriage, you know."

Yes, Levee knew. How differently her life might have turned out if she had been capable of carrying a baby to term. Would she and Liam have lived in a Boston brownstone with their children, or would Liam have insisted on moving to Mexico with his whole family in tow? And if so, would Frank Michaels and his gang still have ended his life—along with the children's?

"Goodness gracious, girl!" Matilda exclaimed. "You look as though you've seen a ghost!" She scooted closer. "I woke a bad memory, didn't I, talking about Susan's miscarriages? Tell me, Levee, have you had a miscarriage, too?"

More than one, Levee thought, squaring her shoulders. "What's done is done," she said, forcing a smile she didn't feel. "So, tell me, has your Mr. Rourke invited you to the church social next month?"

"Oh, you are a brave little thing, aren't you? Lost your ma and pa and your grandparents, then a baby or two and your husband, as well, yet you refuse to wallow in self-pity."

If only Matilda knew how many nights Levee had cried herself to sleep with tears of self-pity!

"No wonder Dan is so love struck."

Levee ignored the comment, mostly because she had no idea how to respond. "So, back to the social, I'm planning to wear my pink dress. I have so few occasions to wear it, and this will be the perfect opportunity. How about you? Have you chosen an outfit that will make Mr. Rourke's eyes pop?"

"All right, then," Matilda conceded, giving Levee a sideways hug, "have it your way. We'll change the subject. For now." She winked. "Well, I asked Sarah to sew me a new frock for the shindig." She slapped her knee before counting on her fingers. "There's material to pick, and buttons and trim to choose, measurements to take, and a fitting…. That will give me several good excuses to visit that ranch, let me tell you!" A merry giggle bubbled forth. "And then, I'll be heading back again in a few days to pick it up." She paused and grabbed Levee's hand. "Say, I have an idea! Why don't you come with me for the fitting? I'd love the company during the drive, and we'd both have a chance to see our men."

"Our men?" Levee echoed. "I'd hardly call them—"

"Levee dear, I feel positively giddy, I tell you!"

"I can hardly wait to meet your Mr. Rourke. He must be quite something to get you this excited."

"Oh, Levee, I've never been happier." She grabbed Levee's hand again. "Pray with me, won't you, so I'll know he really *is* the one God wants me to spend the rest of my life with?"

"Of course, I will!" Her friend's excitement and elation must have been contagious, for Levee thought she might just ask for the some heavenly guidance, too. No sooner had she bowed her head and closed her eyes than the delightful moment of joy dissolved as her feet-on-the-ground brain took over. A few moments of flirtation and several "almost kisses" were hardly enough to justify such a prayer.

But that wouldn't stop her from asking God's blessing on Matilda's blossoming love.

"Heavenly Father," she began, "this obedient servant has lived the upright life You chose for her, sharing all she has to give with the church and its parishioners, with the school and its students, with anyone blessed to call her 'friend.' Show her, Lord, the path You have chosen for her, and guide her steps as she moves toward the bright light of this new love. If Ethan is the one You intend her to share the rest of her life with, give her a sign that she can't help but recognize." *And if he isn't the one,* Levee prayed silently, *grant Matilda the strength to continue without him.* "We humbly ask these things in Your most holy name. Amen."

"A-*men!*" Matilda echoed. She got up and hurried to the door, then turned around to say, "So, will you come with me to the Lazy N?"

Levee got to her feet, too. "You have a legitimate excuse for your visit. What reason can I give for going all the way out there?"

Matilda rolled her eyes toward the ceiling and whispered, "Dear Lord, give me strength." She grabbed Levee's shoulders and gave her a gentle shake. "Do you need an excuse to visit a neighbor?"

"W-well, yes, of course I do! I can't have Dan thinking I'm some sort of man-crazy tart, Matilda!"

Laughing, Matilda said, "Man-crazy tart? You?" This time, she closed her eyes to say, "Dear Lord, *please* give me strength!" She gave Levee another little shake. "He isn't going to think any such thing, you silly, adorable girl, you! And neither will anyone else, for that matter. Why, chances are, he'll be off in a field somewhere, or mending a fence, or tending those horses of his, and you won't see him, anyway." Giggling, she added, "Until you came along, I thought maybe that fiancée fiasco a few years back broke his heart so completely that he—"

"Fiancée? Oh, Matilda, I can barely stand to think that in addition to everything else, he's suffered a broken heart, too!"

Matilda opened the door. "Better a broken heart than a lifetime of misery, if you ask me. That nose-in-the-air little opportunist? Why, she'd have caused him far more pain than anything he'd experienced before meeting her." She picked up her skirts and headed down the porch steps, stopping on the path to say, "I'll bring the buggy to the end of the walk, there," she said, pointing at the spot where the flagstone path met the road. "See you three days from now, eight o'clock sharp! Better bring a shawl. Better yet, wear a jacket. Late January mornings can get mighty cold, and you don't want to catch a chill. Remember that horrible influenza outbreak in Crystal City?"

We certainly don't need that, Levee thought, hugging herself to fend off the chill. She'd seen the inventory of Doc Lane's supplies when she'd met with him to see about assisting him as a nurse, and they were woefully inadequate to handle an epidemic of any size. She could only pray that the rumored influenza epidemic would not reach Eagle Pass.

Back in the parlor, she leaned against the door. "Guess what, Bashful?" she said, feeling almost as giddy as Matilda had acted earlier. "I'm going to the Lazy N in three days, and if I'm lucky, I'll see Dan!"

·17·

*T*he visit never took place because the influenza epidemic did descend upon Eagle Pass. It slithered into town like a snake, striking victim after victim with its poison. Over the course of four days, dozens of people staggered into Doc Lane's tiny office looking for a cure, or, at the very least, something to ease their symptoms. Some were already burning up with fever when they arrived, and those too weak to walk on their own were carried in by family members not yet infected.

When the doctor ran out of space in his office, Matilda offered her house as a temporary infirmary. She took Levee along to help make her case, but the doctor needed no convincing. "It's perfect," he admitted, coughing into the crook of his arm. "Plenty big enough, with lots of windows to let in good light and fresh air." He knitted his bushy, white eyebrows in the center of his forehead. "But you do realize the possible consequences, don't you?"

"Yes, yes, of course. Your patients will leave a mess for me to clean up, and—"

"That's the least of your worries," he said, wheezing. "You could get sick, too."

"A bit of the pot calling the kettle black, I'd say," Matilda told him. "I've always been as strong as a buffalo."

Levee noticed that the doctor's usually robust voice had lost some of its power, and he didn't stand quite so tall, either, as he implored the women to gather up every sheet, blanket, quilt, and pillowcase they could find and ordered the menfolk to shove aside Matilda's fine furnishings to make room for cots and pallets—thirty-nine at last count—which quickly filled with hacking, moaning patients.

Doc Lane was soon among them.

"It's a great relief," he croaked to Levee, "hearing you've been through something similar. So, no need to waste valuable time waiting for me to check your work or give you permission to do what's necessary." Doc muffled a convulsive, phlegmy cough with his pillow, and when the spasm ended, he took a sip from the cup of water Levee held to his lips. "Just do whatever you think is best," he added through clenched teeth. "I trust you completely to take care of these poor people so they get home as soon as possible."

Huddling deeper under his quilt, he struggled to catch his breath. "By the way, Levee, the key to my apothecary cabinet is in my desk, should you need it. Top drawer on the right."

Nodding, Levee put on a brave face, behind which she trembled with fear. Yes, she'd helped out during an influenza epidemic in Boston, but that had been years ago, when she'd been a nursing student. Every action, each activity, had been carried out according to the instructions of experienced doctors and seasoned nurses. She hadn't made a single decision on her own, and her mind whirled now as she tried to remember every command and directive.

But this was no time to panic. The people were suffering and needed to believe that they were in capable hands. "Be with me, Lord," she prayed under her breath. She asked one of the volunteers to take Bashful out to the Lazy N so Willie could care for him. Then, standing as tall as her petite frame would allow, she took a good, long look around her.

There was so much to do! But where to begin?

She remembered that, at the beginning of the outbreak in Boston, the hospital staff had been warned how easily and quickly the illness could spread. Clapping her hands, Levee got the attention of every able-bodied person present.

"I can't tell you how much I appreciate your help," she began. "What we're facing is serious, but together, I believe we can handle it."

She proceeded to organize two lines, one made up of men and boys to keep fresh water coming in as fouled buckets were carried out, another of women to wash soiled bed linens in boiling water, then hang them to dry in the sun. A few individuals were put to work soaking wash cloths and towels that Levee used to cool fevered foreheads.

"Make sure that you drink plenty of water," she advised them. "Wash your hands every chance you get with soap and hot water, and do your best to avoid direct contact with all bodily fluids expelled by our patients!"

Amid the bustle of activity, Levee moved from bed to bed, holding cups of water to trembling lips, tidying covers, and snatching up every bottle of C. I. Hood's TusSano liquid and every vial of Hood's Dyspeplets tablets. The remedies, she'd learned, were more "mind over matter" than medically effective treatments, and for someone who was already dehydrated from expelling bodily fluids through every pore and orifice, the concoctions only exacerbated the symptoms. By lunchtime, Levee had locked at least a dozen pieces of contraband in Doc Lane's desk, and, though it galled her to do it, she promised to return them to those who'd caught her in the act of confiscat-ing their "miracle medicines" once they had recovered.

All through the day and long into the night, Levee tended to her patients, spoon-feeding water to the weakest and deliv-ering mugs of clear broth to those who were able to stomach the liquid. It was early dawn when she stepped onto Matilda's front porch to fetch clean washcloths. Earlier she'd strung a clothesline between the support posts, and as she plucked several cloths from the rope, she noticed Matilda in the big wicker rocker, her head in her hands.

"Dear Lord," she whispered, "please, don't let her have caught it."

At the sight of her young friend, Matilda hopped up and began pacing. "Did you see?" she demanded, walking to the left. "They brought Ethan in a little while ago."

Levee's heart ached for Matilda, whose new romance had brightened every aspect of her world. "I must have been busy with Mrs. Adleman," she said as Matilda turned to the right. "Who brought him here?" *Please, not Dan*, she thought. *Lord, let him be at the Lazy N, safe and healthy and—*

"George and Lucinda," Matilda said, turning to the left again. "They've got a touch of it, themselves." She stopped abruptly and leaned on the banister. "Oh, Levee, he's as pale as a bedsheet and as weak as a kitten."

Levee pictured the burly, red-headed Irishman who'd taken a shine to her dear friend. "He was hale and hearty at church last week, right?" she said, sliding an arm across Matilda's shoulders. "There's absolutely no reason to believe he won't come through this just fine."

For the first time since Levee had met her, Matilda seemed small and vulnerable. It was unsettling to see fear in her dark eyes and terrifying to see the sheen of perspiration on her brow.

"I don't know what I'll do if he doesn't," Matilda choked out. "I've waited all my life for him, and—"

"Let's just have faith and keep thinking good thoughts, shall we?" Levee patted the woman's arm. "I think you need some rest. There's a pallet in the kitchen, and I'll put it beside Ethan's for you."

Matilda shivered and clutched her shawl tighter around her. "I suppose that would be a good idea. I've been feeling a tad dizzy. Can't help you out if I keel over, now, can I?" She paused in the doorway. "Would you mind stoking the fire? And making sure there's enough boiled water?"

Levee stood at attention and snapped off a smart salute. "Colonel O'Reilly at your service."

That inspired a faint smile. "Colonel? That's a pretty high rank for a young upstart like you. I'm almost afraid to ask what that makes me!"

"A general, absolutely."

"Oh, you have enough to do, 'Colonel.' I can manage getting the pallet from the kitchen to the parlor."

Matilda had just disappeared inside when a wagon rumbled up, then screeched to an earsplitting stop in front of the house. Levee recognized the driver immediately. Recognized the man beside him, too. "Oh, no," she rasped. "It can't be!"

Hiking up her skirts, she ran to meet the rig. "Hand him down to me," she said, extending both arms to Sam. "I'll take him right inside, and—"

"No," barked Dan's voice. In a heartbeat, he was beside her, reaching up to accept the small, limp bundle in Sam's arms. "I've got him. Now, where do you want him?" he asked Levee.

She placed a hand on Willie's forehead and held her breath. The poor child was burning up with fever. "How long has he been this way?"

"Better part of a day," Sam said. "Seemed he was fine one minute, and the next...."

She tried not to focus on the way Sam's voice had trailed off. "We're bursting at the seams. I'll need to make up a bed for him, and—"

"No point wasting time with a running itinerary," Dan interrupted her. "Just tell me what I can do for him while you get his bed ready."

She pointed at the wicker rocker Matilda had recently vacated. "Wait there," she said, dashing into the house. "I'll be only a minute."

Levee scooped up an armload of neatly-folded linens from the dining room table and began assembling a crude pallet in the corner of the kitchen, as far away from the rest of her coughing and groaning patients as possible. And since Sam hadn't looked well, either, Levee fixed up a bed for him, too, right beside Willie's.

As she flapped sheets and fluffed pillows, she remembered something Matilda had said weeks ago—that Dan had once confessed to her that Willie was about the closest thing to a son a man like him could hope to have. *A man like him, indeed.* He was a good, decent man, with a big heart and a beautiful soul. *How wrong you are, Daniel Neville!* she thought, smoothing the top blanket. *Anyone with eyes can see that any boy would be lucky to have you for a father!*

An afterthought sent a shiver down her spine. She hadn't known Willie a full year yet. If his fragile condition had shaken her this badly, how much more upset must Dan be? No wonder he'd been so gruff and growly with her just now!

As Levee zigzagged between cots on her way back to the porch, she blotted perspiration from her brow, praying that nervousness and hurrying had put it there rather than the beginnings of the flu. She'd sent every able-bodied helper home in hopes of reducing their risk of exposure. With Doc Lane and now Matilda down with the illness, Levee was the sole caretaker of three dozen patients. What good would she be to any of them if the flu laid her low, too?

"This way," she called, waving the men inside. "Just put Willie here," she told Dan. She watched as he gently laid the boy on the tiny bed of quilts and blankets, and then she lowered herself onto her hands and knees to tuck the covers under his chin. In minutes, the whimpering child quieted and fell into a fitful slumber. Sitting back on her heels, she looked up at Sam. "I've made you a place right here beside Willie."

A look of alarm and disbelief flitted across his haggard features. "Susan thinks—she believes," he stammered, "that labor might have started."

Clearly, the man was torn between staying with his son and returning to his wife's side. Levee stood beside him and laid a reassuring hand on his shoulder. "I'm fairly certain that baby of yours isn't quite ready to come into the world. At least, not just yet," she said, trying her best to sound confident and cheerful. "But even if Susan's right, she has her mother and her sister Sarah there with her, and I happen to know that Lucinda is an old hand at birthing babies." She folded back the top cover of his rough-and-ready bed. "You look as though you haven't slept in days. Why not rest a bit while I fetch you some broth? That way, if Willie wakes up while I'm gone, it'll be a comfort, seeing you here."

Levee glanced at Dan, hoping that he, too, had noticed the dark circles under Sam's eyes and would chime in with a similar exhortation.

"She's right," Dan said, as if on cue. "You look like something a barn cat dragged in. Now lie down before you fall down, will you?"

She might have said he'd come on too strong if Sam hadn't instantly obeyed. "I reckon it can't hurt to catch a little shut-eye," he said, shaking off his boots. He pulled his boy close, lay back on the pillow, and closed his eyes.

Levee turned to Dan and held a finger to her lips, then gestured for him to follow her to the other side of the kitchen.

"Isn't there something we can do for them?" he asked in a raspy whisper.

"I know how difficult it is to watch them suffer," she said, filling two big mugs with water, "but influenza is a virus. There's really nothing we can do but keep them well hydrated and as comfortable as possible."

His frown deepened. "Doc Lane has a cupboard next door with fifty drawers, each one stuffed with powders and potions. Surely there's one among them to—to *fix* this," he said, thrusting out his arm demonstratively.

He was afraid and angry, and he had every right to be. Yes, it was hard watching a loved one suffer, Levee knew. As her grandfather had lain dying, she'd felt powerless, too, when the cancer had drained the last of life from him. That feeling had inspired her decision to attend nursing school, where she had learned the hardest, most frustrating lesson of all: Science and medicine afforded man very little control over health and illness, over life and death. In the end, those matters were in God's hands.

"Will you pray with me?" she asked Dan.

She supposed it might be possible for him to look more stunned, but perhaps only if she were to slap him. Was prayer really such a ludicrous suggestion, especially under these circumstances?

He lifted both arms and let them fall to his sides. "You might as well wish on a star for all the good it'll do you."

His rigid stance and aggrieved expression told her what words needn't: the worries he'd placed at the foot of the cross had not been resolved. At least, not in the way he'd hoped. God had not responded in a satisfactory way, and Dan felt abandoned, alone, and even more powerless than when he'd voiced his pleas. Levee understood something about that, too. Should she tell him about those miserable years when anger and resentment had prompted her to turn her back on God? Someday, perhaps, but this was neither the time nor the place for such confessions. "Well," she said, gazing up into his eyes, "even the wishes of stargazers come true some of the time." She smiled. "What can it hurt?"

A quiet groan issued from him, "Seriously, Levee, I'd—"

"Mrs. O'Reilly, my head hurts!"

In an eyeblink, Levee was at Willie's bedside, fussing over the boy. "Here," she said, handing Sam one of the mugs of water. "Drink it down, but drink slowly, or it'll upset your stomach." Then, supporting Willie's head with one hand, she held the second mug of water to his mouth with the other. "Now then, dear boy," she crooned, "let's get some of this water into you and bring that fever down."

Like odd-sized bookends, father and son obeyed their nurse, then handed back their empty cups. She turned to give them to Dan to refill, but he had gone. *Just as well*, she thought. He didn't need more exposure to the virus.

In the four nights and three days that followed, Levee barely took time to sip water from her own cup. She took no time for sleep, either. How could she rest, knowing that the influenza had taken the lives of two adults and two children?

Then, people slowly got better and went home from Matilda's house. On the morning of the fourth day, Reverend Peterson and his wife tottered home, but not before the good pastor promised to hold a special service over the weekend to pray for those who'd died, for those still suffering, and for protection for anyone who, by God's grace, hadn't succumbed to the virus.

By midday, Levee was left with just five patients: Willie, Sam, Matilda, Ethan, and Doc Lane. The frenzy of running from the broth pot to the washtub, from the water pump to the clothesline, slowed. She was on all fours, scrubbing the floor, when a small voice called out, "Mrs. O'Reilly?"

Thank You, dear Lord, for bringing that precious child through this ordeal unharmed! she prayed silently. "What is it, Willie? Are you thirsty again?"

"No, ma'am, thank you kindly for asking. It's just…."

Getting up on her knees, Levee dropped the scrub brush into her bucket. "Just what, Willie?" she asked, one hand on her hip.

Sitting cross-legged on his mat, Willie smiled. "Well, it's just that your wash water smells real good."

"The boy's right," Sam agreed, propping himself up onto one elbow.

"This place was beginning to smell worse than the outhouse," Willie added, crinkling his nose.

"Well, my chafed hands and sore knees appreciate that you noticed," Levee teased. "I think you're both well enough to go home in the morning. What do you say, Doc? Do you agree?"

"I say it's your call, young lady," Doc Lane said from his bed. "You're the one who saw us all through this disaster, practically single-handedly, I might add."

But four people had died! Levee understood enough about the sickness, and about medicine in general, to know that, yes, she had done everything humanly and medically possible to save them. But that wouldn't stop her from going over and over every single thing she'd done—and the things she hadn't done—searching for reassurance on that score. How long before she found it, if ever?

"It's my professional opinion," said Doc Lane, "that we're all well enough to leave here tomorrow." He aimed a stern look her way. "And I think it's high time you did the same."

"That's right!" Matilda agreed, sitting up on her pallet. "You did the work of ten people. I think you should lock yourself in that cozy little cottage of yours for a whole week and do nothing but sleep."

Levee laughed. "As tempting as that sounds, I have only a few days to get ready for school. The children have been away from their studies too long already. I'd hate for them to fall even farther behind."

"Hogwash," her friend said. "First thing in the morning, I intend to march straight over to the courthouse and have a good, long talk with the mayor. I will insist that he call a special meeting of the town council and demand that they write up a proclamation—or whatever is required—to allow you to stay home for a week. God knows you've earned it, and the children need it, too, even though they've had recess for four weeks."

"Matilda's absolutely right," Doc Lane said. "We all saw the way you worked round the clock for days on end with very little to eat and not a wink of sleep. Your resistance is low, and if you don't build up your reserves, you could very well come down with the influenza, yourself." He turned to face Matilda. "Miss Montgomery, I want you to come fetch me before you head over to the mayor's office, because, by golly, I intend to go along and help plead your case, though I can't imagine any of the council members is ignorant of what you accomplished here."

"Well, now, I'm glad we've got that settled!" Matilda said, then glanced at Ethan before saying, "How would the bunch of you like to be the first to hear some utterly delicious news?"

Willie and Sam wouldn't hear whatever she had to say, for they'd dozed off. But the rest of them smiled and nodded.

"Aw, let me tell 'em, darlin'," Ethan insisted. He perched on the dining room chair beside Matilda and took her hand in his. "See, as a young sprout, I vowed to go to me grave a bachelor. But this dear woman here, she stole me heart, that she did. And with the both of us comin' so close to meetin' our Maker, thanks to this dreadful bout of influenza, I came to realize that time is a blessed gift, and that I don't want to die a bachelor after all." He chuckled, then reached out and took Matilda's hand in his. "I know it must seem sudden to you young'uns, but Tildy an' me, well, we're old enough to know love when we feel it. So, I've asked her to be me wife, and, praise God, she said yes."

He'd barely finished his narrative when Levee began a round of applause. "I'm so happy for you both! Have you set a date? Will you live in this house, or build a new one, so that—" She gasped, pressing both palms to her cheeks. "Goodness! I hope you're not thinking of moving to Ireland, for we couldn't possibly live without our Matilda—or you, Ethan, of course!"

Ethan laughed. "By all that's holy, girl, how'd ye get all that out in one breath?" He turned to Matilda. "Darlin', it'll be the happiest day of me life when you become me bride. You pick the day, and I'll stand at the front of the church in a suit and tie. And I don't give a hoot where I live, long as you're livin' there, too." He hid an enormous yawn behind his weathered hand. "And now if it's all right with the lot o'you, I think I'll catch me a wee nap."

In a matter of minutes, Levee was the only one not snoring, but she didn't mind. Perhaps, if she worked quietly enough, she could restore order to Matilda's house without waking them.

She ached from head to toe, but thankfully, her discomfort was caused not by illness but by too many hours scurrying around on her feet, bending over patients' beds, and standing at the sink or stove. Oh, how lovely it would be to climb into her own bed tomorrow evening for a full night's rest. Grinning, she thought it might just be a good idea to take them up on their offer, because she feared that, once she lay down, she might not wake up for a whole week!

It was dark by the time she finished cleaning the kitchen. *Two rooms down, two to go,* she thought as she filled her bucket with fresh soapy water. In the parlor, as her bristle brush hissed across the wood floor, she wondered where Dan had been for the past few days. She chose to take his absence as a compliment. After all, if he didn't trust her with the care of Willie and Sam, would he have stayed away so long?

"No, I wouldn't have."

She lurched, splashing water everywhere. She didn't know which unnerved her more, Dan's surprise appearance or the unsettling realization that she'd been talking out loud, and that he'd heard her. "Daniel Neville! As I live and breathe, you are—"

He held up a hand to silence her. "I would have made noise this time," he said softly, "but I looked through the window and saw everybody sleeping, and I didn't want to wake them." A sheepish smile lit his face. "It seems that every time I see you, I frighten you. Makes me feel like a brute and a bully, and I'm sorry, genuinely sorry."

"Frightened or not," Levee said with a grin, "I'm always pleased as can be to see you."

Dan chuckled. "I don't know whether to be flattered or worried."

"Worried?" Levee said, bending to pick up the wash bucket. "About what?"

Dan grabbed the bucket, instead, and followed her to the back porch. "About your mental stability. Don't you think it's a little crazy that being scared out of your wits pleases you?"

Levee leaned on the door frame as Dan dumped sudsy water over the rail. She was crazy, all right.

Crazy in love with a cowboy.

18

*A*t the church breakfast social, which he had finally agreed to attend, Dan watched Levee from his seat as she delivered plates of food to elderly parishioners, fetched milk for busy mothers with hungry young'uns, and refilled bowls of fried potatoes and platters of griddlecakes made by the Ladies' Auxiliary. She reminded him of a hummingbird, flitting back and forth, stopping just long enough to share a kind word or a sweet smile.

Like most of her outfits, Levee's dress had seen better days. Yet he'd never heard her complain that the hems were frayed and the cuffs were threadbare. Instead, she seemed genuinely grateful for the hand-me-downs she'd received upon arriving in Eagle Pass.

Dan grinned to himself. In his opinion, even in a skirt too long and a shirt two sizes too big, Levee was still the prettiest girl in the room. The pale blue fabric complemented the violet of her eyes, and the pretty pink posies that dotted the material, beautiful though they were, paled in comparison to her adorable face. Tiny black boots poked out from her full skirt. He'd been in the store when she'd purchased them, looking so proud as she'd counted out three dollars and fifty cents to pay for them. To his knowledge, they were all she'd bought for herself since coming to town.

In all his years, Dan couldn't remember a time when he'd paid this much attention to color and design, and whether a getup flattered a woman or not. But he was paying attention now. He might have smacked his forehead with the heel of his hand in hopes that it would knock some sense into him if she hadn't looked up just then and caught him staring.

Immediately, her smile grew, and Dan sat up straighter and ran a finger under his collar, praying a wisp of air would sneak in there and take his temperature down a degree or two. His temperature only increased when Levee made a beeline for his table. She stopped not two feet from his chair, close enough that he could detect the faint aroma of roses. Had she put a touch of perfume on her wrists, the way his ma often did? Or was it her preference to dab a bit behind each ear, like his sisters?

"You look like a man who could use a cup of coffee."

Until that moment, he hadn't even seen the thick white mug in front of him. "Thanks," Dan said as Levee filled it with the steaming brew. He was glad she didn't say, "Thanks for what?" because his answer would have been lengthy. The coffee, for starters. And that gorgeous grin of hers. The way her eyes couldn't decide whether they were violet or blue. That sweet, lilting voice....

"Well, now," Levee said, pointing. "What do you make of that?"

Dan followed her gaze to see Mack and Sarah standing shoulder to shoulder, piling flapjacks onto their plates. "Looks like somebody woke up with a powerful hunger this morning," Levee said with a knowing smile.

Dan hadn't been a churchgoer for so many years that he'd lost count, and he hadn't planned on breaking with tradition to attend the breakfast. But the influenza scare had shaken him more than he cared to admit. The local population had decreased by four—folks who would have had dozens of good years left in them if not for the virus. He should have been an old hand at dealing with death, but as he had tossed and turned the night before last, he'd realized for the first time just how precious life was. If Mack and Sarah could squeeze a few years of contentment out of it, good for them.

"Do you think...?" Levee giggled and cupped a hand over her mouth.

The music of her laughter made his ears go hot. Made his heart beat harder and his palms get damp, too. Land sakes! What was happening to him? He'd never felt this way around any of the other gals in town, or around any gal in the other towns he'd visited, for that matter. Even Gwendolyn, the woman he'd been prepared to marry, had not roused this strong a reaction from him.

She plopped onto the chair beside his and leaned in close. "You don't suppose...? Has Mack said anything to you about this?"

Dan turned slightly to make it easier to look into her eyes. Amazing,   couldn't-decide-if-they-were-blue-or-violet   eyes. God help him, but now, on top of sweaty palms and a pounding pulse, his throat was as dry as the desert floor. "About what?" he croaked.

He'd never known a body who could frown and smile at the same time and look so all-fired cute doing it.

"The pair of you work together for hours every day. Has he mentioned Sarah at all?"

"Mentioned Sarah?"

She took a quick look back at the couple. "You don't suppose they're courting, do you?"

"Courting? Well, I—"

One delicate brow rose slightly. "I never noticed it before, but there's a *terrible* echo in this room."

For the luvva Pete, what is she babbling about! Now it was Dan's turn to frown. "An echo?"

And then he got it. Grinning, he shrugged. "Sorry. It's just...well, I reckon I'm not much good at noticing details."

"Please," Levee said, crossing her ankles. "Matilda told me that you can spot the Lazy N brand on a horse's withers from a mile off. And your own mother said you had the eyes of an eagle."

"That's different."

"How so?"

He shrugged again. "Don't rightly know. Just is."

She turned in her chair, too, and tilted her head at Mack and Sarah. "Well, I just so happen to think that they are, and I couldn't be happier."

"Courting, you mean?"

She nodded once, then licked her lips. "Mmm-hmm."

Oh, how he wanted to kiss her, right there in the church basement, in front of the whole congregation!

How could he help it that Levee was so stunning? Did she have any idea how fascinating and enchanting and captivating she was? Or that she'd turned him into an addle-brained, poetry-spouting buffoon who behaved more like a knock-kneed schoolboy than any young'un in her class? Only thing left for her to do, he thought, was to brand him with a big, bold *L*, because she'd captured his heart, just as surely as if she'd reined it in with a well-aimed lariat.

She blinked, and so did he.

He swallowed, and so did she.

One of us had better look away, he thought, *or I will kiss her, right here in the church basement, for half the town to see!*

"When you two get through makin' eyes at each other, you think I could ask Dan here a question?"

"Matilda!" Levee stood and wrapped her friend in a warm hug. "I'm so glad you made it." She peered around the woman's shoulders. "Is Ethan here with you?"

Dan got to his feet, too, and pretended to enjoy the syrupy concoction the Ladies' Auxiliary was passing off as coffee.

"No," Matilda answered, "because this slave driver boss of his gave him a list of chores as long as my arm." Winking, she linked her arm with Dan's. "I won't keep your fella long. Promise."

Last thing he saw before Matilda whirled him around and led him toward the door was Levee, eyes wide and lips slightly parted.

"Oh, don't look so down in the mouth," Matilda said, smirking. "She'll be there when you get back."

"Glad you're sure about that."

"Trust me, that little gal is so sweet on you, it hurts my teeth. Haven't you noticed the way she looks at you?"

Well, a man could hope. "So, what's so important you couldn't say it in front of Levee?"

"You asked me to have my nephew, the Pinkerton detective, look into Mack Burdette's background." She reached into her handbag and produced a fat envelope. "This is from him," she explained, handing it to Dan.

"Information about Mack?"

"I aim to please, my handsome young friend, I aim to please!" She looked around, then whispered beside a cupped hand, "I'd wait to read that if I were you. No telling who might look over your shoulder if you open it here, or what they might do with the information."

"Good grief! How bad is this news, anyway?"

"Don't know," Matilda said, chin held high. "As you can plainly see, I didn't break the seal."

He could hardly wait to break that seal, himself. "How much do I owe you?"

"For what?"

"Well, Pinkertons don't work for free."

"They do for folks who paid for their college education." She winked again. "Besides, that boy would do anything for his old Aunt Tildy."

"Let me pay you for the cost of the telegram, at least."

"I won't hear of it, and I'll thank you not to insult me by offering again. When you share what my nephew dug up, that'll be thanks enough. I'm as interested to know about that boy's past as you are." She nodded at Mack and Sarah, who were huddled together, sharing a stack of griddlecakes. "That cousin of yours is getting mighty sweet on him, from the looks of things."

Dan had to agree. "Well, thanks," he said, tapping the envelope. "This will be—"

"There's my sweetheart!" she interrupted him. "Why, Dan Neville, you sly dog! Guess you aren't a heartless taskmaster after all."

And then she was gone, leaving him to decide whether he should find Levee and pick up where they'd left off, or study the Pinkerton's report.

He took the steps two at a time, wincing at the pain it caused his bum leg. But a bit of discomfort was a small price to pay for killing two birds with one stone. He half ran from the basement to his wagon, parked across the way. No reason he couldn't give the information a quick read, then meet up with Levee afterward.

Perched on the wagon seat, he leaned back and crossed one boot over the other as he slid half a dozen stiff pages from the packet. Two paragraphs in, he realized the futility of hoping for a quick scan.

After losing his folks to typhoid fever, the report said, eight-year-old Mack had been sent to live with his paternal grand-father, a wealthy doctor who decided the boy should follow in his footsteps—training at a prestigious military academy, then on to Harvard. During his grandson's first visit home from medical school, the old man introduced Mack to his partner's daughter and inked their wedding date on the calendar. The report didn't say if she'd been as ugly as a turkey buzzard or as hairy as a grizzly. What it did say was that after a bitter argument, twenty-year-old Mack walked away from his first-class education, turned his back on a substantial inheritance, and accepted an assortment of odd jobs that took him West.

How the Pinkerton had unearthed so much information, Dan didn't know, but if the man ever tired of investigating, he'd probably have enough material to write a successful dime novel.

Dan slipped the pages back into the envelope, then hid it under a tarp in the back of the wagon. He breathed a sigh of relief that Mack hadn't been a bank robber, or worse, because he'd come to like and respect the hardworking cowhand. *Sarah could do worse*, he thought as he made his way back to the church basement.

He spotted Levee instantly, sitting with his parents and laughing, probably at one of his pa's corny jokes. *She could do better than the likes of you,* he thought. But, again, a man could hope, and Matilda's observations had given him some encouragement.

Had he been concentrating on Levee so hard that he'd sent a silent message all the way across the room? How else could he explain why she suddenly looked up, as if somebody had banged two pots together, and locked her big-eyed gaze on him? Lifting her shoulders, she smiled and sent him a dainty wave.

Yes, she deserved better than the likes of him. Far better. But maybe, if he went back to praying regularly, and if he went back to Sunday services, God would show him how to be the man she deserved.

A man can hope, he thought again, walking toward her. *A man can hope.*

19

*T*wo days of unrelenting rain had turned the streets into miniature streams and shallow creeks. The grungy, gray clouds overhead seemed impenetrable and all but smothered the town's usually bustling activity. As they waited for the weather to clear, the townsfolk holed up in their homes and businesses, where hints of lantern light, glowing soft and hazily through the sheets of rain, proved there was life on the other side of the windows. Only the occasional soul wearing a duster or using a tarp as an umbrella braved the torrential downpours, scurrying up makeshift ramps or darting around ankle-deep puddles like a frightened rabbit.

Before turning out her lamp for the night, Levee thanked the Lord for the good men of Eagle Pass who, during her first week in town, had repaired her roof. Safe and snug under a thick quilt, she fell asleep to the unceasing, steady beat of fat raindrops hammering down upon the slates. Every half hour or so, window-rattling wind or rumbling thunder shook her awake, and Levee blamed the storm for her distressing nightmares, which echoed with the groan of angry bellows, pounding horses' hooves, and deadly gunfire.

As she struggled to get back to sleep, she thought of Liam. Had paradise calmed his quicksilver temper and softened his hard heart? Had he learned, while surrounded by choirs of angels and loved ones who'd gone to heaven before him, that kindness begets kindness, or that an accumulation of money was no more important than the accolades he'd craved so desperately here on earth?

She lay in that strange, hazy place halfway between deep sleep and awareness, praying that he'd found happiness and satisfaction. He hadn't been the most sharing or caring of husbands, but he deserved peace. Levee prayed for her own cold-hearted soul, too, because he might have been a better husband if she'd been a better wife. Distracted by assignments for her nursing classes, she admittedly hadn't put much effort into making their house a home, and studying had occupied the time she might have spent planting pretty flowers, like his associates' wives had done. True, she'd hoped a nursing degree would earn his respect—and, perhaps, a more obvious display of love and affection. But, in addition to the desire to help others and ease their suffering, her motive for becoming a nurse had become rooted in a self-serving need to safeguard her future, in case Liam left her one day, just as her parents and grandparents had done.

Blessed drowsiness returned as she burrowed deeper under the covers. There, in the warm cocoon that muffled the lightning and thunder, her mother's soft voice wavered on the fringes of a new, happier dream. "It'll soon be morning, Levee-love."

Then, "Levee! Levee O'Reilly!"

Papa? No, her father had been a tenor in the church choir, and this voice—were it singing instead of shouting—belonged in the bass section. She recognized it yet couldn't conjure a matching face or name.

"Levee! Levee, please! Open the door!"

Bashful, who had been sleeping on the rug beside her, jumped up and started barking.

Fully awake now, Levee threw back the blankets and sat up in bed. *Where was a flash of lightning when you needed one?* she wondered, squinting in the dark and patting the bedside table in search of a match. She couldn't distinguish between the sounds of thunder and the pounding on her door, and she barely heard the scrape of the match when she lit it. She lifted the globe of the lantern with one hand and lit the wick with the other. Was it the cold air or her fear that caused her fingers to tremble as she blew out the match?

"Hold your horses!" she shouted. "I'll be right there!" Then, "Hush, Bashful!"

The sharp scent of sulfur hung in the air as she pulled on her thick robe. Carrying the lamp into the parlor with Bashful at her side, she peeked through the curtains and saw a soaked-to-the-skin Sam Rogers, head down, pacing on her small, covered porch.

"Sam!" she said, opening the door. "What in the world are you doing out in this mess? You look as if—"

"It's Susan," he blurted out. "She's in labor. Sent me to fetch Doc Lane, but his missus wouldn't open the door. Only hollered that the doc is in Lubbock, and didn't I realize it's the middle of the night?"

The woman had been a doctor's wife all these years and hadn't grown accustomed to disruptions at all hours? Levee frowned and shook her head as Sam took a step forward.

"It's bad, Levee. Not at all like it was with Willie. Eva thinks the baby's breech. I was hoping, since you're a nurse and all, maybe you could come back to the ranch with me."

"Of course, I will," she said, stepping aside. "Now, come in out of the rain while I get dressed."

As he stepped over the threshold, rainwater poured from the brim of his ten-gallon hat. "Sorry to drench your rugs. Maybe I'd best wait out here."

"Don't be silly. It's only water." Levee opened the door wider. "Stand there by the stove and warm yourself. I'll just be a minute, I promise."

While she changed into a simple, black skirt and calico shirt, Levee heard him walking back and forth, from the parlor to the kitchen, and back again. *Poor Sam*, she thought, picturing his frightened expression as she buttoned her boots. And poor Susan, trying to birth a baby that had decided to come out the wrong way!

Levee had braided her hair before turning in for the night. Now, she wound the long plaits and pinned them in place atop her head, then donned a big bonnet, fastening the strings tightly under her chin.

After the influenza outbreak, the townsfolk had taken up a collection to buy her a medical bag to thank her for all she'd done to see them through the crisis. Inside the bag were a fancy stethoscope and a new thermometer. With those, added to the scissors, scalpels, tape, and liniments from Liam's kit, Levee had enough gear to make any veteran doctor envious.

Hopefully, she wouldn't need any of it.

She moved to the buffet to retrieve the two big oil tarps that had covered the wicker chairs on the porch before she'd moved into the cottage. Grabbing both, she handed one to Sam.

"No sense getting it wet," he said as she bundled herself into the other one. "I can't hold it in place and lead the team at the same time."

"But you'll be soaked to the skin!"

"I'm already soaked to the skin," he reminded her, opening the door. "Besides, it's only water."

Levee told Bashful to "stay." Then, she blew out the lantern flame and followed Sam onto the porch, where the rockers creaked to and fro in the driving gusts of wind. The rain poured down with such ferocity that she could barely see the wagon. Clutching a handful of her skirt, she made her way down the path, now hidden beneath half a foot of mud. With each step, her boot disappeared into the muck. Good thing she'd laced them well, or suction would have pulled them from her feet. Leave it to Sam, she thought, climbing onto the wagon seat, for having the foresight to turn the wagon around before knocking on her door.

Under other circumstances, the characteristically affable Sam would have talked all the way to the Lazy N, but worry, she supposed, rendered him silent. It was just as well, for it gave her time to pray that he wouldn't have a relapse of his illness. The influenza outbreak wasn't that far behind them, and Sam still looked fatigued. She also prayed that Susan's mother had been mistaken, and that the baby wasn't breech, after all. But what if Eva was right? Levee asked God to help her remember everything she'd learned about managing such a difficult birth.

When they arrived at Matthew and Eva's house, half a dozen Nevilles braved the weather to usher them inside. While Sam explained why he had Levee with him instead of Doc Lane, Dan's cousin Josh got straight to work taking care of the horses and wagon while Micah, another cousin, led Sam and Levee down the hall. "Aunt Eva collected some dry duds for you," he said, shoving Sam into the parlor. "Soon as you're out of those wet clothes," he added, jerking the velvet curtains shut, "meet me in the kitchen."

"The kitchen? But—but I want to be with Susan," Sam protested, his voice slightly muffled by the thick fabric.

Micah only grinned and said, "You've been part of this family long enough to know what happens when you go against Eva." Then, he turned to Levee, who was perched on a backless bench, removing her shoes. "Do you need something dry to change into? Sarah's with Susan, but I'm sure she'd tell you to help yourself to anything in her wardrobe."

The tarp had done a good job of keeping Levee dry—from the knees up, at least. Her lower half was soaked clean through. But it was warm inside the house, and her skirt and stockings would dry quickly. Besides, she didn't want to waste time changing. "I'm just fine," she said, hanging her soggy hat and the still-dripping tarp on the coat rack. "Where's Willie?"

"He's in the kitchen with Lucinda. Don't worry," Micah said, winking, "I'll keep Sam out of your hair, too." He gave a jerk of his chin. "You'll find Susan upstairs, second room on the right. Send Sarah down to get me if you need anything," he said when she reached the landing.

Nodding, she hiked up her skirts and hurried upstairs. When she entered the room and swiftly explained why she'd come in Doc Lane's stead, the mother-to-be smiled weakly.

"I'm so glad it's you," Eva said from one side of the bed.

"And so am I," Sarah agreed from the other. "Mother and I have never delivered a breech baby before."

Levee plunked her kit onto the night table, then began rolling up her sleeves. "Susan, I'll need to palpate your stomach," she said, folding back the covers, "to get a feel for where this little mischief-maker has decided to park, and just how soon he plans to make an entrance into the world."

"He?" Susan said as Levee placed her hands on her abdomen.

"I just can't bring myself to call an unborn baby 'it,'" she said, smiling. Palpating every inch of the swollen stomach, Levee felt the baby's contours. Yes, both legs were folded at the knees, and, unfortunately, the child lay right-side up, his head toward Susan's ribs. She had two options: manually turn the baby, or attempt a Cesarean section, which was dangerous even when performed by an accomplished surgeon. She'd observed such an operation on three occasions. The first time, she'd watched as the mother had bled to death. The second time, it had been the baby who had died. The third time, the procedure had been a success, and Levee had assisted. Still, not a great record. *Please, Lord, let the turning work!* was her silent plea.

"Sam tells me you've been experiencing discomfort for days," Levee said, hoping to distract Susan.

In place of an answer, she grimaced at another spasm.

"How long have the pains been this strong?"

"Three or four hours, maybe." She grabbed Levee's hands. "Everything is all right, isn't it? Because I haven't felt the baby move since…I can't remember when!"

"That's perfectly normal." Thankfully, that much was true. "Babies often stop moving when it's time to be born. I think they must sense how much work it'll take to get from the safety of their mothers' wombs into the big, bright world, so they grow still and quiet in the hours just before to store up the energy that will be required of them."

"I like that explanation." A tiny smile lifted the corners of Susan's mouth. "The baby must be a boy, then."

"What makes you say that?"

"Already a master at doing only what's required."

"Susan!" her mother exclaimed. "With talk like that, you'll have poor Levee thinking Sam is a shirker!"

Susan frowned. "If he had taken that job working for his father in Lubbock, we'd have a home of our own right now."

"Yes, and who knows what sort of care you'd be getting right now?"

"Mother, really," came Sarah's harsh whisper. "This is hardly the time."

The disagreement seemed to upset Susan, so Levee said, "Expectant mothers often say such things at times like this. It's very normal. Really. Some who've studied childbirth believe hormones are responsible, while others think the pain and anxiety cause it." She shrugged. "Personally? I'm inclined to believe it's a combination of the two." She met Eva's gaze. "Can you show me where I might wash up?"

The woman held one hand in the air. "Levee, dear, I heard all about how you handled yourself during that nasty influenza epidemic. I'd feel much more comfortable—and I'm sure Susan would, too—if you'd stay here in the room." Eva moved toward the door and gestured for Sarah to come with her. "Sarah will bring you some soap and a bowl of wash water while I'll fetch some towels."

"And some washcloths for Susan's forehead?" Levee suggested.

The minute Eva and Sarah disappeared down the hall, Levee got busy explaining the order of things to Susan. "Your mother was right," she began, taking hold of the young woman's hand. "Your baby is breech. So, as soon as I've cleaned up, I'll need to do an internal examination, to determine just how far along your labor is. I'll leave it up to you who's in the room while I do it."

"I don't mind if Ma and Sarah are here." Susan winced through another spasm of pain. Once it eased, she asked about Sam and Willie.

"I happen to know that Micah has been assigned 'Sam Duty,'" Levee said, smiling, "and Lucinda is keeping Willie busy in the kitchen."

"I'm so sorry to have roused the entire household. The men, especially, need their rest."

Levee patted her hand. "I have a feeling they're only too happy to be part of this miracle you're working so hard on."

Susan exhaled a shuddering sigh and looked away for a moment. "Have you...um," she said, meeting Levee's eyes. "Have you done this before?"

"Yes, as a matter of fact, I have." Not the whole truth, but not exactly a lie, either. "Don't you worry." *I'm worrying enough for both of us!* Would she remember everything she'd learned, watching those skilled practitioners?

Trust in the Lord, and He will guide you.

And guide her, He did.

Levee now had a whole new reason to appreciate the doctors she'd watched during her days of nursing school. Turning the baby at just the right angle to coordinate with Susan's contractions required careful hands and close attention. Too much pressure could cause permanent injury, or worse, to Susan or the baby. Too little pressure might allow the umbilical cord to tangle around one of the baby's limbs or, God forbid, his neck.

In those final moments before the baby's birth, the room quieted, and so did the activity on the first floor of Eva and Matthew's house. Outside, tiny rainbows sparkled as sunshine reflected off each dewy drop still clinging to the windowpanes, while inside, a tiny, warbling cry filled the room.

Eva and Sarah set about freshening up the new mother while Levee placed the newborn in the washbasin on the dresser for a gentle sponge bath.

She took her time counting fingers and toes as she washed the delicate, pink flesh, then bundled the baby into a small flannel blanket. Kissing the tip of a nose no bigger than a sweet pea, Levee closed her eyes and thanked God for the miracle she held in her arms. Thanked Him, too, for all that was good about her own life, for He had blessed her with robust health, a fulfilling job, a sturdy home, and good friends. The only thing missing, really, was a child…a child and a loving husband to share it all with.

She had no idea how many minutes passed while she stood there, swaying to and fro, humming softly, and gazing at Susan's beautiful baby, but a quick glance at the women told her it must have been quite a long time. Laughing quietly, Levee said, "Didn't know I was such a baby hog, did you?"

While they joined in her laughter, Levee reluctantly handed the squirming bundle to Susan, who immediately folded back her nightgown and held the baby to her breast. The beautiful, wondrous picture brought tears to Levee's eyes. Hands clasped under her chin, she bit her lip to still its trembling. "Do you—do you have a name picked out for your pretty baby girl?"

But Susan seemed not to have heard the question, for now *she* was staring into the baby's face as Levee had, moments earlier. Eva and Sarah pressed in closer, oohing and aahing, cooing and crooning, as they admired the newest addition to the family.

Common decency demanded that she leave and let these good women bask in the warmth of family love. She'd return in a few minutes to make sure Susan and the baby were faring well, then see if Josh or Micah could drive her back to town.

Where had Dan been all this time? She knew that he lived up the road with his parents, and not in the main house, but throughout the night, she'd heard the voice of every other Neville man carry up through the floorboards in Susan's bedroom.

Quickly and quietly, she gathered up soiled towels, blankets, and sheets, then stuffed them into a pillowcase, hoping as she worked that he hadn't been out there working while the ferocious storm raged. Lucinda seemed to know everything about the Lazy N. When she inquired about where to put the dirty laundry, she'd ask her about Dan's whereabouts, too.

As Levee made her way down the stairs, a tumult of emotions assaulted her. She was thrilled for Susan and relieved for Sam. Willie had a little sister, and Eva and Matthew, a new grandchild, all because God had seen fit to guide Levee's hands and bless the birthing process. The healthy baby girl had been delivered with a minimum of trauma to her and her mama. So much to rejoice about! So much to thank the Lord for!

So, why the overwhelming urge to weep?

Levee slumped onto a carpeted step and pressed her cheek against the cool wood of the balusters. "You will not cry," she whispered through clenched teeth. "You will not cry!"

She blamed the long hours of watching and waiting and praying she'd execute every procedure by the book, and at the right instant for Susan and the baby. Blamed too many skipped meals and too many nights peppered with haunting nightmares. Blamed the storm's ferocious wind that even now pummeled the Nevilles' house, and—

"I have a clean bandanna, unless you'd rather sit there all night, crying into a sack."

How the voice of a certain man could make her heart soar!

"Sam's about to wear a path in the parlor carpet," Dan went on, "so I told him I'd find out if he's allowed upstairs yet." Planting one boot on the bottom step, he leaned on his knee, putting him nearly nose-to-nose with Levee. "Is everything all right up there?"

"Yes, Susan is fine." Embarrassed at the reedy sound of her voice, Levee cleared her throat. "And so is the baby."

He tucked in one corner of his mouth. "Then, why the tears?"

In truth, she didn't have an explanation. At least, none that made sense, even to her. "Because I'm relieved?" One shoulder lifted in a tiny shrug. "Because, by the grace of God, I didn't make any mistakes, mostly. Even a tiny error could have been costly. Susan had a hard time of it, but with a few weeks' rest, she'll be as good as new." Levee shook her head. "Just one nagging suspicion to take the shine off things."

Concern glittered in his eyes and tinged his voice. "And what might that be?"

"I can't say for certain—I'm not a doctor, after all—but if I had to guess, I'd say there won't be any more babies for Susan and Sam."

Dan inspected his fingertips, then absently picked at a callus on his palm. "So, the baby was breech, after all?" he asked without looking up.

"Yes."

"And you," he said, meeting her gaze. "You made things right." He wiped a tear from her cheek with the pad of his thumb.

"I...I...." She twisted the hem of the pillowcase. "Mother and child are doing well. Exceptionally well, particularly under the circumstances. That's all that really matters."

With a yawn, Levee reviewed all that she had to do before going home: deliver these linens, for starters, before making one last check on Susan and her baby, then gather up the tools from her medical bag—especially Liam's scalpel, which she'd used to perform the episiotomy. Her back ached from hours of leaning over poor Susan, and the soles of her stockinged feet throbbed. Oh, to relax in a tub of hot, sudsy water! No time for that, with lesson plans to prepare and homework assignments to grade. But none of it would get done if she continued sitting here like a lady of leisure.

Levee stood—too quickly, she realized, when the weight of the sack propelled her forward. She grabbed the banister and held her balance, thankful not to have spilled the contents of the pillowcase. "I need to get rid of this," she said, patting the improvised laundry bag. "I need to get cleaned up," she added, indicating her bloody apron, "and find Willie, to let him know that he's a big brother. Then I need to find Sam, so I can send him upstairs to meet his daughter."

"Funny," Dan said, grinning.

"What?"

"Never figured you for a gal with so many needs." Then his eyes widened, and so did his smile. "Wait. Did I hear you right? Did you say Susan's baby is a girl?"

"Yes." Levee pictured the infant whose hair shimmered with the same golden hues as Susan's, whose eyelashes were thick and dark, just like her daddy's. "A beautiful, perfect little girl."

"All thanks to you."

She laughed. "Please! You wouldn't say that if you'd seen me up there, all trembling and stuttering and praying like there was no tomorrow that I'd remember even half of what

I learned in nursing school!" Shaking her head, she freely admitted, "All the thanks goes to God."

He held her eyes in a smoldering gaze for what seemed an interminably long time. "You look dog-tired," he finally said.

"I suppose I am, a little." She sighed contentedly. "I'm so relieved the rain has stopped."

"It quit about an hour ago."

"I was beginning to wonder."

"About?"

"Well, God made the rainbow—remember?—as a symbol of His promise never to destroy the world with water again. But the way that storm was carrying on, I'd begun to wonder...."

Dan chucked. "You must be tired. Tell you what. You fetch Sam and Willie, and I'll hitch the team to the wagon and take you home so you can get some much-deserved rest."

"Y-you're taking me home?"

He quirked an eyebrow. "Why not? You have someone else in mind?"

Someone else? Why, the very notion was laughable! "I can't think of anyone I'd rather spend an hour with."

Her answer erased the worry-creases from his brow. "Two hours, you mean."

"Two? But I thought—"

"The road's a powerful mess. One muddy rut and gully after another." He relieved her of the pillowcase. "Wouldn't want to rush, bog the wheels down, and get stuck, now, would we?"

As they walked side by side down the hallway to the kitchen, Levee's heart fluttered. "No. We certainly wouldn't want that."

*T*he early weeks of March felt downright balmy compared to February's biting winds and fierce storms. While the youth of Eagle Pass enjoyed sun-drenched days and gentle breezes, the town's elder citizens aimed wary eyes at the heavens, wondering if this were just a lull and when spring would finally show its true colors.

Possibly the wariest were the Neville men and their most trusted ranch hands, Mack and George, who'd assembled on Matthew's terrace to discuss the upcoming trail drive. "It's the quiet before the storm," Uncle Matthew said, staring at the cloudless, blue sky.

The concern in his normally composed voice snapped all ten men to attention, and each one followed his gaze. "I almost hate to agree," Dan's pa said, "but the last time it was this peaceful at this time of year, we lost a hundred head of cattle and way too many of our best saddle horses."

One by one, the men listed past calamities, which included buildings collapsing, livestock killed by flying debris, fields flattened by torrential downpours, blistering heat, drought, and tornadoes.

Josh, who'd been appointed scribe at their meeting, put down his pencil and ran a hand through his hair. "Let's pray we won't face any of that on the drive," he muttered.

"And that nothing of the kind will happen here at home while we're gone," Micah added.

A grave hush fell over the group, because two months was an incredibly long time to be away.

"Think word has leaked out about the anthrax?" Dan asked. Just as frightening as natural disasters was the possibility that word of the anthrax epidemic they'd weathered the year before had reached Wichita, which could mean that they'd be forced to turn the herd around and head home. Potential buyers who didn't believe they'd taken every step to stop the disease in its tracks were a scary proposition.

Frowning, Josh shook his head. "Nah, nobody's come through here in months, and it's a sure thing none of us have spread the bad news." His eyes narrowed, and he looked at every man seated around the rough-hewn table, as if looking for a sign, however minuscule, that one of them had suffered a slip of the tongue. It wouldn't be pretty if Josh found that evidence, for, blood kin or not, the guilty man would never live it down.

Uncle Matthew drained his coffee mug and set it down with a thud. "Lord willing, we've managed to keep that bit of awful news under our hats."

Their moods turned as sour as the words he'd left unsaid: If word got out, it would be the end of them as ranchers.

"What about hiring extra hands?" Dan's pa asked.

"I'll do it in San Antone while I'm fetching supplies," Dan offered.

This time of year, men came from miles around and waited in the diners and saloons of every big city in hopes of being hired on for a drive. It didn't matter where the job originated or where the trail ended, because, these days, an honest day's pay was a hard thing to come by. Some had experience, others were green as the grass, but they all had one thing in common: a desire to earn $40 a month.

But Uncle Matthew shook his head. "You'll be of more use to us here, sorting out the horses we'll need." Pointing to his son, he added, "Josh will pull the rations together while Micah rounds up cowboys."

Since his near-fatal accident, Dan hadn't joined them on a drive. But last year, completely recovered from his injuries—and the negative effects of self-medicating with whiskey—he had been entrusted with driving the wagon to San Antonio, where dry goods were more abundant and less expensive than in Eagle Pass. A week later, with a wagonload of supplies and an odd assortment of cowhands trailing behind him, he'd met them on the outskirts of San Antonio and traded the new hires and his purchases for a dependable mount to take him back to the Lazy N. Alone. It hadn't been an ideal situation, but at least he'd had the satisfaction of knowing he'd provided them with everything they'd need for the long, hard journey ahead.

"How many should I sign on?" Micah wanted to know.

On his feet now, Uncle Matthew began gathering his paperwork. "Ten, twelve…." He shrugged. "What say you, Mark?"

"Ten sounds reasonable to me." Laying a hand on Dan's shoulder, he said, "We'll need your best horses, son. How many are ready for the ride?"

Just yesterday, he'd worked up those numbers, knowing that each man needed four or five mounts per day, thanks to the long hours and the pace the horses were expected to maintain. Wild mustangs would have been naturally well-suited to the work, if not for their willful ways. For every ounce of muscle and dexterity in their powerful bodies, the beautiful animals possessed twice as much pigheadedness. A dangerous trait, Dan had learned the hard way. Instead, he put them to better use, siring foals that, when grown, could be trained to dart in and out and alongside a herd, starting and stopping, often reacting instinctively rather than at the command of their riders. But, as strong and dependable as they were, not even the sturdiest of them could last more than a few hours on the trail. "Shouldn't be any trouble," Dan said, "making sure each man has four ponies to get him to Wichita."

"We'll leave it to you to decide which ones we'll bring," his pa said.

"How many cows this time?"

"Thirty-two hundred."

"And how many miles a day?"

"Twelve, fifteen at most."

Any more than that, and the cows would lose weight during the arduous, two-month trip from Texas to Kansas. And what right-minded businessman would pay $40 a head for skin-and-bone animals? Dan worked the numbers in his head. Even if things went flawlessly, they'd probably lose some cows to illness or injury.

It would be an important drive for the family, and not only because it would replenish their losses from the anthrax outbreak. Everyone knew that this drive could very well be their last, thanks to the railroad, the advent of barbed wire, and fences being erected all across the prairie. Every man standing there knew this to be true, but not one could bring himself to admit it out loud.

"So, who's staying behind this year?" Dan asked, mostly to change the gloomy subject.

His pa took two pencils, broke one exactly in half, cracked the other so that one stub was noticeably shorter than the other, and then bundled them into his fist. From youngest to oldest, his brothers selected nibs, leaving Uncle Matthew holding the shortest. A noisy round of guffaws drifted across the lawn as Uncle John said, "Looks like you're caught this year, big brother."

"Seems only fair," Uncle Luke put in. "I drew the short one three years running and got stuck looking after the Lazy N all by my lonesome." He reminded them that on the last occasion, his wife and children had been in Houston, visiting his wife's parents. "Why, if it wasn't for Matilda Montgomery stopping by now and then with vittles, I might've starved to death!"

"Speaking of Matilda," Dan's pa said, "who's going to the wedding?"

A chorus of moans floated around the yard, followed by heavy sighs. "Not that I begrudge Ethan or Matilda a happy marriage, but they'd be just as married taking their vows in the pastor's office," Uncle Luke said.

"You got that right," Dan's pa agreed. "Now we'll all have to suffer right along with them, dressed up in our Sunday best."

"Tell me about it!" Uncle Matthew chimed in. "Eva's got herself all in a lather over it." He shot a guarded glance over his shoulder to see if the coast was clear. "Sarah sewed up new frocks for herself and Susan. Made one for her mama, too. I'll be on the poorhouse if they keep buying bolts of fabric and fancy trim at this rate!"

"Can bonnets and earrings and purses be far behind?" Dan's pa asked.

Uncle John chuckled, too. "And let's not forget gloves and lacy handkerchiefs!"

"I fail to see the humor," Uncle Luke put in. "They're gonna expect us to put on starched shirts."

"And spit-polish our own boots."

"Scrub our fingernails."

"Shave."

"Wear suit coats and ties!"

A moment of absolute quiet preceded another round of boisterous laughter.

Dan grinned so as not to call attention to himself, but he didn't understand what all the grumbling was about. Every last one of them had attended no fewer than a dozen weddings and, to the best of his recollection, had seemed to enjoy the festivities wholeheartedly, despite being forced into bathtubs and then clean duds.

Bottom line: he'd never seen Matilda happier. What else mattered?

"It's all that *should* matter," Eva said firmly.

Dan decided that he needed to get more sleep. To stop skipping meals. And to ask God to guide his words. Because until he'd heard Aunt Eva's voice, he hadn't realized he'd spoken aloud.

The Neville men spun around to see her, each standing with one shoulder pressed against the porch rail, one boot crossed over the other.

"Eva, darlin'," Uncle Matthew said, pulling nervously at his collar, "how long have you been standing there, eavesdroppin'?"

She gave one nod of her head. "Exactly long enough to know that Dan, there, is the only man among you with a lick of sense." She matched his grin, tooth for tooth. "Besides, I'd hardly call it 'eavesdropping' when the wind likely carried your caterwauling straight up the road and clear into Eagle Pass."

Crossing both arms over her chest, she concluded, "I hope you don't mean to imply that I need permission from the Neville men to stand on my own back porch!"

A succession of muttered "'Course not's" and "No, ma'am's" scattered across the yard, and when it ended, she gave them all a piece of her mind.

"Matilda has single-handedly done more for Eagle Pass than the lot of you put together. Is it odd that she has decided to take a husband during the autumn of her life? Perhaps. Is it a surprise that a rough-and-tumble Irish cowboy has stolen her heart? Yes. But if the dear woman can find joy and companionship with Ethan, I say, good for her."

"Aw, Eva," Dan's pa said, "we didn't mean to imply she didn't deserve to be happy."

Uncle John nodded. "We just don't fancy gettin' all gussied up for her weddin'!"

Dan studied the facial expressions and postures of his uncles and cousins, and he could predict the turn this conversation would take the instant his aunt went back inside. And, having no desire to be the butt of "Dan is Aunt Eva's favorite!" jokes, he decided the time was ripe for a hasty departure.

Head down, he did an about-face and set off toward the barn. "See you at supper," he said, waving.

"Not if we see you first!" Mack bellowed.

Dan turned just long enough to say, "You might do well to give some thought to how you'll deliver your own marriage proposal, don't you think?"

In the ensuing silence, the men considered Dan's suggestion. Then, quick as an eyeblink, Mack became the target of their good-natured jokes. Dan might have felt guilty, trading his own discomfort for his friend's, but the cowboy's blushing, grinning face was all the proof he needed that he'd correctly guessed why Mack and Sarah called a halt to their whispering every time he approached them. Unless he was mistaken, they'd exchange "I do's" in the not-too-distant future, bringing the total number of Neville bachelors to three: Paul, Micah, and Dan.

Oh, he could just hear his cousin Paul now, thanking the good Lord for giving him the freedom to come and go as he pleased, with no young'uns to worry over and no wife carping at him for tracking mud into her kitchen or sitting down at the supper table without washing his hands first.

Dan couldn't admit it out loud, of course—at least, not without inviting a volley of jibes and barbs from his uncles and cousins—but he hungered for a taste of the abiding love shared by his parents, his aunts and uncles, and his married cousins. And he would gladly trade his best horse and his favorite saddle for a slice of that sweet family pie.

Dan could think of only one woman worth sacrificing his so-called freedom for. Yet the admission hit hard, like a painful punch in the gut, because he couldn't imagine a woman like Levee—smart, capable, and every bit as lovable as she was beautiful—settling for a man like him.

That being the case, he figured he'd better give some serious thought to spending more time at church. A lot more time. Maybe if God saw him on his knees at the altar, He'd see fit to bring him back to a state of contentment with his solitary existence.

Because if he couldn't share his life—its ups and downs, his hopes and fears, himself—with Levee, then he didn't want to share it at all.

21

*D*espite the chill wind blowing west toward the Rio Grande, it was stifling inside the church, where nearly a hundred people had gathered to witness the marriage of Matilda Montgomery to Ethan Rourke.

Dan had deliberately arrived late, thinking if he slipped quietly into the last row, he could sneak out unnoticed. If he'd known the ceremony would drag on this long, he would have shown up later still. Running a finger under his collar, he did his best to ignore the sweat beading on his forehead and tracking down his spine. Tried not to wince at Opal Henderson's off-pitch rendition of "Holy God, We Praise Your Name." Tried to tune out the sour notes spewing from the old pipe organ, too.

He focused, instead, on the list of excuses he'd offer up— from tending a mare's skinned shins to figuring out how he'd get the trail ponies ready for the drive—in case anyone asked why he intended to skip the reception at Matilda's house.

Correction: Matilda and Ethan's house.

Pinned between the pew's carved wooden armrest and Mack's beefy arm, Dan chuckled softly, picturing the big Irishman clomping through rooms decorated with velvet and lace, where delicate porcelain figurines and fragile lamps balanced on doily-covered tables. Why, the chair legs were so skinny that he couldn't help but wonder how long the furniture would support the new master of the house.

Without turning his head, Mack whispered out of the corner of his mouth, "What's so all-fired funny?"

Dan shook his head, hoping the gesture would convey his silent "Can't talk about it here and now." He'd never know for certain if the cowboy picked up on the cue, because Fanny Martin chose that moment to faint dead away, falling from her pew into the aisle.

A small crowd of men gathered around her, one fanning her with a program, another patting her chubby, dimpled hand.

Her husband groaned, then said, "I'll need help carrying her out of here."

The crowd couldn't have dispersed more quickly if a skunk had sauntered up to Fanny's inert body.

Mr. Martin looked around, hoping to make eye contact with someone…and failed.

"You up for it?" Dan asked Mack.

"I reckon."

Fanny was beginning to come around by the time they stepped into the aisle. "You take one arm," Dan said, "and I'll get the other." Together, with a little help from Fanny's own efforts, they moved her down the aisle and out onto the front stoop, her husband close at their heels.

"I don't know what came over me!" Fanny exclaimed, plopping herself down on the top step.

"You're not pregnant, are you?" her husband demanded.

"At my age?" she grumbled, waving him off. "Please."

"It's probably just the heat." *Levee.* Dan had been feeling cranky and on edge for days, and the sound of her melodic voice was all it took to dissolve his surly mood.

"Fresh air is good," she added, sitting down next to Fanny on the step. "Some cool water would be even better."

"I'll get it," Mack offered, then leaned closer to Dan and quietly gave him back a piece of his own advice: "You might do well to give some thought to how you'll deliver *your* own marriage proposal."

Dan might have laughed out loud if Levee's big, violet eyes hadn't crinkled with confusion. Had she heard Mack?

"I'm so embarrassed!" Fanny exclaimed. "Landing like a sack of grain in the center aisle of the church, and during Matilda's wedding, no less!" She buried her head in her hands. "I'll never forgive myself for ruining her special day."

"Now, now," Levee said, sliding an arm around the woman's shoulders. "I have a feeling it'll take a lot more than your swooning to ruin her day."

Fanny gave a grateful nod. "I suppose you're right." Brightening a tad, she added, "The dear lady has waited so long for this. Imagine, finding her one true love after all this time!"

"Oh, I know," Levee cooed. "I haven't known her as long as you have, but I've never seen her look happier. And is it any wonder, the way Ethan stole her heart?"

Her one true love. The phrase echoed in Dan's head and sparked a glimmer of hope in his heart. Maybe claiming his slice of that "happy family pie" wasn't an impossibility, after all.

What are you thinking? Get hold of yourself, man! For his foolish thinking, Dan blamed the occasion. The happy banter of the two women seated side by side on the church steps. His too-tight shirt collar.

"Doesn't Matilda look beautiful today?" Levee asked.

"Oh, yes," Fanny gushed. "Beautiful and radiant and, you're so right, happier than I've ever seen her!"

I'll tell you who looks beautiful, he thought. Levee had worn that outfit before—another hand-me-down from a church lady—but there was something different about it today. The pink fabric seemed pinker, somehow, and brought out the rosy glow in her cheeks. And that hair.... In San Antonio, he'd seen plenty of fashionable ladies in mink stoles and beaver capes, but he doubted the pelts were anywhere near as luxuriously soft as that gleaming ebony mane. More than ever, he wanted to run his hands through it, find out for himself if—

"Here's your water," Mack announced, unceremoniously passing the mug to Fanny.

"Why, thank you," Fanny said, gulping down the liquid. "It's been a long time since a handsome man treated me with such chivalry."

Her fluttering lashes and girlish giggle set Mack to back-pedaling so fast that if he'd been wearing spurs, he would have carved up his own calves.

"Good grief," her husband said, slapping a hand to his forehead. "Let's get you back inside, shall we?" He offered his elbow, and Fanny took it.

"I hope they haven't exchanged 'I do's' yet," she said, handing the empty mug to Levee.

The organ thundered the first rib-shaking bars of "What Wondrous Love Is This."

"Oh, for shame!" Fanny whined. "We've missed the best, most romantic part of the ceremony!"

"Good grief," her husband repeated. "Romantic, indeed. Come along, now, Fanny. At least you can offer the bride and groom your best wishes."

As if on cue, Sarah appeared in the doorway. She scanned the tiny group assembled on the steps, then met Mack's eyes. "There you are," she said, smiling. "I thought you'd slipped out to avoid the reception."

Mack, blushing and grinning like a schoolboy, shook his head. "Now, why would I go and do a fool thing like that? I hear-tell Matilda had some special grub shipped in all the way from Abilene."

Now it was just Dan and Levee, alone on the steps. He leaned back against the railing and looked at Levee, who smiled. The breeze picked up, blowing the hair back from her face. It also made the breath catch in his throat. The poetic notions that rolled through his head whenever she was around were foreign and absurd, yet he was powerless to control them. *Must be all those second helpings of rice pudding that awake these sweet feelings and tender thoughts.*

"So, you want to go in and congratulate the happy couple?" Dan didn't want their time alone to end, but he wasn't sure what else to say.

"Matilda asked for my help getting out of her wedding gown and into her party dress," Levee explained, standing beside him. "I'll have plenty of time for that later."

"Plenty of time for that later," he echoed absently.

"She made a very lovely bride, don't you think?"

He crossed both arms over his chest. "Yes, very lovely." *Not as lovely as you—not by a long shot.* Dare he voice his thoughts? He decided to take a chance. "But nowhere near as beautiful as you."

Her cheeks flushed and her shoulders lifted, making her look shy and girlish and exquisitely alluring at the same time.

"Bet you were a vision in your wedding gown," he added.

"I didn't wear one."

"Why not?"

"Because I didn't have a wedding like Matilda's."

What had she meant by 'a wedding like Matilda's'? Didn't every wedding consist of two people in love, a pastor, and vows?

"Liam always said it was a sin to waste money on frivolous things like gowns and veils and flowers and such." She shrugged. "So, we were married in the rector's office, wearing our Sunday best." On the heels of a barely audible sigh, she added, "Afterward, he told me he couldn't be prouder of his plain and prudent bride."

Prudent? Dan could agree with that, because from all he'd seen and heard, Levee had a good head on her shoulders. But plain? He harrumphed. "You didn't tell me that your husband was blind."

"Blind? He wasn't—" When she understood his joke, her laughter danced across the church lawn, reminding him of the pure, round notes of the chimes hanging outside his ma's kitchen window. All too soon, it ended, and he found himself holding his breath again in the hope of hearing the music start up again.

Instead, the chattering voices of parishioners spilled from the church, and he fought disappointment as people filed past them down the stairs and onto the lawn. The only positive thing about the interruption, from his point of view, was that to make room, Levee had turned sideways and pressed close to his side. It seemed the most natural thing in the world to wrap his arms around her to shield her from elbows and shoulders, purses, and Bibles…and, oh, how cold and lonely his arms felt when the last of them passed and he was obligated to let her go!

Reverend Peterson stepped out and stood on the stoop. "Ladies and gentlemen," he announced, "I give you Mr. and Mrs. Ethan Rourke!"

As he moved aside to make room for the newlyweds, Levee grabbed Dan's hand. "Come on!" she said, tugging him along. "Let's make way for the bride and groom!"

He followed her, though he had chores waiting back at the ranch, and in spite of his earlier decision to skip this part of the festivities. Would she expect him to follow her to the reception, too?

The part of his brain that considered such revelry a waste of time and hard-earned dollars agreed with Liam, but his heart held more power over his decision-making abilities. If she asked him to go, he'd say yes in a heartbeat. Especially if she asked while still holding his hand.

He'd follow her to the ends of the earth if he could be sure she'd never let go.

$\mathcal{Y}$ou're a dear to help me out this way," Matilda said as Levee carefully unfastened the dozens of tiny, satin-covered buttons down the back of her wedding gown.

"It's my pleasure," she said, and meant it. She hoped her friend would remember this when she unwrapped her wedding gifts, for it seemed hers needed a supplement. With a paltry teacher's salary that provided barely enough to stock her pantry with the most rudimentary items, and with every extra penny going toward supplies for the school, Levee had very little left with which to buy a proper wedding gift.

She'd quickly discovered that a lack of money inspires creativity. It had taken an entire evening to unravel the knit coverlet one of the church ladies had donated for Levee's bed and another dozen evenings to crochet an afghan that featured the entwined initials of the bride and groom. Later, at the reception, she'd find out how her gift held up among the rest of the presents stacked in Matilda's dining room.

"Why so quiet all of a sudden?" Matilda wanted to know.

Levee couldn't answer directly, not without sounding like one of those pathetic people who will stop at nothing to encourage a compliment. "Just thinking about something I overheard while I was waiting for your wedding ceremony to begin."

"Oh?"

"You and Ethan aren't taking a honeymoon?"

"'Course we are, just not right away. He feels duty-bound to go on the trail drive with the Nevilles. Could be his last—the last for them, too—and he doesn't want to miss it. I think he rather likes being called 'Cookie,' and I know he's proud that he can drive a four-up."

"A four-up?"

"Four mules, pulling the chuck wagon. I tried it once. Got the reins so tangled up, it's a wonder the poor things didn't trample one another!"

Levee traded Matilda's puffy gown for the pale blue walking suit she'd chosen as her reception outfit. "How soon will they leave?"

"Three days, at dawn."

"So soon? How long will they be gone?"

"Hard to say. But even if they don't have swollen rivers or rustlers and only the good Lord knows what else to contend with, I don't expect we'll see them for fifty or sixty days."

Fifty or sixty days? Having finished unbuttoning the gown, Levee began pacing. If the thought of not seeing Dan for two whole months upset her this much, how must poor Matilda feel? "Oh, my goodness, and you, a newlywed! I'm so sorry, Matil—"

The woman grabbed Levee's hands. "Easy, now, honey," she said. "It's fine—really, it is. Ethan and I will have a few days of marital bliss before he and the Neville men head north. To be quite frank, I've never shared my house—or myself, for that matter—with anyone for more than a few hours at a time. And the same is true of Ethan. All that togetherness is likely to take some getting used to, so the temporary separation might be a good thing for us both!" She chuckled. "Besides, once he's home again, we'll have the rest of our lives to spend together."

Matilda kicked off her tall, white boots and exhaled a long sigh. "Will you just listen to that wind!"

"Yes, and the sky over the river looked almost as black as night."

"Well, let's hope the storm holds off, at least until everybody is home safe and sound, *after* the reception."

"The food smells delicious," Levee said. "I can hardly want to sample those fancy finger sandwiches you ordered."

"I'll tell you what I can hardly wait for—seeing those big, strappin' cowboys trying to look brave and bold, munching on the dainty things!" Her laughter bounced off every wall.

Levee giggled as she laid the wedding gown on a bed of crisp white tissue paper. Then, grabbing a match, she lit both lanterns on Matilda's dresser, bathing the room in golden light. "There. Much better," she said.

But Matilda had turned her attention to the billowing black clouds that loomed outside. "Mighty dark out there for one o'clock in the afternoon," she muttered, frowning out the window. Then, turning to Levee, she grinned. "Bet you didn't know what a wonderful cook my new husband is, did you?"

"No, I didn't."

"That man can whip up a tasty, rib-stickin' meal from nothing but flour, bacon, and beans, I tell you! I hope he'll carry on the practice once he's home for good."

"Oh, so he isn't going to stay on at the Lazy N?"

"He would, I suppose, if I hadn't asked him not to." She threw back her head with a vigorous laugh. "I told him that since we have only a decade or so before we're too old and feeble to travel, we should make the most of every day.

All my life, I've wanted to see the world but never had anybody to share the sights and delights with. Now that I have Ethan...."

Matilda's expression grew dreamy. Levee was happy for her friend—and a little envious, too, because she'd never experienced joy like that, not even on her own wedding day. But then, whose fault was that? No one had forced her to choose financial stability over heart-pounding love. What pounded in her heart now was guilt, pure and simple. *Lord, please forgive my self-centeredness!* she quickly prayed.

"I heard a bit of gossip the other day that just might interest you," Matilda said.

Levee had never been one for idle chitchat but hoped the news would get her mind off of self-pity.

"Seems Dan isn't going on the drive."

A flash of joy sparked in her heart. "Because of that stampede a few years back?"

Matilda shook her head. "Last year and the year before, he wasn't healthy enough, physically or mentally, to spend so much time on the trail. So, his uncles put him in charge of buying supplies and hiring extra cowhands, and he delivered both when they met up, north of San Antonio." She paused for a moment. "Don't know why, but this year, they gave that job to Josh, one of his cousins. That's gotta hurt."

Torn between sympathy for Dan and relief that he wasn't going, Levee didn't know how to reply. "I'm sure he's hurt, and disappointed, too," she said carefully.

"Which is exactly why it's good that you'll be here for him."

"Me? What help could I possibly be to—"

"He'll need somebody to lean on, somebody who won't judge him—or his past—and who cares about him."

Oh, Levee cared about him, all right—far more than was healthy for Dan or herself! But what made Matilda think he would come to her for support, or that he'd share his thoughts and feelings?

"If you want my honest opinion, those other invites from his Neville kinsfolk were nothing more than afterthoughts. I expect Dan feels the same way." She shrugged. "But, by golly, when they asked for his help, he gave it without questioning or complaining about it, so I'm at a loss to explain this latest turn of events."

During past visits, Matilda had told her that Dan had made a few mistakes—costly ones that had mostly hurt himself—but he'd righted them all and had lived by a strict "do the right thing" code ever since. "I don't understand. Seems very unfair, doesn't it?" Levee said.

"Well, they've got Mack to help out now, for starters."

It seemed harsh—no, it was downright cruel—to replace one of their own with a near stranger. "What would make them do such a thing? I'm sure Mack is dependable and capable, but Dan—Dan is family!"

As Matilda stood in front of the big, oval mirror, buttoning the jacket of her walking suit, Levee caught sight of her own reflection. Hands on her hips and scowling, she looked like a woman on a mission—and with a score to settle.

"Now do you see why I think you'll be a help to him?"

"No, not really," Levee admitted.

"Just look at you, all riled up and ready to stand against anyone who so much as considers harming Dan!" Matilda nodded approvingly. "I can't decide if you're more sentry than advocate, or the other way around."

A clap of thunder shook the house, startling Levee so badly that a tiny yelp popped from her mouth. For a moment,

Matilda stood stock-still, her eyes wide and unblinking. Then, she bent at the waist, put her hands on her knees, and laughed until tears coursed down her ruddy cheeks. Gasping for breath, she wrapped Levee in a motherly hug. "Oh, Levee, darlin', I'm afraid the job of 'guard' just isn't in your nature!"

Next, lightning sliced the sooty sky, filling the room with bright, white light. This time, even Matilda shuddered. "Let's get downstairs. I'm dying to see how many reception visitors have decided to brave the storm."

"Lots, I expect. Isn't every day the good citizens of Eagle Pass have an opportunity to dine on fancy foods, imported all the way from Abilene!"

But when they got to the first floor, the women saw that only the townsfolk who lived within walking distance remained. In the parlor, Doc Lane and his wife sat chatting with Reverend Peterson, and in the dining room, Mr. and Mrs. Riddle, each balancing a plate of food on an upturned palm, stood talking with Ethan.

Levee looked around and, sadly, didn't see Dan. She made a quick mental list of all the important chores that no doubt had necessitated his return to the Lazy N, but not even logic and common sense could ease her disappointment.

Then, she saw the loving exchange between Ethan and Matilda, and her mood improved.

"There's me beautiful wife," the big Irishman said, crossing the room to greet her at the bottom of the stairs.

Blushing and twittering like a schoolgirl, Matilda accepted his noisy, affectionate kiss.

He took her in his arms to say, "I'm sorry yer party broke up early, m'love. Everyone said to extend their regrets—"

"Oh, it's all right. Really. If they'd stayed, we'd all have been miserable, wondering what sort of bedlam the storm might deliver while they were trapped here."

She'd no sooner spoken the words than the last of the partygoers hurried out the door. Levee might have pitied the bride and groom if they'd looked the least bit disappointed by the empty rooms. Smiling, she decided to give them some privacy in the parlor and made herself useful tidying the dining room and kitchen. At least she had peace of mind knowing Dan was safe at the ranch, seeing to his horses. She hadn't even filled one tray with tumblers and teacups when Ethan said, "Isn't that just the way of nature? Now the sky brightens, after all the guests have left!"

Levee glanced out the nearest window. "Thank the Lord," she said, remembering the frightful thunderstorm that had welcomed Sam and Susan's baby into the world. "I've had enough miserable weather to last me a while!"

Matilda's gritty voice halted their relieved laughter. "I've seen this before, far too many times."

"Seen what, m'darlin' wife?"

Flinging open the front door, she stepped onto the porch. "Smell that?" she asked, sniffing the air. "What time is it?"

Ethan followed her outside and checked his pocket watch. "It's ten minutes past one. But what, exactly, are you smellin', m'dear?"

Levee peeked at the tiny timepiece attached to her necklace. It, too, said ten minutes past one.

"Feel that?" Matilda asked her.

Levee shook her head. "Feel what?"

"Hush. Listen…." She held up one finger. "See how completely still and silent things have become?"

"Still?" Ethan echoed, and in the same moment, Levee said, "Silent?"

Matilda tilted back her head, and, eyes closed, expelled a quiet groan of frustration. "Listen to the pair of you, one from Ireland, one from Boston." She looked at Levee, then at Ethan. "Neither of you has the slightest idea there's a tornado brewing, do you?"

A tornado! The very word struck fear in Levee's veins, thanks to the newspapers. Some articles called them cyclones and detailed the massive destruction left in their wake, while the headlines in others said things like "Twister Destroys Texas Town" before painstakingly listing those who'd died or had gone missing in the whirlwind. Once, during recess at the schoolhouse, she'd heard two of her older students bickering about which would use his "I survived the tornado of '86" tale to complete an essay assignment. The descriptions were so frightening that she forbade either of them from writing about it!

Matilda pointed. "See how the sky has an odd green cast to it?" She sniffed again. "And the air smells a little like a spent match. And see here?" she added, drawing their attention to the gooseflesh on her arm. "There's just something strange and crackly in the air. Any minute now, you'll hear a roar like nothing you've ever heard before." Hands clasped as if in prayer, she looked from Levee to Ethan and back again. "Don't tell me you can't feel that!"

Levee had to agree. The atmosphere definitely had turned eerie and ominous. "What can we do to prepare, to protect ourselves?" she asked, trying not to panic.

Matilda raced back inside and began snapping the curtains shut. "We'll wait it out in the root cellar, that's what."

She handed Levee a lit lantern and a box of kitchen matches, then gave her a gentle shove. "At the end of the hall," she said, "first door on your right. There's a trap door in the closet floor. Pull it up and climb down the ladder. Once you're down there, you'll find another lamp, hanging from the rafters. Take care not to thump your head, now, because the ceiling is low, even for a little slip of a thing like you."

Levee stopped halfway down the hall. "But—but where are you and Ethan going?"

"Ethan will finish closing the shutters on this floor while I get the ones upstairs. Then—"

"Let me help," Levee interrupted her. "We'll get the job done faster with three of us working together."

"No!" Matilda thundered. Then, hiking up her skirts, she started up the steps. "Trust me," she said, "you're more use to us getting things ready in the cellar. Once we're finished here, we'll need to scramble down that ladder, ourselves. We'll be in the biggest hurry of our lives and might get our feet tangled up on a rung or drop a lantern." She hesitated on the landing and glowered down at Levee. "Get moving, girl! We'll be with you in two shakes of a lamb's tail!"

And with that, she disappeared into one of the bedrooms as Levee stared up at the now-empty staircase.

"Better do as she says," Ethan said, grinning as he shut the panels hanging at the parlor windows. "I've yet to see her truly angry, but something tells me she's even fiercer than a tornado when riled."

"You're probably right," she agreed. "Be careful," she said, "and I'll see you in a few minutes."

After making her way down the rickety ladder, Levee held the lantern high and spun in a slow circle, casting light on the back wall, where sagging shelves held jars of fruit and vegetables and tins of lard. As Ethan hurried back and forth above her, the ceiling rained powdery dirt onto Levee's head. *When was the last time someone came down here?* she wondered, cringing and brushing grit from her hair. She put the lamp in the center of the wobbly wooden table and separated four chairs that were stacked together. Her watch now said twelve minutes after one. *Any second now, surely, Matilda and Ethan will come down the—*

The spongy dirt beneath her feet pulsed and throbbed, as if a mighty, furious beast was straining to free itself from the earth's crust. "Oh, Lord! Oh, Lord! Oh, Lord!" she chanted, "Keep them safe! Keep them safe!" Crouching, she hugged her legs to her chest, hid her face in the gap between her knees, and shut her eyes tight. The scream of a thousand nails ripping simultaneously from their boards was trounced by a clamor so deafening that Levee thought she'd die of fright. The only noise in memory that came even close to matching its ferocity was the water's roar at Niagara Falls, where Levee had taken a trip with her grandparents at age ten. But even that paled by comparison.

And then, there was sudden, absolute silence.

She opened her eyes, sputtering and blinking as silt sifted from her lashes to her lips. Shards of light painted the grimy cellar floor—light far too bright to have come from the dim glow of a single lantern.

Levee looked up. "No, it can't be," she whispered, rubbing her eyes.

Slowly, she stood. Why she glanced at her watch again, Levee didn't know, but one peek at the tiny clock made her heart pound harder still. Had the gears stopped, or had it been only three minutes since she'd last checked the time?

The sound of a dog barking in the distance drew her gaze upward once more.

No, her eyes weren't playing tricks on her, after all.

There, where grimy boards had been home to spiders and mice, Levee saw nothing but the blue-gray Texas sky.

*D*an saddled Biscuit the minute he spotted those swirling black clouds in the distance.

Thankfully, his dependable mount knew the way into town as well as he did, because he couldn't pry his gaze from the twister, which bounced through Eagle Pass with a path no more predictable than a child's spinning top. Each time its narrow bottom touched down, wood shards—some as big as wagon seats—swirled in every direction. He couldn't distinguish between the dust kicked up from the road as the cyclone hurtled through the streets and the smoke of fires fanned into flame by its chugging winds.

Quick as a rattler's strike, the tornado leaped high into the sky, dragging with it stones and tumbleweeds and a Stetson or two. It churned and spiraled up there for a full minute, grinding and groaning as if struggling to retain its strength. And then, in a blink, it was gone, like the whiff of a snuffed match.

Dan brought Biscuit to a halt, dismounted, and tethered him to the hitching post outside J. W. Riddle's grocery store. Doc Lane hurried past, medical bag in one hand, shovel in the other. "If I live to be a hundred," he said, "I'll never understand things like this."

Dan thought he knew exactly what the man meant, because it took only a glance to see that the schoolhouse and teacher's cottage had remained untouched, yet right beside them, where Matilda's house had been, nothing but a pile of rubble remained. Beyond that, the church, its steeple catching a ray of sun, stood proud and strong against the backdrop of blue sky.

Mr. Riddle stepped into the doorway of his store, wiping a bloody palm on his apron.

"Are you okay?" Dan asked him.

"Window blew in back there," he answered, tossing a thumb over his shoulder. "Put my hand up to block the little woman from flying glass."

"She's all right?"

"Oh, yeah, yeah. Scared, but otherwise fine."

Dan nodded. "I'm going over to Matilda's."

The grocer stared at the empty lot where, just moments ago, their friend's house had been. "Awful quiet and still over there." He met Dan's gaze. "Why don't you wait, let me get this hand taken care of? No telling what you'll find over there...."

Wait? Was the man daft, or had something hit him in the head? Dan ground his teeth. The last time he'd seen Levee, she'd been with Matilda, a woman he'd known since childhood. "Can you loan me a shovel?"

Mr. Riddle's expression said "Have it your way, then" as he shrugged and then grabbed a spade from the rack on his porch. "Now, don't this just beat all?" he said as Dan took it. "Blasted twister tears an entire house from its foundation, yet leaves this spindly li'l thing right where I put it this mornin'."

Dan started across the street but stopped mid-step. "Don't suppose you've seen Levee."

"The schoolmarm? No, can't say as I have."

Good God in heaven, Dan prayed, *let her be all right.*

"Doesn't appear there's too much damage here in town. Good Lord willing, we'll have just a few buildings to repair and replace once the dust settles."

"Good Lord willing," Dan repeated.

"Take care where you put that shovel, now, hear?" Mr. Riddle called after him.

He kept moving but acknowledged the advice with a wave of his hand.

A moment later, he found himself picking his way through mangled wrought iron and wicker that had furnished Matilda's pride and joy—the veranda, where she loved to sit and rock, watching the comings and goings of Eagle Pass residents. On the other side of the threshold, in her parlor, the blood-red velvet sofas and gold brocade-upholstered chairs looked exactly as they had the last time he'd visited. One wall hosted the curved-front curio, where she housed her collection of porcelain dolls. Across the room was her rolltop desk. To his left was a wall of windows covered by thick curtains, and at his right, the brass pendulum of the grandfather clock still counted out the minutes. Except for the steady ticktock, ticktock, ticktock, not a sound was heard, save for a faint humming.

Craning his neck, Dan followed the sound. He skirted the dining room table, which had been set with china, crystal, and silverware for the wedding guests. There, in the ruins that had been the kitchen, Levee sat on her heels and cradled Matilda's head in her lap as she rocked to and fro, picking wood shards and sawdust from the woman's hair. Tears had carved pink tracks in the grime that coated her cheeks. "It's all right," she chanted, her voice a mere whisper. "It's all right, it's all right…."

His knees went weak at the sight of her. If he'd ever been more thankful to see someone, he couldn't say when. Part of him wanted to sing out with joy because there she was, safe and sound. He shoved aside an upside-down table, hell-bent on getting to her as fast as his bum leg would carry him.

"Please, Dan, be gentle with her things," she said without looking up.

How calm she sounded, how serene she looked, even sur-rounded by the wreckage. Had what she seen driven her mad, or had something thumped her on the head? He got down on one knee beside her, laid a hand on her shoulder, and did his best not to stare at her blood-spattered skirt. At the wedding, he'd noticed how she'd tied up her hair with a pink ribbon that matched her pretty dress. Now, both were a shade of gray, thanks to a layer of grit and grime. "Are you hurt?"

When she shook her head, a curl sprang free from her coiffure. After two failed attempts to shove it back into place, Levee let loose a growl of frustration.

"Let me help." How ironic, he thought, tucking it behind her ear, that after all his dreaming and scheming of ways to touch her beautiful hair, it had finally happened—when the tresses were matted with sweat and tears and dirt. "Are you sure you're all right? There's blood on your apron." He didn't mention the streaks of blood in her hair.

"Yes. Yes, I know. It's Matilda's." Head down and voice low, she said, "You can't see it now, but…." Her tears came faster, and she wiped them away with the back of one hand. "She was im—impaled." A reedy cry squeaked between her trem-bling lips as she pulled back the coverlet draped over Matilda's motionless body.

Like most ranchers, Dan had seen some grisly sights in his day, but nothing that compared to this. "Good God," he muttered, grimacing at the lance-like board that had run clean through his dear friend. "Good God in heaven," he said again, pulling the coverlet back over her.

When Levee found her voice, it was to say, "I heard her, heard her calling from under a mountain of...." She glanced around at the upturned tables and legless chairs, at the fringed curtains, hanging like tattered rags from bent and twisted drapery rods, and at the fragments of shattered glass and mirror, which reflected the mayhem from odd, chaotic angles. "I—I dug her out, tried to stop the bleeding...."

Eyes closed, she shook her head. "But I—I couldn't."

The only time Dan had felt this helpless had been when Daisy had lain dying of hydrophobia and had called for him. Back then, he hadn't been able to think of a single meaningful thing to do or say, either. But he was older and wiser now. Shouldn't he have sense enough to give Levee a scrap of reassurance, at least? "There's no doubt in my mind that you did all you could, and then some," Dan said, giving her shoulder a gentle squeeze.

When Levee looked up at him, he thought he might drown in the sorrow that brimmed in her big, damp eyes. A huge, crystalline droplet clung to her tear-spiked lashes, and when she blinked, it rolled slowly down her cheek. "Have you...?" She swallowed. "Have you seen Ethan?"

Dan swallowed, too, suddenly aware of the pent-up sob aching in his throat. "Where was he last time you saw him?"

"Matilda sent me to the root cellar to light the lamps, and she sent Ethan to close the shutters on the first floor while she closed the ones upstairs."

The story spewed from her quivering lips like water from a geyser.

"I couldn't imagine how we'd all fit down there, small as that root cellar was." She described spider webs and mouse nests and snake skins she'd seen hanging from the rafters. Told him about the rickety table and chairs and jars of food, all coated with what looked like a decade's worth of dust. "I kept checking my watch, wondering why it was taking them so long to come down. If I'd stayed up there and helped them, like I'd offered to, maybe we could have made quicker work of all that time-wasting, stupid, stupid, *stupid* shutter-closing Matilda insisted on doing."

"She did it to keep glass from blasting into the room," Dan explained.

"Well, a fat lot of good it did!" she shouted, looking around her. Then, hands balled into tiny fists, she pounded her thighs with each emphasized word. "I should have *refused* to go to the cellar, should have *insisted* on helping. Instead, I behaved like a silly, obedient child, and—"

"Levee," he said, gently taking hold of her slender wrist, "nothing that happened today was your fault." He didn't think she was ready to hear the truth, as he saw it: If she *hadn't* gone into that root cellar, she'd be dead, too! "Now you listen to me, Levee O'Reilly," he said, giving her hand a little shake. "This isn't your fault!"

But she seemed not to have heard him. In place of a reply, Levee laid her free hand atop his. "Oh, Dan, it just…it all happened so *fast*. One minute, Matilda was describing how it smells and looks just before a tornado hits, and the next…."

And in the next, he finished mentally, *it hit, ripping the house from its foundation.*

Dan got to his feet. "Come with me," he said, extending a hand. "We'll look for Ethan…together."

Levee hesitated, but only for a moment. He watched as she eased ever so gently out from under Matilda's body, then tidied the coverlet, the way a doting mother might do to tuck in her napping child. Scooting back, she sat on her heels for what seemed to Dan a full minute, staring at the woman's bruised and abraded face. Was Levee praying, he wondered, or simply searching her soul for the strength to stand and walk away from her friend?

At last, Levee let him help her to her feet. She reeled, and although she quickly regained her balance, Dan grabbed hold of her elbow anyway.

"I'm all right," she said.

But she wasn't. How could she be, after what she'd just been through? Dan stood there, staring like a simpleton at the small, slender hand that patted his thick, calloused one. He couldn't move, and even though she'd told him she was fine, he couldn't let her go, either. He needed time. Time to console her. Time to wrap his mind around what had happened to Matilda, to her beautiful home. To figure out how he'd talk Levee out of helping him look for Ethan. What if the man was in worse shape than his wife? Levee was a tough, hardy little thing, to be sure. Her pluck and fortitude had seen the town through a ghastly bout of influenza and helped her survive more than her fair share of heartache and misery. But how much more could one human endure?

Dan didn't want to put her to that test. He tightened his hold on her elbow, determined to lead her straight through the mess and outside, into the sunshine, where townsfolk who hadn't been directly affected by the cyclone could get some water into her, help her get cleaned up.

Halfway to the door, he spotted Ethan, who looked more like a heap of rumpled laundry than the big, strapping man he'd been mere hours ago. He turned a tick too late to protect Levee from the heartbreaking sight but just in time to catch her as she crumpled in his arms.

*I*t seemed wrong, somehow, that the weather was so beautiful.

Overhead, the crisp blue sky stood in stark contrast to gauzy black veils and ebony skirts of mourners, and the temperate breeze did little to warm the dour mood set by eleven wooden caskets lined up in a tidy row near the cemetery gates.

Levee stood at the back of the congregation, directly behind the Riddles and the Lanes, twisting her handkerchief as Reverend Peterson led congregants in a doleful rendition of "Holy God, We Praise Your Name." Today, not even the mayor's wife, whose quavering soprano always hovered above altos, tenors, and baritones, sang with her usual verve.

The tornado had spared most of the ranchers—a rare occurrence, from what Levee had heard in town, and those who weren't planting hay or oats for livestock feed were busy preparing for another onerous trail drive. The demands of their jobs explained and excused their absence at the service.

But Matilda had been more family than friend to the Nevilles, so Levee wasn't surprised to see them standing across the way, and as the next hymn began, Dan looked more sad-faced than any of them. But then, Levee happened to know that, over the years, he'd developed a deep and abiding friendship with Matilda.

Levee didn't even bother to mouth the words to "O God, Our Help in Ages Past," for she simply didn't feel that a note of music remained in her soul. Too much suffering. Too much death and dying. First, her brother, parents, and grandparents. Then, Liam. And now Matilda, more a sister to her than a friend.

She'd held her tears in check during the long, awful days while the undertaker had prepared the tornado victims' bodies for burial, but when her fellow parishioners reached the last phrase of the first verse, "…our shelter from the stormy blast, and our eternal home," her tight control on her emotions began to evaporate.

Levee gritted her teeth, knowing that if she hadn't been in that cellar, safe from the cyclone, she'd have joined Matilda, Ethan, and nine others in paradise. "…our shelter from the stormy blast," they sang again, "and our eternal home." If she never heard the word *shelter* again….

She couldn't cry—*wouldn't* cry. Not here, not now, with her innocent young students gathered all around her. At the thought of them, Levee wondered where she'd find the courage to stand at the front of the schoolhouse tomorrow, teaching fractions and conjunctions, as if nothing had happened!

The pastor's voice rang out with a powerful "Amen!" which set off a succession of slapping noises as hymnals were shut.

When he launched into his prayer, saying, "We thank You, Father, for the blessings of family and friends," Levee stared at her shoes. *Why can't preachers just be honest?* she wondered. *No one came here today to celebrate, and who wants to express gratitude to God for the tornado that ended the lives of eleven of our loved ones?*

The reverend continued. "We look to You, Lord, for the peace and understanding we will need today, and in the coming days, for no matter how deep or broad our faith, the loss of our loved ones cuts deep. It hurts. We miss them. We grieve that they were taken from us so quickly and so cruelly."

Levee looked up into the tear-filled eyes of Reverend Peterson and gave her handkerchief another wring. Maybe he knew how to be honest, after all.

"Look around you, dear friends, at the people who have gathered here today to share your loss. In them, you will find strength. With them, you will find the courage to continue. Because of them, you'll find the love required to encourage one another, and this is a beautiful thing to behold!

"God provides healing, but we cannot know how quickly He will administer the balm of His mercy. Let us boldly come unto the throne of grace, that we may find grace in time of need. There is nothing wrong with mourning, dear friends. I could cite dozens of passages from His Word that teach us about death. Remember what Samuel said? *'There is but a step between me and death.'*"

How true, Levee thought, remembering how close she'd come—two times in less than a year—to meeting her Maker face-to-face.

"We hate facing death, for we know that when we die, there will be judgment. It is that fear which overshadows our grief— the fear that our loved ones did not know Him and therefore may not be joined with Him in heaven. And so we must trust, friends, that each and every one of them did know Christ our Lord and is happy with Him now and for all of eternity!"

Whispers of "Amen!" and "Praise the Lord!" rippled through the congregation.

"We come humbly to You, o Lord," the reverend contin- ued, "and ask that You mend our broken hearts and bind up our broken spirits. Come to us now in Your mercy, dear God, and dry our tears as we stand sad and silent beside these open graves. We entrust the bodies of our loved ones into Your loving hands, just as we entrust their spirits into Your keeping."

One by one, the coffins were lowered into the ground, and then, one by one, the good people of Eagle Pass filed by to toss a handful of Texas earth onto the closed caskets.

"Deal with us mercifully, o God, our almighty Father, and keep us in Your grace and glory until we, too, come to our final resting place. Oh, dear friends, let us not be lonely or sorrowful for long. Let us instead remember that He is here with us and calls us to find our refuge in Him."

Levee waited for the stirring "Amen" that would conclude the service. Instead, a powerful hush fell over the graveyard as every head bowed, all hands folded, and the worshippers filed slowly and silently toward the church, where a hearty meal of eggs and flapjacks awaited them in the basement. She had decided earlier not to attend the breakfast, because she couldn't bear to listen to the "Remember when…" and "I'll never forget…" stories about the dead. Instead, she'd decided to hide in her little cottage, put pen to paper in her diary—it had been months since she'd written in it—and sit for a spell with her Bible in her lap.

Sit for a spell, she thought, smiling faintly. The Boston accent that had been the butt of many good-natured jibes when she'd arrived in Eagle Pass had all but disappeared, replaced by witticisms and adages preferred by the locals. But what was she saying? She was a local now, too, a fact happily confirmed by every greeting of "Howdy, Levee!" and "Hello, Mrs. O'Reilly!" wherever she went.

As she made her way down the center of Main Street, Levee smiled and waved at the people she passed. No one asked why she seemed in such an all-fired rush to get away from the church—something else to be thankful for. *Maybe you should have attended the breakfast*, she thought as she neared her cottage, *to forestall the inevitable*.... Walking up the curvy flagstone path that led from the road to her house required her to pass Matilda's house—rather, what used to be Matilda's house. The men of Eagle Pass had held a meeting the day before yesterday and voted to start cleanup on the property the day after tomorrow. Well, tomorrow couldn't get here fast enough for Levee, because the sodden heaps of wood and once-plush carpets and the remnants of what had once been the finest hand-carved furnishings ever delivered to Eagle Pass acted as a constant reminder of the tornado's wrath.

She walked quickly, head down and eyes on the toes of her boots, deliberately averting her gaze from the part of the house where she'd found Matilda, and where she and Dan had spotted poor Ethan. If anyone had told her a cowboy could pray like that, she might have said, "Impossible!" But there, amid mounds of wood fragments, brightly fringed shawls, and Sunday-go-to-meeting hats, he had hunkered down, reached out with a trembling hand to coax the Irishman's eyelids closed, and prayed with a quivering voice, "Dear God, we pray that Ethan died easy and fast, and that he didn't suffer a moment's pain before You took him home." So much for Matilda's theory that Dan had parted ways with God....

"Levee! Levee, wait up!"

She turned toward the animated voice and returned the happy smile of Dan's cousin-in-law. Of all his relatives, Levee had a soft spot for Kate. The young woman had put her own life on the line to save Josh, and in so doing, had put a stop to the ruthless rampages of the infamous outlaw, Frank Michaels. "Kate," Levee said as the pretty blonde approached.

Kate stopped not two feet from where Levee stood on the path. "I'd say it's good to see you, but with everything that's happened, it seems a tad inappropriate."

"Not at all," Levee said, hugging her. "It's a horrible reason that brings you to town, but I'm happy to see you, all the same." She faced the cottage. "I was just about to put a kettle on for tea. Would you care to join me, or were you headed to the church for breakfast?"

Laying a hand on her slightly rounded tummy, Kate groaned. "Please. The smells of bacon and sausage and greasy potatoes turn my stomach these days." Laughing, she linked her arm with Levee's. "A cup of tea sounds delightful. Besides, it'll give us a chance to catch up. It's been months since we've talked!"

Inside, while Levee filled the teapot with water, Kate took two cups and saucers from the shelf above the stove. "So, tell me," she said, arranging them on the tiny table near the window, "where have you been hiding these days?"

"I haven't been hiding," Levee replied. "I've just been busy, is all." She reached into the icebox, removed the tiny pitcher of milk, and held it aloft.

"None for me, thanks, but please, help yourself," Kate said.

As Levee put it back and latched the icebox door, Kate added, "Something else we have in common! I prefer mine black, too."

"Something else?"

"We both seem to have a fondness for Neville men," Kate said with a wink.

"Heavens. Does it show that much?"

"No, no, of course not. At least, not to the untrained eye."

Levee was far more concerned about Kate's physical condition than the way either of them felt about the cowboy cousins. When she'd first seen her friend on the path, she had blamed the bright sunshine for the waxy pallor to Kate's usually pink-cheeked complexion. "So, Kate," she said, joining her at the table, "have you been feeling all right?"

The merest hint of a frown etched her brow. "Oh, I hear it's perfectly normal to feel this way."

Levee pretended to concentrate on adding sugar to the tea leaves and steaming water in her cup. "And what way is that?"

A short burst of nervous laughter preceded Kate's answer. "Well, I can barely hold down a meal. I'm dizzy all the time. And I do believe I could sleep for a week straight and still wake up feeling dog-tired!" She sipped her tea. "That *is* typical, isn't it?" she said, looking serious again.

Weariness was, indeed, a common symptom. The rest of it, though, filled Levee with concern, but she kept her fears to herself. The last thing the poor girl needed was something else to worry about. "Yes, for some women, fatigue is a routine part of pregnancy." She gave Kate's hand an affectionate pat. "Your body is going through some miraculous changes, and that baby of yours will, by nature, take what he needs and leave whatever is left for you." Levee sat back and took a sip from her cup. "Remind me," she said, placing the cup in the saucer, "when do you expect this little bundle of joy to arrive?"

"Doc Lane says I might have my baby by Mothering Sunday."

Levee tried to calculate the weeks remaining in Kate's term. "Mathematics was never my best subject," she said, grinning, "so I'll just have to guess that you have almost two months before your big day?"

"Pretty close for not being good at arithmetic! But I'm surprised to hear you aren't gifted with numbers. I thought nurses and doctors were born ciphering!"

"I hope I can trust you with my little secret, because if my students get wind of my inadequacies, I'll never live them down."

"Don't worry. Your secret's safe with me."

"So, did Doc Lane tell you what to expect? When your time comes, I mean."

"No, but Lucinda and Eva and Susan did, and I don't mind telling you, they scared me out of my wits!"

Levee clicked her tongue. "I wish I understood why women seem to delight in terrifying one another half to death. Having a baby is one of the most natural and normal functions a woman can experience. Trust me, when it's over, you'll forget all about the little bit of pain that goes along with labor and delivery."

"I don't suppose you could be there, could you, like you were for Susan? She told me if it weren't for you, she might have died of pure, unadulterated fright."

Levee remembered all too well the ordeal that Susan Rogers had survived. Hopefully, she hadn't shared too many of those details with Kate. "I don't know if you're aware," Levee began carefully, "but before my husband's death, I had two miscarriages—the first when I was just two months into the pregnancy, and the second"—she couldn't very well say that she'd been about as far along as Kate was now, not without adding to the poor girl's fears—"when I was about halfway to my due date."

"Oh, Levee," Kate said, patting her hand. "No, I hadn't heard, and I'm so sorry."

"Ancient history," Levee said dismissively.

"What was it like? I mean, if it doesn't pain you too much to talk about it."

Levee had been hoping Kate would ask, to spare her the effort of devising a subtle way to bring up the warning signs of a miscarriage. "The first time, I noticed a dull ache in the small of my back, and then some bleeding—a pinkish-grey color instead of red. That went on for a few days before, well, you know."

Kate nodded sympathetically. "And the second time?"

"That time, I had a fever and felt nauseous, and the pain was in my abdomen rather than my pelvis." *Goodness, Levee! Don't sound so cold and clinical, or you'll be the one to terrify her!* "Please bear with me," she said, laughing. "It isn't often I get to practice all the terms I learned in nursing school!"

Now that Kate knew what to be wary of, Levee could breathe a sigh of relief. "And to answer your question, I'd love to be with you when the time comes. When Josh rides into town to drag Doc Lane back to the ranch, tell him to fetch me, too."

"Oh, Levee, you have no idea how that comforts me!"

"Well, just keep in mind that for all we know, your baby has plans to come right out, just like a popover from a muffin tin. You might not need any help at all!"

Kate refilled their teacups, and, for the next thirty minutes, the women spoke only of happy, hopeful things, like the nursery Kate had been preparing, the Nevilles' annual Fourth of July pig roast, and whether or not Mack and Sarah would marry when he returned from the trail drive.

When the carriage clock struck two, Kate stood. "Josh will think I've fallen asleep in the wagon again," she said, carrying her cup to the sink. "Won't you come with me to the breakfast?" Winking, she added, "You know better than I do that the whole town expects the schoolmarm to show up at such functions. If you don't go, they might think you've run off with that sleazy snake-oil salesman who passed through town yesterday!"

"Goodness, we can't have them thinking that!" Levee agreed. "All right, I'll join you, but I'm staying only a little while." She feigned exhaustion by holding her hand to her forehead. "Pregnant women aren't the only ones who get tired, you know!"

Arm in arm, they giggled and chattered all the way from the cottage to the church, and Levee barely noticed the rubble that had been Matilda's house when they walked past. Reverend Peterson had been right, she decided, for she had found respite from her grief in her friendship with Kate. She didn't think it possible to feel more content until she saw Dan, leaning against the railing of the front porch of the church, exactly as he had on the morning of Matilda's wedding. Oh, how handsome he looked in his neat black trousers and starched white shirt. The roguish tilt of his hat only added to his appeal, but it was that slanting grin aimed right at her that made her heart thump wildly against her ribs.

"Oh, my! Would you look at that?" Kate whispered.

In all honesty, Levee hadn't seen anything else since spotting Dan. "Look at what?"

"Why, Dan, of course! He's got it bad, I tell you. Real bad."

Her heart nearly stopped and her mouth went dry. "Wh-what?" she stammered. "What does he have? I—I had no idea! How long has he been sick?"

The young woman's laughter bounced off every storefront on Main Street. "He isn't sick, you silly goose!" She gave Levee a sideways hug. "The man is as healthy as a horse, except maybe for a raging case of heartsickness. And you, m'dear, are the one who infected him!"

Levee didn't seem capable of tearing her gaze from his. Feeling giddy and girlish, she grinned. *From your lips to God's ears*, she thought as the heat of a blush crept into her cheeks.

25

*D*an hadn't seen Levee since the day of the funeral service, and he'd spent the days that followed wishing he'd at least made a short appearance at the breakfast, where he might have had a moment to tell her how sorry he was that she'd lost her dear friend. He'd lost a good friend in Matilda, too, of course, but something told him it was very different for him, because his family overflowed with loving women, from his ma and sisters to his aunts and cousins, while neither Matilda nor Levee had been blessed by such warm family ties. He figured it was only natural that they'd so quickly bonded, one to the other.

Besides, a dozen chores had lured him back to the ranch—tasks that, no matter how demanding, still left him feeling addle-brained, as not one of them managed to distract him from the way she'd looked, standing across the way.

She'd hidden her hair under a wide-brimmed hat, and although her face had been concealed by black netting, he had a pretty good idea what he'd see if she lifted it: Big, purplish-blue eyes brimming with tears, just as they'd been when he'd found her leaning over Matilda's lifeless body.

It had been a blessing that she'd fainted in his arms, because after delivering her into the care of Doc Lane, he'd gone straight to work, helping dig through the rubble in search of mothers and fathers and children missing since the tornado. Knowing Levee, she'd have been smack in the middle of it, skirts tucked into her waistband and sleeves rolled up, clawing through the mud and the muck right alongside the able-bodied men of Eagle Pass. Each time they uncovered another body, Dan had found himself saying a prayer of thanks that Levee wasn't there to witness it.

But one victim in particular had made him especially grateful that she'd lost consciousness. After the Christmas pageant he'd overheard Levee talking with the Boones. *"Tim is so smart and capable,"* she'd told them, *"and there's just no limit to what he might accomplish if he stays in school!"* Whether the notion that their boy could become a doctor, lawyer, or teacher had convinced them that he was better off attending classes than helping out on their humble farm, Dan couldn't say, but he remembered thanking God that he wasn't Tim's pa, because between Levee's lovely expression and animated gestures, she probably could have talked him into giving away his share of the Lazy N, lock, stock, and barrel!

At the graveside service, it hadn't escaped his notice that she'd positioned herself halfway between Matilda's casket and Tim's. He'd thought about shouldering his way past the other mourners so that he could wrap her in a comforting hug. But the way she'd stood, so still and straight-backed, had told him Levee wanted—no, needed—those moments all to herself.

Thankfully, Dan would see plenty of her today, because Josh had sprinted into the barn, red-faced and breathless, to beg him to ride into town to fetch Doc Lane. "Kate made a point of saying you should bring Levee, if you can find her."

According to the calendar, it was too early for Kate's baby to come. Way too early. Evidently, the child would take after his daddy, with a mind of his own and a timetable that didn't take anyone else into consideration. Dan's plan had been to hunt down the good doctor, who hopefully was not occupied with another family emergency, and send him to the ranch in his own buggy.

As it turned out, Doc Lane had been at the McAllister farm since dawn. Fortunately, Dan found Levee at home. He knew, even as he parked the wagon alongside the road, that he'd find her out back, where Bashful yipped happily to every word spoken by his mistress.

It seemed that every time he approached her, he startled the poor girl. *Seemed?* Why, he couldn't think of one occasion when his sudden appearance hadn't scared her! "Levee," he called softly as he made his way toward the cottage. "Levee, it's Dan Neville...."

She peeked around the corner of the little house, smiling and waving. "Well, hello," she said. "What brings you to town on a Saturday?"

"Josh sent me, and—"

Instantly, her smile vanished. "Oh, dear. Oh, my. Just let me put Bashful inside and grab my medical bag. I'll meet you out front in two minutes."

She was gone before he could say a word, and, as he made his way back to the wagon, he marveled that Levee knew without his having to tell her why she was being summoned to the Lazy N. *For a li'l gal who rarely goes more than half a mile from her house, she sure is in tune with the goings-on in town.* He didn't have time to puzzle out the how or the why, because she ran out to the wagon in less than the estimated time.

He took her bag and put in on the floor under the wagon seat, then hoisted her up before climbing up, himself. The instant Dan took up the reins and released the brake stick, Levee scooted closer. "What time did her labor start?" she asked. "Was there much blood? How long has she been experiencing pain? I told her just the other day that—"

"Easy," he said, steering the wagon into the traffic. "I never saw her. Josh ran into the barn, face red as a beet, and breathing like he'd just run a country mile. Asked me to fetch Doc Lane, and said Kate made a point of asking for you, too." He shrugged. "So, here I am."

She turned in the seat as they passed the doctor's house. "But aren't you going to—"

"He's out at the McAllister place. His missus didn't go into details, and, frankly, I didn't see much point in pressing her for more information."

"Oh, dear," she said again. "Oh, my."

"I'm sure it isn't serious. And even if it is, Doc's an old hand at tending—"

"It isn't that," she interrupted him. "Of course, he can handle whatever happened out there. It's just...."

He thumbed his Stetson to the back of his head. "Just what?"

Levee's shoulders slumped. "Well, the whole thing with Susan's baby, for starters. I don't know how much longer my luck can hold out, performing all these 'doctoring tasks.' I'm just a lowly nurse, you know?"

"First of all, when it comes to describing anything about you, the word 'just,' well, it *just* doesn't belong in the sentence."

She grinned and patted his knee. "Flatterer."

The gesture seemed so innocent. So friendly. And yet, so very warm and intimate. And wifely. He'd seen his mother pat his pa's knee that way. If he hadn't needed both hands to control the team, Dan might have given hers a gentle squeeze. *Might have?* Dan harrumphed. No question about it: he would have taken that little hand in his, and no telling when he might have turned it loose!

"I sense a 'second' is on its way."

Dan had almost forgotten the other point he'd wanted to make. "Oh. You're right." He chuckled again. "Second, where's your faith? Luck didn't have a thing to do with what you did for Susan and her baby girl. Your instincts were sound. It's as simple as that."

"Everything I did that day—that night, to be more accurate—was an answer to prayer. God directed me every step of the way. If I deserve any credit at all, it's for having the good sense to ask for His guidance."

"You're something else, Levee O'Reilly."

If Levee heard his sideways compliment, she gave no sign of it, for she was too busy digging in her medical bag, whispering the name of every item inside, then thanking the Lord for reminding her to sterilize each tool and replenish rolls of gauze used on the night little Beth Rogers had been born.

Once they arrived at the Lazy N, Levee wasted no time in hopping down from the buckboard and rushing into the house. In the minutes it took Dan to unhitch the team, stow the wagon, and hobble up the walk, she'd painted her special brand of serenity everywhere, except for the bleary-eyed face of the worried father-to-be, who greeted Dan on the front porch with a steaming mug in each hand.

"Care for some coffee?" Josh asked, handing Dan a mug. "Careful, it's strong."

Dan thanked him with an expectant look. "Well?"

"Levee says the baby will be here in a matter of hours, and things will be fine, just fine." Josh dropped heavily onto the seat of a tall-backed rocker. "But how's that possible when the little guy is almost two months early?"

Dan sat down beside his distraught cousin. "If Levee says it, you can believe it. Surely, I don't need to remind you how she handled things when Susan's baby came breech…."

Josh nodded and ran a trembling hand through his tousled blond locks. "Yeah, I reckon."

The cousins rocked in companionable silence, sipping their coffee and staring at the horizon, where the cows Josh would soon take to Wichita grazed contentedly. He got up and started pacing the length of the porch. After about five minutes, he stopped in front of Dan's chair. "I can't go to Kansas."

"What? You've got to be joking! George has never led a cattle drive, and Mack sure isn't ready to handle a herd," Dan said, more to himself than to his cousin.

His cousin smiled. "That leaves just one person to do it."

Dan expected Josh to suggest one of their fathers, who'd deliberately stepped back from driving to give their sons more experience and allow them more control in running the ranch.

Instead, Josh pointed at him and said, "You."

"Me? Now I *know* you're joking! I haven't been on a drive since I got sucked into that stampede. There's not a chance in—"

"Every man on the ranch knows you can handle it with both hands tied behind your back. Besides, you've used that bum leg of yours as an excuse long enough." Josh paused a moment, then added, "You're ready. I know it, and our pas know it, but, more important, so do you."

Dan had been in attendance at every meeting regarding the drive; however, knowing his participation would be limited, he'd paid very little attention and knew next to nothing about the plan. He would have pointed that out, but Josh beat him to it.

"Our pas can hire extra hands, and Mack will do just fine, rounding up supplies."

"What about the chuck wagon? Who'll do the cooking and tend to the injuries, now that Ethan's—"

"Oh, let me do it!"

Both men faced the door and saw Levee, wiping her hands on a big white towel. "And you thought *I* was joking," Josh said, grinning at Dan.

"What's so funny?" Levee asked, narrowing her eyes.

"You are," Josh said. "God bless your spunk, Levee O'Reilly, but a trail drive is no place for a woman. 'Specially not one who's no bigger than a minute."

She took a step closer and draped the towel over one shoulder. "And why not?" she demanded, hands on her hips.

"If I wrote up a list, it would be as long as you are tall!" Josh said.

"Isn't easy driving a four-up," Dan said, hoping to soften things for her.

"Bet she doesn't even know what a four-up is."

"I most certainly do," Levee insisted. "And, by the way, Joshua 'Know-It-All' Neville, you might be interested to know that your wife just gave birth to a healthy baby boy."

Eyes wide, Josh said, "A—a boy?" He started for the door. "I can't believe it! The baby's here already? He's all right, isn't he? I mean, he's way ahead of schedule!"

"He's tiny, very tiny, but his heartbeats are regular, and that's a good sign. A really good sign."

"Can I—can I see them?"

"Of course, but Kate is plumb tuckered out, so don't stay too long." Her smiled dimmed when she placed a hand on Josh's forearm. "Don't let on when you see her, but the baby isn't out of the woods just yet."

She didn't need to say more, for the potentially grim prognosis was written all over her face. "Doc Lane will have the final say on that, of course. As soon as I see him, I'll give him a detailed report. I'm sure he'll come out here and see Kate and the baby for himself."

Nodding, Josh put one boot on the threshold, but Levee's voice stalled him. "I can bake and cook with the best of them, and Matilda taught me to handle a four-up, and how to shoot, too. And, don't forget, I have a nursing degree."

He stood in the doorway, slack-jawed and wide-eyed, for all of a second, then met Dan's gaze and lifted both shoulders. "I'll leave it to you to talk sense into her, since you're running the drive." And with that, he left them alone on the porch.

"How soon before you're ready to head back to town?" Dan asked her.

"As soon as Doc Lane gets here, I'll be free as a bird."

"Then get to flappin', li'l bird, 'cause here he comes now."

Once Levee brought the doctor up-to-date, she turned to Dan. "I'll just be a minute. I need to fetch my bag and take one last peek at Kate and the baby."

"I'll bring the wagon around, then, and meet you here in...."

But she was gone before he could finish his sentence. Dan pocketed both hands and headed for the barn, grinning all the way, because something told him that this ride from the ranch to Eagle Pass would be one for his memory book.

*L*evee decided that it would be best to ease her way into the subject of going along for the trail drive, but it wasn't easy finding topics to redirect Dan's attention. The moment she'd overheard Josh saying that he couldn't make the trip, it had seemed like the answer to a dozen prayers. She couldn't think of a time when she'd needed a diversion more. Besides, what better way to find out if her feelings for Dan were genuine, or if she'd been behaving like a starry-eyed schoolgirl with a crush on the cute boy in class?

"I heard in town that Matilda was the richest woman in these parts," she said, opening yet another item for discussion.

"She was well off, that much is true."

"But with no husband, how'd she come by all her wealth?"

He cast her a quick sideways glance. "I would have thought she told you all that, considering how much time the two of you spent together."

He had a good point. "It wasn't something I thought to ask," she admitted, "and a proper lady surely wouldn't volunteer such information."

Shrugging, he looked forward again. "Way the story goes," he began, "her daddy owned half the State of Maine, made his fortune selling lumber to England and Ireland and other countries where wood wasn't plentiful. After he died, her mama pined away and left the keys of the kingdom to Matilda and her brother, who took his share of the estate and went to Alaska."

"So, it's his son who's the Pinkerton?"

He shot her another wary glance. "You know about him, too?"

"I didn't realize it was a secret. His being a detective, that is."

Dan looked thoughtful for a moment, then said, "I don't suppose it is."

No doubt his apprehension was rooted in the fact that he'd hired Matilda's nephew to dig up information about Mack. Levee decided to keep what she knew about that to herself, at least until he agreed to let her go with him to Kansas.

"Is it true you can shoot?"

Nodding, she grinned. "Matilda is a very good, very patient teacher."

"Speaking of teachers, who'd teach your students if you were to go to Wichita?"

If? Did that mean what she hoped it meant? "Your mother told me just the other day that she has begun to miss her old job, especially now that her leg is healed. She says she's bored to tears with mending socks, and that your father threatened to burn her needles if she crochets even one more doily."

Dan harrumphed.

"What?"

"Oh, just marveling at your ability to worm secrets out of people, even the most tight-lipped of individuals."

"I've never thought of your mother as tight-lipped."

He shrugged again. "Well, she never told me she wanted to go back to teaching."

Point taken. But, were his feelings hurt because Judith had shared information with her before discussing it with her son, or was he insinuating that she was nosy? "Can I help it if I'm curious? My grandfather used to say that I should get a job writing for the newspapers." Laughing, she added, "Trouble is, I can't write a concise sentence to save my soul. My style is too poetic for the papers."

She could tell, even in profile, that he was smiling. *Good.* Levee needed him in a happy mood to convince him she had what it took to make the drive.

"You realize, don't you, that even an easy trail drive lasts six, maybe eight, weeks?"

"Oh, yes. Matilda told me all about the ones she went on in her youth. She said that it was dirty and hot and so dusty, you sometimes couldn't see your own hand in front of your face. That when it rained, there was no place to go to get in out of the weather. And that it was dangerous, too, what with snakes and flooded rivers and—"

"Matilda was twice your size, Levee."

"She stood taller, maybe outweighed me by a few pounds, but she was hardly double my size."

"How tall *are* you?"

"Five foot one."

"Standing on tiptoe, maybe."

"I don't have much cause to measure myself."

"And if you had to guess, what would you say you weigh?"

"I have no idea." And it was true. "Don't have much cause to—"

"I'd say a hundred pounds, soaking wet."

Another giggle, and then, "Please. How could you possibly know a thing like—"

"Because I lifted you into the wagon today, remember? I've lifted sacks of grain and bales of hay that weigh a lot more than you do."

"Don't know how I feel being compared to sacks of grain and bales of hay."

"Can you ride? Can you saddle a horse? Can you replace a thrown shoe?"

"Yes, I can ride, and, yes, I can saddle a horse." Levee tidied the folds of her skirt, then froze. Would he see the gesture as too delicate, too feminine, for someone hoping to sign on for a trail drive? "And I thought shoeing was the cowboys' job."

Dan steered the wagon to the roadside, brought the team to a halt, and wrapped the reins around the brake stick.

"Why are we stopping?"

"So you can prove to me you can handle a gun." He jumped down, then walked around to her side of the wagon and extended both arms.

"Oh, no, you don't, mister," she said, grinning. "I aim to prove more than that, starting with getting myself into and out of wagons." She joined him beside the wagon and held out her hand. "Give me that peashooter, cowboy."

He unholstered his six-shooter. "Careful," he said, putting the grip into her palm. "It's got a hair trigger."

"Pick a target," she said, narrowing both eyes.

Dan scanned the area. "See that cactus blossom over there?"

Levee nodded.

"Take off one of the petals."

Matilda, she mused, *if you're not busy telling stories to the angels, I could use a little help right about now.* She tossed her bonnet to the ground and stood, feet shoulder-width apart, and pulled the hammer back. Then, raising both arms to shoulder height, she took a breath, held it, and closed one eye.

Dan hadn't been kidding. The revolver did have a hair trigger, which made firing round after round much easier than anticipated. When all six chambers were empty, she turned the gun around and handed it to him, grip first. "Satisfied?"

"We'll see," he said, reloading the weapon as he walked over to the cactus. All the way back, he shook his head and reholstered the gun. "Clean up your brass, missy," he said, then strode toward the wagon.

She retrieved the still-warm spent shell casings, then joined him on the wagon bench. "What do you want me to do with them?"

He shot her a wry smile. "Don't tell me Matilda didn't teach you that, too."

She ignored his gentle teasing. *Better get used to it*, she warned herself, because there was bound to be a lot more of the same if he let her accompany him on the drive—and not just from Dan, either.

He waited for her to get settled, then handed her the reins. "The road's good and straight for a couple of miles. Let's see what you've got."

Levee handed off the spent shells, and as Dan dropped them into his shirt pocket, he said, "Can't expect a girl from Boston to have learned everything about living in Texas in just a few months." He patted the pocket and set the brass to jingling like loose coins. "When we get to Eagle Pass, I'll give them to Mr. Riddle. He'll refill 'em and resell 'em. Lots cheaper than brand-new bullets."

Levee frowned and wrapped the leather straps around her hands, just as Matilda had shown her. "But what if he puts in too much gunpowder? Or not enough?"

"Don't rightly know," he said. "Hasn't happened. Yet."

She signaled the team forward with a quiet clicking sound, and they rode along in comfortable silence for half a mile or so.

"Can I ask you a question?" Dan asked.

"I can't promise you'll get an answer that'll satisfy you, but fire away!"

"How does a gal no bigger than a ladybug saddle a horse that's twice as tall as she is?"

She felt her cheeks go hot with the beginnings of a blush. "I hate to admit it, but…." *Lord, please don't let this give him the grounds to say no.* Levee cleared her throat. "I stand on a crate. Or a fence rail. Or lead the horse to a hill, and—"

"Funny, but I've never seen you ride." One eyebrow inched higher on his forehead. "You sure you know how?"

From the corner of her eyes, she saw that he'd furrowed his brow. "Yes, but I won't take offense if you decide to put me to that test, too."

A second, perhaps two, ticked by before Dan let loose a rip-roaring round of laughter, startling a jackrabbit that had been hiding in the brush. While she watched it dash left, right, and then into another thicket, he added, "I've said it before, but it bears repeating." He looked right at her to say, "You're something else, Levee O'Reilly."

Had she convinced him to take her on the trail drive, or did it just seem that way because of his good mood?

"Can I ask you another question?" he asked.

She was almost afraid to say, "I suppose."

"Why would a beautiful young city girl want to go on a drive in the first place?"

It was a good question, one Levee didn't quite know how to answer, because she wasn't at all sure she understood the reasons, herself.

"If you think the drive will distract you from everything you've lost, well, you've got that right." He grabbed her hands and helped her pulled back on the reins, slowing the horses' pace. "But those things will distract you from the trail, too." Dan patted his bum leg. "I learned the hard way that you can't hide from heartache."

If he thought that would talk her out of it, he was sadly mistaken! Feeling more confident than she had since the subject first came up, Levee began citing additional reasons why it made sense for her to go. "You have my word that you won't need to spend a minute seeing to my needs. You know from personal experience that I can cook, and you've seen me shoot and drive a—"

"You're controlling two well-trained horses, here. Four big oxen will be out in front of the chuck wagon, and they're nowhere near as easy to control as these mares. When we stop for the day, it's the cook's job to tie 'em up, feed 'em, check their legs and hooves for—"

"I'm stronger than I look, Dan," she interrupted him. "I won't need help carrying sacks of flour or cornmeal or stacks of iron pans, and I won't need help with the team, either." If only Levee felt as certain of that as she'd made it sound! "I'm not afraid of hard work, and I'm deft with my hands. I'm a fast learner, too, so what I don't know, I'll pick up quickly. I'm not scared of bugs or snakes, though I'll admit that scorpions make me squirm, and, after that tornado, I can't imagine being rattled by anything else Mother Nature might throw at us. And," she added, pointing a forefinger in the air, "I'm a trained nurse. If anybody gets hurt, who better to have along to tend their injuries?"

Dan wrapped a gloved hand around her finger and gave it a gentle squeeze. "Didn't your mama teach you it isn't polite to point?"

"Yes, she did," she admitted, her heart skipping a beat. "Sorry."

Another moment of agreeable silence passed before he said, "What about your dog?"

Goodness. Now *there* was something she hadn't considered. "You don't have a herd dog. Maybe I can bring him along to—"

"That pup has a lot of good traits, but a cattle dog, he ain't, despite what my pa once thought."

"How do you know without testing him? Doesn't he deserve the same chance you gave me?"

"Levee, Levee, Levee," he said, sounding more like a patronizing parent than a potential boss. "That mutt is afraid of his own shadow. Isn't that why you gave him that name?"

As much as Levee hated to admit it, Dan was right. And the last thing she wanted was for her sweet, fuzzy companion to be trampled or to cause a panic and start a stampede. "Well," she said tentatively, "Doc Lane has always seemed fond of Bashful. Maybe I can talk him into keeping him while we're gone."

Dan aimed a skeptical glance her way. "And if, God forbid, you die out there? What'll become of him then?"

"Well," she said on the heels of a tiny gasp, "aren't you just the master of subtlety?"

He slapped his leg again, the second reminder in as many minutes. "Bad things happen out there." He shook his head. "I dunno, Levee. You've already been through so much—losing your folks, then your grandparents and your husband, and then Matilda." With another shake of his head, he added, "How much more can a li'l slip of a thing like you take?"

It seemed to Levee he'd given the matter an awful lot of thought. But how could that be, when she'd made the decision to join the trail drive only an hour ago? "I'll tell you what," she said carefully. "With everything else you'll have on your mind, how about if you let me worry about that?"

"All right."

All right? *All right?* "Does that mean—? Are you saying—?" She heard herself giggle. "I can go?"

"Something tells me I couldn't stop you if I tried." A moment ticked by before he groaned softly. "I just hope all the way to heaven and back that I won't be sorry."

That could have meant any one of a dozen things, and Levee had no intention of asking what those things might be. "So, what does this job pay, if you don't mind my asking?"

"Fifty dollars a month, same as the cowhands."

"Really? I'd think they'd earn more, since their jobs are more difficult and more dangerous. And since they've all done the work before—"

"Trust me," he said dryly, "you'll earn every dollar, and then some."

She ignored the implied warning and concentrated instead on trying to figure out what in heaven's name was wrong with her. The very idea of driving a wagon into strange territory, cooking for and cleaning up after several dozen rowdy cowboys, and facing wild weather should have scared her witless.

And why didn't she dread the notion of spending forty, fifty, even sixty, days exposed to whatever nature—and possibly outlaws—decided to toss at them?

Oh, what did it matter? She was going on a trail drive. She'd have plenty of time to wonder about those things on the way to Kansas.

Hopefully, she'd be too busy to think about all the loved ones lost and buried. If the trail drive didn't put an end to the morose mood that sometimes overtook her, Levee didn't know what would! "Oh, and by the way?"

Dan's head swiveled slowly. "Yes?"

"I can sing, too."

He stared for what seemed a full minute before another round of wonderful, masculine laughter bounced off of every cactus and tumbleweed in the vicinity.

27

*D*an kept a close eye on the lumbering chuck wagon as it pitched and rolled across the prairie. He'd assigned George to ride alongside it, partly because the man knew the trail as well as just about anybody, and partly because the keen-eyed old Mexican could spot a rustler five miles off—and shoot the eye out of a rattler from a hundred yards. His ability to do both meant Levee couldn't be safer.

True to her word, she piloted the team of oxen as though she'd been born for it. And, to her credit, she hadn't uttered a word of complaint, even when the reins had rubbed blisters on her hands clean through her leather gloves. He wouldn't have noticed her discomfort at all if she hadn't darted behind the wagon, looking guiltier than a child sneaking cookies before supper. Dan had spotted her in the nick of time to catch her shoving both hands into the wash water, then wincing and sucking air through her teeth when the soapy water made contact with her raw skin. Thankfully, she'd been too preoccupied with rubbing liniment into both palms to notice him at all, and he'd managed to creep away before she noticed him.

Or so he'd thought.

"Being the trail boss," she'd said later, "doesn't entitle you to special treatment."

For the first time since they'd met, Levee had startled him. "Special treatment? I don't know what you're talking about."

"I can't think of any other reason you'd skulk around my cook wagon, except that you think your rank buys you that privilege."

Since she'd had him, dead to rights, Dan had decided not to belabor the point. "You might want to consider wearing a double layer of gloves," he'd told her.

Levee had given her hands a quick glance, then hidden them in the wash water again. "Not a bad idea," she'd said. "Thanks for the advice." Levee had winked as she'd shaken water from the tin plate she'd just scrubbed. "And here's a bit of advice for you: Take care where your shadow lands in the future."

His shadow?

"If I'd been an outlaw or a diamondback, you'd be sportin' a couple of holes that weren't put there by the good Lord."

He'd smiled then, and every time the dialogue came to mind.

Much to his dismay, Dan hadn't seen her since, unless he counted casual nods and fleeting glances exchanged in the food line. And, oh, he counted them, all right. He'd liked Levee before setting out on the drive, and now? Well, now he couldn't think of a female he admired or respected more.

He'd taken a lot of heat from the boys when they'd found out he'd hired a woman as camp cook, and he'd threatened to visit the nearest zoo and replace them with monkeys if they so much as mentioned it in front of Levee. He'd never admit it because of his "tough guy" reputation, but his decision had been the result of heartfelt prayer.

It hadn't taken them long to realize it had been the right choice. Levee worked from sunup till long past dark, churning out delicious stews after keeping pace with the herd, even on days when they'd moved fifteen miles instead of the usual twelve. The work seemed to agree with her, and so did the territory, for her skin glowed with healthy radiance, and, though she seldom took off her big, floppy hat, the sun had painted cinnamon-colored streaks through her long, dark hair and dotted her cheeks and the bridge of her upturned nose with freckles.

Long before noon on the first day, she'd traded her full skirt and dainty belt for trousers and suspenders and swapped her frilly bonnet for a wide-brimmed hat. Yet, despite her rugged outfits, Levee's presence had a calming, civilizing effect on the men. She hadn't demanded it—and, to Dan's knowledge, she hadn't so much as mentioned it—but those prone to tussling found other ways to settle their disputes, and the boys who were known for their spicy language chose gentler words, even when Levee wasn't within earshot.

Dan's favorite time of day was after supper, when the pots and pans hung neatly in the wagon and the herd had bedded down for the night. While half a dozen men rode slowly and quietly alongside the snaky parade of slumbering cattle, the rest found out-of-the-way places to spread their bedrolls and, using their saddles as pillows, set up a symphony of off-key snorts and snores. Amid those was one exquisite voice, softly crooning ballads and hymns.

Tonight was no different from the other nights, and Dan sprawled out under the endless black sky, closed his eyes, and waited. Three tunes, four, and then Levee's natural vibrato began to lose its trill, and the melody grew faint and slow, signs that told him fatigue had finally sapped the last of her energy. *So*, he thought with a grin, *even young beauties with seemingly boundless energy need to wind down, like clocks that have counted out too many hours.* He wished her deep and dreamless sleep, but that didn't stop him from missing the soothing, sultry sound of her voice.

With his hands clasped behind his neck, Dan stared at the wide, starry sky and hoped this weather would hold all the way to Kansas, because they'd started out three weeks late, thanks to the deadly tornado and the damage it left in its wake, and definitely didn't need storm-swollen rivers and lightning-induced stampedes putting them even farther behind.

As youngsters, Dan, Micah, and Paul had envied Josh, who had enjoyed privileges the rest of them would not receive for years. But, as he matured, Dan learned that every opportunity comes with monumental responsibilities. When Josh had taken himself out of the running as trail boss, the duty had naturally fallen to Dan, the next in line, and he understood only too well the importance of this drive.

These past few years hadn't been easy on the Lazy N, what with drought and prairie fires and frosts demolishing feed fields and tornadoes and anthrax destroying huge portions of the herd. Getting these cows to Kansas would turn things around. One mistake could be fatal—for the cows, the hands, and the ranch, itself. Dan had more to prove than the rest of them. They'd stood by him through thick and thin, and he couldn't—wouldn't—let them down. When it was his turn to catch a few winks of sleep, he spent most of the time wide awake, plotting out their course, coming up with ways to prevent a stampede, and making sure they found ample pastureland so that the cows would be fat and healthy and worth every dollar on the pound once they got to Wichita.

Tomorrow, he'd send Micah out as point rider to scout out watering holes and a good place to bed down for the night. In spite of the late start, they'd made steady progress, tallying a good twelve miles a day on average. If things continued this way, Dan could cut the number of night drives from fifteen or twenty to just eight or ten.

Nobody liked traveling at night, when lantern signals at both ends of the cow line were their only means of communication, because it made the already hard, dangerous work even more so. Gopher holes were hard enough to spot and harder to avoid in the bright light of day, let alone at night, and rattlers and scorpions routinely curled up under bushes and rocks during the evening hours. If man or beast stepped into either, things could get downright ugly. And the cows were more fidgety and more easily spooked at night, making the hours between dusk and dawn the choice of bandits or rustlers for when to strike.

He'd drive himself crazy dwelling too long on things like that. When all was said and done, there was no escaping the fact that things were in God's hands. Besides, Dan reminded himself that Micah had hired seasoned cowboys— three swing riders who'd run the Goodnight-Loving Trail half a dozen times, two wiry drag riders who'd helped blaze the old Chisholm Trail, and one old cowpoke who, at first glance, appeared too ancient to hoist himself into the saddle but who'd earned the men's respect on their first day out by fetching a calf even before anybody else had noticed it'd strayed from its mama. Added to the Nevilles born and bred on Lazy N soil, they were a trustworthy bunch of drovers. Yes, good Lord willing, they'd be just fine.

"You told me to tell you when it's your time," Paul said, kicking the sole of Dan's boot. "Well, it's your time."

"Aw," Dan groaned, propping himself up on one elbow. "I didn't catch a wink of sleep."

"Your own fault," his youngest cousin said, chuckling, "for bringin' your sweetie along to addle your brain."

"She's not my sweetie," Dan growled, gathering his bedroll.

"Could'a' fooled me." Paul spread his blankets where Dan's had been and wasted no time lying down. "Ground's still warm. Thanks, cousin," he said around a yawn.

"Where were you night hawkin', left or right?"

Paul pulled his Stetson down over his eyes. "Left side of the herd," he said, crossing both arms over his chest. "And now, if you don't mind, I'd like to try to get a little sleep."

Dan started walking toward the horses but slowed when Paul added, "Unlike you, I'll be snorin' in two minutes 'cause I had the good sense to leave my sweetie at home."

"Hmpf," Dan shot back. "I would've sworn I saw her with the horses."

"Huh?"

"Yeah, she was swishin' flies with her tail and had her face buried in a feed bag of oats."

"Funny," Paul said, rolling onto his side. "Real funny."

Grinning, Dan made his way to the horse line. "Which one's rested the longest?" he asked.

The night wrangler pointed to a buttermilk dun, and Dan smoothed a hand over its back, inspiring a soft nicker of appreciation. Grabbing a blanket, he let the horse have a sniff of the fleecy plaid. "Purty, ain't it? Now, how 'bout you and I take a li'l walk around cow town?" he said, easing the blanket across the horse's back. Head bobbing, the animal snorted and held its ground, even as Dan eased the saddle atop the blanket. He made quick work of lowering the stirrups and buckling the cinch, and then, with his right arm between the mount's ears, he seated the bit in its mouth with his left hand. "Good job," he whispered, sliding the bridle over the dun's ears. After finger-combing the horse's mane and forelock, he patted its neck. He poked the pointy toe of one boot into a stirrup and swung his bum leg over the saddle and, taking care not to let his spurs gouge the animal, urged it forward.

Soon, he found himself fighting drowsiness, thanks to the steady rhythm of the horse's footfalls and the quiet squeak of saddle leather. The plaintive cry of a whip-poor-will competed with an elf owl's haunting cry. Then, the gentle sounds of the night went quiet, silenced by the hoofbeats of an approaching horse.

Side by side, both steeds automatically syncopated their unhurried pace. Dan hid a yawn behind one gloved hand. "What's up?"

With no more than the hint of a nod, Micah indicated the bluff about a hundred yards ahead. "Been noticin' that movement yonder?"

Dan followed his cousin's gaze and spotted several men on horseback, moving unhurriedly toward the herd. If not for the bright light of the moon, glinting occasionally off their spurs, he might not have seen them at all. "Reckon they're point riders for another ranch?"

"Not likely. I didn't see signs of other drovers when I was out there earlier." Micah hesitated, then added, "Think it's rustlers?"

Rustlers. The very word made the hairs on the back of Dan's neck stand up. Unconsciously, he wrapped his fingers around his pistol grip and mentally tallied the shadow riders. "How many, you reckon?"

"Eight, maybe ten, by my count."

"Same here." Instinct made him want to bolt left, tell Micah to go right, and alert the rest of the men. But any sudden movement or noise would spook the herd. The last thing they needed, especially if there were poachers out there, was a night stampede. Dan turned his horse around slowly, and Micah followed suit. "Pass the word," Dan told him. "Everybody stays quiet, and nobody shoots unless I give the signal."

"Which will be...?"

"The first gunshot."

Nodding somberly, Micah peeled away at an easy canter, picking his way through the slumbering longhorns.

Dan moved out at the same speed, intent on warning the men on his own side of the herd that they might be in for a fight. Experience had taught him that a few of the ranch hands might decide the fifty dollars a month they'd get at the other end of the trail wasn't worth their own spilled blood. But it was just as likely that every man they'd hired would exhibit loyalty to something other than the almighty dollar.

His biggest fears weren't with the drovers but with his cook. He'd tacitly given his word to keep his distance from Levee so that she could prove herself by dint of her own hard work and determination rather than because he treated her with deference. And, while she was capable, when he'd tested her shooting skills, she hadn't been under pressure. Granted, she'd handled the heavy wagon as well as any man he'd worked with, but the trip had been uneventful to this point. She had been born and raised in Boston. What experience could she possibly have with the kind of men who steal livestock?

And then he remembered that men like that had put her in Eagle Pass in the first place.

The realization did nothing to sooth his ragged nerves.

He leaned down from the saddle and rapped lightly on the half-door at the back of the chuck wagon. "Levee? You asleep?"

"No," she said, "I'm wide awake."

Had she heard something, too? If so, he thought admiringly, maybe she'd make a halfway decent cowpoke, after all.

"How anyone can sleep with those coyotes screaming, I'll never understand." She lifted the canvas that covered the wagon. "Sounds like a woman being tarred and feathered! What *are* they caterwauling about tonight?"

"Could be rustlers skirting the perimeter of the herd."

A sliver of moonlight sliced its way through the wagon's rough side boards, reflecting brightly from her shirt and illuminating the left side of her face. If she didn't look like a vision, her hair gathered up loosely behind her head and both elbows propped on the big wrought-iron latch, he didn't know what did.

"I'll load both shotguns," she said matter-of-factly, "and the rifles and revolvers, too."

She knew as well as any of them that because the drovers stashed their bedrolls and wallets in her chuck wagon, it would be the first place the rustlers would target after scattering the herd. If anything happened to her, Dan would never forgive himself.

He shook his head. The time to worry about that had been before he'd agreed to her ridiculous proposition to come along on the drive. Now, he had no choice but to hope and pray that he and the boys outnumbered the rustlers, and that they could shoot straighter, too.

Dan tightened his grip on the reins and leaned a forearm on the pommel. "One shot," he said, raising a finger. "That'll be my signal."

He watched Levee's delicately arched brows rise higher. "Signal?"

"To shoot first, ask questions later."

She lifted her chin a notch, brought it down with a resolute nod, and then leaned to the side to peer around him. "Where are they?"

He jerked a thumb over his right shoulder. "Moving in slow and easy, east-southeast."

She'd kept a level head during the influenza outbreak and the tornado, so Dan had no reason to believe she'd panic. Still, he didn't reckon she'd seen anything like this back in Boston. "Maybe I oughta climb in there with you, give 'em the surprise of their lives when—"

"You wouldn't even consider such a thing if my name was Ethan."

Dan couldn't help smiling. "If your name was Ethan, I'd have no choice but to inquire about your mama's sanity on the day you were born."

"You can joke all you please," she retorted, "but you're not setting foot in this wagon. I can take care of myself just fine, thank you very much!" She sniffed. "Besides, there's scarcely room for me in here with the camp stove and pots and pans, and I don't think the boys would like it very much if I tossed their bedrolls out to make room for the likes of you."

She made a good point, but that wouldn't stop him from worrying about her. Especially if and when the shooting started. He narrowed his eyes "Keep your head down and your eyes peeled, you hear?"

When she nodded, Dan turned his mount around and headed for the invisible boundary beyond the cattle line. There, he pulled up alongside Micah. His voice was barely a whisper when he said, "Round up Paul, Mack, and George, then meet me back here."

"What for?"

"We're gonna ride straight up to 'em, let 'em know if it's a fight they want, it's a fight they'll get."

In a matter of minutes, the cousins were flanked by Mack and George. As the ground between the Neville outfit and the menacing strangers shrank, Dan hoped the rustlers would see their united front, turn tail, and run.

But the closer they got, the more apparent it became that no such thing would happen on the prairie this bright, moonlit May night.

28

W ell, boys," said the biggest man. "Looky what we've got here."

There was something familiar about his gravelly Texas drawl. With his innards quivering and his heart beating hard, Dan felt his brain buzz with memories of all the ways he'd almost died, from falling off the barn roof, to nearly drowning when the Rio Grande overflowed its banks, to being trampled in a stampede—and the coma and months of whiskey-numbed recuperation that went with it. If not for the generosity of an Abilene barkeep who'd insisted Dan wasn't the type to cheat at poker, a cardsharp would have drilled him with a sawed-off shotgun.

He'd read about the gunfight at the O.K. Corral, but never in his wildest nightmares would he have expected to die in a showdown. Yet, here he sat, face-to-face with a row of what looked like weather-beaten outlaws, prepared to do just that, if need be, to save Neville cows and his beloved Lazy N.

Gun hand on his pistol, Dan pulled back the hammer. One by one, so did the men on either side of him.

"Hey, now," said the raspy voice. "There's no call to get your neck hairs bristlin'."

Dan might have asked the man to introduce himself if he hadn't added, "You boys blind? Can't you see our stars?"

Paul, Micah, Mack, and George looked every bit as bewildered as Dan felt. "I'm in no mood to puzzle out a riddle," Dan said.

"Lord, help us," one of them complained. "The prairie's rife with idjits these days."

One by one, the threesome shoved their vests aside to expose their badges. "Gus Applegate," said the biggest, who then proceeded to introduce the men on his right and left. Dan remembered two of them, who went by Stretch and Shorty, from the run-in with Frank Michaels the year before.

Paul grunted. "You'd think a Texas Ranger would know better than to sneak up on a trail drive."

"I'll thank you not to lecture me, boy," Gus said. "We was just bein' respectful and courteous, is all, on account o' we didn't want to spook your cows."

"Seems to me you could've found some way to signal us," Mack said.

And Micah added, "You boys have been movin' parallel to us for nigh on to two days now. Mighty suspicious, if you ask me."

"Well, I didn't ask you," Gus snapped. "We was just makin' sure you're the rightful owners of these longhorns. Lucky for you, I recognize that one." He pointed at Dan. "You were there the night Frank Michaels got shot."

"Yessir, that I was."

"Well, son, we come to tell you to be on the lookout for the Ketchum Gang."

"Black Jack Ketchum?" Micah asked.

Gus nodded. "The one and only."

"I heard-tell that bunch mostly robbed trains."

"They're outlaws," said Gus, "and they'll take whatever they need to get by."

Dan had tired of the back-and-forth discussion. It was time to let these men know who was in charge of this drive. "Not much point settin' out here in the middle of nowhere, bumpin' our gums," he said. "If you boys have a mind to bed down here for the night, you're more than welcome to a piece of our trail."

"We'll just take you up on that, Neville." Gus winked merrily. "Especially if there's breakfast in it for us in the morning."

As Gus and Dan rode side by side toward camp, the Ranger said, "Not to add to your worries, son, but Ketchum and his gang ain't the only ones you need to be on the lookout for."

Dan clenched his jaw and waited to find out what other varmints the prairie was hiding.

"The U.S. Cavalry has just about cleaned up all the Indian problems, but they've yet to get a handle on the strays. They're fumin' mad that the government took their land and forced their people onto reservations and takin' it out on any white man they come across."

Dan had heard comparable news in San Antonio and Lubbock, and the details of those stories weren't pretty.

"They partnered up with Mexican *banditos*, and there ain't a man with a heart among 'em. They won't steal your beeves so's they can take 'em to Kansas and keep the profits," Gus said. "No, siree. They kill every man, then use the cows for target practice."

Similar reports about the unnecessary slaughter of entire buffalo herds had reached the Rio Grande, and every rancher Dan knew had pulled in his belt to be able to afford hired hands who knew how to shoot to kill.

"How many guns you boys got?"

"Two pistols and a rifle for each man, maybe half a dozen shotguns."

"How you fixed for ammunition?"

"I'd have to take that up with my cousin back there. He's in charge of supplies."

Gus only nodded, and they rode the rest of the way to the horse line in silence. When they reached the chuck wagon, Gus didn't give Dan time to explain why he'd brought Levee along. Instead, he slid from his saddle and threw his hat on the ground. "Why, of all the.... You mind tellin' me what in blue blazes a woman is doing out here? You got killers and rustlers and train robbers on the loose, and—"

Levee stepped forward and, as calm as you please, picked up Gus's Stetson, dusted it off, and returned it to the Ranger. "The name is Levee O'Reilly," she said, extending her arm for a handshake.

He stood, blinking and staring at it for a full five seconds, before reaching out his hand. "Gus Applegate," was his gruff reply. "Wish I could say it's my pleasure to make your acquaintance, ma'am, but...."

Smiling, Levee motioned him and his comrades to the camp stove, where a pot of coffee steamed on the grate. "You've already made your position on the matter patently clear. I appreciate your concern—is it Captain Applegate?"

"No, no," he chuckled. "I'm nothin' but a lowly lieutenant. Feel free to call me Gus."

She filled a blue enameled mug with coffee. "Well, Gus," she said, handing it to him, "I hope you'll feel free to set your worries aside where I'm concerned. I may not be the typical camp cook, but I can handle the duties of the job—and a few that don't usually go with it."

Dan stood, watching and listening, as Levee changed the man's mood from grumpy to chivalrous. He added "charming" to his list of reasons Levee was likable and wondered what other talents she'd reveal before they made it back to Eagle Pass. *If we make it back to Eagle Pass*, he corrected himself, remembering Gus's warning.

"Tell him, Dan," Levee urged him.

If he hadn't been woolgathering, Dan might have had half a notion what she was talking about.

"Tell him about Ethan, and—and things."

Like an obedient pup hoping for a bone, Dan complied. "You likely heard about the tornado that blew through Eagle Pass awhile back?" When Gus nodded, Dan continued. "Well, it didn't just destroy property. That cyclone killed eleven people, including our camp cook."

"That's right," Levee put in. "The funeral services and cleanup efforts delayed this drive, and I'm sure a native Texan like yourself understands what that means." Both shoulders rose in a delicate shrug. "There wasn't time to hire another man, so I volunteered."

Gus harrumphed, then took a sip of his coffee. "Say," he said, smacking his lips, "this is right tasty. Better than the brew they serve at that fancy restaurant in Amarillo." He aimed his next comment at Dan. "You don't really expect me to believe one of these other fellows couldn't do the job, do you?"

Frankly, Dan didn't give a hoot what the Ranger believed. He understood—and even appreciated—the man's concern for Levee's safety. He shared those concerns, after all. But, just as it was Applegate's duty to protect the good citizens of Texas, it was Dan's responsibility to look after every living being on the drive. Well-meaning or not, the Ranger had crossed the line when he'd poked his nose into Lazy N business, and Dan aimed to set him straight. "Tell me, Applegate, how long you been a Ranger?"

The question hit a nerve, as evidenced by the change in Gus's stiff-backed stance. Dan wouldn't have been at all surprised to see the man salute, too.

"Goin' on twenty years, now."

"Careful there, Gus," Stretch said. "You push your chest out any farther and the buttons will start poppin' off your shirt."

Shorty snickered. "I was just about to say he's lucky it ain't rainin'."

"Rainin'?" Gus echoed.

"You'd drown for sure, with your nose poked up in the air thataway."

The group shared a round of quiet laughter, which came to a halt when Gus announced, "I'm headin' for my bedroll. Sun'll be up before we know it, and we need to make tracks first thing."

"Breakfast is at dawn," Levee told them. And once they'd stepped out of earshot, she turned to Dan. "I have a confession to make." Looking right, then left, she whispered, "I was so relieved when you came riding up with those Rangers on your heels instead of some brand of outlaws that I nearly jumped up and down for joy!"

He might have pointed out that he and the boys could have held their own, even against outlaws. Might have admitted the relief he also felt. But the sight of her standing in a pool of moonlight took his breath away. The idea that bandits might harm one hair on her pretty head roused a fearsome ache that pulsed from his Stetson to his spurs and left him feeling weak-kneed and feebleminded.

When he realized he was staring like a simpleton, he dropped his gaze. And then, not knowing what to else say, he walked away without so much as a "Good night."

But who was he kidding? He knew exactly what he'd wanted to say, which opened the door to a whole new set of problems. He hadn't come anywhere near close to getting over the sins of his past, for starters, and until he did, it just wouldn't be right to put into words the sentiments swirling in his heart. Yes, he believed what the Good Book said about forgiveness. Trouble was, he didn't believe he could live long enough to ever forgive himself.

It had been a mistake to bring her along—one of his biggest to date—and the Lord knew he'd left a passel of them in his wake! Back home, even when it had been just Levee and he on the seat of a buckboard or a porch swing, good manners and respect for her had helped him keep an emotional arm's distance.

Out here, despite the miles of prairie that stretched between the chuck wagon and whichever position he'd chosen, Dan remained keenly aware of her presence. If she hadn't managed the team and dealt with the men so ably, all the while looking more beautiful in her dusty dungarees than a bride in her wedding gown, maybe he could ignore his growing feelings for her. Yet, no matter how glum or tired or overburdened he felt, a glimpse at her ever-smiling face was all it took to lift his spirits.

Lest his scales of justice get out of whack, Dan made a point of balancing every stirring moment of contentment with what he saw as the bare and ugly truth: He was a man scarred inside and out, a man who, time and again, had let down the people who loved him, and he didn't want to add Levee to that list. It had been more than a year since he'd taken a sip of whiskey, yet not a day went by that he didn't crave its mind- and muscle-numbing powers.

He cared deeply for her.

But she deserved far better than the likes of him.

He wanted to share his life with her.

But what kind of life would that be for Levee?

He'd risk life and limb to keep her safe.

But he wouldn't have to if his spine hadn't turned to jelly when she'd offered to take Ethan's place.

Now, really, how was a man supposed to keep his eye out for gopher holes with all that to distract him?

*J*ust days ago, while cleaning up a rib-sticking supper of pan-fried biscuits and hearty stew, Levee had over-heard the men discussing the peculiar things they'd witnessed on past trail drives. A few had hallucinated entire pools of cool, clean water rippling on the horizon, while others talked of having seen loved ones waving hello.

"The heat can fry a man's brain like an egg on a griddle, I tell you," Micah said.

"And the dust," Paul put in. "If the dust doesn't drive you mad, your powerful thirst is sure to do the job."

Though she'd been careful not to intrude on their conversa-tions, Levee found it hard not to admit to them how fortunate she felt riding up front, where her only grievances were gnats and horseflies. The men seemed not to notice them, though how they managed to keep their eyes on the trail through the narrow openings between their hatbands and bandannas, Levee didn't know.

"Saint Elmo's fire," said one of the tough old cowhands who'd signed on for the drive. "That's the thing sets my nerves to janglin'."

Micah agreed. "Not many things as spine-tingling as light-ning flashing from the cattle horns."

Levee thanked the Lord for the memory of that quiet conversation, for without it, she might have gone mad as the hours cranked by, with only the sound of the wagon wheels biting into the sandy soil and the constant clip-clop of oxen hooves to keep her company. Now and then, a horse's whinny or the blat of a longhorn broke the monotony. Rarer still, the two-note whistle or singsong "yip-yaw!" of the cowboys signaling to one another could be heard. Oh, how she missed the merry laughter of her students frolicking during recess!

It would probably take months to rid her nostrils of dust and the stink of the trail. Would she recognize the delicate fragrance of a rose or the odor of a spent match? It wouldn't really matter if she couldn't, because nothing from her previous life could compare to the sights, scents, and sounds of the trail.

She'd discovered a whole different side to her personality out here. City born and bred though she might be, it pleased her no end to admit that she had earned the respect of seasoned cowboys. When they got back to Texas, no one would look at her the same way again—especially not herself!

Levee had seen a different side of Dan, too, and she liked what she saw. Liked it very much! Oh, she had appreciated the finer qualities of his personality long before starting out for Kansas, to be sure. But it seemed he walked taller and limped less out here, and when he talked, there was a certain resolute confidence in his voice that she hadn't noticed before. The men respected him, that much was clear, for whether he asked them to take up the point, flank, or drag position, they went immediately and uncomplainingly to the task.

Dan was everything Liam had not been, and the thought inflicted many a sting of guilt on her conscience, because it seemed treacherously disloyal to entertain anything other than happy, complimentary thoughts about her poor, dead husband. Yet the trail drive only magnified Dan's superior qualities. As the herd lumbered from Texas to Oklahoma and finally into Kansas, she couldn't help but observe—and admire!—how the strong, stoic cowboy courageously led his men with equal ease through swollen, fast-flowing rivers and over parched plains. And if the Rangers' warning about bandits and rustlers had put him on edge, Dan hadn't let it show.

Oh, to spend the rest of her life with a man like that, who knew the right thing to do and did it, even in the face of incredible odds!

Maybe when the drive was over and they got back to their normal routines, he'd see her as more than a fragile woman too delicate and frail to handle any job more demanding than tending the sick or teaching little children. Hopefully, at trail's end, the hard work she'd done would prove to him that she had what it took to be his partner, in work and in life.

She hadn't given him a single reason to regret taking her along—at least, none she was aware of. So, she wondered why it seemed that, since the Rangers' departure, Dan had gone out of his way to steer clear of her. Why, when he couldn't avoid an encounter, it seemed as though he would do anything, short of turning himself inside-out, to avoid talking to her!

Levee had put a lot of effort into performing her duties as well as any man might have. And she'd put just as much effort into making sure Dan never noticed that her heartbeat accelerated and that she found it difficult not to stare whenever he was around. She made sure always to have something useful to do so she could pretend to focus on scrubbing pots or folding blankets rather than make it obvious that she hung on his every word. The men didn't say much, but they noticed everything, and Dan was sure to be the butt of every campfire joke if they caught sight of her mooning over their trail boss.

Maybe he's figured out that one of the main reasons I volunteered to come along was to avoid two long, lonely months in Eagle Pass without him, and he doesn't like—

Something bobbing on the horizon seized her attention. "It can't be," she muttered, squinting through the haze. The cowboys' earlier talk of mirages came to mind as she craned her neck left and right to get a better look. Was she seeing things, or was it really what she thought it was? "Bashful?"

Every muscle tensed as the dog moved closer and closer to the wagon. Dozens of questions swirled in Levee's mind, starting with how he'd managed to follow the herd this far. What had he been eating and drinking, and what shape must his poor paws be in after covering so many miles?

She prayed he wouldn't bark when he saw her, for that would surely spook the cows. When he remained silent and merely wagged his tail, she said a prayer of thanks. Oh, to have the freedom to stop the wagon and gather him close for a big, furry hug! But that, she knew, would start a jam of monumental proportions.

Levee squinted through the murk, hoping for a glimpse of Micah. If he still rode near enough, perhaps she could signal him and talk him into grabbing the dog and putting him on the wagon seat beside her.

As if in answer to prayer, Micah came into view with a happily grinning Bashful draped across his saddle.

"Appears you've lost something," he said, guiding his mount as close to the wagon as he could. "Wrap your reins around the brake stick. Not too tight, now—leave enough slack so the beasts won't notice anything's afoot."

Once she'd done it, Micah leaned in and, holding Bashful by the scruff of the neck, handed him off to Levee. "I reckon it won't be long before Dan finds out we've got another mouth to feed," he said with a wink, "so if you mention I had any part in this, I'll deny it." With that, he galloped away and quickly disappeared into the thick, floating cloud of dust.

"Well, aren't you a sight for sore eyes?" she said, ruffling Bashful's thick, silvery fur. If she'd had any doubts about her olfactory senses, they died with the first whiff of her canine companion. "Oh, dear," she said, wrinkling her nose. The stench didn't stop her from accepting Bashful's eager affections, though. Soon, he was asleep on the floor of the wagon. Levee smiled to herself, knowing that when they stopped outside Clearwater for the night, ample water awaited them on the banks of the Ninnescah, according to the cowboys. "Enjoy your nap," she said, bending to pat the dog's head, "because you're only a few hours from a belly-filling meal and a thorough scrubbing."

As for what Dan might say when he realized Bashful had followed them all these miles? "We'll just cross that bridge when we come to it," she said, laughing, as she thought of the trestle the railroad was building across the Ninnescah River, not far from Clearwater.

As they neared Clearwater, five riders approached, and it was obvious at first sight that the one in the middle wasn't in good shape.

Dan hoisted his shotgun and pressed the grip tight to his shoulder. "You don't want to come any closer, boys," he said. "I've cut down my share of good-sized trees with this thing."

The four who were able slowly raised their hands. "Don't shoot," the tallest one said. "We've got a wounded comrade, here."

"What happened to him?" Micah asked, using the barrel of his rifle to point to the man.

"We don't want no trouble," the fat one said. "Just a place to hole up for the night, and maybe some vittles."

"Was he shot?" Paul wanted to know.

"'Fraid so," the tall one said. "Bandits snuck up on us in the middle of the night. Stole everything that wasn't tacked down before we woke up."

"Sounds to me like maybe you should've put the whiskey away a mite earlier," Micah observed.

The man only shrugged. "They would'a' got our horses and saddles, too," he said, "iffen we hadn't scared 'em off with a stick of dynamite. Our last one, too, blast 'em." He snickered. "No pun intended."

"Only reason I can think of that you'd need dynamite is to blow up tracks," Dan said. "To make it easier to rob trains."

"Whether that is or that ain't the reason," the fat one said, "we're unarmed. I give you my word."

God be with us. Dan lowered the shotgun, but only slightly. "Can't say the word of a pack of train robbers eases our minds, but I reckon putting you up for the night would be the Christian thing to do." Without taking his eyes off the rough-around-the-edges men, he told his cousins, "If it ain't nailed down or tied on, keep it in your shorts till these boys hit the road at sunup. That goes double for firearms and ammunition."

He let his chin serve as the go-ahead sign. "You first," he told them.

As they moved toward camp, the fat one said over his shoulder, "Don't mind admittin', I'm not overly fond of havin' so many guns pointed at my backside."

"Don't mind admittin'," Dan retorted, "you've got nothing to worry about, as long as you behave yourselves."

"You wouldn't be that Ketchum bunch they were talkin' about in the last town, would you?" Paul piped up.

"Would," the tall one said. "My brother and me, we worked many a ranch in our day. Ran many a cow up the trail, too. Developed a powerful respect for the work, so we don't mean you no harm."

"Unless you've got Derringer pistols tucked away in your boots, I reckon we can take your word on that, at least," Mack chimed in.

They were half a mile from the chuck wagon when Dan nodded for Mack to ride ahead. "Let Levee know we're heading in and tell her what's what, so she'll have time to dig out her medical bag."

The wounded man finally found his voice. "Her?" he rasped.

"Yeah," Paul barked. "Her. And don't go gettin' any ideas, either."

From the moment they rode into camp, Dan decided, somebody would have a loaded gun aimed at this bunch, especially while Levee was tending the wounded one. As for himself, he had no intention of resting or relaxing until the pack of thieves made tracks out again.

Just as he'd expected, Levee had everything ready when they arrived. "Put him down right here," she said, pointing at the pile of clean blankets she'd spread on the ground. One look at the bloody, oozing hole in the man's shoulder made her scowl. Out of earshot of the robbers, she said to Dan, "Live by the bullet, die by the bullet?"

He chuckled, but only until he realized that in seconds, she'd be nose-to-nose with a wanted man.

She got down on her knees and, with a filet knife, made quick work of slicing through the man's shirt. "Goodness!" she said once the wound was exposed. "Look at the size of this!" She looked up at Ketchum. "What kind of gun did they use? A cannon?"

The injured man's companions chuckled, and as Ketchum opened his mouth to reply, Levee frowned at Dan. "Is it your plan to stand there pointing that thing the entire time it takes me to remove this bullet?"

Patting the shotgun, he gave one short nod. "It is."

She sighed. "Well, then, would you mind moving to his other side? You're casting a shadow, and I need all the light I can get."

Grinning, he did as she requested.

"Mack, scrub your hands in that bucket, there," she said, pointing, "and then hand me those tools as I ask for them, one at a time."

The cowboy eyed the white towel where she'd arranged scalpels, clamps, black thread, and what looked an awful lot like a fish hook.

She poured ether onto a gob of cotton and, after recapping the bottle, held it over the man's nose and mouth. "I want you to count backward," she told him, "starting at a hundred."

The fat one said, "Lady, I doubt he could count forward from one to ten, even on his best day."

"Comedian," the man mumbled into the cotton. As he began counting, Dan noticed that every man who'd gathered around was mouthing the numbers right along with him. By the time they reached eighty-five, the fellow was fast asleep.

Levee got right to work and, with Mack's help, had the hole cleaned and closed up in a matter of minutes. It took less time, in fact, to repair the gash than it took to bandage it, wrap the shoulder, and put the man's arm in a sling.

"Is he right-handed?" she asked Ketchum.

"No, ma'am."

"I didn't think so." She gave an approving nod.

Ketchum took a step closer. "How would you know which hand he favors, if y'don't mind my askin'?"

She turned the unconscious man's left hand so that the palm was facing up. "There are a lot more calluses here, see?" She turned his hand over again. "Once you leave here, you'll need to see that he keeps this arm immobile for as long as possible. Otherwise, he'll start bleeding again. I'm guessing you don't have a doctor friend in every county, and you don't want his condition calling attention to your whereabouts by having to visit any who might turn you in." On her feet now, she added, "And you'll need to stop in the next town you come to, for gauze and whiskey—not for drinking, mind you, but to pour on this wound to keep it from becoming infected."

"Yes'm." He frowned. "You've done a fine job. If those pole-cats hadn't took all our money, I'd pay you for—"

"That isn't necessary. And I apologize if I seem tactless or insensitive. I tend to be a little gruff when I'm digging bullets out of train robbers' shoulders." Batting her eyelashes, she smiled prettily. "But how insensitive of me. I'd almost forgotten that *you* were the recent victims of a coldhearted robbery."

"Point taken," the leader said, grinning.

Levee gathered up a small package of gauze and a small vial, which Dan recognized as carbolic acid. "I don't have any whiskey in my kit," she explained, holding up the bottle, "but this will work even better at keeping the germs at bay." She rolled it all in a clean rag and tied it up with a leather shoelace before handing the bundle to Ketchum. "It should last until…well, at least until you board your next train to…um, to secure the funds to buy more."

"Well, don't she just beat all?" Ketchum said, chuckling.

Yes, Dan agreed silently, *she surely does.*

Ketchum tipped his hat to Levee. "Thank you kindly, ma'am."

Levee took off her apron and draped it over one shoulder. "You're quite welcome," she said, submersing both hands in the sudsy water in the bucket. "You boys might want to consider taking a quick nap, since it'll take your friend there an hour or so to come around. He'll be in some pain, I'm afraid, and you'll need some rest if you plan to distract him from it."

"If I know him," Ketchum said with a wry smile, "you'll be more than distraction enough."

The fat one expelled a growly laugh. "Yeah, he won't want his purty nurse thinkin' he's a sissy, so he'll be all bad 'n' brave till we head out." He chuckled. "Bet you'll hear him caterwaulin' five miles out." With that, the robbers meandered toward the trees where the night wrangler had tethered their horses.

"If you're hungry, it won't take but a minute to heat up some stew," Levee said, smiling up at Dan. "You look a bit ragged around the edges, yourself. Afterward, maybe you ought to try to get some sleep, too."

Dan couldn't remember the last time he'd snoozed for more than an hour at a time, so it didn't surprise him a bit to hear that he looked as tired as he felt. Didn't make much sense going to the trouble of removing his spurs to bed down, especially when he knew good and well that sleep wouldn't come. What did surprise him was the strange sensation awakened by her concern for his well-being. But he couldn't afford to let down his guard. Couldn't afford to fall any deeper in love with her than he already had, because it would be tough enough pretending he felt nothing when they got back to Eagle Pass.

Frowning, Dan growled under his breath, turned on his heel, and walked away, knowing even before he got to where the horses and the Ketchum gang stood that it would be a long, long time until he could put her wide-eyed, wounded expression out of his mind.

Lord, he prayed silently, *help me learn to live without her.*

31

*W*hen they were seated around the fire for supper, Ketchum nodded toward the horizon. "You seein' what I'm seein'?"

Dan barely looked up from his stew plate. "Rustlers," he said. "The boys and me have had our eyes on 'em for close to four hours now."

"Looks to me like there's half a dozen of 'em, and by my count, we number fourteen, not countin' Bob and his bandaged shoulder, over there. But if push comes to shove, I guarantee he could hold his own with—"

"We?" Slowly, Dan met the man's eyes.

"Least we can do," he said, nodding toward his pasty-faced comrade, "is help you fight 'em off. Can't pay for the medical supplies, can't pay for the food, and there are few things I hate more than feelin' beholden to another man."

The sky was aglow with the slate-gray light of the setting sun, reflecting off the bellies of low-lying storm clouds. "Maybe they'll head for the hills once the rain starts in earnest," Dan mused.

Ketchum scoffed. "You don't believe that any more than I do. Best time to attack is when drovers are busy keepin' those dumb animals from scatterin' to the four winds." He whistled. "Never did understand how a critter that big could be scared of its own shadow, and just about everything else that moves or breathes."

As much as Dan hated to admit it, Ketchum was right. But that didn't mean he and his gang could be trusted with loaded weapons. For all Dan knew, this bunch was in cahoots with the rustlers.

"If I was in your boots," Ketchum said, sopping the last of his stew with a griddle-cooked biscuit, "I know what I'd be thinkin' right about now."

Dan drained his coffee, set the mug down with a tinny clank, and waited to hear what the man would say next.

"I'd be thinkin' that me and my boys, here, was nothin' more than forerunners for them cow thieves."

Dan grunted. "If you ever decide to retire from train robbing, maybe you can sign on with a circus, put that mind-reading act of yours to good use."

Ketchum showed his appreciation for the joke with a moment of grating laughter, but he got real serious, real fast. "Look," he said, plopping his plate onto the table beside Levee's stove. "I don't mean to sound all uppity here, but stealin' cows is for brainless idjits. I can make a hundred times more money in a tenth of the time without even breakin' a sweat." He paused long enough to dig a cigarette from his pocket. "It'll be my pleasure," he said, lighting it, "to help you get your longhorns to Wichita. Like I said, it's the least we can do." He gave a one-shouldered shrug. "And if I pick off a few of them rustlers in the process, so much the better." He squinted through the cloud of his own smoke. "It's boys like them give cultured criminals like me a bad name." This time, he punctuated the pause with a gravelly laugh.

Dan didn't know that he agreed with the concepts of cultured versus uncouth criminals, but the part about drovers being so busy they were easy pickin's? Ketchum hit the target with that one, for sure.

"Looks to me like they're fixin' to move in with the storm," Ketchum said.

It looked that way to Dan, too.

Micah chose that moment to join them. "What're we gonna do about that?" he asked, nodding his head toward the ambling shadows, closer than ever now, on the rise ahead.

"We're gonna sit tight," Dan said, "and let them make the first move." Paul, Mack, and half a dozen other ranch hands walked into the circle. "We've all been down this road before," he continued, "and lived to tell our tales. We'll have this one to talk about, too, if we keep our wits about us."

"I reckon," Micah said. Then he slapped a hand to the back of his neck. "They've got a spyglass trained on us. I can feel it in my bones."

"Which means they know how many of us there are, and how many guns we've got, too," Ketchum said. "But they're counting on storm power to help hide 'em when they sneak on in. What they don't know," he said out of the corner of his mouth, "is we're countin' on brainpower." He tapped his temple. "Me and my boys will circle around and rush 'em the minute they break rank."

"You and your boys?" Micah said.

"Y'all can't do it alone. Think about it for a minute. They'll be so busy watchin' where you are that they'll never expect us to slip up behind 'em." He tapped his temple again. "The element of surprise. It'll work, I tell you!"

Lightning flashed up ahead, but thankfully, it was far off enough that the cattle didn't seem to have seen or heard it. "Y'know," Paul said, "that idea is just crazy enough that it might work."

"If it don't," Ketchum said, "I'll eat my hat. And then I'll eat yours!"

Grinning, Paul removed his Stetson and pressed it possessively to his chest. "I'll have you know I paid five dollars for this in Lubbock."

Dan hoped and prayed these moments of tomfoolery would bond crook to cowboy. Maybe then, when the rustlers made their move, his men would have half a chance of saving the herd—and one another, too.

"All right, boys," Dan said. "You know what to do."

One by one, they headed for their posts—some on horseback, others on foot.

"Better warn your purty li'l sweetheart, there," Ketchum said with a nod, "to keep her head down and her eyes peeled."

Dan gritted his teeth. He was about to issue six-shooters, rifles, and ammunition to this band of renegades, and it was hardly the time to rile them. Yet, he couldn't resist saying, "You've got a few years on me, Ketchum, I'll give you that. But I'm still trail boss."

The man lifted his hat for an instant and put it back on again. "Sorry, Neville," he said, grinning. "Guess I've been in charge of my own bunch for so long, I don't know when to button my lip."

"And—not that it's any of your business—she's not my sweetheart."

Ketchum whistled and mimicked Dan's tone as he said, "Then, if you don't mind my sayin' so, you might want to think about how you look at her."

"How I—" But Dan didn't need to finish the sentence. He was looking into the eyes of a man who'd made a career out of reading people's faces, and the skill had probably saved his own neck more times than he could count. He'd be more careful about how he behaved around Levee from here on out, but he didn't have to admit that to Ketchum. "We'd best get you and your men outfitted," he said, walking toward the chuck wagon. *Lord*, Dan prayed, *don't let me be sorry for what I'm about to do.*

"Don't tell me you're still hungry," Levee said when they approached.

"We're not here to eat," he all but snarled, forcing a frown onto his face. Reaching into the artillery trunk, he pulled out four pistols, two rifles, and enough ammo for each weapon. He was about to hand them to Ketchum when Levee grabbed his arm.

"Dan, surely, you're not thinking of—"

"Have to," he interrupted her. "There are rustlers off to the east."

"That's what we thought before, and they turned out to be—"

"This time, we're sure." Shame coursed through his veins. He hated being so cross with her. Almost tenderly, he peeled her fingers from his shirtsleeve and gentled his tone to say, "When I give you the signal, I want you to get into the wagon. Bring that mangy mutt with you and hit the floor. Stay there until I come back for you, okay?"

"What about you?"

Fear flashed in her big eyes. Fear, and a mix of care and concern for his well-being. If only he could take her in his arms and reassure her that she'd be all right—as would he. Scowling, he faced Ketchum. "Who's the straightest shot in your bunch?"

"That'd be me," said Ketchum, accepting a rifle and a revolver from Dan.

The fat partner stepped up. "And I'm the next straightest."

While they loaded their weapons and strapped on their holsters, Dan started toward the horses.

"Dan," Levee said, running up behind him. "Dan, please, wait!"

He didn't know where he'd find the strength to look into that pretty face and behave like a cad again, but for her sake, as well as his own, Dan did his best to look surly. "What now?"

Her eyebrows went up in response to his abrupt tone, but to her credit, Levee shook it off quickly. "The signal— What—? I...."

"I'll fire two shots in the air, one right after the other." He paused. "You remember what my pistol sounds like, compared to the other boys'?"

She looked away for an instant, and when she did, he was reminded of how he'd felt as a small boy when his mama would blow out the lantern at night and throw his room into darkness. He probably could have stood there staring into those enormous lavender eyes for the rest of his life if he thought for a minute he deserved a woman like her.

He cleared his throat, mostly to clear his head, but Levee must have read it as a sign to snap to attention and answer his question. She stood taller and said, "Yes, I remember."

"Good." And with that, he walked away.

"Until now, I didn't take you for a fool, Neville," Ketchum said, coming alongside him.

"Why 'until now'?"

"Had me a dog once I talked nicer to than you did to that purty li'l gal."

"Ketchum, I—"

He held up a hand. "Far be it from me to meddle in another man's affairs of the heart. But if she's in love with you, and you're in love with her, well, doggone it, what's the problem? Life is short, man, and pretty girls don't grow on trees."

In love with him? He'd suspected for some time that Levee had feelings for him, but *love*?

"Well?"

Well, what? Dan wondered.

"As you so rightly pointed out earlier, you're the trail boss."

And so he was. Dan took stock of the situation and, satisfied that his men were in position to coax the cattle into a smaller, tighter herd, climbed onto his own horse.

Ketchum snapped the cylinder on his rifle shut and propped it against his shoulder. "Mind if I ask you a question?"

"Long as it isn't about my love life."

"How'd you come by that bum leg?"

"Stampede," Dan said matter-of-factly, and rode toward the back of the herd, grinning to himself at the memory of Ketchum's admiring nod.

32

*T*he streets of Wichita bustled with cowmen and range bosses, and the sounds of cattle and horses rolled up from the back alleys in waves. Levee stood with the rest of the hands, waiting, as Dan doled out the money he got from the man at the meatpacking company. One by one, the cowboys pocketed their cash. Some headed for the saloon, while others claimed that the only liquid they yearned for would be found at the bathhouse.

Levee aimed to spend the first of her pay in the little dress shop she'd seen on the way into town, because what she craved more than anything else was a clean, dry outfit that wasn't caked with trail dust. Maybe she'd buy two outfits, or three, and wrap the ones she wasn't wearing in canvas, so that—

"Hey, there, li'l lady."

Ketchum. Levee didn't know what to make of a fellow who robbed trains for a living and was also capable of the selfless act of helping a bunch of cowboys protect their herd from a band of rustlers.

"Got me an appointment with the barber," he said, scratching his whiskered chin, "and after a long soak in a hot tub, I aim to get me some vittles at a fine restaurant."

"Sounds delightful," she said.

He pulled at his thick, dark mustache. "I don't s'pose you'd do me the honor of joining me for a steak dinner?"

Levee tried to conceal her surprise at his invitation. If she was going to share a restaurant meal with anyone, it would be Dan, not some common criminal!

"Ah, I take it you've heard some of the stories that malign my character."

As if being an admitted train robber isn't enough! Levee thought.

"Some of the newspapers call me 'Black Jack.' That's 'cause they think I've killed folks, but they're dead wrong—if you don't mind the pun." He whipped his dusty hat from his head and bowed. "Name's Tom, not Jack, and I ain't never killed a man."

Why did she get the feeling it would have been far more accurate if he'd added "on purpose" or "yet" to his sentence? "I heard you telling the men that you drove cattle to market a time or two, so I'm sure you won't take offense at what I'm about to say. After almost two months on the trail with nearly a dozen grimy cowboys, I'd rather dine alone."

"I thought for sure you'd say you were saving yourself for Dan Neville."

Saving herself? Had Dan said something to this scruffy thief, something that involved her? "I'm sure he feels exactly as I do and intends to find some much-needed time away from the rest of us. After all, first thing in the morning, we'll be Texas-bound, and that means constant togetherness, and more dust and grit, and—"

Laughing, Ketchum said, "I get the picture." He started to walk away, then turned around to add, "I don't mind admitting, you're just the sort of gal who could set a crooked man straight. If Neville doesn't marry you, he's a bigger fool than those rustlers were."

Then he tipped his hat and disappeared into the hotel, leaving Levee alone to wonder what Dan had said to put that in his head.

All night, she tossed and turned, remembering those harrowing hours when the clouds had pelted them with rain while the rustlers had tried to shower them with bullets. They'd never gotten the chance, thanks to Ketchum and his gang. As predicted, their surprise attack thwarted any idea the cow thieves might have had about spooking the herd. By morning, their biggest problem had been the mud and muck that bogged down the trail.

After the skirmish, Dan had gone on ahead to talk beeves with the meatpackers in Wichita. Last thing he'd told her was that he'd see her at the auction barn. Now that the cows had been traded for cash, he'd disappeared again, but not before promising to meet up with her, Micah, Paul, George, and Mack at first light. The hired hands would scatter to the four winds, and the rest of them would head for home.

Early in the morning, with two cowboys on either side of the wagon, Levee followed as Dan led the way. Off and on, Bashful leaped down to trot alongside his horse. The distance prevented her from hearing what Dan said, but she could tell by the wagging tail of her furry pal that his words had been gentle, maybe even a bit playful. If only he'd talk to her that way again!

Levee supposed she had no one but herself to blame, considering she'd come out here dressed like a boy to do a man's job. If it was true that absence makes the heart grow fonder, she was out of luck!

Dan trusted her to keep up, and keep up she did. With no worries that too many miles at too fast a pace would burn the fat from his beeves and turn them into worthless skin-and-bone critters, Dan pushed his ragged little group hard, stopping only to water the horses and to sleep.

His pace put them back in Eagle Pass in record time, and when Levee opened the door to her little cottage, all she wanted was to curl up in bed and stay there for a whole week. Maybe more!

She might have done it, too, if Mack and Sarah hadn't surprised them all on the night of their homecoming: they were getting married on Sunday, immediately after the church service. Levee was thrilled for them and happy that the money Dan had paid her meant she could afford a proper dress and shoes to wear, as well as a gift for the bride and groom. Best of all, he'd have no excuse to avoid her, because he was Mack's best man!

At the ceremony, Levee sat on the aisle, about midway between the vestibule and the altar. From her vantage point, she could see Sarah's happy smile and Mack's nervous twitching—and Dan, looking positively regal in his trim black trousers and bright white shirt. He'd worn that bolo tie she liked so much, the one with the turquoise stone in the cinch that brought out the magnificent blue of his eyes.

It must have been ninety degrees in the little church, yet every time he looked at her with those glittering, black-lashed eyes, Dan set her heart to thumping and made gooseflesh appear on her skin as if it were midwinter.

Luckily for her, the reverend wouldn't hold a quiz at the end of the ceremony, because Levee had been so engrossed in staring at Dan that she hadn't heard a word between "We are gathered here today…" and "You may kiss your bride."

What a silly little twit she was to imagine herself up there beside him, holding hands and looking deeply into his eyes as they exchanged those oh-so-special words! Silly or not, it would be a dream come true if, after the reverend pronounced them man and wife, Dan leaned in and whispered "I love you," then kissed her so long and so sweetly that the whole congregation broke into happy applause, just as they had for Mack and Sarah!

She'd rarely envied other women, but oh, how she envied Sarah! Not her flowing white gown or her gleaming golden hair. Not because it was plain to see that Mack cherished her, and she treasured him, too, but because from this day forward, Sarah would never be alone again. Even if Mack spent months on the trail, the two of them were united, now and forever, as companions, as partners, and as mates who'd share joy and sadness, triumphs and tragedies.

Tears filled Levee's eyes as the organ pumped out the resounding strains of "Amazing Grace." She loved the song and would have sung it at the top of her lungs if a pent-up sob hadn't clogged her throat.

Reverend Peterson hurried toward the back of the church, smiling and nodding at the congregants as he passed. On his heels were the joyful newlyweds, followed by Susan, Sarah's matron of honor, and Dan, the best man, who sauntered slowly down the aisle. Levee poked around in her purse, looking for her handkerchief. She simply had to dry her eyes before he reached her pew!

"I've never seen you looking more beautiful," he said, stopping beside her seat.

When she looked up, they bumped noses.

"Levee," he said, pulling her into the aisle. "You're crying." He slid an arm around her and led her outside, into the hot, early June sunshine. "Is everything all right?" he asked, turning her to face him.

"Yes," she sniffed. "Of course, it is. A wedding is a happy occasion, a blessed event." Oh, where was that handkerchief? She dug madly through her purse again. How could something so large get lost in a bag that was no bigger than her fist?

"Here." Dan rested one hand on her shoulder and held out a huge red bandanna in the other.

Levee took it and almost laughed out loud, for while all the other ladies were dabbing the corners of their eyes with dainty, lace-trimmed linen, she was blubbering into a—a *mankerchief*! She supposed it was fitting and proper, since, of the dozens of females gathered on the church lawn, only Levee had donned trousers and gloves and driven a team of oxen across the wild prairie.

The only thing that kept her from racing up the street and locking herself in her cottage was the fear that she'd cause a scene. It was Sarah's special day, after all, and Levee would never want to detract from it by drawing attention to herself. She took a deep breath and held it, closed her eyes tight and clenched her jaw. *Stop your sniveling*, she ordered herself. *Turn off the waterworks and get into a cheerful mood, or—*

"You're coming with me," Dan said, gently taking her wrist in his big hand.

Levee had to half run to keep up with his long-legged stride, and when he finally stopped on the porch of J. W. Riddle's grocery store, she was gasping for breath.

"Sit down," he said, scooting a rocker closer to the rail. As she did, he slid up another chair and dropped into it, then pulled an envelope from his pocket and handed it to her. "I'll just sit here quietly," he said, propping both boots on the banister, "while you read it."

She glanced at the postmark. "Boston?" Levee didn't recognize the handwriting, and said so. She knew only two people back in Massachusetts. "How did you get this?"

"Somebody got the cockeyed notion you work for me." He paused. "Well, aren't you going to open it?"

Levee broke the seal and slid the pages out of their wrapper. Was it the breeze that made the paper flutter like the wings of an injured bird, or had his nearness caused her hands to tremble? Again, tears filled her eyes, and no amount of blinking seemed to clear her vision. "Would you—would you please read it to me?" she asked, handing the paper to him.

She couldn't decide if he looked more worried or annoyed. Under other circumstances, she might have tried to figure out why he had cause to be either. Or, she might have grabbed the letter back from him and run into her cottage. As it was, she breathed a sigh of relief when he cleared his throat and began to read.

"Dearest Levee, It's with a heavy heart that I write to you today. Mother hasn't been well since she heard of Liam's untimely illness…." He stopped and looked up at her. "You didn't tell them how he really died?"

"I—I couldn't. I wouldn't have been able to live with myself, knowing the truth would expose them to the same nightmares that haunted me for so many months." She felt the heat of a blush creeping from her throat into her cheeks. Why, oh why, was he scrutinizing her so?

Dan went back to reading. "I'm sorry to tell you that she passed away a week ago today." He looked at the top of the page. "She wrote this more than a month ago."

"Goodness!" Levee managed to squeak out. She was closer to her cottage than she'd been at the church. If she made her

292 ～ LOREE LOUGH

getaway now, no one would see it as a disruption. *I could just grab the letter, make a beeline for my door, and—*

"You're all the family I have in the world, dear Levee, and the only comfort I get these days is thinking about how you used to call me your little sister. Remember the telegram I sent? The one in which I told you that if I didn't hear from you within the month, I'd take it to mean it's all right with you if I buy a train ticket and join you in Texas? Well, my sister, I have to admit I was hoping you wouldn't answer, and now I'm happy to say I'll arrive in your quaint little cowboy town on July twentieth."

Dan pulled his watch from his pocket. Levee nearly giggled aloud, wondering if he really thought he'd see the month and date etched on its pearlescent face.

"You were on the trail when she sent that telegram," he said, more to himself than to Levee. "That's why you never got it. That's why you couldn't reply."

"If I'd been here, I would have told her to come. What choice would I have had, knowing I'm the only family she has?"

His expression said, "That's a shame." But his voice said, "How old is your sister-in-law?"

"She's twenty. Her name is Bonnie."

He inhaled an enormous breath and let it out slowly. "July twentieth," he repeated. "That's just—"

"Two weeks off." Levee clutched the envelope so tightly that it all but disappeared in her hand. So much to do to prepare for Bonnie's arrival! She'd need to find a cot of some sort, because the girl was as tall as a tree, and both feet would poke through the rails of Levee's bed. She'd need to stock the pantry, and clean the cottage, and plant flowers, and—

"I can't tell you how much I'm looking forward to seeing you, Levee dear. You have no idea how it warms my heart to know you'll be there to welcome me with open arms. I love you and I'll see you soon. Bonnie."

Dan sat back. "Well," he drawled, handing her back the letter. "Feeling better now?"

"Yes," she admitted, tucking the letter back into the envelope. "I suppose."

He stood up and held out his hand, inviting her to join him. "Are you going to tell me what got you all weepy in the first place?" he asked once she took his arm.

Where to begin? Levee wondered. Should she tell him that she'd fallen bonnet-over-boots for him on the day they'd met? That every time she'd been with him since, she'd fallen even deeper in love, or that out there on the rugged trail, she'd figured out that he was the man she wanted to spend the rest of her life with?

"I thought not," he said, giving her fingers a gentle squeeze. "Maybe another time."

Maybe, if the good Lord suddenly decided to shower her with the courage of David and the strength of Job. What if she spelled it all out for him, and he said he didn't want to share his heart with a woman who behaved more like a maverick than a wife?

Thankfully, the crunch of gravel under their boots drowned out the sound of her distraught sighs. She prayed that her tears wouldn't start up again when she saw Mack and Sarah together at their very first function as man and wife, for if Dan cornered her in the church basement and demanded to know what she was crying about this time, she might just tell him the truth!

33

It was no secret that Bonnie didn't like summertime in Texas, and, for the first time since moving to Eagle Pass, neither did Levee.

The cottage was small, but she'd always seen it as cozy—before Bonnie had moved in, that is, with steamer trunks and stacks of valises. Gowns and dresses of every fabric and hue hung from the drawer pulls and doorframes, and it had been weeks since any sunshine had peeked through the windows, thanks to blouses, jackets, and skirts hung from the drapery rods. Hats lined the top of the buffet and china closet, and Bonnie had draped silk scarves over the lanterns, leaving just one in each room to provide light once darkness fell. Fur stoles had been flung across the back of the sofa, while shoes, slippers, and boots stood in a tidy row, toes to the baseboard, along the dining room wall. Jewelry dangled from the upper corners of every picture frame, giving a haphazard tilt to each landscape and still life.

Levee quickly went from feeling like a substitute older sister to a nagging shrew. "One of these days," she warned Bonnie no fewer than two times a day, "you're going to step on one of your umbrellas you've left lying around, and it's going to pop open and whack you square between the eyes!"

"Oh, Levee," Bonnie would say, giggling. "Don't be such a worrier!"

She'd brought crates of books with her, too, and their musty smell permeated the air. "Mama kept some of them in the attic and some in the cellar," Bonnie explained. "I didn't mind leaving the furniture and knickknacks behind, but I couldn't part with Papa's beloved tomes!"

As if it wasn't bad enough that the girl's possessions ate up every extra square inch of space, she went to town nearly every day and bought new things to add to the mess! Levee feared that soon, if things kept up this way, her adorable little house would burst at the seams, and, like the steam from a locomotive's smokestack, ruffles and lace and leather book bindings would spew into the air and rain down upon the streets. Such an event might have been viewed as a blessing by the women of Eagle Pass if all of them stood five foot eight and weighed a hundred pounds soaking wet.

Levee found herself looking for reasons—any excuse at all—to escape the mayhem. By the end of Bonnie's first month in Eagle Pass, Levee had worn out her welcome just about everywhere she'd gone to seek refuge, from J. W. Riddle's grocery store, where she'd volunteered to dust shelves and scrub floors, to the hotel, where she'd run the carpet sweeper in the lobby. Why, even poor Bashful had taken to wandering the streets in search of just two feet of space where he could lie down without something falling on him.

One morning at dawn, when the coffee finished perking, Levee looked forward to taking her mug to the front porch and sitting on the swing to soothe her jangling nerves with the morning breeze and birdsong. She shoved the screen door with her shoulder, expecting it to open wide, the way it always did. Instead, it thumped against something hard and bounced back, causing hot coffee to slosh over the rim of the cup and down the front of her favorite robe.

"What in the world?" she mumbled, pushing harder.

But whatever it was had no intention of budging.

Levee set her mug atop a teetering pile of books and shrugged out of the now-stained robe, groaning when she saw that the coffee had seeped through to her nightgown, too. The sight riled her enough to put more effort behind the next thrust, and this time, the obstruction slid just enough for Levee to squeeze through the opening.

"Of all the…." She stood, hands on her hips, inspecting the big wooden container that dominated the front porch. "Why, you could fit a piano in there!"

"There *is* a piano in there," Bonnie called out to her.

It was a good thing Levee wasn't still holding her coffee, for she'd have slopped more of the stuff on herself in response to her sister-in-law's announcement. "Bonnie," she said, pressing a palm to one cheek, "just where do you plan to put it?"

Bonnie squeezed through the door and onto the porch. "Oh, we'll figure something out. You'll see!"

"No."

Bonnie's eyebrows inched higher on her forehead. "No?"

"Absolutely not."

"But—"

"No buts. There's barely enough space in there for the two of us. You'll have to take it back."

"But I didn't buy it here; I sent away for it!"

"You what? From where?"

"Well, Boston, of course!"

"When?"

"Oh, three weeks ago or so, give or take a day."

It had taken Bonnie's letter more than a month to arrive, but the piano had made the trip in a matter of days?

"I can't send it back. The catalog said 'All Sales Final.'"

Levee ran down all four porch steps and into the yard, the only place that provided enough space to pace. "Think," she told herself. "Think!" She stopped dead in her tracks. "I know! You can donate it to the church. I'm sure they'd love to—"

"Oh, Levee," Bonnie said, hurrying down the steps and throwing both arms around her. "I'm so sorry. So very sorry. How thoughtless of me, barging in here with all my things and turning your world upside down." She held Levee at arm's length. "In another week, you'll have your tidy cottage back, because I've bought the Collins place at the edge of town. I'm going into business with Sarah, you see, and we're going to turn the entire first floor into our boutique."

A house? And a business? With Sarah? What was the girl talking about? She hadn't been in town for two whole months yet! "When—? How did all of that happen?"

"Oh, Levee, you've been so busy getting the schoolhouse ready for classes in the fall, helping your friends, and volunteering at the church…. I would have felt horribly guilty bothering you with my silly little plans. It was bad enough the way I moved in and just took over."

"Your—your silly little…." Levee grabbed the girl's hand and half dragged her back onto the porch, where they sat for the next half hour, Bonnie assuring Levee that the banker hadn't taken advantage of her in the house deal, and Levee apologizing for having been inhospitable and aloof.

After a warm, sisterly hug, they headed inside and cleared enough space in the kitchen to bake a dessert for the church social that afternoon. While they worked, Bonnie described how she and Sarah would set up the shop, with the front half dedicated to books, handmade jewelry, and bric-a-brac, and the back half serving as a dress shop and fitting room. Sarah, Bonnie explained, would put her sewing talents to work making one-of-a-kind outfits for the women of Eagle Pass. "And I'll order all supplies and keep the ledgers in order," Bonnie added.

"How exciting!" Levee exclaimed. "You know, I think you're going to be a very welcome addition to this town."

"Oh, I hope so! You know, it's the strangest thing," Bonnie said as she arranged rows of freshly baked cookies on a cooling rack, "but I feel as if I've been here for ages instead of only a few months."

"I know exactly what you mean!" Levee said. "Why, I remember my first day here, when I arrived all—" She bit her lower lip. If she told Bonnie about the day when she'd turned up with little more than the clothes on her back, she'd have to tell Bonnie the truth about how her brother had died. And she'd vowed out there on the prairie, even as Mack had pounded the makeshift grave marker into place, that Liam's mother and sister would never hear the ugly details of his demise. At least, not if she had anything to say about it.

Thankfully, Bonnie didn't seem to have noticed that she'd ended her sentence abruptly. "I think it's going to be quite a scorcher today," Levee said, in case she had noticed. "I'll be glad when all this cooking and baking is done!"

"We should leave the windows and doors open while we're at the church. The breeze will flow through here and cool the place off."

Levee sneaked a broken cookie to Bashful, who gobbled it up whole. "Windows, maybe, because they have screens," she said. "But if we leave the doors open, a scorpion might just wander in."

"Ooh, good point," Bonnie said, wrinkling her nose. "Have you chosen what you will wear today?"

"I haven't really thought about it." Levee remembered Dan's remark about how her blue walking suit brought out the color of her eyes, and she was tempted to wear it for that reason alone. But flannel on a day this warm? Not unless she wanted to faint dead away!

Together, they tidied the kitchen, chattering the whole time about clothes and coiffures, earrings and rouge. Then, dressed in their Sunday finest, they headed for the church, each carrying a basket of cookies. "You know," Levee said as they approached the back door of the church, "I'm really going to miss having you around once you move into your own place."

"Bet you won't miss the big mess I've made of your cottage, though!" Bonnie said, giggling, as she set her basket on the dessert table. "Besides, I'll be only half a mile up the road. We'll probably see each other more once I'm gone than we do now!"

"Who's your pretty friend, Levee?"

Turning, Levee smiled at Dan's youngest cousin. "Paul! It's good to see you." She put an arm around Bonnie. "This is my sister-in-law, Bonnie O'Reilly."

"Ah," he said, grinning, "the one from Boston." He tipped his hat. "Pleased to meet you."

"Likewise, I'm sure."

Levee had never seen Bonnie blush before and thought she looked quite pretty, all pink-cheeked and giggly. Maybe these two would make a match. And, if her prayers were answered, and things went as she hoped they would for Dan and herself—

"Don't think I've ever met a gal tall enough to look me in the eye before. Least, not one with hair the color of a carrot."

Uh-oh, Levee thought as she saw Bonnie stiffen. *She's misunderstood*. Levee knew Paul well enough to realize that his statements had been nothing more than his clumsy way of saying that he liked tall women and, unless she was seriously mistaken, that he liked Bonnie's red hair, too. She should have warned the girl that sometimes, what cowboys said didn't accurately express what they meant.

Bonnie lifted her chin. "And I've never met a chap with tiny wheels on his boots."

"Wheels?" Paul looked at his feet and chuckled. "Oh. They're called spurs." He spoke loudly and slowly, as if Bonnie were hard of hearing and feebleminded, to boot. "I don't s'pose you know what they're for, being that you're from back East."

As Paul explained the purpose of spurs, Bonnie gasped and raised her eyebrows. "Why, that's—that's positively uncivilized! And ghastly! And the most inhumane thing I've ever heard!"

"Ghastly?" Paul frowned. "Inhumane? Well, don't you beat all?"

Levee noticed that heads were turning toward the agitated voices, and she decided to put an end to the discussion before it got completely out of control. "Oh, look," she said, grabbing Bonnie's elbow. "I see Judith Neville. She's Sarah's aunt, and until she broke her leg, she was the schoolteacher here in Eagle Pass." She didn't give her sister-in-law time to react. "Come with me," Levee said, tugging her arm. "I'll introduce you. You're going to just love her!"

In no time, the women were talking about the Boston Tea Party and Plymouth Rock, and Levee breathed a sigh of relief as she left them to get better acquainted. Head down, she made a beeline for the table of lemonade pitchers and big glass tumblers, trying to think of ways she could fix things between Paul and Bonnie. Before she reached the table—or a solution—she walked headlong into Dan.

34

Levee would have landed square on her backside if Dan hadn't grabbed her by the arms. He looked into her pretty face, now tanned and more beautiful than ever, thanks to long days spent on the trail. Oh, how he'd missed her! "Whoa," he said. "Where are you headed in such an all-fired hurry?"

"To get something to drink." She grinned. "And thanks. If not for you, I'd have a dusty bustle right about now."

Dan didn't want to turn her loose, but if she stood there much longer, looking up into his face with those dazzling eyes of hers, he might just do what he'd been dreaming of doing from the moment he'd first seen her—gather her close so that he could kiss those pretty pink lips. *Lord, give me strength.* He cleared his throat and let her go, then took a step back.

"Won't you let me pour you some lemonade?" she asked, grabbing a tumbler from the table.

If she'd asked him to lasso the moon, Dan didn't think he could have said no. "Sure."

Levee pointed at the door. "I'm going outside to sit for a bit. Want to keep me company?"

"Sure," he said again. It wasn't like he had a list of other things to do. Besides, he'd missed her. A lot. "Why not?"

In the yard, Levee sat down on a long wooden bench beneath a tree, leaving about three feet on her right and a good eight feet on her left. Should he plop down at the other end or sit close to her?

Before he could decide, Levee patted the smaller space, and Dan breathed a sigh of relief.

"Take a load off, cowboy," she said, grinning, "and tell me what's been going on in your part of Texas since we got back from Kansas. It seems like I haven't seen you in weeks and weeks."

That's because he'd made a point of avoiding her. Now, however, he was close enough to smell the delicate scent of lilacs. She'd probably splashed some perfume on her wrists, the way he'd seen his sisters do while primping themselves. He could see her earrings, too, which shimmered in the bright sunlight like silvery rainbows. Did she have any idea what she was doing to him?

"I was beginning to think you were avoiding me."

That's because I have been, Dan thought. How else could he have hoped to take control of his emotions? "Aw, just been busy, that's all." And to take the edge off his curt reply, he added, "So, how is it, having your sister-in-law around?"

"Oh, she's a delight!" Levee leaned closer to whisper, "But, just between you and me, as much as I adore her, I think I'd go stark mad if I had to live with her permanently. Why, she's got clothes strewn everywhere, and would you believe she ordered a piano? It's sitting on my front porch as we speak!"

"A piano? Outside? But, what if it rains?"

"Let's just hope the skies cooperate with Bonnie's big plans." She turned a bit to look into his eyes. "She bought the old Collins place, you know, and next week, she'll begin moving her things in."

He nodded. Sarah had told him about the deal she'd struck with Bonnie. "Think they can make a go of it?"

"Oh, I doubt either of them will get rich, but I think they'll stay afloat financially." She shrugged. "What do you think?"

"Sarah's never had much of a head for business, but from what she tells me, Bonnie has everything figured out." It was his turn to shrug. "I suppose as long as they're willing to keep their noses to the grindstone, they'll do fine, just fine."

"I envy Bonnie a little," she said with a sigh.

"Oh? Why's that?"

"Because I've come to love the Collins house."

There was something about the soft, dreamy tone of her voice that made him ask, "What's so special about that old place?"

"It reminds me of my grandparents' house. So many happy memories of time spent on their big porch." She sighed. "And that turret! When I misbehaved, Gran would send me to the third floor to sit in the window seat and think about whatever I'd done." She stifled a giggle with her hand. "I hate to admit it, but I spent a lot more time pretending to be Rapunzel, waiting for the handsome prince to climb up and rescue me, than I did mulling over my misconduct!"

The image of little-girl Levee staring out of the window of her imaginary tower put a smile on Dan's face.

"The house wasn't far from the Orpheum Theater, and my bedroom faced the street, so I could watch the fancy carriages riding up and down. Sometimes, when the weather was nice, people would leave their buggies in the park and walk, and I'd picture myself all dressed up in silk and satin." She adopted a thick British accent to say, "And I'd cling to the arm of an elegant tuxedoed gentleman…." Laughing, she clapped her hands. "And Gramps had a library on the first floor. Once a week or so, his friends would gather in there behind closed doors and smoke pipes and cigars." She leaned in again, this time to whisper near his ear, "Gran never knew it, of course, but they sipped cognac and sherry in there, too!"

Her merry laughter danced around the churchyard. Dan could almost picture her with her ear pressed to the door of her grandfather's study. He liked what he saw. Liked it so much, in fact, that the image touched a faraway chord that made his heart swell with affection.

"Sometimes, the noise in the street seemed to go on and on, all night long," she said. "The constables tried to keep it under control, but there wasn't a blessed thing they could do to silence the motorcars or the horsecars." Another musical strain of laughter bounced across the lawn. "It must have been difficult to accept that, after fastening all those shiny buttons on their coats and putting on their important-looking hats, their main job was scooping dung!"

"Do you miss Boston much?"

"I miss my grandparents, of course, and, oh, how I miss that house! But no, I don't miss the city." She took a drink of lemonade. "You've seen a lot of places, delivering cattle and whatnot. What's your favorite city?"

"Eagle Pass," he said without even thinking. Now that Levee called it home, too, it was truer than ever.

"Look," she said, pointing. "There goes Paul. I'm surprised to see him smiling."

"Why?"

"The poor thing had quite a run-in with Bonnie earlier."

"Oh?"

Levee gave him a detailed description of the exchange, and the story compelled Dan to say, "A lesson learned for both of them."

She sighed again. "I suppose. Still, it seems a shame, doesn't it, that they got off on the wrong foot? I, for one, think they'd make a lovely couple. Don't you?"

He honestly hadn't given it a flicker of a thought, mostly because he'd been too distracted thinking about what the future might hold for him and Levee. He cared for her, a fact he'd acknowledged to himself and accepted long ago. But she was too good for the likes of him, and he'd been trying to puzzle out how to tamp down his feelings and get busy getting by without her.

It seemed to Dan that everybody was pairing off, leaving Paul, Micah, and him as the last bachelors standing. Maybe it was true, and misery really did love company. One thing was certain: Without Levee, he sure was miserable!

"What is it about you women that makes y'all want to match everybody up?" he asked, somewhat surprised by his own vehemence. Still, he went on. "Did you ever stop to think that maybe some folks are better off alone? And that maybe," he added, standing up and plunking his glass on the table behind them, "some of them like it that way?"

Levee sat quietly for a long, uncomfortable moment, and he supposed her silence meant she was trying to make sense of his outburst. He didn't have much hope that she'd figure it out. The words had come out of his mouth, after all, and if he couldn't understand what had prompted his own flare-up, what made him think she could?

She stood, too, picked up his tumbler, and faced him head-on. "Well, thank you, Dan Neville," she spat, eyes narrowed, "for turning this sweet day as sour as this lemonade." With that, she turned and stalked off.

Dan sat down again and wondered as her little boots pounded over the lawn how feet so small could keep her upright.

Suddenly, she whirled around and marched back toward him, stopping a good ten feet away. "And thank you, too, for adding something to my prayer list."

"Your—"

"Starting tonight, I'll pray every day that you and all those like you who prefer to live out your lives alone will never have to bother with annoying little nuisances like me, who seem intent upon playing matchmaker because, unlike you, they like to see others happily united and often dream of the same thing for themselves!" With that, she spun around and stomped away.

He should have gone after her. Should have admitted how sorry he was. Goodness knows he hadn't intended to get her all riled up. Instead, Dan just sat there, hoping she wouldn't turn around again and catch him smirking. If the powers that be gave out awards for ludicrous notions, Dan would earn one today for sure, because all he could think while she made her little speech was that she looked as beautiful all riled up as she did when she was calm and content.

He'd seen her happy as a lark, and he'd seen her faced with great adversity. As petite as she was, Levee was a woman to be reckoned with. While doling out medical care, she had a capacity for tenderness, even when the patient was a known felon. When crossed, she wasn't afraid to go head-to-head with grown men, even if her head barely reached their shoulders. No wonder she'd played Rapunzel instead of figuring out ways to make up for the wrongs she'd committed as a little girl.

Suddenly, an idea began to formulate in his head—amazing, considering how crowded it was with thoughts of Levee—and Dan grinned. In fact, he couldn't remember a time when he'd felt happier. If this wasn't a sign from God, he didn't know what was.

He sure as shootin' didn't deserve a woman like her right now, but he'd work toward earning her love. If she'd have him, warts and all, why, he'd have plenty of incentive to become the man she deserved!

And he'd start right this minute.

35

*L*evee had all but given up hope that Dan would forget the heated exchange at the church social that had sent her stomping off in one direction and sent him back to the Lazy N. Evidently, that's exactly where he'd stayed, because if he'd come to town at all during the past two months, wouldn't she have caught at least a glimpse of him?

She tried telling herself it had been for the best. That God, in His infinite wisdom, had orchestrated the set-to, to give her a good taste of what life with a short-tempered, know-it-all cowboy would be like.

That worked for a while. That's when Levee told herself that she'd done Dan a colossal favor by going along on the trail drive because, now that he knew what real women were capable of, he wouldn't settle for second-best if he ever changed his mind about spending the rest of his life alone.

When Bonnie told her that Eva Neville had invited both of them to join the family for Thanksgiving at the Lazy N, Levee had refused, even though she would have loved to see everyone, especially Susan's little girl and Kate's baby boy. It wasn't until both new mothers guaranteed that Dan would be in Amarillo on ranch business that she agreed to go, and to bring those frosted sugar cookies everyone at the ranch had come to love.

Some weeks ago, Bonnie had decided that it made good business sense to buy a wagon and a couple of strong horses. She'd struck a deal with Otto the blacksmith: all the dresses and knickknacks his dear wife could possibly want in exchange for a place to stable her mares and store the buckboard. "I'll stop by to pick you up at ten o'clock," she told Levee over dinner the night before Thanksgiving.

The next morning, like clockwork, the crunch of gravel signaled her sister-in-law's arrival as the mantel clock chimed its tenth note.

They arrived in time to help set the big table, using every plate and bowl in Eva's cupboard. If Levee were ever lucky enough to fall in love again and start a family of her own, this is what she wanted—a home with room for a table that could seat all of her children and grandchildren.

Eva had put out one too many dishes, but since no one else seemed to notice, Levee kept it to herself. When everyone finally sat down, someone would notice the little counting error and move the place setting to the buffet.

Much to her surprise—and dismay—Levee soon realized it hadn't been a mistake, after all, for Dan sat down directly across from her. She leaned to the right and whispered to Bonnie, "Did you know about this?"

But her sister-in-law, involved in an animated conversation with little Willie, ignored the question. Leaning to the left, she repeated it to Susan, who seemed too preoccupied with filling Sam's plate with food to hear a word. "It's a conspiracy," Levee muttered, frowning at her empty dish.

Her discomfort only grew as the meal progressed, which seemed as ridiculous as the argument itself had been. It wasn't as though she or Dan had resorted to name-calling. Why, neither of them had even yelled...much. While bowls of beans and platters of meat traveled up and down the table, Levee carefully avoided Dan's gaze, meanwhile trying to remember what, exactly, she had to be angry about.

And the answer, unfortunately for Levee, was nothing. Unfortunately for her because, as the one who'd said the most, she was the one who should apologize. It wasn't likely they'd pick up where they'd left off, wherever that had been, but once the deed was done, she'd at least be able to look at him when he came to town. *If he ever comes to town again.*

After dinner, while the young mothers put their children down for naps and the men retired to the parlor, the rest of the women gathered in the kitchen. "I need to talk to you," Levee told Bonnie, pulling her aside. "Don't try to deny it—I know you were part of getting me here under false pretenses. And I'm glad."

Bonnie's eyes widened. "Y-you *are?*"

"Yes. Being here today made me realize I need to apologize. But to do it, I'll need your help getting Dan alone."

"Apologize? Are you serious?"

The two had discussed the quarrel a dozen times, if not more. "You know very well that I behaved like a spoiled little girl that day. I can't stand having something so petty and ridiculous between Dan and me. It wasn't so hard pretending it was as much his fault as mine when he was here at the ranch and I was in town, but seeing him again after two months...." Levee exhaled a sigh of frustration.

"Don't give it another thought," Bonnie said, hugging her. "Fetch your shawl and go for a walk."

"A walk? But—but it's cold outside, and—"

"That's what the shawl is for, silly! Now, trust me and do as I say."

Levee had never been one to go along with others' ideas so easily, particularly those as vague and peculiar as Bonnie's.

"The fresh air will be good for you," the girl added. "Now shoo, before I drag you outside, myself."

Levee grabbed her shawl and stepped onto the front porch. She might have changed her mind if the door hadn't clicked shut behind her. Maybe Bonnie was right, and a walk in the fresh air would clear her mind.

"I'm glad they were able to talk you into it."

Levee yelped at the sound of Dan's voice. "They? Talk me into wha—"

"Bonnie, Kate, Susan, Sarah, Ma, Aunt Eva...they promised to get you out here, but I was beginning to think they'd reneged on their end of the agreement."

"Agreement? What agreeme—"

He took her hand, and she let him lead her to a buggy at the end of the driveway. "Your carriage awaits, m'lady," he said, bowing low.

Levee put her hands on her hips. "Just where do you think you're taking me?"

He smiled mischievously and moved to help her into the buggy.

Oh, what could it hurt to humor him? she thought, allowing him to hoist her up. Besides, she couldn't deny how thrilled she was to see him, how delightful it was to spend a few minutes alone with him. "Really, now. Where are we going?" she asked as they began to move forward.

"Not far. I want to show you something."

And before she could ask what, he said, "It's a surprise."

They rode in silence for a mile or so, then passed the next mile talking about Thanksgiving dinner, the ruts in the road, and whether the upcoming winter would be easy or hard. It broke Levee's heart that her little tantrum had set them back in a position of blathering on about unimportant things, the way two strangers might. "Dan," she blurted out, "I have to tell you—"

"We're almost there," he interrupted her. He looked at her then—really looked at her—for the first time that day. "Whatever you were about to say, well, it'll just have to wait."

Just then, a beautiful two-story house came into view. It had bright-white siding, black shutters, tall, narrow windows, a stunning turret, and curlicue trim along the roof. On the wide covered porch, matching rockers swayed forward and backward in the chilly November wind. Levee knew the ranch was a maze of roads and paths that crisscrossed Neville land, but she thought she'd traveled all those leading to their houses. "Oh, Dan," she exclaimed, "it's just beautiful!" She swiveled in the seat to face him. "Who lives here?"

"I do."

"You?" Eyes on the house again, she said, "But I thought you lived with—"

"Some folks don't mind living with their parents once they're married, but I've always believed that a man and woman ought to have a place of their own." He paused and looked deep into her eyes. "Don't you?"

"Well, yes, I suppose, but—"

He climbed down from the wagon and took his time getting around to her side. He lifted his arms up and helped her down, then led her to the porch. "Will you sit with me for a minute?"

Something about his eager expression made her agree. "Just for a minute. If we don't get back to your aunt and uncle's place soon, Bonnie will have to maneuver that rutty road home in the dark, and she isn't the best driver, even in the bright light of day!"

He took her hands in his. "I've had a lot of time to think and pray since the last time I saw you. Building this," he said, nodding toward the house, "has been the cure for a lot of what's been ailing me."

He told her about his twin, who'd died a horrible, painful death so many years ago, and although Matilda had already shared the story with her, Levee didn't interrupt him, because it seemed that he needed to tell her about it, himself. He told her about the stampede, too, and the injury that had made him turn to whiskey for comfort.

"I lived most of my life carrying the blame for what happened to Daisy. Guess I spent so much time telling myself what a bum I was, I started to believe it. Believed that after the sort of life I've lived—gambling and drinking, fighting and carousing—I wasn't good enough for a woman like you.

"But as the idea for this house started to take shape, I realized that a man can build his future just as surely as he can build a house." He gave her hand a gentle squeeze, then got onto one knee and, without letting go of her hand, fished something out of his pocket. "I realized something else, building your dream house…." As he slipped a ring onto her finger, he said, "I realized I'm a selfish man. A very selfish man."

Levee pressed a palm to his cheek and shook her head. "You're nothing of the kind! Why, you're the most—"

"Hush, woman," he said, "and let me finish, please?"

Oh, how she loved that enchanting smile!

"I don't deserve you," he continued. "Might never deserve you. But I want you, anyway."

He spun the ring around a time or two, and when he looked up, she saw tears glistening in his eyes.

"Well, you haven't taken it off and tossed it back at me," he said, chuckling. "I'll take that to mean you'll spend the rest of your life with this selfish cowboy?"

He'd built her the house of her dreams. That's why he'd been mysteriously absent for so long! She turned his hands over and ran her fingertips across the calluses worn into both palms. "It doesn't seem fair to keep you from living in the house you built with your own two hands."

Dan looked disappointed and a little bit hurt. "But—but I built it for you, Levee."

"I know. And I love it. No one has ever done anything this generous, this thoughtful, or this loving for me, so you'd better believe I aim to live in it!"

He grinned. "Then, why do I get the feeling you're about to add a 'but' to that sentence?"

"I aim to live in it, but…how would it look if we lived here without getting married first?"

"Are you asking me to marry you?"

She put both hands on his shoulders and gave him a gentle shake. "I suppose I am."

In place of a response, Dan slowly shook his head. "The way you took to the prairie, like a beautiful mustang… I didn't know if I had what it took to tame you, or if you would ever see me as worthy of that honor. I only knew that I had to try."

Levee had the rest of her life to explain how she'd seen him as the untamed one, and that she'd been right there all along, just waiting for him to put his loving brand on her. "Is that a yes?"

He answered with a lingering kiss, holding her so close that not even the prevailing Texas wind could have slipped between them, so close that she could feel the drumming of his heart...his wild, maverick heart.

About the Author

Long before becoming a writer, best-selling author Loree Lough literally sang for her supper. She enjoyed receiving rave reviews and applause and touring the country but sensed it wasn't what the Lord had in mind for her. She tried everything from shrink-wrapping torque wrenches to spinning pizza dough to working as a chef in a nursing home kitchen, to name just a few, without finding one job that fit her. Then, while visiting her parents in Baltimore, Loree worked for an insurance corporation, where she met the man she would marry.

Loree began writing when her husband, Larry, had a job change that moved the family to Richmond, Virginia. She started out writing a neighborhood column and soon began getting assignments from the publication's editor—as well as the editors of other publications. But it wasn't until she penned her first novel, the award-winning *Pocketful of Love*, that Loree finally understood what the Lord had in mind for her: seventy-five books (and counting) later, she's still touching the hearts of readers worldwide. *Maverick Heart* is the second book in her Lone Star Legends series, which opened with *Beautiful Bandit*.

In addition to her books, Loree has sixty-three short stories and 2,500 articles in print. Her stories have earned dozens of industry and Reader's Choice awards. Loree is a frequent guest speaker for writers' organizations, book clubs, private and government institutions, corporations, college and high school writing programs, and more, where she encourages aspiring writers with her comedic approach to learned-the-hard-way lessons about the craft and industry.

An avid wolf enthusiast, Loree is involved with the Wolf Sanctuary of Pennsylvania. She and Larry, along with a formerly abused, now spoiled pointer named Cash, split their time between a remote cabin in the Allegheny Mountains and a humble house in the Baltimore suburbs.

Loree loves hearing from her readers, so feel free to write her at loree@loreelough.com. To learn more about Loree and her books, visit her Web site at www.loreelough.com.

Coming Soon...

Unbridled Love
Book Three in the Lone Star Legends Series
by Loree Lough

*L*ife seemed like a dream come true for Callie Roberts—until her worst nightmare ruined the fairy tale. A boiler explosion on a steamboat kills her parents, her older brother, and her beloved fiancé, Seth. It also deafens her younger brother and leaves Callie with an unsightly scar from cheek to chin, a haunting reminder of the tragedy, which might have been prevented had she not convinced her brother to feed the boilers so that she could have a tryst with Seth.

She settles with her brother in Eagle Pass, Texas, where the two set up shop designing and sewing fine dresses and hats. Business takes off, but the same is hardly true at the nearby Lazy N Ranch, where the Neville family's herds are in trouble. Micah volunteers to go to Lubbock for seed, but he doesn't share his ulterior motive for traveling there. He mistakenly intercepted a letter for Dan and fears that his cousin is in trouble. And for all that Dan has done for him, Micah intends to set things right.

It's a shock to everyone—including Micah—when he returns to Eagle Pass with not only the seed but also a baby boy in tow. But he'll do anything to protect Dan's honor, even if it means pretending to be the father. He can handle the gossip and glances just fine—until he meets Callie Roberts and learns the meaning of love at first sight. Will the misguided decisions these two have made keep them apart, or can they face the truth about each other—and themselves—and discover a love they never could have imagined?

Beautiful Bandit
Loree Lough

Having escaped a gang of robbers who forced her to participate in a bank heist, Kate Wellington adopts an alias and decides to flee to Mexico. Lost and hungry, she stumbles upon the camp of a man named Josh Neville who offers to escort her across the border. But when she injures her ankle, the kindly cowboy takes "Dinah" home to his ranch to heal, instead. As the two grow closer, Josh realizes he's fallen in love, even as he learns the truth about Dinah. But does he know the whole story? And, after the truth comes out, will he put his life at risk to keep her with him?

ISBN: 978-1-60374-225-2 ✦ Trade ✦ 400 pages

WHITAKER
HOUSE